ERROR
IN
JUDGMENT

ERROR IN JUDGMENT

D.C. Brod

TYRUS
BOOKS

Published in electronic format by
TYRUS BOOKS
an imprint of F+W Media, Inc.
10151 Carver Road
Blue Ash, Ohio 45242
www.tyrusbooks.com

eISBN 10: 1-4405-3320-2
eISBN 13: 9781440533204

POD ISBN 10: 1-4405-5407-2
POD ISBN 13: 978-1-4405-5407-0

This work has been previously published in print format by:
Walker Publishing Company, Inc.
Print ISBN: 0-8027-5763-4

For Donald, with love

Chapter One

YOU ARE what you own. I once worked with a guy who was the human version of his Saint Bernard. Behind the massive build, the craggy, jowled face, and the thundering bark was a man who couldn't bring himself to set a trap for a mouse. And I dated a woman who was a lot like the obscure foreign sports car she drove—exotic exterior but not much under the hood. With Mason Burke it was his office.

It was a refurbished home about a half century old, the exterior warm and comfortable—pale yellow paint and contrasting brown shutters—making you think about picket fences and fresh-baked cookies. Then you got inside and bam!—steel file cabinets, Plexiglas fixtures and stark furnishings. Even the artwork was impersonal to the point of being sterile: framed, angular swatches of colors with no apparent purpose except to complement the room's pale grays and greens. That was Mason—warm and friendly on the surface, but turn him inside out and you had one big chunk of ice.

For all her warmth and personality, Mason's secretary might have been hanging on one of the walls. "Mr. Burke will see you in a moment. He's taking an important call just now."

Mason always happened to be on the phone at the precise moment I walked into his office. And it was always important. Never calling to check the time and temperature or to find out what was playing at the cinema.

I tried to be inconspicuous as I watched his secretary go about her business. The jacket of her navy suit had slash pockets piped in white and her skirt was pleated. I'd been to Mason's office about a half dozen times and I still didn't know the woman's name. She was fairly young—maybe late twenties. Too young to be so intense, I thought.

She cleared her throat without looking at me. "Is there something I can do for you, Mr. McCauley?"

"How long have you worked for Mason?"

She turned toward me and said, "Four years," adding in a silent stare that it wasn't any of my business. Some invisible signal saved us from further pleasantries. "Mr. Burke will see you now."

"C'mon in, Quint," Mason said as I entered. He stood, cigar in one hand, pocket watch in the other. Noting the ten minutes he'd successfully kept me waiting in his outer office, he snapped the watch shut and inserted it into his vest pocket. Smiling, he motioned for me to sit. The smile, pleasant and unforced, somehow didn't mesh with the rest of him.

Mason Burke was not an attractive man. He was thin and wiry with wispy red hair and huge freckles that blended into his receding hairline. I'd once heard another lawyer say that Mason had a face like the back end of an Appaloosa. But Mason had energy and an easy confidence that more than compensated for his physical shortcomings. Not only was he one of the most successful divorce lawyers in the county, he was married to a former fashion model who was about a half foot taller than him. He was also a descendant of one of the first families in Foxport.

Mason opened a silver case filled with Cuban cigars. "Care for one?" I shook my head and sat in the chair across from his desk. "That's right," he nodded, "you like something you can inhale. Well, I know where you're coming from. I used to smoke three packs a day myself." He shook his head at his imprudence, as he did every time he admitted this lapse in his otherwise exemplary life. "These things," he gazed lovingly at the cigar. "A man can take his time enjoying one of these works of art and not have to worry about coughing up blood twenty years down the road." The sweet, stale smell that permeated his office attested to the fact that he had, indeed, spent plenty of time appreciating this art. Mason lowered himself into his chair and watched as I lit a cigarette and inhaled deeply. The smile deteriorated a bit.

To hear him talk, Mason believed that he and I were right on the same level: a high-priced lawyer and a reasonably-priced private investigator, both professionals, both performing a vital service. But judging from the covert inventory he took of his desk whenever I placed papers or photographs on it, he really put guys like me on a level with subway pickpockets. And I guess that's why I called him Mason instead of Mr. Burke. He couldn't correct me without slipping out of character.

"Here's what I need, Quint." He spoke slowly at first, as if he hadn't already rehearsed and refined this speech. "I'm defending Scott Markham, the circuit judge who's been indicted for accepting bribes." He paused and lit his cigar, puffing on it several times to get it going. He watched me as he shook the match out. "Stop me if I'm boring you with something you already know."

"You are a lot of things, Mason; boring isn't one of them."

He smiled and continued. "I'm looking out for my client here. Don't want to see him burned, you know. And if I were Mrs. Markham, I'd be bailing out of this marriage as soon as I could. Don't know if you heard what happened to Carl Wittenger. Had a construction business that was going through some tough times and, to ease the pain if you know what I mean, he had a little something going on the side. Wife found out and before he knew what hit him he was filing for bankruptcy. Lost everything. Now, I don't want anything like that happening to Scott Markham. You understand?" When Mason tried to ingratiate himself with me, he had a lot of trouble with eye contact.

I nodded, realizing that I'd been treed and there wasn't a damned thing I could do about it.

"I'd like to see what you can dig up on Lorna Markham. Boyfriends," he shrugged, "girlfriends, whatever. Drinking habits. Any bad habits will do, really."

In the few seconds I could take before he'd know I was stalling, I considered my options. If I told him I didn't have time, he'd know I was lying and probably conclude that I was already working for his client's wife. I was pretty sure he suspected that anyway. And if I said no, that'd clinch it for him. I'm not in the habit of turning down cases. However, there was at least one other good reason for turning this one down.

I leaned forward, resting my elbows on my knees and stared at my folded hands before I looked up at him. I spoke slowly, not so much for effect as for time to figure out how I was going to end this speech. "You mean to say that you want me to dig up dirt on this woman, this Lauren Markham, just so you have something to use against her if and when she files for divorce?"

"Lorna," Mason said. "Her name's Lorna."

I nodded and looked at my hands again. "And her husband? He doesn't know about this?"

Mason shrugged and smiled. "Like I said, I'm just looking out for my client's interests."

I shook my head and leaned back into the chair. "I can't do that. It's one thing to follow some woman around when her husband's been staying up nights thinking she's sleeping with his best friend. It's another thing to follow a lady trying to catch her spitting on the sidewalk. Jobs like that give people in my business a bad name." I shook my head. "I'm hungry, Mason, but I won't do it."

Mason smiled. "You're working for her, aren't you?"

I swallowed hard. "It doesn't matter."

He stared at me for an uncomfortable amount of time, still smiling but slightly distracted, as if he were looking for the answer to something. Then he nodded and said, "Don't get moralistic on me. You and I aren't so different, you know. We both make a living off people's misfortunes. Oh, maybe every now and then you get a missing person to dig up, just to make you feel respectable. But the real meat of your business—and mine—comes from getting the goods on some poor slob so his spouse can stick it to him."

I would have liked to refute that observation, but couldn't. So I said, "Seems like you got all the answers. Why am I here?"

Mason laughed. The sound was full but without warmth. "Why Quint, we both know why you're here. In fact, I can only think of one reason for you to turn down a job like this. What you people call 'conflict of interest.' I'm right aren't I?"

"You seem pretty convinced," I said.

His smile faded a bit and his eyes narrowed, trying to read my mind. I thought about a white dog in a snowstorm.

He leaned back into his chair and folded his arms across his chest. "Quint, we're both professionals here. And I'm sure it isn't necessary for me to remind you that I tossed you a lot of business when you were trying to get established here. Even after that bad start you got off to. Back when you were the new boy in town. Not so long ago. Am I right?"

"Yeah, Mason, you helped me out. But I think the 'support your local gumshoe' spiel is a little out of line. You wouldn't have hired me a second time if I hadn't produced results the first."

Mason studied the glowing tip of his cigar, then turned back to me. "Perhaps. But I don't think I need to remind you that you're a little old to be starting a new business in a new town. It helps to have lots of time on your side. Takes a while to build relationships. To learn the ropes, so to speak. Things you can't pick up in the P.I. manual or whatever it is you folks call your Bible. So, when you don't have all kinds of time on your hands, you have to take advantage of opportunities that come your way." He leaned forward and stared into my eyes for several long seconds. "You know what I'm saying, Quint, don't you?"

Sure I did. At my age, most career types were either scaling peaks or learning to enjoy life on the plateaus. They weren't trying on new hats hoping there was still a chance they'd find one that fit.

Mason must have interpreted my silence as agreement. He nodded. "That's good." Then he leaned back into his chair and gazed at the ceiling while drawing on the cigar. "You know, there's another reason you should help me out here. I think it takes a reasonable, sympathetic man like you, Quint, to fully appreciate Scott Markham's situation. I don't have to tell you, this guy's in a bad way. You wouldn't be trying to make things worse for him, now would you?" Mason emphasized his point with a conspiratorial wink.

I was hungry, but I wasn't starving. I stood. "Mason, why would I try to make things worse for him? He's got you. What more does he need?"

As I left, Mason fired the last salvo: "Hope you're not getting too attached to this town. Don't think there's much future for you here." I didn't look back at him, but in my mind's eye, a scrawny, spotted, cigar-smoking Cheshire cat watched me leave.

I'd parked my car directly across from Mason's office and as I crossed the street I glanced up and down at the cars and looked for something out of place. Mason was either incredibly canny or he had someone tailing me. There was a red Jaguar parked halfway down the block and it looked like there was someone in it, but I dismissed that as a possibility. Bad form to tail someone in a car like that.

As I got into my car I wondered who could possibly have known that I'd been hired by Lorna Markham to discover the identity of her husband's latest flame. The only one I could come up with was the lady herself. That made no sense. Maybe I'd uncover the informant when I started tailing Markham.

He was out of town until the next morning so Lorna wasn't going to start paying me until then. I thought about what there was to eat in my refrigerator and came up blank. I could either go home and try my luck or stop someplace where I knew I could get decent food. I mentally tossed a coin and was relieved when it turned up heads. I turned onto Stone Avenue and headed toward a riverfront restaurant called The Den.

As I drove, I considered Scott Markham's choice of attorney. Why would a circuit court judge, indicted for accepting bribes, his career on the line, hire a divorce lawyer like Mason Burke to defend him? Especially when the lawyer Markham had practiced with before he became a judge was one of the best criminal lawyers in the state, let alone the county. That was sort of like hiring some guy who advertised on the side of ambulances when F. Lee Bailey was your fishing buddy. Go figure. Anyway, Mason Burke had done all right by Scott Markham as far as Lorna was concerned. Mason couldn't prove it, but he strongly suspected that Lorna had hired me. I'd probably have a lot of trouble catching Markham in the act after Mason told him to cool it. But then, you never know. One thing I've learned in handling divorce investigations: hormones die hard.

The hostess escorted me to my favorite table—nice view of the river and in the middle of the smoking section. I ordered a drink and lit a cigarette. When the drink came, I sipped it without looking at the menu. I wondered if Mason did have the clout to destroy any chance I had of building a business in this town. He probably did if he cared to bother. Maybe he was right: I should have tried this years ago when I wouldn't have given time, or the lack of it, a second thought.

There wasn't much light left in the mid-March day. As I sipped my drink, I watched a jogger make his way down the bike path along the river. Maybe it was time to take up jogging. The exercise wouldn't hurt. I'd been lucky in that I'd managed to close in on middle age without ever having to be a fanatic about what I ate and how much I exercised. But that wouldn't last. All my life people have been telling me that I look like my father. And I guess that's true. We've got the same deep set eyes and the same way of looking at someone who's full of shit. But lately when I see my dad, I see a tall guy with skinny legs who can't suck his gut in anymore. Maybe I'd start with situps.

Pushing unpleasant thoughts from my mind, I continued to stare at the river, mesmerized. I put myself in the middle of it, flat on my back, just floating.

"You slimy bastard. Who in the hell do you think you are?"

One hundred and twenty pounds of fur-clad fury landed in the chair across the table from me. I tried not to choke on my drink and failed.

"I hope you die," she said as, between gasps, I drained a glass of water.

When my eyes cleared, I focused on Lorna Markham. I could think of only one reason for her assessment of me. Only one she would know of anyway. I motioned to the waitress and asked Lorna what she was drinking.

"Scotch on the rocks. Just make it the bar scotch. I'm going to dump it on this bastard's head."

The waitress emitted an uncertain giggle, glancing first at me, then Lorna. Her expression sobered and she hurried away to fill the order.

"I should have known better. You private investigators are all alike. You go straight from my place to see Mason Burke. You just work for the highest bidder don't you? Does Mason pay you with drugs and bimbos?" Although the venom in her tone was unmistakable, she took care not to raise her voice much above a sharply-delivered whisper. Even so, a couple of tables were unable to ignore the exchange.

"Lorna," I tried to interrupt but she would hear none of it.

"Have I been stupid? And don't call me Lorna. It's Mrs. Markham to you. To think I thought that since you'd only been in town a few months you wouldn't have been poisoned yet by that scum." There was a special hatred in her voice when she referred to Mason. "That was a mistake I won't make again.

That son of a bitch is like a cancer." She seemed to drift off for a minute. The waitress brought the scotch and set it in front of her. She grasped the glass so tightly I thought it would shatter. I put my hand on her wrist. She recoiled a little but didn't pull away.

"Listen to me for a minute, okay. Then, if you want to, you can dump the drink on my head. In fact, I'll do it for you."

She glared at me but didn't speak. I took her silence as my cue to go ahead. "Yes, I have worked for Mason Burke. Yes, he asked me to his office today to find out if I was working for you. No, I did not tell him that I am working for you. Yes, he does suspect as much, but at this point he has no proof."

"What else did he say?"

"Not much. But it took him a long time."

She didn't loosen the grip on her glass, but her eyes softened a little. "Why should I believe you?"

I shrugged. "Because I've only been here a few months. I've worked for Mason, but I've also worked for several other lawyers. You and I probably have the same opinion of Mason, but, unlike you, I can't afford to be real fussy. On the other hand, I've only been in this profession a few months so I haven't lost all my scruples yet." I glanced at her scotch. "It's up to you, Mrs. Markham. It's your choice." Then I added, "And on second thought, if you want to douse me with that drink, you gotta do it yourself. 'Cause I don't deserve it." I released my grip on her wrist.

Her eyes narrowed and she pushed her shoulder-length brown hair off her face. She lifted the drink and hesitated. "So, what do you do now that Mason knows what you're up to?" The anger had evaporated and she might have been inquiring about how the Cubs looked for the season.

"Nothing different. If Mason tips your husband off, maybe he'll cool it." I shrugged. "Maybe you've got him back."

"I don't want him back." She drank some of the scotch, and set it down, taking care to place it in the ring of water it had left on the table. Then she stared out the window, tapping her nails against the side of the glass. They were short and painted a deep shade of red. Sighing, she said, "He's as predictable as they come. He likes to screw around. That's a given." Then she turned to me. "I just need proof so I can destroy him." She waited for me to respond and when I didn't, she acknowledged my choice with a nod and continued. "I put Scott Markham through law school—I helped him build his career—I told him what moves to make, what friends to have. Without me, he'd be some minor corporation's flunky lawyer. How does he thank me? He blows it all to hell and gone. Just like that." She snapped her fingers and continued making her point. "When I'm through with him, I want a destroyed man. A man with nothing. Do you have a problem with that? If you do I'm sure I can find someone who's not so squeamish."

Inwardly I sighed. Of course I had a problem with that. But I had a bigger problem with starving to death. "I'll let you know if I can't keep it down."

She nodded and looked out at the river again. "I know my husband. He can't handle failure. He's never had to. All I have to do is set it in motion. He'll self destruct."

I nodded and picked up the menu. "You sure there's only one 'other woman'?"

"There may be more than one, but I doubt it. If there are, I'd like to know about all of them. Who they are. What they do." She smiled, "And maybe I'll let her . . . or them . . . know that I was never fooled. Not for a second. Those little bimbos. They think they're so damned discreet." She rested her chin on a fist and stared at the breadsticks. When she spoke again her tone was more reflective. "You know, I could forgive him the women. I know my husband and I know he never seriously considered monogamy as a way of life. But his career," she shook her head, "I can't forgive him that."

"Did he take the bribes?"

"Of course he did." She pushed away her drink and looked at me. For a second I thought she was fighting back tears, but I might have been wrong. She slipped her coat on and glanced around the room. "I'm leaving. It was stupid of me to come here in the first place. I don't need people talking right now." Had she considered what action she'd take once I got the information she sought? I guess that wasn't my problem.

"One question, Lorna. Why did your husband hire Mason Burke—a divorce lawyer—to defend him on a bribery charge?"

She looked at me hard, as though she were trying to tell whether I already knew the answer and was just testing her. Finally she said, "They go way back." She stood. "Call me as soon as you have something. Or if anything else happens with Mason." With that she left.

It was dark now and the river looked cold and black and uninviting.

"Would you like to order now?" I looked up at the waitress who seemed relieved to find me alone. I asked her to bring me a turkey sandwich and another scotch.

As I drove home, I wrestled with the fact that I'd been hired to facilitate a man's destruction. That bothered me. Even if he *was* a corrupt philanderer. It bothered me a lot. Maybe this private investigator hat didn't fit quite right either; there might be worse things than punching a clock and doing the corporate shuffle. But, I allowed myself, this hadn't been a particularly rewarding day. I hoped tomorrow would be better.

When I unlocked the door to my apartment and stepped into its cool emptiness, I fought the urge to go out and look for a friendly bar. Maybe the place wouldn't seem so hollow if I had some area rugs. It didn't smell like home yet either.

I turned on the television—more for the noise than entertainment. If that's all you ever ask of your TV, it'll never let you down.

I studied the apartment, trying to decide what I needed to do to make it more livable. I'd left Chicago and my job as head of security at a large department store a few months ago. At the time, I wasn't sure where I was heading. I just decided to go west until I hit water and was relieved to stumble on the Fox River before the Mississippi. Actually, I was only an hour out of the city.

For the first couple months, I lived out of a suitcase in one of those *Psycho*-type motels on the eastern edge of town. Then I found this apartment—in one of those large building complexes catering to singles and couples without kids. The location was nice, with a view of the river if you stuck your head out the window and found a gap between buildings. But the rooms seemed sterile. I'd always traveled light and the few pieces of furniture I had—a bed, a small couch, a couple of chairs, and a coffee table—had been donated by family and friends. Yet I knew it wasn't just the scant furnishings that made the place feel empty. All that awful, unbroken beige reminded me that I wasn't used to being alone. It hadn't bothered me so much in the motel. You don't expect to have someone to come home to when you're living out of a suitcase.

I thought of Elaine. She seemed to always be in my thoughts, sometimes just below the surface, but there. It's amazing how little time it takes to mesh your life with another's; how deeply you can feel separation after only a month together. Maybe we'd been scared off by the intensity of the relationship. Things had happened fast and when they'd cooled off a little, we'd both clutched. Then she announced she was moving to Santa Fe. Well, I guess one of us had to do something. Since then I've spent a lot of time wondering what it would take to get her back. Maybe all I had to do in the first place was ask her to stay. And to think, we're the intelligent species.

There I sat on my couch, telephone in my lap, debating whether I should call Elaine. But she was staying with a friend until she got settled, and I felt awkward talking to this friend. She had gotten Elaine the job in Santa Fe, and I held her responsible for Elaine's departure. Small of me, I realize, but hell, who else could I blame? Not me. No way.

I put the phone on the floor, my feet on the table, and closed my eyes. There were worse places to settle in for the night. I was nearing that twilight area just this side of sleep when inspiration struck. I sat up and grabbed the phone book. Quint McCauley wouldn't be alone for long.

$\triangledown$

CHAPTER TWO

FOR TWO DAYS, Scott Markham behaved himself. I watched him execute the duties assigned to him as an indicted judge. He wasn't presiding over a courtroom but was busy making contacts. Of all sorts. He came and went, meeting with lawyers, having a drink with his former partner, Judd Townsend, whose offices he had moved back into after the indictment. The guy had one thing going for him—loyal friends. Although I couldn't help but wonder if Townsend felt like an empty nester who reluctantly clears the junk out of the guest bedroom so the divorced kid can move back in. I watched Markham and Townsend, intense in conversation, down several drinks along with a four-course meal while I sat at the bar feeding on soda water and baskets of popcorn. And I had a chance to observe Scott Markham, the man.

He was aging the right way, going gray with a full head of hair. I wondered how much of that gray he'd acquired since the indictment, but he laughed and talked like he hadn't a worry in the world. People liked him. Each time he was addressed, by a bartender, another lawyer, or whoever, he gave that person his full attention, as if what they were saying was the most important thing at that moment. I heard the bartender telling him about his kid's science project, and Markham hung on every word. He listened, nodded, made eye contact, asked the right questions. Everything. It seemed to come so easily to him that I couldn't help but wonder if this indictment had ruined a brilliant political future.

The more I watched Scott Markham, the more I was able to justify to myself what I'd been hired to do. Here was this guy who had looks, a better than average personality, and a wife who knew how to put spontaneity into a situation. And now he'd blown it all for accepting bribes from drunk drivers who wanted their licenses back.

It was also becoming easy to believe that this man would never settle for one woman. From the way he watched a waitress leaning over the next table to the way he exchanged what I would call "meaningful glances" with a woman seated at the bar, it was obvious he enjoyed women. He charmed them, he flirted with them, and he always left them smiling. Well, almost always. I wouldn't have been sitting there taking notes if he hadn't fallen out of favor with the one at home.

Finally, on the third day—a Sunday—his hormones kicked in. He arrived at his office at about ten thirty A.M. Townsend was out of town for a long weekend. The building was on a quiet, partially residential street and their offices occupied the first floor's southwest corner. They shared the south entrance with the Beck' and Call Answering Service. There was a door on the east side which was used by an architect who occupied the east end of the building. Markham, Townsend, and their secretary came and went via the main door on the south side. The second floor was a private residence, accessed by stairs from the parking lot. It was pretty easy doing surveillance since I could view the entrance and the small parking lot from two streets, and was able to vary my position.

I was thinking maybe my new partner was itching to stretch his legs, when I saw Markham leave the building. He wasn't carrying the briefcase he had brought in with him. It was eleven o'clock. My companion and I followed him to a florist's shop. He came out after a few minutes carrying a bundle of flowers. Bingo. Next, he led us to a six-flat building in the northwest corner of town. It was an older building with one main entrance and no balconies. Markham glanced around as he got out of his car and walked into the building. The picture I took of Markham looking over his shoulder as he pushed the door open was one Lorna was sure to like. He barely hesitated at the inner door. Either it wasn't locked or he had a key.

I traded seats with my new carmate, opting for the passenger side. This was the first time he'd accompanied me on surveillance and I was learning a lot about him. For one thing, he liked to sit on the driver's seat with his paws propped in the lower arc of the steering wheel, looking like he was ready to pop the car into gear and go cruising for young terriers.

The woman at the animal shelter had said he was mostly border collie and assured me that he was full grown. He was black with a white ruff and couldn't have weighed more than forty pounds. My only hesitation in adopting a dog from the pound was that I might get one of those little ones with paws the size of frying pans. They tend to grow into those paws. This fellow had been abandoned by his owner who'd moved out of their apartment and left him there on the chance that the maintenance man would find him before he starved. That had presented me with a situation I hadn't counted on. When I tried to leave the dog in my apartment to do surveillance on Markham, he put up such a fuss that there was no way I could leave him there alone. Not yet anyway. I wondered how long dogs remembered.

So the two of us sat in the car. He had moved to the back seat where the view wasn't as good but there was more room. He paced back there for about ten minutes, then found a comfortable spot for a nap. I read a book called *Know Your Border Collie* and began to realize that there was a lot about this breed that the woman at the shelter had neglected to mention. Like the fact that they needed a lot of exercise, having been bred to work ten to twelve hours a day. Just what I needed, a dog that made me feel like a bum.

I dug out a roast beef sandwich and realized I hadn't packed anything for the dog, so I gave him half. He gulped it in two bites and gazed greedily at the half I'd only taken one bite from. It was our second test of wills. The score was even now.

I popped a cassette tape of Italian guitar concertos into the portable tape deck I carried in the car, adjusted the volume to low and tried to make myself comfortable. It was a Sunday so there was no telling how long he'd be. We waited almost two hours. At one fifteen, he left. I followed him back to his office where he parked his car in the small lot behind the building. Hoping he'd stay put for a while, I drove back to the six-flat.

Lorna Markham had been real specific about her reasons for hiring me. She wasn't only interested in photos of her errant spouse crawling out of a bedroom window. She wanted the goods on the woman too. When I got out of the car, the dog seemed wary, but was otherwise calm. Maybe he figured I might abandon him, but not my car.

The six-flat was a security building and none of the names next to the buzzers gave me a clue. Just last name and initials. I started ringing doorbells and hoped that, on a pleasant Sunday afternoon, there wouldn't be a lot of people home.

"Who's there?" a woman's voice, emanating from apartment 3A, crackled over the intercom.

"Oh, hi. I understand one of the units in this building is for rent. It wouldn't by any chance be yours, would it?"

"Nope."

"Oh," I tried to sound disappointed. "Darn," I added. "Uh, listen. This is probably way out of line, but could I just look at your place? I don't want to come in or anything, I just want to see it. From the doorway." Christ, I thought, after that speech she was probably breaking out the mace with one hand and dialing 911 with the other. I didn't know if she still had me tuned in, but I blundered on. "You see, I'm moving here from out of town and don't have much time to find a place. This address was listed in the *Chronicle*. I won't be a minute."

A long hesitation, then she came back on. "Why should I?"

A good question. I checked my resources. "Twenty dollars," I said, figuring that would leave me just enough for dog food. She buzzed me in.

As I rounded the corner to the third floor, I saw the body behind the voice and understood two things. One, this was not Scott Markham's mistress and two, there was a very good reason for this woman not to be nervous about letting a complete stranger into her apartment. I'd been watching Markham watch women for several days and I was reasonably certain this one wouldn't have made the first cut. She was probably around sixty, short and plump and wore a pair of tight purple polyester pants with a red and white striped top. Her hair was hidden by a red bandanna. The reason she feared no mortal man was the creature straining at the collar she gripped in her right hand. The doberman's red bandanna was tied around its neck, draped over its chest cowboy style—sort of like a canine John Wayne. Unlike the woman, the dog was smiling at me. I smiled back.

"Hi," I said, "I'm Roger. Roger Kafka."

She stepped back from the doorway, holding her hand out

for the twenty. "There it is." She thrust the bill down her velour top.

I peered into the room. It was cluttered and smelled moldy. Not that I cared. "Is this a one or a two bedroom?"

"Two," she said.

"Oh," I shoved my hands in my pants pockets. "I thought the one advertised was a one bedroom. Are there any one bedrooms here?"

"Yeah," she jerked the dog back as he tried to sniff my feet. "Across the hall. All that side of the building." She and the dog crossed in front of me to the other apartment. "I doubt it's her place that's for rent. I think she just renewed her lease." She rapped on the door. "Robyn, you there? It's Wanda."

There was silence for a few seconds while Wanda and friend eyed me, then the sound of a chain being released. The door opened and I mentally crossed my fingers. She was young, mid to late twenties, with long, thick hair parted in the middle. It fell loose and straight, and reminded me of the way my sister wore her hair at a time when she also wore a head band and love beads. Her eyes were warm, brown and, even behind a thick pair of lenses, remarkable.

"This guy wants to rent one of these apartments. You're not leavin' are you?"

"No," the woman spoke softly. "Must be one of the others." She eyed me from top to bottom.

I was beginning to feel uncomfortable under her scrutiny. If this wasn't going to be an easy decision for her I didn't want to push so hard that I appeared desperate. "That's okay," I said. "I don't want to be any trouble. I'll call the number." Then I tried a self-conscious laugh. "Just like I'm supposed to do."

Before I could turn away she responded with a little "who cares" shrug and, stepping into the hallway, gestured toward her living room. "Look if you like. I guess they're all the same." She wore a pair of faded, comfortable-looking jeans. And she wore them well. She hung her thumbs in the pockets and waited.

I stood in the doorway and surveyed the sparse furnishings. It reminded me of my place—make-do furniture and a sense of impermanence.

"Want to see the rest?"

"Here," the older woman said, "take Fiscus with you." She offered her the dog's collar.

"That's okay, Mrs. Buchholz," she smiled. "I think he's safe enough."

"You never know, honey. I used to think that about my husband. Ex now. Boy was I wrong."

I laughed and Fiscus growled. That made Robyn laugh and pretty soon we were all yucking it up. Except for Fiscus, that is.

Mrs. Buchholz moved back toward her apartment. "Just leave your door open, honey." Then she looked at me. "And remember, anything happens to her, I know you've been there."

I nodded solemnly and entered Robyn's apartment.

It was small, but clean, and totally devoid of personal touches. As if the person living there didn't intend to stay long or was a meticulously private person. On the other hand, maybe she'd just moved into town with a few hand-me-down sticks for furniture and was trying to establish herself as a private investigator.

"Nice place," I said, taking in the counter that separated the kitchen from the living room and the vase full of fresh-cut flowers sitting on it. I gestured toward the flowers. "Nice. They sure give the room some color."

She seemed far away somewhere and had to drag herself back in order to respond. Then all she said was, "Yes, aren't they?"

She studied me for a few moments and I wondered if maybe I shouldn't have mentioned the flowers. Finally she asked, "Where'd you say you heard about this place?"

"The *Chronicle*," I repeated the lie and hoped she wasn't a subscriber.

She nodded. "Listen, I don't know the other people who live here, so I don't know who it is that's moving out, but I'll be happy to take your name and let the other tenants know you were looking."

"That'd be great." She gave me a piece of paper and a pen. "I'm staying with a friend. This is his number." I hesitated a second then wrote down my own number. Then I handed her the paper. "Name's Roger Kafka. I wrote that down too. What was your name?"

"I didn't say." She took the paper and studied it. "It's Robyn Fosse."

"How do you like living here in Foxport? Seems like a nice town."

"It's okay I guess. More like a small town than it seems." She shrugged slightly then eyed me. "You transferring here?" I nodded and she said, "From where?"

"Santa Fe," I congratulated myself on coming up with the name of a city on such short notice, and hoped she had never been there.

All she said was, "It's probably better than Foxport." Then she turned and walked to the door. "I have to get ready for work. Sorry if I seem rude, but . . ."

I held up my hands. "No problem. You've been a big help." Then I apologized for taking her time and left. On my way out, I knocked on Mrs. Buchholz' door and wished her a good day.

As frequently happens in the Chicago area, the weather had taken a sharp left while I'd been in the apartment building. The sky had clouded over and the temperature had dropped. Mother Nature's way of reminding us who held the cards. My jacket was suddenly inadequate, but it looked like it would be a while before I got home.

I returned to my car and prepared to wait for Robyn to go to work. The dog acted like I'd just made it home unscathed from the Trojan War. I scratched him behind his left ear and he leaned against the car seat. He didn't have a name yet. I thought I'd wait until he grew into one. That's what I'd wanted as a kid. No eight-year-old wants to be named Quintus. Not when there were names like Rex and Bart and Diego for the asking. My parents were wise in the ways of small boys having had four before me, and they humored me and made a real effort to call me by my chosen name of the moment. I'm not sure how old I was before I realized it was just easier to settle for what I had.

The dog ended a wide yawn with a whine and gazed expectantly out the window. I was beginning to learn the disadvantages of taking a dog on surveillance. Just as I was about to let him out, Robyn left her apartment. "Sorry, boy, you'll have to wait." We exchanged seats and he whimpered his disapproval.

"It can't be far," I tried to assure him.

It was farther than I thought. I followed Robyn as she drove east of town. The dog voiced his urgency with soft but steady whines.

We drove about ten miles before Robyn pulled into a parking lot next to a restaurant called The Nordic Loft. I parked in an adjacent lot that backed into a wooded area and, using a 1000 mm lens, snapped some pictures of her as she got out of her car and walked into the building. While my dog took advantage of the woods, I copied her license number.

On the way back to town, I picked up a hamburger for each of us—tomorrow I'd start him on a sensible dog-like diet—and drove back to Markham's office. Lorna Markham might have been skeptical about her husband seeing more than one woman, but I'd been watching the guy in action for the past few days. I wasn't so skeptical. And if Robyn worked in a restaurant, she'd probably be tied up for the night. So Markham had a whole evening to kill.

There was something else about Markham that really bothered me. Something I couldn't quite focus on. Maybe it was his air of confidence. Nobody in the kind of trouble he was in had any right to carry on as if the world were his party and he was being a great host. Maybe if I sat there long enough I'd learn the secret to living under stress.

I didn't see any activity in his office, and his car was the only one parked in the lot. He was probably in there by himself not making much noise.

Shortly after three, a man entered Markham's office building. He sort of bounded up the steps, taking them two-at-a time. The guy must have come on foot. I'd been watching for cars and I almost missed seeing him. Not that it would have mattered. I wasn't getting paid to observe the men that Markham was seeing; only the women. He left the building a few minutes later and cut across the next door lawn and parkway heading east. I only saw the back of him. He wore a short, tan jacket that might have been suede, and had a distinctive spring to his walk. And while he wasn't running away from the building, he did seem to be in a hurry. He could have been there to see Markham or Beck' and Call.

Then it started to get dark and I wasn't seeing any lights in the office. He was out. I was tempted to go in but reminded myself that I was hired to find out about his girlfriends, not his judicial business. Still, you can tell a lot about a man by what's on his desk. To take my mind off breaking and entering, I thought about where he might have gone. Maybe he'd gone out to dinner with someone who drove. Maybe that someone was woman number two . . . or number three if you counted Lorna. All I could do was stay put until she dropped him off. I could wait him out. As long as his car was in the lot, he had to come back.

An hour and a half later I had just about convinced myself that this was a stupid idea. The dog was going stir crazy and I'd walked him as far as I could while still keeping the entrance in sight. He wasn't the only one getting restless. I was tired and thirsty and wasn't being paid by the hour. As I sat there, the urge to get a look at Markham's office grew so that I was going to have to act on it soon. And the longer I waited, the better the chances of him walking in on me. I tapped my foot to Willie Nelson's wailing and the dog curled up in the back seat, probably wondering why he had tried so hard to be appealing when he first saw me in the shelter. Finally, I removed the flashlight from my glove compartment and entered the darkened building.

▽

Chapter Three

IN THE FLASHLIGHT'S BEAM he looked, at first, like he was sleeping. His head rested on his folded arm—the telling portrait of an overworked public official. He'd wake in a half hour or so and immediately focus on the word that had lulled him to sleep. But when the light didn't rouse him, I moved closer and realized that wasn't it at all. The first thing that was wrong with this picture was that nobody sleeps with his eyes open. Then I saw the small black hole in the middle of his temple and the thin, dark line that trickled from it and I knew this wasn't the kind of sleep you wake up from. Not in this dimension anyway.

Lorna had been right about his self destruction mechanism. Only thing was, he apparently didn't need her to grease the wheels. His right hand barely brushed the handle of the .25 automatic that lay on the desk in front of him. His pulse was gone and his eyes were dilated. What was it, Markham? Was it the idea of doing hard time in a minimum security country club? Or maybe knowing that you'd have to settle for the lecture circuit rather than the campaign trail and couldn't handle the trade off? Maybe I was just being bitter because I knew I'd never have that much to lose.

I thought about the story I'd give the police and hoped that this was Chief Carver's night off. It probably wouldn't matter, though. I'd heard that he once left his son's little league playoff game in the bottom of the ninth inning with his son, representing the go-ahead run, at bat. He'd surrendered that moment in order to oversee the arrest of three teenagers who ended their brief and not so profitable burglary spree by stealing the radar detector out of a councilman's BMW. A guy like that wasn't the type to take a pass on the suicide of a judge.

Damn. I decided I'd better check out the office now because I wouldn't have a chance later. After a moment's consideration, I switched on the lights. To a passerby, room lights attract a lot less attention than the beam of a flashlight.

There was a familiar smell to Markham's office and, using a handkerchief, I lifted the lid of a leather-bound humidor. Seemed that Mason and Markham shared a taste for the same expensive cigars.

Markham's desk bore the marks of a much-used piece of furniture. Only one of the heavy, deep drawers had a lock on it and it was open. The drawer was crammed with hanging files, each labeled according to its contents. Using one of Markham's cigars as a maneuvering device, I picked my way through the files. One of them was devoted to Mason Burke and, using my handkerchief, I removed it from the drawer. It seemed to contain only information pertaining to Markham's indictment. There was a three inch gap behind the rack that held the files and the back of the drawer. I reached behind it and withdrew a large brown envelope with a metal clasp. Inside it were four business size envelopes. The first of these smaller envelopes contained five photos featuring Robyn Fosse in various stages of undress. They weren't the sleazy kind of photos you find in some magazines. I wouldn't call them art either, although that was probably what he was shooting for. They were black and whites. Somehow that tends to give a photo respectability, whether it deserves it or not. A color photo of a bare-breasted woman licking an ice cream cone is a girlie shot. Do the same thing in black and white and you've got a serious attempt at art. Go figure. A glimpse inside a couple of the other envelopes revealed more attempts at art with different women. Before I had time to consider the implications, I put the smaller envelopes back into the larger one, which I folded so I could cram it in my inside jacket pocket. At the time, it seemed the thing to do. No one needs their nude photos found in the contents of a suicide's desk.

There wasn't much else in Markham's office that you wouldn't expect to find in a judge's place of business—law books, journals, *Supreme Court Reporters,* and a good stock of liquor. He had one of those elaborate appointment books on his desk—the kind with so much going on you have to load one month at a time. It had been looking pretty empty lately.

I noticed that not all of Markham's photographic efforts were hidden in a drawer. A couple of enlarged photos framed in chrome dominated the walls. Both were black and white. One was a Chamber-of-Commerce type view of the Fox River—shot upriver from the town. Duck-filled parks banked the river and none of the people glimpsed in the scene appeared to have anything better to do than look at the ducks and the water. The other photo was of a pheasant being shot in midflight. Markham had captured that split second the bird was hit—feathers and down erupting—and it was frozen in that piece of sky, neither rising nor descending. I wondered if the pheasant had known yet that it was dying. It was a powerful but very uncomfortable image.

In a corner was a wooden safe which doubled as a stand for a particularly prosperous jade plant. The safe was designed more for looks than function. The combination lock looked cheap and unchallenging. But that didn't really matter because the door was wide open. I rummaged through the contents, which appeared to be mostly stock certificates and contracts.

Markham's office was the smallest in the three room suite. Townsend's was large and ordered with a secretary's desk in the reception area. There was a large closet with supplies and metal files in it. The old cabinets seemed to contain only closed cases.

It would have been easier to leave Markham for the cleaning people or his secretary to find. I doubted if he'd care one way or the other and I wouldn't have to come up with a reason for being there. But in the end, I called the police. While I waited for them to show up, I stashed the envelopes full of photos and the cigar in my car and brought the dog into Markham's outer office. I did that for two reasons. One, he was getting antsy being cooped up in that car and really seemed to like being with me. How could I fault him for that? And two, it occurred to me that they might be more inclined to believe my story if I had a dog with me. Nobody robs an office, let alone kills a man, if he's got a dog with him. Just isn't done.

I sat in the secretary's chair and, after a cursory inspection of the office, the dog curled up on the floor next to me. I idly rubbed his back with my foot and thought about Markham. He hadn't impressed me as the type to take his own life. From my observations, he seemed too sure of himself. Like he was playing this hand with an ace up his sleeve. Besides, Lorna hadn't even played her card yet. Maybe something had happened between Markham and his mistress. Something big enough to make him put a gun to his head and pull the trigger. Not a split. That wouldn't be enough. A guy who stored his current girlfriend's nude photo along with those who had gone before her (I assumed they were former friends) wasn't the kind of guy who let anything get close enough to his heart to break it.

The sound of approaching sirens cut short my reverie. I barely had time to run through my story once more before the first squad car pulled up and a man stepped out. I'd only met Chief Carver once before, but I knew, even without the benefit of sunlight, that the tall, lanky figure approaching the office was his. Damn. Our one meeting had not been under the best of circumstances. And, although I was more than willing to chalk the whole thing up to an unfortunate misunderstanding, Carver didn't quite see it that way. In fact, he specifically noted that he would see me in hell before he let me forget.

Carver climbed the stairs two at a time, stepped into the outer office, and took in the room without appearing to give any more consideration to me or my dog than he did to the coat rack.

"Markham's in the office to your right," I told him.

Without a word, he entered the office. Two police officers, one a detective, the other a patrolman, followed several paces behind him. The detective nodded at me on his way. The uniform scowled at me. I waited, reasonably certain I wouldn't be ignored for long. I was right.

"McCauley." It was not a request. When I entered Markham's office, Carver looked at me for the first time since he'd arrived. "This how you found him?" I nodded. "You touch anything?"

"I know the procedure." I tried to sound appropriately offended by his question.

Carver approached me. He was a few inches taller than my six feet, and he stood close enough so he got to look down to address me. His eyes had the hardness and intensity of steel bearings. "You touch anything?" he repeated.

"Just the light switch." There was no way I was going to hand Carver those photos.

He didn't back up an inch and didn't change the inflection in his voice when he said, "What were you doing here?"

I cleared my throat. "I was on a job. Working for my client."

Who's that?" Carver asked.

"Can't say. That's confidential."

"Well unless you're a lawyer, you'd better say." He paused and his scowl deepened. "Because you're sure as hell no priest."

Damn. Sometimes, if a cop doesn't know any better, that works. "Lorna Markham. She thought her husband was having an affair."

Carver looked over his shoulder at Markham's body, then back to me. "Was he?"

"I have no proof," I lied, thinking that it couldn't possibly matter anymore.

I explained my entry into the building, adding that since Markham's car was in the lot and I hadn't seen any lights go on, I'd started to wonder. When I began to tell him about the man I'd seen go into the building, Carver walked over to one of the windows and looked out. "You call anyone else?" he interrupted me in mid-sentence.

"No. Why?"

He turned back to me as if by reading my expression he could tell if I was putting him on. "We got company." He turned to the scowling policeman who stood in the doorway to the outer office. "Henninger, Barlowe's here. Keep him out." Henninger was a big man—shorter than Carver but with about fifty pounds on him. He responded with the speed of a large snake with a full stomach. Carver regarded him with a mixture of disgust and wariness but kept silent.

"Who's Barlowe?" I asked Carver.

"Newspaper," he said like he was talking about rat droppings.

There was some commotion in the outer office followed by the protest, "Hey, man, I've gotta right to be here."

I stepped into the office to get a look. The reporter barely came up to the deputy's chin but had stepped right up to him and was using Henninger's discomfort at the proximity the same way Carver had intimidated me with his height. The reporter was slight of build as well, with longish dark, curly hair. He wore a corduroy jacket over jeans and had wire-rimmed glasses. He saw me step into the room and moved toward me before Henninger could stop him.

"And who are you? Where's the judge?" It took him about three seconds to cross the room. That was one second longer than it took my dog to lunge between us, growling and threatening the reporter. Barlowe stopped and bounced back a step like he'd just hit an invisible shield and held up his hands, one holding a pencil and the other a spiral notepad. "Whoa. Nice dog." He looked up at me. "Does he bite?"

"What d'you think?" I said, noting that his lenses magnified the size of his eyes. He reminded me of someone, though I couldn't place who that someone was.

I heard Carver behind me. "Nice. A dog that eats reporters."

Barlowe ignored him. "Okay, let's start over here. I can see I've gotten off on the wrong foot. No threat intended." The dog had quieted down and was watching Barlowe with immense interest. "I'm just trying to get a story here."

"No. You're digging for a sensational headline so you can sell more copies of that rag you work for." It was Carver again. He continued, "I may not be able to stop you, but I don't have to make it easy for you either."

Barlowe sighed and put his arms down at his sides. "Chief, we could stand here and debate freedom of speech until one of us dies of old age, and neither of us would budge an inch, but that isn't going to change what I've got to do here." He gestured toward Markham's office. "There's a body in there, isn't there? And it belongs to Judge Markham, doesn't it?" No one said anything, so Barlowe continued, "Did he die of a heart attack? Was it a suicide? Was it murder?" He looked at me. "Did you kill him?"

"No," I said, realizing it was the first straight answer in the last fifteen minutes. Then I said to Carver, "He does have a few rights, you know. First Amendment and all that."

"Why, thank you, Mr. McCauley, defender of the Constitution."

I shrugged, Barlowe looked amused and I didn't have eyes in the back of my head, so I couldn't tell what Carver was doing. Smiling fondly at me, no doubt.

The young detective who had been inspecting Markham's

office stepped out, saying, "Looks like a clear case of suicide to me, chief."

Barlowe's eyes widened and Henninger smirked. I turned to look at Carver. This I didn't want to miss. He turned the full force of his steel gaze on the detective. "Who died and made you coroner, Rand?"

Rand looked at the reporter, at me, then back to Carver. "You're right, sir. Of course. Sorry," he stammered and cast his eyes toward the carpet.

Carver turned on me. "What were you saying about this guy you saw?"

Barlowe jumped on that before I could answer. "Who did you see?"

I shrugged. "I didn't get much of a look at him. There was quite a distance between us. He was wearing a tan jacket. Could have been suede. Maybe someone else around here saw him."

Barlowe was getting everything down. Carver looked at him and shook his head. "We'd appreciate it if you'd keep a lid on this at least until we notify the widow."

That comment struck me as ludicrous and before I could stop myself, I said, "What're you going to do? Drop her a note in the 'out of town' mail slot?"

Carver turned on me abruptly and the dog growled. Just as quickly, he dropped his gaze to the snarling animal. "If you don't shut that mutt up, I'm gonna kick its ass up the river." I had to kneel down to do it, but I placed a restraining hand on the dog. Carver towered over me. "I'm running the show here, not you. Not Barlowe and," he turned to Rand, "certainly not you." He turned back to me. "McCauley, I want your address and phone number. I want you to go home and stay there until tomorrow morning at nine o'clock when I want you to come down to the station to make a statement. You got that?"

"Yeah," I said, more confused than surprised that he was letting me leave. Perhaps I'd underestimated my ability to get on his nerves.

"And when we're finished with you, it'd just make my day if you'd get the hell out of Foxport."

Carver had me outclassed when it came to cold stares, but I did my best. "I'll bet it would," I said, removing a business card from my wallet. I placed it on the secretary's desk and started to walk out, wishing I'd left Markham for the cleaning people. Barlowe stopped me. "Could I have one of those cards?"

"Sure," I said, glancing at Carver who was probably thinking about the virtues of a police state. I handed Barlowe another card.

When I got back to the apartment, I didn't go right in. Instead, I took the dog down to the river and walked south for about a half mile. I wasn't going anywhere; I just needed to feel the air and smell the river. The dog seemed to need that too. He tried to herd a bunch of ducks that had bedded down for the night. One of the drakes went after him with a nasty rattling noise. The dog didn't back off though, just changed direction and, moving in a low-to-the-ground crouch showing remarkable speed, worked the group from a different angle. It was fascinating to watch and I wondered if maybe I should invest in some sheep so he could stay in practice. I sat on a picnic bench, hypnotized by the stars and the reflection of the lights in the river, and thought about what didn't fit with Markham's suicide. I didn't care what Lorna said. I'd spent the last few days following a man who wasn't acting like a judge with an indictment hanging over his head, much less like a suicide candidate. But then that wasn't my problem, was it?

Carver was though. I could understand the guy's hostility toward me. The fact that he'd misread the whole situation during our first encounter wouldn't have mattered to him at the time. And then, after a while, it doesn't help to explain. Maybe I should have tried.

It was almost ten thirty before we got back to my apartment. We walked in and the dog trotted over to his bowl of water. I picked up a folded sheet of paper that had been inserted under my door. It was from the apartment management. It read:

Dear Tenant,

As you know, pets are prohibited in the River's Edge Apartments.

Normally, any tenant found keeping a pet is subject to a fine. However, we value you as a tenant and feel that such drastic measures are not necessary.

You have one week to dispose of the pet. If, after this time, you still have the animal, you will be subject to eviction.

We appreciate your cooperation and look forward to serving you in the future.

Thank you,

The Management.

I crumpled the note and hurled it against the wall. "Damn." Then I took a beer out of the refrigerator and turned on the radio, tuning it to a local station. I was just in time to catch the news. They were reporting Markham's death as suicide pending the coroner's verdict, but they had not ruled out foul play.

I sank into the couch. The dog hopped up next to me and I scratched him behind the ears. "Let's see," I said, "what's the score here? Mason wants me out of town. Carver wants me out of town. And by tomorrow I'll bet that Lorna Markham wants me out of town. That's three for me. And how are you doing?" The dog didn't seem to care, but I continued, "The management at this river dwelling wants you out of town. That's one for you. So far. I don't think Carver's crazy about you either. Barlowe may come around, though." I took a long drink off the beer. "I don't know about you, but I'm beginning to wonder why I'm trying so hard to stay in a town where nobody likes me."

▽

Chapter Four

I WAS UP EARLY and decided to see what the papers had to say about Markham's death. I could have taken the dog along but I figured it was a good time to start weaning him. I felt like his mother. Every time I got up or turned around, there he was. He curled up outside the bathroom door when I showered. I'd tripped over him a couple times, not realizing he was right behind me. I had to start to rebuild the trust that someone had done such a good job of eradicating. He might bark and cry and put up a fuss, but I'd take the car so I'd only be gone for ten minutes. I wasn't too concerned about the management hearing him. They were already going to evict us. What more could they do? I gave him a new rawhide bone just before I left.

The story only made the suburban section of the Chicago papers but topped the front page of the *Foxport Chronicle*. There was a large photo of the judge that might have made a good campaign poster—smiling and confident—above the headline: Judge dies of gunshot wound. The article, which appeared under Jeffrey Barlowe's byline, described the incident and said that although authorities were still investigating, the death was believed to be suicide. Only a brief mention was made of the man I saw leaving Markham's office. But Barlowe referred to my role as a private investigator following Scott Markham. I imagined Lorna would be pleased to see that.

The more I thought suicide, the more it bothered me. If you're shooting yourself in the head, you're pretty serious about it. As far as you're concerned, it's over. Why put the gun to your temple? There's always a chance you'll survive a shot like that and spend the rest of your life as a vegetable. If you put the barrel in your mouth and blasted away, you can just about guarantee you won't be taking up space in a nursing home.

When I got home, the dog was lying by the door and was a good way into his rawhide bone. His greeting was enthusiastic but showed no signs of desperation. We were improving.

On the way to the police station, I debated what to do with the photos I'd found in Markham's office. I was already regretting my action. I should have left them there and let the cops use them or ignore them. But there was no easy way to undo my mistake. The fact that they were calling it suicide didn't help much. Because I couldn't get around the idea that every woman in those pictures or, if any were married, every one of their husbands might have had reason to want Markham dead. I'd only looked at the pictures briefly and, although Robyn was the only woman I recognized, maybe if I weren't brand new to Foxport, I would have recognized others. It did occur to me that I might have hit the mother lode in terms of usable material for blackmail. It didn't take a criminal mind to figure that out. Maybe if Markham's death was officially declared suicide, I'd destroy them. But there was the problem. If the police knew of the existence of the photos, would they be so quick to make that statement? Or was Markham's death to be investigated and closed as quickly and unobtrusively as possible?

Foxport was known as a quaint, river town; the kind of town that liked to keep a low profile on its scandals and disgraces. Just by being indicted for bribery, Judge Scott Markham had put the town's public relations people into a dither. Now he had died violently and there wasn't a rug big enough to sweep that one under. The one labeled "suicide" seemed to be the most convenient. And I guess that was why they thought it would help if I called it suicide too.

Detective Rand took my statement and I couldn't help but notice that he was painfully young. He constantly fidgeted with the knot in his necktie and recited the procedures like he was reading them out of a manual. It was strictly business. No smile, no attempt at making me comfortable. He must have been trying to atone for his slip of the tongue at Markham's office. "Mr. McCauley," he was saying, "if you'll just tell us exactly what happened. Speculations and theories really aren't appropriate here. Do you have any questions?"

"Any leads on that guy I saw at Markham's office?"

"Nobody but you saw anything."

"In other words, 'no'."

Rand switched on the tape recorder. "Just tell me what happened, all right? Why were you there?"

"I was working for my client."

"And who's your client?"

"Lorna Markham," I said and before he could ask why, I continued, "Here's what happened," and told him most of it. Afterwards, I asked to see Carver.

"He's not around," said the detective, rewinding the tape. "Why do you want to see him?"

"I got tickets to the Cubs opener. Thought maybe he'd be interested." I shrugged. "That's okay. He's probably busy anyway. Just tell him I asked for him."

I walked out of the office and the detective followed me. "Uh, McCauley, he just went into a meeting. He should be out in five minutes. Ten at the most. Why don't you wait?" He gestured toward a bench out of the traffic area.

I glanced at my watch. "Ten minutes?"

"No more."

I nodded and took a seat on the bench. The detective started to go back to his desk, hesitated, and turned toward me. "How many tickets do you have?"

I smiled apologetically. "Just two. Sorry."

He nodded and left. Call it a death wish, but here was a chance to talk to Carver; a chance to set things straight. And maybe, if the water tested out okay, I could drop a few hints about the photos and try his reaction.

In just over five minutes, the desk sergeant directed me to Carver's office. I spent a solid three or four seconds praying that Carver didn't think I was serious about those tickets. From the look on his face as I walked into his office, I'd say he knew I was kidding. I'd also say that he wasn't the slightest bit amused. If a hatchet were to be buried here, it would be in my head.

Carver was only a few years older than me, and I was the one who had initiated this meeting, but I felt like I'd been called down to the principal's office for cutting class. I closed the door behind me. We were still visible to the outer office because of the glass panels that made up the upper half of the walls and the door.

From the set of his jaw and his eyes, he appeared more tightly strung than usual. He swept me with his gaze and said, "You've got three minutes to convince me I shouldn't have you arrested for obstructing justice." He moved a pile of papers from his "In" basket to the center of his desk and began to go through them one at a time. He spoke as he did this, frequently pausing and muttering, wanting to make it obvious that what was on his desk was a lot more important than what was standing in front of it. "I don't appreciate your lying to my men . . ." long pause while he studied two lines on a piece of paper . . . "The only reason you're in here . . . ," he jotted a note on his calendar, ". . . the only reason you're in here is because I'm available to anyone in this town." He stopped shuffling papers and looked up at me.

"Nice speech," I said and continued, "I guess I just want to know why when a prominent citizen—an elected official yet—dies in what appears to be a suicide, but which could just as easily have been made to look like a suicide, the authorities are ready to classify it that way before the corpse is cold."

Carver used up about ten of my seconds before he said, "Give me a reason why I should believe otherwise."

"He wasn't acting like a guy about to kill himself."

"I see. And you're qualified to make that statement." He paused, then added, "He had reason to."

"If your career's your whole life, maybe, but I don't know if that was the case with Markham."

"How well did you know the guy?"

"Not well." Ideas weren't coming to me fast enough. "But I'd think you'd talk to some people who knew him before you jumped the gun on this one."

"How do you know we haven't?"

He had me there. "Well, did you find anything out about that guy I saw going into his office?"

"We learned that no one besides you saw him, and that doesn't bother me too much. He probably had business there and when he figured nobody was there, he left."

"Nope. He took too long."

"There was no sign of a struggle and it was Markham's own

gun." He checked his watch. "Your time's almost up McCauley. I'm not impressed yet."

I tried again. "Well, if I were going to kill someone and wanted to make it look like suicide, I sure wouldn't buy a special gun for the occasion."

He pointed a finger at me. "I don't owe you an explanation. I don't care if anything about this bothers you." He started to go back to his papers when another thought occurred to him. "And I'll tell you, I don't owe you a warning either, but I'm giving you one. Keep out of this. Find yourself another client. Preferably in another town."

"I like it here."

Carver slammed a hand down on his desk. "Why am I wasting my breath with you? I don't give a damn what you think about this investigation. I'm not here to humor some minor league detective with an overactive imagination."

The intensity of his reaction helped me decide that now was a good time to go for broke. "Yeah, well I guess I shouldn't be surprised that you aren't interested in the facts surrounding Markham's death. You've never let the facts get in your way before."

In less than a second, Carver had himself under control again. "So this is what we're all about here." He smiled and nodded as though he now understood the score and could predict the winner. The temperature in the room dropped. "You know, in some cultures I would have been justified in killing you."

I leaned on his desk. "Well, isn't it just your luck that you're in a country sane enough to make that illegal but crazy enough to make you chief of police." I sat down and continued before he could interrupt or deck me. "Look," I said, "I didn't know she was your wife, okay? How could I have known? I'd been in town all of four days. I'm sitting in this bar and this attractive, very pleasant woman starts talking to me. She's not with anyone, not wearing a ring, and not wanting to be alone. I'm not with anyone, I'm not married and I definitely don't want to be alone. How am I supposed to know she's married to the chief of police and there are three off duty cops in the bar?"

"You took her to a motel."

I shrugged. "That's where I was living."

"And I suppose you were going to give her a nightcap and call her a cab."

I leaned back in the chair, determined not to put myself on the defensive any more than I already had. "What do you think?" I asked quietly.

Carver's glare didn't soften and he didn't say anything.

Maybe defensive wasn't a bad way to be. "I had no idea she was married, let alone married to the police chief, until you showed up at the door and made it abundantly clear. Look, I'm not saying I'm blameless here. But, no matter how convenient it is for you, maybe you should quit dumping it all on me." Still no response. I cleared my throat and changed position in the chair. "Well, I'm glad I got that out in the open. I sure feel better, don't you?"

This was the point where Carver would either arrest me, throw me out of his office or tell me we should just forget our past differences and start from scratch. Realistically, the most I could hope for was the middle option. For a few seconds, Carver looked genuinely confused. Then, abruptly, he looked away. He might have been studying the watercolor of the river hanging on the wall, but I didn't think so. Without turning toward me, he said, "Get out of here, McCauley. We've got no more to say to each other."

Assuming that our exchange was over, I got up to leave. "McCauley," he stopped me before I opened the door. "If I see any of your half-assed theories turning up in the newspaper, there won't be a town far enough away for you." Then he went back to his pile of papers and wouldn't look at me again. That was when I decided that if they wanted to call Markham's death a suicide, who was I to argue.

On my way back to my apartment, I stopped in the manager's office to plead my dog's case. A young woman was talking with a guy I'd seen walking around with a tool belt. She was seated at a desk and he was slumped on a couch with his feet on a two-drawer file cabinet. The woman's blonde hair curled slightly just past her shoulders. A startling rainbow of colors was painted on her eyelids so her actual eye color didn't register. The desk in front of her was bare except for a lusty paperback lying pages down to mark her place. The title had something to do with desire and conquest and the concept was illustrated on the cover with a man and a woman wearing lots of clothing except in the places where it counts. The man and the woman who weren't on the cover of the book looked up at me, clearly annoyed that I'd interrupted what was, no doubt, a thoughtful discussion of contemporary fiction.

Neither of them spoke so I took the initiative. "Hi. I'm Quint McCauley. Apartment 510B. I received a letter from management yesterday." The woman raised one manicured nail, indicating I should wait. She opened a desk drawer and thumbed through its contents. Finally she removed a single file folder and opened it, riffling through the papers until she found the one she was looking for. "You've got a dog." She raised her eyebrows as if concealing a dog on your premises was right up there with exposing yourself to nuns. "They aren't allowed here."

The maintenance man made a disgusted noise and shifted his bulk on the couch. "Damned animals. They crap and piss all over the carpets. Can't ever get the smell out. Dog'll trash a place in a week."

"Yeah," she said, "we don't allow cats either." She and the lump on the couch shared a conspiratorial smile. I wondered how many notches he had in his tool belt.

I asked how they knew about him.

"Neighbors." She smiled and I wanted to torture their identity out of her. Then I thought about pointing out that while there was a strictly enforced pet ban, the owners of the complex apparently didn't have any standards as far as hiring people to run their operation. Unfortunately, I didn't have the wording down until later that night after a couple beers. What I wound up saying was, "My dog has a lot more class than the people who run this place."

The maintenance man finally moved. He stood up. He was about six inches shorter than I was and most of his bulk came from beer rather than muscle. No problem.

The woman was not so aroused by my statement. She shrugged slightly and returned the letter to my file. "Either you get rid of the dog or you move."

"Oh, yeah," I said. "Well, one of my rules is that I won't live in a place that isn't good enough for my dog." I nodded to both of them. "Thanks for your time." I heard them laughing as I walked out and realized the futility of insulting someone who didn't know it had happened. I congratulated myself on burning yet another bridge.

Moving is a pain; an expensive one at that. According to the balance in my checking/savings account, I was good until the end of the week if I skipped one meal a day. Of course, that didn't count breakfast which I didn't eat anyway.

My dog was uttering little growls as he gnawed on his rawhide bone, which, like my bank account, had shrunk considerably. He appeared oblivious to our financial distress. Things were pretty bleak, but I had a couple options. Lorna owed me money, but there was something about dunning a widow the day after she'd attained that status that went against my grain. I could also do some cold calling. Aside from Mason, there were four other lawyers I'd worked for in Foxport. Maybe one of them would have something for me. I walked to the window and watched a row of ducks waddle between buildings. Phoning people to drum up business or to collect debts was almost worse than starving. The idea of resorting to telemarketing made me feel miserable right down to my socks. Was there a way to put this off for a few minutes? I turned to the dog. "You have to go out?"

I took the dog for a run in the park and dredged my brain for other options. I could try to find somewhere else to live in Foxport. But, I'd checked the classifieds and there were damned few that didn't specify "No pets." The rest probably didn't allow them either, but didn't want to spend the extra buck to have the words printed. Well, there was at least one building that I knew allowed pets. I had a hunch though that a border collie and a doberman named Fiscus might not hit it off. My other option was to leave town. I was pretty sure a number of people would be more than happy to help me pack.

The thing was, I liked Foxport. Something drew me to the river. It revitalized me, calmed me. I liked the smell, the ducks, the canoers, the fishermen. The way the moon cast its reflection on it. The way it just kept flowing, working its way around the obstacles, never faltering or flailing.

A movement out of the corner of my eye jerked me around. My dog stood, ears perked, frozen. I looked for a duck that had unwittingly strayed from its herd. All I saw was a man about fifty feet south of me with a young Irish setter. It wasn't the setter that had attracted my dog's attention, though. The man was throwing a red saucer-shaped object which sailed maybe a hundred feet then glided to the ground. The setter was having a whole lot of trouble grasping the concept of this Frisbee. We stood and watched them for several minutes. The guy would throw it and point after it, trying to cue the dog. The dog showed extreme interest in the pointing finger, but was unable to connect it with the soaring object. Both dog and owner were getting frustrated. The dog, being a dog, wanted very much to please, but couldn't figure out how to do it. The owner couldn't believe his dog was that dense. And the owner was getting pretty tired of fetching the Frisbee himself.

Finally, on about the fifth attempt, he threw the Frisbee in our direction. My dog couldn't take it anymore. He bolted after it and as it curved back to earth, leaped up and caught it in mid air. It was quite a sight. Then he dropped it on the ground and waited for the pitching machine to do it again. The Irish Setter and its owner trotted up to us. Maybe I was reacting to my run-ins with mankind over the last few days but I was half expecting this guy to trash both me and my dog for appropriating his Frisbee. He was big enough and, from what I could see, strong enough to pull that off. Even though it was a brisk day, he wore cut off jeans and a cut off sweatshirt. His legs and arms were corded with muscle and his neck, what there was of it, looked like a tree stump. He looked at me and my dog, then turned to the setter. "See, stupid, that's how it's done."

The setter sat down and wagged its tail. The man shook his head. "I love this dog. But he's the dumbest thing." He looked back at me. "How'd you teach your dog?"

I shrugged. "I don't know. I got him used."

He nodded and neither of us said anything for a minute.

"Maybe," I suggested, "if he watched my dog catch a few he'd learn by example."

He looked down at his dog who obviously wanted nothing more than to make this guy happy. "What do you think?" He turned to me. "Can't hurt." Then he held out his hand. "Name's Mike Richardson."

I shook his hand. "Quint McCauley."

The dog's name was Dallas and he did, indeed, learn how to catch a Frisbee. But he was a slow learner and it took a while. I learned that Mike was a computer consultant and not, as I had suspected, a professional wrestler. He worked out a lot because he didn't want anyone to put him in the "computer geek" mold. I certainly wouldn't have tried. He thought that being a private detective was probably the next best thing to being a cowboy and I told him that it paid just about as well.

After a half hour or so, Dallas had the art down pretty well. However, he seemed to be reluctant to let go of the Frisbee after he retrieved it and thought that sometimes Mike should be the one to come to him. One thing was very clear. Dallas was never going to come anywhere near my dog when it came to catching Frisbees. Although mine was a smaller dog, he would jump higher, sometimes twisting in mid air, to execute some stunning catches. As we walked back to the apartment, I felt pretty good about a couple things. First, I had met the first person in Foxport who, after an hour, hadn't offered to help me pack. And he had given me the name of a good bar. And second, my dog now had a name. I'd only seen one other creature who was able to shag flies like that and he did it for a living. Harry "Peanuts" Lowrey had been an incredible outfielder for the Cubs during the '45 season that everyone still talks about. I'd thought he was fantastic even though most of what I'd seen of him had been in film clips. His name fit my dog and he seemed to respond to it. Or maybe he didn't care who he was named after. Maybe he was just relieved to finally have a name.

When I got back to the apartment, I forced myself to place the call to Lorna Markham. I assumed that my services were no longer needed, but I had the information she'd hired me to get and I wanted—no I needed—to be paid. A man answered the phone, from the sound of it a young man. It might have been her son, Eric. I asked for Lorna and identified myself. He came back a minute later. "She says she doesn't know you."

"Would you please tell her it's important."

There was a long, irritated pause and finally he said, "Just a minute." He was gone a little longer this time, but brought back the same answer. And he didn't wait for my protest before he hung up.

It was possible that Lorna was just saying this for the benefit of her family and would be more than happy to settle up as soon as I could meet her in private. But I hadn't been doing well in the human relations department lately and I wasn't optimistic.

Next I pulled out my list of lawyers, swallowed hard, and started dialing. I shouldn't have bothered. The first one sounded nervous and said he'd get back to me; the second and third weren't in for me; the fourth was the only one to level with me.

"What in the hell did you do to irritate the Napoleon of Foxport?" Clayton Peterson sounded both amused and incredulous.

"The word is out on you, McCauley. You're going to have a tough time getting someone to hire you to catch flies."

I wanted to yank the phone out of the wall and put it through the window. "Tell me, Peterson, how is it that Mason Burke's got so much power? What's the guy got?"

Peterson's laugh was low and without humor. "Don't underestimate the man. That's dangerous. Besides," he hesitated, "the truth may hurt, but here it is. You're simply not worth taking a stand for. No offense or anything, you're a good investigator and all, but decent investigators aren't exactly tough to come by. The fact is, nobody's going to put up a fuss because this is not a major issue."

I didn't respond. What could I say?

"I'm really sorry. I'd like to hire you, but, well I think you understand. The success of one investigator is not worth me losing clients over."

"How long does Mason hold a grudge?"

He paused before he said, "A long time. A very long time."

As I hung up, I wondered if maybe it wasn't time to move west again until I hit the next river and then maybe I'd just keep going until the water hit my ears. Or maybe I should head the other way. Go back to Chicago. I called an acquaintance on the Chicago police force. He wasn't exactly a friend—we weren't on each other's Christmas card list—but we had a healthy respect for each other.

"What in the hell are you doing way the hell out in Foxport? For Christ's sake, you might as well live in Nebraska," was O'Henry's greeting when I told him where I was calling from. "What's this I hear about you starting your own business? How's that going?"

"You know of any agencies in the city that are hiring?"

"That good, huh?"

"Well, let me put it this way. They're taking up a collection to send me to Nebraska."

"Wouldn't happen to have anything to do with that judge's suicide, would it?"

The last few months hadn't changed O'Henry. He still didn't miss a thing. "It might." Then I said, "He died yesterday. They closed the case today. Does that seem fast to you?"

O'Henry made some thinking noises, then said, "Maybe. It depends on who the guy is and if they're getting pressure to close it or to investigate it. What's it seem like to you?"

I wasn't inclined to spill my guts. "They're probably right."

"Well, back to your question, I don't know offhand of anyone hiring, but I can check around." He paused. "You using me as a reference?"

"Sure am."

"Hmph. Can't guarantee you'll impress anyone."

Before we hung up, O'Henry asked me about Elaine. "Hey, how's that lady friend of yours?"

I sighed. "She's in Santa Fe."

"Santa Fe? What's in Santa Fe?"

"Not me."

"Oh," was all he said before telling me he'd call if he heard of any work.

All the fresh air had made me hungry and nothing in the refrigerator inspired me so I dug out of my jeans pocket the name of the bar that Mike had mentioned and decided that tomorrow would be a good day to fast. Peanuts had crashed after the workout in the park and barely lifted an ear as I left to celebrate the plight of the working man.

CHAPTER FIVE

MIKE RICHARDSON was right. The Tattersall Tavern was just the ticket for a beer and a sandwich. They had Guinness stout on tap and I was pleasantly surprised to find they served it the right way—somewhere around basement temperature. I had a cold turkey with Swiss sandwich that was as generous as it was good. The tavern was fairly small. A big dark wood bar dominated the room and there was space for about ten small tables. They'd managed to cram fifteen in, however.

The place was pretty crowded—especially for a Monday night. The tables were filling fast and there were only a couple seats left at the bar when Jeff Barlowe walked in with a tall, slender woman. He scanned the room, spotted me sitting alone at a table with four chairs, and said something to his companion. Then they both looked back at me and nodded.

At Markham's office the night before, I had been impressed with Barlowe's aggressiveness. Not just in the way he conducted an interview but also in his walk, his posture and the way he left anyone who couldn't keep up with him in his wake. He reminded me of a small feisty terrier that would take on a dog twice its own size because it had never occurred to it that size made a difference.

"We weren't exactly introduced yesterday," he said, extending his hand. "I'm Jeff Barlowe." He gestured toward the woman behind him. "This is Anne Phillips. She's a photographer for the *Chronicle*. Mind if we join you?"

"Is this business or social?" I asked.

Jeff's shrug was almost apologetic. "Well, maybe a little of both. Reporters are like cops. We're never off duty."

"Okay," I said. "Just so I know the ground rules."

They hadn't been sitting more than a half minute when a waitress was there. After she joked with Jeff and left to fill the order, I said, "It pays to be a regular, doesn't it?"

"Jeff's a regular customer in about five bars here in Foxport." Anne laughed a little when she said that, but it was a forced laugh. She seemed tense. Jeff was slouched comfortably in his chair but Anne was perched on the edge of hers, hands in her lap.

Jeff raised his hands in self defense. "Hey. Gotta know what's going on. Bars are a great source." Anne laughed again and there was something about the way she had to pull her gaze away from Jeff—it seemed a conscious effort—that made me suspect there was something more than a professional relationship going on there. While Anne was intent on drawing beer up from under its foam, I watched her, and tried to figure out why she looked familiar. Up close, she was much more attractive than she had appeared at first, but she was doing her damndest to conceal that fact. Her hair was short and dark and hung in her face, with no apparent attempt at a style, as if its sole purpose were to screen her from the world. She didn't seem to have made even a half-hearted effort to enhance her looks. In spite of that, there was an attractive woman buried there. She had small, sharp features that softened a lot when she smiled. She wore a down vest over a turtleneck sweater and carried no purse. When the waitress had brought their drinks, she'd dug into her pocket and paid for her own.

"So," Jeff said after securing a basket of popcorn, "this one's wrapped up nice and tidy."

"It's official?"

He nodded. "Just talked to your buddy Carver," he spoke with a mouth full of popcorn. "The official word is suicide."

I nodded and realized my glass was dangerously close to empty. Jeff noticed and flagged the waitress down. "What makes you think Carver's my buddy?" I asked as if I didn't know.

Jeff smiled. "Like I said, I know the bars around here pretty well. Lots of sources." My drink came and he paid for it before I could get my money out. "One thing, though," he said.

I waited, not touching the beer.

Jeff leaned forward and kept his voice down. "Did you know she was the police chief's wife?"

I took a long drink before I answered. "You must think I've got sawdust for brains."

Jeff settled into his chair, smiling a little. "That wasn't exactly a first for Ellie. She usually targets guys who are new in town."

I nodded. "I think I can figure that out."

Jeff continued, "I suppose being married to Carver could make a person crazy in a lot of ways." Then he looked at me and added, "No offense intended."

I shrugged and turned to Anne who seemed to be only half listening to the exchange. "Did you take that photo that was in the *Chronicle* a couple weeks ago? On the front page. The one with the ice melting on the river?"

"Yeah," she brought herself back to the present with an effort, "that was mine."

"Real nice." I began to ask her about the photo equipment she used. This was not the way Jeff wanted the conversation to go.

"Uh, Quint," he interrupted. "What do you think about Markham's death?"

"This off the record?"

"Hey," he lifted his hands to show me they were empty. "I'm not taking notes."

"From what I hear, Truman Capote never took notes either."

"Okay," Jeff said, "I'm fishing. It's just that I heard you were causing a minor fuss down at the station. Questioning the suicide verdict and all."

I didn't know if I believed the "off the record" part, but I decided I didn't much care if he quoted me. "Well, I'm looking at it this way. If I wanted to kill Scott Markham—and there was probably one huge sigh of relief when he turned up dead— if I wanted him dead, I might consider a faked suicide to be a perfect solution." I paused. "On the surface, the guy had a real good reason to blow it all away."

"So. Maybe that's what he did." Then he shrugged and added, "He stood to lose everything. People have blown their brains out over less. What makes you think he didn't? Anything to do with that guy you saw?"

"No. Not really. Just a hunch, that's all. Or maybe it's not so much a hunch as a basic distrust of neat packages. Take that guy I saw for example. Why isn't anyone making an effort to find out who he is? Maybe he saw something, someone. But it's like the cops are saying he didn't leave a business card, so they're not going to bother. Doesn't make sense." I shook my head and looked at Jeff. "You've got to think they closed this whole thing too fast."

"Probably." He helped himself to a couple kernels of popcorn, washing them down with some beer. "That's the way this town is, though. Sensitive when it comes to corruption."

"Whatever happened to the crusading press?"

He didn't speak for several seconds and when he did he sounded like he was reading lines. "Newspaper's part of the community. Right now, public sympathy is with Markham and his family. We could really hurt ourselves if we didn't let this slide." He looked at me as though daring me to argue, which I intended to do, but he changed the subject before I had the chance. "What did you see when you walked into Markham's office? Anything out of the ordinary? Aside from Markham, that is."

"Can you be more specific?"

Barlowe wet his lips. "Oh, any drawers that looked like they'd been sacked. Any gaps in files that maybe looked like something had just been yanked out."

"You mean like legal briefs?"

"Yeah, something like that."

"Or appointment books?"

"Yeah, or . . ."

"Maybe an entire file missing on someone?"

"Yeah."

"Photographs?"

He didn't say anything that time and I glanced at Anne. She was looking down at the table. Finally I said, "No, nothing like that."

Jeff sighed. He glanced at Anne who was filling her hand with popcorn one kernel at a time. I wasn't sure why she looked vaguely familiar to me, but I had a pretty good idea, and was starting to feel like a jerk. I fought it though.

"Even if I wanted to keep going with this story, I couldn't." Jeff said. "You're probably right. It shouldn't be finished. But it is. And you're not going to find many people, friends of Markham's, who want to talk about it."

"What about Mason Burke?"

Jeff rolled his eyes.

"How powerful a guy is Burke?" As if I didn't know.

"Very. And it's all because of the family name. I mean it's really got nothing to do with his talent as a lawyer. Which is minimal."

"What do you make of that?" I asked. "Markham's got his choice of all the lawyers in the county and he picks one who makes most of his income off bad marriages. Mason's that powerful?"

"The two of them go way back." Barlowe crammed his mouth full of popcorn and wiped his hand on his jeans. After he'd swallowed some beer, he continued. "Law school at least. Maybe further. When Markham came to town about fifteen years ago, Burke had a lot to do with his becoming a judge as fast as he did." He turned thoughtful for a moment. "I think Burke used him to get respect for himself. Let's face it, Mason's not exactly the charismatic type. Maybe Markham had the presence that Burke needed. They fed off each other."

"Hard to figure though," I said, "who was doing who a favor when Markham hired Burke to defend him."

"That may be where another idea comes in. Word is that there were a number of lawyers involved in this bribery thing. Maybe some other judges. Even some of the ones that weren't involved in this one might be thinking 'there but for the grace of God' and all that stuff. Maybe nobody wanted to get anywhere near him. You know, guilt by association."

"What about Markham's former partner, Judd Townsend?"

"He's still out of town, I hear. Townsend's always seemed pretty straight. Hard to say though."

I led the discussion back to Markham's death. "I suppose Lorna Markham's making herself real accessible to the press."

Jeff smiled. "Nobody can get in the house. That kid of hers is like a trained pit bull."

"Is there *anyone* interested in keeping the investigation open?"

"Besides you? I doubt it."

"Is there an edict coming from somewhere that I should know about?"

Jeff stared at his glass and slowly shook his head. Then he looked at Anne for a few seconds before he shrugged and said,

"It's that kind of town." He took a healthy swallow of beer and added, "There are times when I feel like I should've gone into public relations."

"Who's sending the word down? Off the record, of course."

"My guess is it's either the gang at the mayor's office who doesn't think murder is good for commerce or," he leaned forward, "there is the school that believes Markham was going to sing for a reduced sentence. Like I was saying, all those lawyers were keeping their distance from Markham. And it makes sense. In order for there to be a bribe, there've got to be a lot of bribers. I talked to Janet Miraldi. She's madder than hell about it. She was just planning to start with Markham. That wasn't where she wanted to finish."

"Who else?"

"You'd have to ask her."

"She's the State's Attorney?"

"Assistant."

"You know, it's funny," I said. "Markham's death doesn't seem to have affected anyone on a personal level. Just seems like at best, it's very inconvenient or, at worst, it's very fortunate. Nobody seems genuinely sorry that the guy's dead."

Jeff signaled for three more beers. My head was getting a little fuzzy, but I didn't try to stop him. "You didn't know Markham, did you?" he said after they arrived and he paid for them.

"I've seen him around, that's about it."

He glanced at Anne. "Kind of a strange dude." Then he turned back to me. "Let's just leave it at that." He drank off his beer and changed the subject. "You live in those River's Edge Apartments, don't you?"

I nodded. "I do now."

"How d'you like them?"

"It's a large box, but the river's nice. I've gotta move though. They don't like my dog. I don't like the management much either."

"What kind of dog is it?" Anne spoke for the first time in a while.

"A border collie."

"How big is it?"

"Not very," I said. "Bigger than a piece of carry on luggage; smaller than one you'd have to check."

She nodded slowly and, after a few moments, said, "My aunt has a place on the east side of the river. It's really a two-story house. She rents out the second floor—it's got its own kitchen and everything. It's empty now." She smiled, "Aunt Louise is very particular about who she rents to. No kids and no weirdos, she says. And she's suspicious of young couples because they have 'kid potential'."

"Are pets okay?"

"She's got, at last count, three cats, two cat-sized dogs and a piranha."

"Bet the cats only tried to have him for dinner once."

It was almost eight o'clock when I left the bar with Aunt Louise's name and phone number in my shirt pocket. I was counting on the walk home to clear my Guinness-shrouded head. I wasn't a quarter of a block from the bar when Jeff caught up with me. At first I thought I'd forgotten something.

"You got a second?" he said as he sprinted up to me.

"Sure," I shrugged. "Don't need another beer though."

"No," he said pulling me into a store's doorway. "I didn't want to talk in front of Anne."

"Okay," I said, waiting. I had a hunch I knew why he'd called this meeting.

"This is totally off the record," he said. "Okay?"

"What is it?"

"Back in there," he gestured toward Tattersall's. "You mentioned photographs."

"Yeah, but you were leading."

He shook his head. "I'm not trying to get a scoop here. I swear. It's for Anne." He looked away for a second, searching for the words that would cut right through to the part of me that was softer than the rest.

"I know what you're talking about," I said before he had to find another line.

That statement seemed to bring him some relief, but he waited for me to continue. I glanced across the street and then back at him. "Don't worry. I don't know what I'm going to do with them, but no one'll see them."

"Were there others?"

"Not that I know of." I should have told him I didn't know anything about pictures of Anne and gone home and burned them. Burned all of them for that matter.

We both stood there for a minute. I was wondering how many people Markham was going to take down with him before this was over.

Finally he said, "Thanks, Quint. I owe you."

I studied him briefly, trying to figure out what emotions he was feeling right now. "You and Anne. Are you two a couple?"

"No. She's a friend. That's all." The way Jeff said it, as a flat statement, I believed him. I wasn't sure Anne was that casual about the relationship, but that wasn't any of my business. "Markham did a number on her," he added. "Anne. She's real," he groped for a word, "sensitive. Too sensitive to be very good at survival."

I nodded.

"What are you going to do?" he asked and quickly added, "About Markham."

"I guess nothing," I said to Barlowe. "Not much point in it."

There was something about the way he nodded in agreement that made me think he was relieved to hear that. Under the circumstances, maybe that was understandable. "I gotta get back," he said and thanked me again.

I had about four blocks to spend wondering whether agreeing to either return or destroy Anne's photos was a very bright thing to do and had just about convinced myself that, although it wasn't, if I had it to do again I'd do it the same way. With age comes predictability. The idea of getting rid of the rest of them was starting to sound better and better.

By the time I turned into the parking lot next to my apartment, I had decided that all there was left for me to do on the Markham case was collect my money. Debating the suicide verdict would be a waste of time. Besides, I hadn't convinced myself that it wasn't suicide. I was probably just looking for a way to keep working on this case because it was the only one I had, and it beat spending the day watching game shows and soap operas. I focused on the task immediately at hand: collecting my money. That looked like it might become a problem. But if that phone call I made was any indication of her accessibility, I'd have to put on my tough guy hat. I didn't want to intrude on her grief or whatever emotion she was feeling, but I didn't think a "we missed your payment" note was going to be strong enough.

Then something out of the corner of my eye caught my attention and, as I looked in that direction I had only one thought: Lorna Markham needed a crash course in the art of subtlety.

▽

CHAPTER SIX

I HAD TO GIVE her credit for choosing the dimmest part of the parking lot. But the way she was leaning against the red Jaguar, one hand on its hood, the other in the pocket of her fur coat, made it look like she was posing for a car ad and the lighting had been chosen intentionally for its dramatic effect; as though it never occurred to her that I might see her.

I wasn't looking forward to meeting with Lorna again, but the figure leaning against that import was my opportunity to earn a living. I'd get through this.

She waited for me to approach her before she said, "We have to talk."

"I know." I gestured toward my apartment building. "My place okay?"

"It will have to do," she said, leaving her car and walking a half step ahead of me. "Why don't you have an office like other detectives? Doesn't make for a very professional appearance."

"It's part of my no frills package. For an extra hundred a day, I rent office space and go through the motions—secretary, telephone with a hold button, the works. I'm not any more effective though."

We'd reached my apartment and I inserted my key in the lock and opened the door. There was another piece of paper waiting for me on the floor. I picked it up and tossed it on the coffee table. Then I greeted Peanuts and offered to take Lorna's coat. She hesitated then removed it and handed it to me.

"Drink?"

She nodded. "Brandy, please."

"Sorry," I said. "All I've got is Scotch."

51

"That will be fine," she said without hesitation.

I poured the Scotch from the crystal decanter Elaine gave me when I got my private investigator's license. She had said that it might take a while for the public to realize this agency was a classy operation but that the decanter would help establish that as a fact. Whatever.

I handed the glass of Teacher's to Lorna and said, "I don't stock the cheap stuff, so you're going to have to control yourself."

She smiled stiffly and I pulled up a lawn chair and lit a cigarette. Lorna made an unpleasant face and said, "Do you mind? Smoke bothers me." She said it as if I were sitting next to her in a public restaurant instead of across from her in my own apartment. I extinguished the cigarette.

Looking at Lorna, I noticed that the past two days had taken their toll on her. Her hair, hanging limp, had lost some of its sheen and makeup hadn't succeeded in covering the shadows beneath her eyes. She was tense and it was obvious that she was putting a lot of effort into holding herself together. She wore a dark green v-necked sweater over a pair of jeans that were cut tight. I couldn't help but notice that she had a figure a woman half her age would be proud of. Peanuts apparently thought she was okay too, for he sat on the floor next to her. She set her drink down and began to pet him. He obligingly offered her the portion of his neck that he most liked to have scratched and seemed pleased that she was a quick learner. Finally Lorna looked up at me. "I apologize for avoiding you this afternoon." She paused as though waiting for me to say something. When I didn't, she continued, "My son, Eric, doesn't know I was having his father followed by a detective." She made a gesture with her body that was either a shrug or a shiver. Then she removed an envelope from her purse and dropped it on the table. Hallelujah.

Next to it, I placed the envelope containing the photos I'd taken of Robyn and Markham. Lorna stared at it without moving. I retrieved the one she'd offered, glanced in it, and deciding this wasn't the time to put it in the shoebox with the rest of my earnings, dropped it back on the table. Lorna still hadn't moved and continued to stare at the eight by ten envelope. "You paid for them," I said.

"I know. I guess I don't know whether I want anything to do with them now."

I nodded and muttered something about understanding, removed a cigarette from its pack and held it without lighting it.

She stared at me for several seconds then said, "You must think me a class A bitch."

"I don't get paid to make judgments." When that came out it seemed harsher than I'd intended. I smiled and added, "If I did, I doubt I'd be any good at it."

"But you are a thinking human being. You do have opinions, don't you?"

"Sure. But why should you care what I think of you anyway?"

Sighing, she crossed her arms over her chest. "I guess I don't." Then she looked out the glass balcony doors, even though there was nothing but black out there and said, "I didn't expect this to happen. I really didn't. Not this. When I said I wanted to destroy him, I meant what's inside him. I didn't mean I wanted him to die." Leaning forward, her eyes locked onto mine, she was asking me to absolve her of her guilt.

Who was I to say? "He was ultimately responsible. No one else can accept the blame." I hesitated. "Unless of course, he didn't kill himself. Then someone else is definitely responsible."

Sitting up, she raised her eyebrows, as her eyes widened. I might have just told her she'd won the lottery. When she finally spoke, the words had a breathless quality, as though she were afraid that once uttered, the spell might be broken. "Do you think it's possible that Scott was murdered?"

Forgetting our agreement, I lit the cigarette I'd been rolling in my hands. It didn't taste very good, but I inhaled deeply. She didn't make a face or turn her gaze from me and all she wanted from me right now was a yes or no answer. "Yeah," I said. "I think so."

Suddenly she became intense, and I felt I was being cross-examined. "Why? Why do you think that?"

I wanted to know why she was asking me these questions, but I could wait. "I followed your husband for three days. He didn't impress me as being a man with insurmountable problems. In fact, he acted like he didn't have a care in the world."

"What else?"

I smashed out the cigarette and poured myself a short glass of Scotch. "I don't know. It just seems like they wrote this one off to suicide so fast that someone should be asking questions." My first sip of the drink didn't set right and I pushed the glass away. Then I shrugged and ended my eloquent defense with, "That's all."

Lorna wasn't finished. She'd gotten hold of something and she was going to work it until she had it set right. And all I could do was play along. "According to the police report, the gun was next to his hand. They, the police, said he must have released it after he pulled the trigger." She described the events of her husband's death without a glimmer of emotion. "Is that possible?"

"Yes," I tried a little more Scotch. It went down better this time. "But it seems to me that someone ought to consider another obvious possibility. . . ."

Before I could finish the sentence, she did it for me. "That someone shot him and put the gun next to him. To make it look like he'd released it." Her eyes were wide with excitement.

Nodding, I said, "It's possible. But at the risk of bursting the bubble that's got you up in the stratosphere, remember they might be right. He might have had everyone fooled about his state of mind. Maybe he was so depressed he couldn't even think of a decent suicide note."

"You don't understand." She was shaking her head and smiling.

"I know. And I want to so bad it scares me."

She leaned back into the couch, folded her arms and crossed her legs, effectively shutting herself down. After a couple minutes, she looked at me, eyes narrowing. "Are you a betting man?"

"Depends on the odds and what's at stake."

Lorna unfolded herself. "Here it is." She leaned forward again. "About six months ago, Scott canceled the life insurance policy we'd had for years and took one out through a local company—Dieken Insurance Agency, owned by John Dieken. It was for a million dollars. And unless I can prove that my dear, dead husband was murdered, I won't see a penny of it." She took a few seconds before continuing. "There's some clause in the policy; they call it a suicide/self-destruction clause. And it means if you're stupid enough to kill yourself within the first two years, all you get is what you've put into it, which, after six months, isn't a whole hell of a lot."

Seeing no easy way to argue the logic in that clause, I waited.

"I got a visit from one of John Dieken's little helpers this afternoon. She said how sorry she was about Scott's death and how it really troubled her to have to tell me that Dieken Insurance Agency wasn't liable to pay Scott's survivors a cent. Then she gave me a Bible. The bitch." From the way the corners of her mouth tightened as she told the story, I believed she had some ideas on what the woman could do with that book.

"So here's my offer." She turned back to me. "If you are able to prove—to the satisfaction of the insurance company—that Scott was murdered, I'll collect the million dollars and I'll give you twenty-five thousand."

Before I could respond, she continued. "On the other hand, if it does seem to be suicide or if you are unable to prove it's murder, I . . ." she paused and gave me an apologetic smile. "I don't think I can afford to pay you a cent."

I studied her as I rolled twenty-five grand around in my imagination. Then I said, "You have nothing to lose."

She smiled. "True. And you have a great deal to gain."

I still didn't answer. Not that the offer wasn't interesting and I wasn't tempted to take it. It was and I was. The thing was, I didn't know how to ask her if she could give me a small advance. I figured if I put about five hundred dollars with the money she'd just paid me, I'd have enough to move—and to eat for the rest of the week.

Apparently she interpreted my hesitation in another way. "All right," she said, "I'll go up to fifty grand. But that's it."

I nodded. I'd sleep in the car for a while. "Okay. You're on. But tell me this. Do you really believe he might have been murdered or are you just playing a long shot?"

"A little of both. On the one hand, I can't believe Scott would be that stupid. I mean, I can see him leaving me nothing, but not his son. Not Eric. On the other hand I can't think of anyone who would kill him. Besides me."

This was an awkward question, but since I'd been hired for nothing, I should get to ask a few awkward questions. "Tell me. You said without the million, you're broke. How can that be? Surely you must have some money stashed away."

She shook her head slowly and spoke like someone who had already accepted a horrible fact. "We don't. I don't know what happened to our money, but it's not there."

I waited and she finally continued. "We had money in stocks, bonds, and certificates." She looked at me. "In the last few months, Scott cleaned most of it out. I didn't know. I don't know where it went."

I lifted the glass of Scotch to my mouth and set it down without drinking. "I don't get it. Shouldn't you be hiring me to find out what happened to your money? Maybe it's not gone forever. Or do you know what happened to it?"

"No. I have no idea." She smiled at me. "Would you do that for me on speculation as well?"

Now I understood. "I'd do it for five hundred dollars. Up front." I never would have said that, but I had the feeling she had a little stashed away.

I must have been right because she hesitated only a moment before agreeing to my terms.

Peanuts had moved over next to the sliding glass doors. He was licking his paw and using it to scrub behind his ear. Three licks, three rubs, three licks, three rubs, and so on. He was so wrapped up in his ablutions that I was sure it was the only thing occupying his mind right now. I sort of envied him.

I got up and began to move around. Peanuts immediately ceased his task and looked at me, ears perked. Now his only thought was: What is this guy going to do next? Pick up the Frisbee? I walked to the glass door and looked out toward the building that stood between me and the river. The movement seemed to clear my head a little.

She sighed and didn't say anything at first. Although I had my back to her, I could see her reflection in the glass door. She was leaning forward, holding her glass of scotch between her two hands, poised above the coffee table. "I've been stupid. Really stupid. I put him through school and ran the house. Then when he got his degree, I turned all the financial matters over to him while I tried to have his children. I thought that was all he wanted. Isn't that all anyone's supposed to want? If that's not enough, then isn't there something wrong inside of you? Maybe I just don't understand the way the game's played." She set her glass down with an abruptness that startled both me and the dog. "No, dammit," she said, "I'm not going to let that man get to me anymore." I turned to her and saw that she was watching me with an intensity that demanded my attention. "I spent most of my life letting that man get to me. I loved him when he didn't deserve it. I looked the other way when he cheated. I had plenty of practice at that. Then I watched him destroy everything we had." She leaned back into the couch, leaving her drink on the table. "I just want what's coming to me. The next time I do something for someone, it's going to be for me."

"Tell me about Eric." I returned to my chair. "How was he handling the indictment? All the accusations against his father."

"Eric," she said with, it seemed, a touch of bitterness. Then she added, "He's a senior this year."

"High school?"

She nodded. "Scott was worried about what his indictment might do to his son's future as a lawyer. Because, of course that is what he must become. But this kind of thing can be devastating to anyone it touches."

"Did Eric know about the bribery charges?"

She smiled a little and, again, there was that touch of bitterness. "Eric knew about the indictment, but it never occurred to him that his father might be guilty."

"Can you tell me more about the indictment?"

She shook her head. "Like I said, we barely discussed it. You might say it wasn't my concern anymore. You're going to have to get the gruesome details from Mason Burke."

"Is Eric your son too?"

She jerked her head up, surprised and a bit angry. "Of course he is. Why do you ask?"

I shrugged. "I don't know. I guess it's the way you referred to Scott as 'his father' and to Eric as 'his son'. It's like you don't include yourself in the family unit."

She eyed me and there was a touch of distrust there. Maybe she suspected me of reading her mind, but couldn't figure out how that was possible. Finally she smiled. "You're very perceptive, Mr. McCauley." She ran her hands through her hair, pushing it back from her face until she captured it in a knot at the nape of her neck. Then, sighing, she shook it out and looked up at the ceiling. "I don't know. I've never been very close to my son. And he and Scott were so close. I suppose I resented the blind devotion. I mean, for a very long time—forever really—I loved Scott in spite of his flaws. Eric never saw the flaws. Any of them. So it was easy for him to love him."

Abruptly she stood, brushing dog hairs from her dark pants. "Speaking of Eric, I have to get back. I told him I wouldn't be late. Not that he's at all concerned."

I helped her on with her coat. "What can you tell me about Mason Burke?"

She adjusted her collar and fanned her hair over it. Then she said, "When Eric was little there was one kid I didn't want him hanging around with. Nothing specific, but I knew the kid was trouble. Well, that's how I feel about Mason." She shrugged. "Nothing I can be specific about, but I don't like the man. And, I'm sure he's not terribly fond of me either."

She gave Peanuts a goodbye pat. "That's a nice dog." Then she added, "They're a lot less trouble than people."

"That's usually true. Only this one's the exception." I explained the situation with the apartment.

Shaking her head in sympathy, she said, "Just be sure you give me your forwarding address."

After she left, Peanuts hopped up on the couch and sniffed the place where Lorna's fur coat had been. "Smell anyone you know?" I asked.

Now I had a reason to be interested in the Markham murder theory. Proving it was to be something else again.

I retrieved the folded note from the table. It was from apartment management and, as I suspected, a reminder that our days were numbered. I scrounged in my pack for another cigarette and came up empty. Peanuts lay down on the couch and looked up at me. I found myself studying his intelligent eyes and thinking how nice it would be if we could carry on a conversation. That was when I realized how badly I needed to hear the voice of a friend.

I'd been on the verge of calling Elaine so many times that I'd memorized her new number. I dialed and counted the rings, thinking that if she wasn't home maybe her roommate would talk to me.

▽

CHAPTER SEVEN

LOUISE ORWELL wasn't the type of person you'd expect to harbor a vicious fish. And it looked especially out of place in a room that smelled like a candle shop and overflowed with dried flowers, needlepoint coasters and afghans. But when you learned how the piranha had found its way into the twenty gallon aquarium in her living room, it said a lot about the woman. Her niece, Megan, "the spoiled one" had bought it on a whim, because it glittered so and was such an oddity. But it had never warmed up to her and she quickly grew tired of supporting a fish that ate raw meat and flashed its incisors every chance it got. ("I don't know what she expected it to do," Louise told me, "roll over and play dead? Fetch?") Megan had been about to flush the fish into oblivion when Louise stepped in. "We don't much care for each other." She paused and clarified. "The fish and I that is. But we've developed an uneasy rapport. Someday he'll die, and I don't suppose I'll miss him much." She looked at him swimming lazy circles in the tank. "He does sparkle so in the sunlight though, doesn't he?" She spoke with a clipped English accent that was captivating.

"Can I get you an ale?" she said rising and dropping an orange tabby to the floor on her way to the refrigerator. I'd seen one other cat strolling through the room and the dogs had joined us like they were part of the family greeting a visitor. One was a fawn-colored pug and the other some kind of cocker mix. The latter must have been quite old. It spent a long time and considerable effort climbing into a chair and didn't look as though it would move for a while.

Louise had just showed me the second floor she was renting and we were getting the details out of the way. It was a great

59

place—one small bedroom but a long, narrow living room and a big kitchen. At the end of the hundred foot stretch of backyard was the Fox River. And Peanuts was welcome. I had the feeling that Louise closed a lot of deals with a beer or some other kind of liquid refreshment. It was difficult to pin an age on her. She had a vivacious, youthful quality that might have belied her years. She could have been anywhere from ten years older than me to somewhere in the vicinity of my mother's age.

She set the drink down in front of me. "Tell me. How do you know my niece, Anne?"

I explained how I'd met her at the Tattersall Tavern.

"Who was she with?"

"Jeff Barlowe, a guy from the paper."

She nodded. "He's her friend." The way she spoke seemed to imply that he was her only friend, but I might have read the inflection wrong. "I do worry about Anne. She's so naive and trusting. Just waiting, wide-eyed, for Prince Charming to arrive on his white steed. As much as I hate to say it, she should take a few lessons from her sister, Megan. Now there's a woman who won't be kept waiting for anyone." She shook her head, held onto that thought for a few seconds, then changed the subject.

"Is it true that none of you private detectives ever really charge anyone for your services?" She paused. "What I mean is, you seem like such a nice young man, isn't it difficult to ask for money from indigent widows and wronged persons?"

I smiled. "I don't think so. My desire to eat regularly overcomes my inclination to be a nice guy." Louise seemed to buy that and I was pretty sure I had passed the credit check. I felt more than a tinge of guilt. At this point in my life I was hardly a good credit risk.

"How long have you been doing this?"

"Not long. About four months."

"Is that so?" She nibbled on a cracker from a basket she'd placed on the table. "What did you do before then, if you don't mind my asking?"

"Not at all." I took a drink of the ale which tasted faintly of ginger and said, "I was head of security at a department store for a while. Before that I spent some time as a cop. And before that I pitched in the minors."

"Baseball?"

I nodded.

"Splendid," she leaned forward in her chair and clapped her hands. "I find that a delightful game to watch, although," she leaned back now, slightly subdued, "I must say I don't always know what's going on. And it seems some of them spend a frightful amount of time scratching themselves in odd places. Take that fellow who crouches behind the plate . . . the wicket keeper?"

"The catcher?"

"Yes, I suppose so. Well, he's not even subtle about it. There he is, I mean he must know the camera's on him, and he's making odd gestures in his crotch area."

I choked on my beer and came up laughing.

She gave me a quizzical look and, not wanting the situation to turn awkward, I quickly said, "I'm sorry. I guess I never looked at it that way. But, what the catcher is doing there is signaling the pitcher, suggesting a certain kind of pitch. One finger usually means fast ball, two a curve ball and three's whatever else he's got. You see, if the catcher doesn't know what kind of pitch he's getting, he's going to have a lot of trouble catching it."

"Oh," she said, suddenly enlightened. Then she added, "I feel altogether different about that young man now." She sipped on her glass of ale like it was a cup of tea.

I arranged to move my things the next day and, in exchange for a security deposit and a month's rent, Louise gave me the key. I hoped I'd get Lorna's advance before the check cleared.

Before going home to pack, I stopped at Dieken Insurance Agency. The small office was one in a row of convenience stores adjacent to Foxport's only mall. Charm hadn't found its way to this part of town.

"Looks like he's on the phone now," the secretary said after glancing at the red light on her phone. It was a small, cramped reception area, but was dotted with personal touches that were a nice contrast to the institutional exterior. A nameplate, which read Lucy Summers, was about an inch away from toppling from her desk.

I told her I'd wait. I didn't feel like sitting so I turned my attention to a grouping of extremely heathy-looking plants.

"It's silk," she laughed as I bent over a spider plant. "They all are. I always kill the real ones, but they look so pretty."

She was young, early twenties at the most, and cheerful. She offered me coffee, which I refused.

"Is there anyone here besides Mr. Dieken?"

"No. Not today. Mary Carlson comes in a couple days a week, but she's just part time. For the most part, Mr. Dieken handles everything." She drank from her mug of coffee and set it down on one of the many piles of papers covering her desk. Barely making an appearance for all the rubble was a Wookie pencil holder.

She saw I'd noticed it and said, "Isn't he great? I read somewhere that George Lucas has one on his desk."

I wasn't sure what that had to do with anything, but this was a pleasant enough conversation to keep going. "I'll bet his was free."

"Lucy." She swung around as John Dieken stepped from his office. "Where are the . . ." He stopped when he saw the two of us chatting and shot Lucy a look that might have wilted a less resilient person. But she just smiled at him and said, "This is Quint McCauley. He'd like to see you."

"In regards to . . ." Apparently he wanted me to fill in the blank.

"Scott Markham's insurance policy."

It took him less than a second to respond. "She's got no case. We told her that. It's unfortunate, but that doesn't change anything. We go by the police report, which in this case says suicide." There was no glimmer of sympathy in his words.

I hadn't expected such an immediate and forceful explanation. "I understand that. I'd still like to talk with you for a few minutes."

Dieken turned to Lucy. "Is my schedule clear for the next ten minutes?"

"Sure is," she said without consulting an appointment book. Dieken glared at her. Lucy smiled back.

He stepped out of his office's doorway and motioned me in. When he spoke again, he didn't sound quite so rehearsed. "I suppose I've been expecting someone like you. Did Mrs. Markham send you?" In his own office, Dieken wore his suit jacket, which was a very dark gray, almost black. With the white shirt and the subtly patterned dark tie, this guy's person literally screamed for color. Even his thinning hair was a non-descript shade of brown.

"Can you blame her?"

His smile was curt. "I suppose not."

I looked around the unimpressive executive office in this even less impressive store front space. The wood-paneled walls looked cheap and at least one of the panels wasn't aligned correctly, creating an odd off balance effect. The walls were bare except for the one behind the desk which boasted a large rather gruesome oil depiction of the crucifixion. It had one of those little lights beaming down on it; the kind that seem to belong in funeral homes. With the exception of a leather-trimmed blotter and an empty in basket, Dieken's desk was bare.

"Tell me about the policy."

He sat behind his desk and tightened the knot in his tie. "What would you like to know?"

"For starters, what kind was it?"

"Term life. Five year renewable."

"What company?"

He swallowed before he said, "Metro Mutual."

"Don't most companies discourage term life policies?"

"Some do. Some believe a term policy isn't in the best interests of the client. It's a temporary, renewable policy as opposed to universal or whole life." The tone with which Dieken finished a statement reminded me of a kid who's always saying "Wanna make something of it?"

"When Markham came to see you about the policy, didn't you think that a million bucks was a bit steep?"

"He had his reasons. And they seemed like good ones to me."

"For instance?"

He seemed to be debating whether to share this tidbit with me, but finally he said, "Scott Markham said he planned to take on some relatively risky financial ventures within the next couple of years and he wanted his family to be adequately compensated if anything were to happen to him."

"You have any idea what these ventures were?"

"No, I don't."

"So you cut him a million dollar policy. Just like that."

"Yes I did."

"The policy has to state who recommended the amount, doesn't it?"

After a moment's hesitation Dieken said, "Yes that's right."

"Who recommended a million bucks for Scott Markham?"

Raising his chin a half inch, Dieken said, "I did," and went on, "He was in good health. An excellent risk."

"If Metro Mutual had been socked with a million dollar claim, that wouldn't have made them too happy, would it?"

"Insurance companies understand these risks."

"Which in this case paid off."

"If you want to look at it that way."

"So really, Markham killing himself after paying six months worth of premiums, that's really the best thing that could have happened, isn't it? Well, I guess it would have been even better if it had happened the day before the suicide clause lapsed. But you can't have everything, can you?"

Dieken folded his hands on top of his empty desk. "I don't believe I care for what you are implying."

"What's that?"

"That I benefited from his death."

"No," I said. "That's not what I'm saying at all. It just seems so unlikely that someone would go to the trouble of seeing that his family will be well provided for if he should die and then go ahead and kill himself. He leaves them in the worst possible situation."

Dieken's gaze flickered over me. "Apparently Scott Markham was a troubled man. It's unfortunate that he chose to sin against God by taking his own life, but it's not my place to make judgments." He paused and said, "Now may I ask a question?"

"Go ahead."

"Why did Mrs. Markham hire you?"

"She's not convinced it was suicide. Neither am I."

Dieken smiled as if I'd just gobbled up the bait. "And you accuse me of benefiting from this man's death. While you're taking money from a widow when you know there's no way you can earn it. The simple fact is that Scott Markham shot himself."

I didn't bother to explain.

When I left Dieken's office, I wondered how much convincing he had needed to recommend a million dollar policy for his client, a man who understood the power of a well-placed bribe.

The light on my answering machine was blinking and I hoped without much faith, that it was Elaine calling me back. Our conversation the night before had been less than satisfying. I had been a little drunk and she had sounded like she was on her way out the door when I called. Or maybe she had company. I don't think she used a sentence with more than five words in it. She said she'd call me back "when she had more time," but I suspect she figured that was the most expedient way to get me off the phone.

There were two messages. The first was from my old police contact O'Henry telling me to call him back.

The second caller had been a woman, dying to see me, but it wasn't Elaine. Her name was Janet Miraldi, she was Assistant State's Attorney, and she was presumptuous as hell. In the recorded message she told me to meet her at her office at two thirty. It was a struggle. Half of me wanted to tell her, by my no-show approach, that Quint McCauley was not to be ordered around. And half of me was real curious about her reason for wanting to see me. Actually, I guess at least fifty-one percent of me must have been curious, because I wound up going. My only nod to whatever percentage was left was that I arrived some thirty minutes late. I'd actually only intended to be twenty minutes late, but I had trouble finding the building and her office. It's great being new in town.

▽

Chapter Eight

IF THERE WAS any part of Janet Miraldi that was not strictly business, it was too small to be seen with the naked eye. I was pretty certain that this woman would cut me no slack.

Her office was wedged in a second floor corner of an annex to the courthouse. There was no surface in the office that was not used to hold papers, files and law books. And for every gray metal file cabinet there was a single-drawer cardboard file that didn't close flush. The only thing in the Assistant State's Attorney's office that didn't appear to be bordering on chaos was the Assistant State's Attorney.

After I'd taken a seat in one of the two green vinyl chairs, she maneuvered around her desk to close the door. I could have done it from where I was sitting, but she didn't ask. As she sat at her desk again, it occurred to me that I could have done just about anything do-able in that office from where I was sitting.

"Nice place you've got here."

"Thank you," she said dryly, eyeing me over the top of her dark-rimmed glasses. I'd made a point of dressing for the occasion—gray corduroy jacket over a good pair of jeans. I'd even worn a tie. She was giving me the once-over, but I had no idea how I was doing. From my corner, and from what I could see behind the glasses, she was doing all right. Her hair was dark and shoulder length with feathery bangs brushing the tops of her frames.

She cleared her throat, "I know that you were hired by someone to keep Scott Markham under surveillance. I'd like to know a few things about those last days. Who he saw, what he did, where he went. Things like that."

66

I didn't answer right away. She'd made her request like she was asking me for my flu symptoms, and she was following through like a pro—hands folded on the desk in front of her, head cocked slightly—the interested, sympathetic ear. But she had to be thinking that if I gave in without batting an eye, she was either very lucky or was being lied to.

"Why?" I asked.

"I'm investigating the bribery charges that were brought against him." She didn't act for a moment like this was slightly unusual.

"You do know he's dead, don't you?" I said. "It was in all the papers."

She stared at me for several seconds. Then she said, "Mr. McCauley, don't screw with me. I won't allow you to waste my time."

"Waste *your* time?" I leaned forward. Because of the close proximity of the office, we were face to face little more than a foot apart. "Whose idea was this meeting anyway?" Neither of us spoke or moved for a few seconds and I noticed that her eyes were very large and so brown they were almost black. Finally I leaned back in the chair and continued, "And now you're sitting there, in your pseudo authority position trying to bully all kinds of information out of me."

When she spoke again, her tone had softened slightly. "We believe this bribery thing was very far-reaching. Others were involved. We want them to answer."

That might have been true. I knew little about Markham's indictment and there might very well have been a whole lot of lawyers stuffing bills in his pockets. On the other hand, the prosecutor was going to have a hard time convicting the bribers when the bribee was dead. I had a hunch that Janet Miraldi was still interested in Scott Markham for the same reason I was still interested in Scott Markham. Only the motivation was different.

"You don't believe Markham committed suicide," I said.

"I didn't say that," she raised her chin slightly.

"You didn't have to. No thinking person without a motive would have chalked this one off to a depressed guy trying to get away from it all."

The door opened and a man stuck his head into the office. "Got a minute, Janet?" When he saw me, he straightened up and edged his way into the room. Once in, he immediately assumed an air of authority. And even though he wore no jacket and his tie was loosened, there was no doubt in my mind that this guy ran things. His eyes were sharp and hooded with heavy gray brows. And he was very interested in this guy in Janet Miraldi's office.

"This is Quint McCauley." She hesitated and I could tell she wasn't sure where she was going with this. "He's a friend. We're going to lunch."

I smiled and nodded. He returned the nod and introduced himself as Jack Alden. I knew the name and if my memory served me correctly, he was the State's Attorney, Janet's boss.

He sized me up quickly and looked at Janet. Then he glanced at his watch. "I've got to leave in a half hour. We'll talk at nine o'clock tomorrow." Janet nodded.

"Well, Jan," I stood and turned to her, "I don't know about you, but I'm hungry. Let's move."

Without a word, she pulled her purse out of her desk and grabbed a khaki trench coat off the coat hanger nailed into the wall. "I'll see you tomorrow then," she said to the man we left standing in her office.

We were in the stairwell on our way down to the first floor when she stopped and grabbed my arm so I had to come to a stop with her. When she had my attention she said, "It's Janet. Not Jan. Janet."

Janet had parked her car in the municipal lot behind the courthouse. She had her own space. I let her lead. She seemed comfortable in that role. We drove in her white Toyota to a restaurant called La Primavera that was small and comfortable and smelled of garlic and olive oil. It was about four blocks away on a side street wedged in between a shoe repair shop and an antique dealer. I hadn't realized the place existed. But I was sure there was a lot I didn't know about Foxport. We were both silent on the trip over, both, undoubtedly, strategizing.

When we sat down at a table with a red and white checkered tablecloth, we still hadn't spoken. I had decided to play it close to my chest. She was the one who wanted information, but I was reasonably certain she could supply me with a few morsels as well. There was no way she was still interested in prosecuting a dead man unless somewhere in the lake, there were bigger fish to fry.

This place wasn't new to her and she exchanged a few pleasantries with the waiter, Tom, a young man I guessed to be college aged.

She ordered a bottle of Chianti Classico and spoke to me for the first time since we'd left the courthouse. "Do you drink wine?"

"Sure."

"Two glasses," she instructed the waiter.

When the waiter left to fill the order, she removed her glasses and placed them on the table. Gazing at some object over my shoulder, she said, "We can help each other." Then she looked at me and I tried not to think of how she looked better without the glasses because more of her face showed. It was an excellent face.

"Maybe," I said.

"Who hired you to investigate Scott Markham?"

I smiled. "Isn't this where we were back in your office? You think it's going to work any better now that we're sharing a bottle of wine?" She stiffened slightly and I was surprised that brown eyes could turn so cold. I continued before she could blast me. "I'm not sure that the identity of my employer is all that important to you right now." For some reason I didn't want her to know about the fifty thousand motivations either. I sensed that this woman's motives never dropped to anything so base as money. "Besides," I added, "it's in the police report."

She studied me for what seemed like a long time. "Why do you think Markham was murdered?"

The wine arrived and the waiter uncorked the bottle with clean efficiency and presented the cork to Janet. She fingered its damp end while he filled the bottom of her glass. Then she tasted it and smiled as she nodded her approval. "That's fine." Tom filled my glass and allowed himself a quick perusal of this guy that Janet Miraldi had brought in with her.

When he left, I said, "It's not so much that I think he was murdered, as that I don't think he killed himself."

"Why not?"

"He seemed to be having a real good time being Scott Markham."

The wine was good and I helped myself to a piece of bread. I hadn't eaten since beer and crumpets at Louise's and didn't want my head to go fuzzy on me. Not yet anyway. While I ate and drank I considered how much I should tell Janet. Finally I said, "Apparently the only thing wrong with his life was the indictment and he wasn't acting like that weighed too heavily on his mind either. He had a devoted son, a wife and a mistress."

She raised her eyebrows. "Who was she?"

I held her gaze for a long moment, trying to convey the fact that this tidbit was going to cost her. "Robyn Fosse. Lives in the west part of town. Works at the Nordic Loft." I finally said.

"Interesting," she said and added, "although from what I've heard, she wasn't his first."

"Can you name any others?"

"Yes," she said and looked at the menu.

We sat in silence for several moments. Tom came to take our orders. Janet ordered veal picante and I opted for spaghetti.

"Did he meet with anyone other than his mistress?"

"Judd Townsend. A few other cronies."

"Interesting."

I refilled our glasses. "Now it's your turn. But first let me see if my suspicions are correct. You've been told to drop this investigation, which would be the logical thing to do seeing as Markham's dead, but you aren't satisfied. You think there's more to it than a single indictment. And you suspect that there may be more than bribery involved here. You could get in considerable trouble if your office knew you were still nosing around the ashes." I drank some more wine and when she didn't respond, asked, "Am I warm?"

She glanced around the room. It was mid-afternoon and there were few remaining from the lunch crowd. The table that Janet had chosen was against the red brick wall in the back and she had a view of the door. Only two other tables were occupied. Two elderly women wearing tweeds with shopping bags stacked about their chairs shared a table near the door, and a casually dressed man reading a newspaper sat next to the opposite wall. Some kind of nondescript music filtered in through speakers mounted near the ceiling. It was the kind of noise you had to make an effort to notice but it kept the place from becoming cavernous in its silence.

Janet turned her gaze back to me. "You're hot." Then she added, "Now that you know how to pull the plug on me, are you going to exercise that option?"

I lit a cigarette before I answered. "Hell no." I shook the flame from the match. "I'm new in town. I need all the friends I can get."

She smiled and I noticed that she had a dimple on one side of her face and not the other, giving an appealing, lopsided quality to that expression.

I looked for an ashtray and found none. "Are we in the no-smoking section?"

"Yes, but no problem." She motioned with her hand at someone behind my back and within moments there was an ash tray at my elbow. I nodded my thanks to the busboy and said to Janet, "You must be a regular customer here."

She shrugged, "I don't cook and this is the closest I've found to my mother's cooking in an area populated by and for WASPs." Pausing, she released an almost imperceptible sigh and added, "One needs an anchor." She shook her head, forcing her thoughts back to our discussion.

I picked up. "Is Jack Alden your boss?"

She nodded. "He's okay. He knows I put a lot of work in on this Markham indictment. I've got a right to be a little suspicious." She didn't sound like she'd convinced herself of that yet and I waited for her to continue.

Finally she said, "There's no way you write off the suicide of a judge as fast as they did this one. The fact is, if a murderer knows what he's doing, it's relatively simple to make it look like suicide."

"Tell me something I don't already know." I broke off another piece of Italian bread.

She frowned a little and studied me. Then she too tore at the loaf of bread.

"Was Markham going to cop a plea?" I prodded.

We were interrupted by the arrival of the minestrone soup and, being an observant kind of guy, I noticed that the wine bottle was almost empty. I ordered another. Janet didn't protest.

"It was being negotiated." She set her soup spoon on the

table and picked up her glass of wine, collecting her thoughts. Finally she said, "Bribery is a strange offense. Everyone does it to one degree or another and it's been going on since the beginning of recorded history. Let's face it. Influence is a commodity that can be bought and sold. And it's not always illegal." As she spoke, she talked with her hands, using the wine glass as an instrument of emphasis. "For example, you can't walk up to your senator and hand him one thousand dollars and tell him to vote no on the tax increase. But you can make a 'campaign contribution' of a thousand dollars and mention that there ought to be other ways of funding the schools than to raise taxes. It's done all the time. Bribery is one of the things that makes the system work. And even though bribing a judge to disallow a piece of evidence or paying him off so your client gets the lightest possible sentence, even though that kind of behavior is totally illegal not to mention unethical, it's not that easy to prove. A defense attorney is visiting with the judge, waiting for the prosecutor to arrive for the plea bargain. He mentions he's got a nice condo and a thirty-foot cruiser up on the lake and loans it out to friends for a week or two at a time during the summer. Technically the bribe hasn't been made, but it's there."

Our wine came and we were silent during the opening ritual. The waiter let me taste it this time. We were starting on our first glass when I said, "There must have been a specific bribe made and accepted if Markham was indicted."

She nodded. "We'd heard rumors and we got a defense attorney to go in there as a plant. A mole. Whatever you want to call him. Markham took the bait like a greedy bass."

I smiled at the image. "Who was he?"

Janet frowned then shrugged slightly. "Knox Ferris. I doubt that you've met him. He's a nice guy and it's too bad all the work he did was for nothing. There were several instances of bribery we were able to get Markham on."

"Did you get anyone besides Markham?"

She shook her head. "Somehow the word got out on Knox. I'd give a month's pay to know who leaked it. We had to bring Knox in. But there were a number of lawyers Markham could have implicated. And the way to do that was to dangle the carrot of freedom in his face. Work with us and we'll go real easy on you."

"You bribed him."

"Precisely."

"I don't suppose you'd be willing to share the names of the people Markham was going to exchange for leniency?"

"No, I wouldn't," she smiled. "I have to have something left to negotiate with, don't I?" Then, almost as an afterthought, she added, "We also had him on income tax evasion."

I nodded. That made sense. All that extra income isn't easy to declare.

Tom removed our bowls, mine empty and Janet's barely touched, and replaced them with our entrees. For several minutes we both ate as if starved. The meat sauce was either delicious or its flavor had improved with my intake of wine.

"So," I said after consuming a good portion of the plate, "what you seem to be hinting at, is that it would have been in the best interests of certain members of the legal profession to have Markham commit suicide."

She wiped her mouth with a red cloth napkin. "It would seem that way, wouldn't it?"

"Okay, then explain to me why everyone else is so eager to classify Markham as a suicide. Wouldn't it be a real nice feather in the prosecutor's hat to be the one to solve a judge's murder?"

"It sure would," she said, and I noticed that her eyes weren't focusing quite as well as they were a half bottle of wine ago. Or maybe it was mine that had the problem.

"Okay," I said, "I'll bite. Why is everyone backing off?"

"I don't know," she giggled a little, a sound I figured she didn't make much. "I was hoping you could help me there."

I shrugged. "Sorry to be useless. Tell me about Markham."

She raised her eyebrows. "What do you want to know?"

"What was he like? As a woman how did you react to him?" I probably wouldn't have said that without benefit of the wine.

If the question bothered her, she didn't let on. "Well, he was attractive, vital, intense. There was something very sexual about him." She paused and stared at the brick wall for a few seconds. Then she turned back to me and said, "No. Maybe sexual isn't quite the right word. Maybe sensual is closer. Yes, sensual."

"As a judge?"

With a wry smile, she said, "I think he used his attractiveness to compensate in areas where he wasn't so hot. Never underestimate how far good looks will get you." She put the glass to her lips, then dropped it an inch as she said, "Take Mason Burke for example. The guy's a pretty good lawyer, better than Markham ever was. But he never had what it takes to pass yourself off in public. So he's had to depend on his brains, which aren't remarkable but are adequate and his family's name, which is more than adequate." She took a couple sips of wine.

"How did Markham's colleagues see him?"

"Aloof, but pleasant. Not overly competent, but complex."

"Complex?"

She nodded and set the glass down, empty. "He had an interesting past. He was in Vietnam as a photographer and was quite a good one. He's had a couple books published. He was also involved in land conservation. He killed a man once." She glanced at me for my reaction.

The wine had dulled my brain enough for me to react like a hardened P.I. An "Oh?" was all she got out of me, but that was all she needed.

"Yes. It was in self defense though. It happened about seven or eight years ago. Long before I got here. I read the account in an old issue of the *Chronicle*. I guess I was curious. A man was upset because his child was run down by a drunk driver who'd been let off a previous Driving Under the Influence charge on a technicality. I guess 'upset' is an understatement. He blamed Markham for letting the guy off. Pulled a gun on him in his chambers. Fortunately for Markham, he had a gun in his desk. It was a pretty clear cut case of self defense."

"The guy must have had a strong reason to believe Markham was responsible."

"No one could prove there was anything funny going on."

After a minute I asked Janet what she thought of Markham as a professional.

"There was a lot to admire. Unfortunately for Markham when you break the law you don't get to offset the damages with an impressive set of credits."

As I finished the last of my wine, she asked me again who I was working for.

I shook my head. "Sorry. Still classified."

Smiling, she said, "I don't suppose you're getting much co-operation from the police."

I signaled for coffee and the check. "Is there an underground newspaper in this town that I should know about?"

She laughed, apparently enjoying herself.

I continued, "Wouldn't it be in the best interests of Carver's men to keep their mouths shut?"

Janet stopped laughing and went into a reflective mode. Tom served us our coffee and put the check in the middle of the table. "Ellie Carver's a friend of mine," Janet said quietly, and placed a VISA card on the check.

I watched the way the hologram on her credit card shimmered and changed shape. "What do you think of Carver?"

"As a cop or as a human being?"

"As a cop."

"Dedicated. Tough. Not easily influenced." She stressed 'easily' and watched to make sure I noticed.

"Are you saying someone's got him by the privates?"

"I'm not saying anything." She glanced at her watch. "Jesus, it's late. I should get back to the office."

We walked out to her car and the blast of cool, early spring air helped revive me some. It also drove home the fact that I'd consumed more than my usual amount of wine. I couldn't believe that Janet was faring any better. I took her arm. She didn't need steadying; it just seemed the thing to do.

When we got in her car, I said, "Are you sure you have to go back to business?"

She had just inserted the key into the car's ignition on the second try and now she looked at me. "What did you have in mind?" She started the car and pulled away from the curb.

I shrugged. It had really been an innocent statement. "I don't know. I guess I just figured that it's six o'clock and we've just consumed a big meal and a lot of wine. There have got to be better things to do than go back to work. We could always use another drink." I was making this up as I went along.

She glanced at me then turned back to the road. I had no idea what was on her mind until she spoke. "I've got some brandy at my place," she said and I still wasn't sure. Was it an invitation? If so, how much of it was the liquor talking? Maybe it was just a simple statement of fact. What was I expected to say here?

I swallowed. "I like brandy. It's good stuff." She smiled and didn't change direction.

Her place, a small apartment above a dry cleaner, turned out to be just a few blocks away. Her bed wasn't much farther. For a long time we lay on the down comforter, propped up with pillows and cushions and sipped coffee made out of some Mediterranean roast, alternating with a snifter of brandy. The combination was delicious and I knew it wasn't the wine this time. We talked for a long time, and everything she said was wise and wonderful and everything I said seemed to reaffirm my existence. And even before we shed our clothes and moved the relationship up one notch, I thought I'd found the part of Janet Miraldi that was too small to be seen with the naked eye.

CHAPTER NINE

I'D FORGOTTEN about Peanuts. I burst into my apartment at seven in the morning half expecting to find a note telling me he'd gone to find someone who would understand that he was incapable of using the toilet. Instead, he was cowering in the bedroom corner, expecting to be punished for the puddle he had left on the kitchen floor. I almost would have preferred the note. I bent down and scratched his neck and once he realized I wasn't going to beat him, he changed his attitude. I think if he could have given me hell, he would have. I took him out and threw the Frisbee for him for about twenty minutes.

Packing to move when you are nursing a hangover is an experience not to be missed. I showered and shaved, downed several aspirin and made an eight-cup pot of coffee. Then I started throwing things right from the drawers into the boxes I hadn't gotten rid of after my last move. I was finished in less than an hour.

I sat on the couch, drinking my last cup of coffee, and felt my head begin to clear. I thought about two things. One: how was I going to get all this stuff moved? I had hired a mover to take it out of storage and move it in here. That was a luxury I couldn't afford more than once every ten years or so. And two: Janet Miraldi. I thought about calling her at work, but decided to give her time for a cup of coffee first. Maybe then.

I swept the kitchen floor and decided that, since I had never used it, I could forgo cleaning the oven. Maybe I'd blown this whole thing with Janet out of proportion. We'd just gotten a little drunk and hadn't interfered with instinct. We were both lonely and alienated and not bothered with proprieties. No shit. Most made-for-TV movies take a more leisurely approach to courtship. The thing was, I had serious doubts that Janet Miraldi would have invited me home with her if she hadn't just consumed a bottle of Chianti. And that bothered me.

Cleaning took less time than packing. There was one advantage to living in a place for less than a month. I hadn't been there long enough to get it dirty.

I'd made arrangements to keep my phone number, but the phone wouldn't be hooked up until the next day. I hated the thought of being without a phone and decided to wait to unplug and pack this one until I was on my way out the door.

What was left of the coffee in my mug was cold, but I drank it anyway. Maybe a phone call wasn't enough. I dredged my brain for the name of the florist that Scott Markham had used. My recall failed me and I unpacked the phone book and leafed through the Yellow Pages. Foxport Florist. I knew it was something subtle like that. I hesitated. Maybe not. Last night had been wonderful. This morning had been less than wonderful. On waking, Janet had looked at me, slightly confused, as if trying to figure out where she'd seen me before. And once it had registered, I'm not sure she was relieved. Then I didn't help matters any when my first, no make that my second waking thought was of a dog I had neglected. I'd quickly gotten dressed and, refusing her offer of a ride back to my car, walked the six blocks. Maybe I should have explained the reason for my speedy departure, but somehow I just couldn't tell this beautiful, desirable woman that I was leaving her for a dog. Maybe now wasn't the time to do anything concerning Janet Miraldi.

When I pushed Janet from my mind, Elaine crept in. She was probably dating some sun-tanned physicist from Los Alamos who would fill her head with visions of neutrinos and quarks. I hoped he wouldn't ask her why she never went to college. She was real sensitive about not having a degree—as if she thought it made her less significant.

In order to get Elaine out of my mind, I dumped the photos out of the large envelope I hadn't packed yet. I hadn't looked at them since the day I'd taken them from Markham's office and then I'd only glanced at them. I felt a little sleazy doing so now. But I told myself I was doing this in the interest of justice. That helped some.

There were four envelopes in all—each containing several

three-by-five photos. Each envelope was devoted to a different model.

On second viewing, I had to admit that some of these photos weren't half bad—if your tastes ran in this direction. He'd done some interesting things with lighting and textures. A couple of them—a woman I didn't recognize—were a bit too strange for my taste and suggested a darker side to Markham's imagination. The woman was blonde with extremely short hair. In both photos she posed with a .25 automatic—just like the one I'd last seen on Markham's desk—and in one of them the barrel of the gun was in her mouth and she looked into the camera's eye with a taunting expression. Call me old fashioned but there's something about a naked woman and a gun that goes against my grain. But then it's so easy to be a critic.

The only models I recognized were Anne and Robyn. And as I studied Anne's photo, it was easy to see why I hadn't instantly recognized her at the Tattersall Tavern. The photo was of a provocative woman; the person I'd met in the bar was a mousy little girl.

When I returned the envelopes to the larger one, I noticed there was one loose photograph. I let it drop onto the coffee table. Then I picked it up for a closer look. This woman made the one with the gun look like the girl next door.

She was young with very long, light colored hair. She had a pretty face that might have made her appear younger than she was. She looked barely out of her teens. Unlike the other models, she was a bit on the plump side. Not obese, but definitely plump. But it was her eyes—wide and glazed—that commanded my attention. They reminded me of that shot from *Psycho* where Janet Leigh, just murdered in the shower, is lying on the tiled bathroom floor and the camera zooms in on her eyes—surprised, horrified and quite dead. She had been posed to look as though she had died violently. Either that or she had died violently. There was no blood or sign of violence, but that wasn't necessary to convey the concept. All it needed was a chalk outline around her body. She was wearing only a garter belt and stockings and was draped half on and half off a bed so that her long hair cascaded to the floor like a waterfall. Except, that is, for a lock of it, which was wrapped around her neck.

Was she dead? There was no way to tell. She looked it, but then so did Janet Leigh. Either way, this added a new dimension to Markham's personality. And I didn't care to think about the position this picture put me in.

Fortunately, I didn't have to right then. There was a knock at the door that sounded like the first four notes of Beethoven's Fifth. I stashed the photos in a box and opened the door. It was Jeff Barlowe. He stood there with a sixpack of beer in one hand and a newspaper in the other. He handed me the newspaper as he brushed past me on his way to the kitchen. "I hear it's moving day," he said removing two cans and putting the other four in the refrigerator. He popped the tops and asked, "You pack the glasses yet?"

" 'Fraid so." I was still at the door. "I don't usually drink before noon," I said, accepting the beer.

"Neither do I." He took his first gulp. "Moving day's the exception."

"Oh. Okay," I said, following suit. I was surprised at how good it tasted.

We both sat on the couch. Peanuts came up to him, tail wagging. "Hey," he said, turning his attention to him, "I remember you. You almost took my head off. Not quite so defensive now. So you're the troublemaker."

"Yeah," I said, "he's the riffraff."

He laughed. "What's his name?"

"Peanuts."

"Peanuts?"

"I named him after a Cubs centerfielder. He's dynamite with a Frisbee."

He continued to rub the dog's neck, and looked over at me. "Let's see, that must be Peanuts Lowrey."

I nodded, a little impressed.

He returned his attention to the dog. "I used to cover sports," he said and no further explanation was necessary.

"Thanks for the beer," I said and added, "I think I know why you're here."

"Yeah? Well you probably don't know all of it." He gave Peanuts a final pat and leaned back into the couch. Then he looked at me. "You're a real cynic, aren't you?"

I shrugged. "Life brings fewer disappointments that way."

Jeff nodded in agreement. "Well, you did tell me you'd give me the photos of Anne."

"I thought I'd just send them to her."

"Oh. That's cool." But it was obvious that it wasn't. It was like I'd rebuffed him. I waited. I wanted to see how bad he wanted those photos. He continued, "It's okay with Anne, you know. You can call her if you want." He shrugged. "Just thought it'd be easier for her. I know her pretty well. You don't."

"Maybe she'd just as soon get them in a plain brown envelope."

"Yeah, but the thing is, she lives at home. With her mom and sister. They might, you know, ask her what she was getting in the mail."

I was going to suggest that she tell them it was none of their business but, realizing how difficult that would be for someone like Anne, I didn't.

Finally Jeff said, "Well, whatever. Just give 'em to her as soon as you can. She's walking around like a spooked cat.

"Anyway," he changed the subject. "I've got a Chevy S-10 parked in the loading zone and if you need help moving, I'm your man."

I looked at him and tried to figure out if this guy sitting next to me, drinking a beer at ten A.M., and tapping out the rhythm to some song inside his head on the arm of the couch, was really on the level. Then I decided that I didn't care if he was or not and said something to myself about gift horses' mouths and said, "Thanks. I can really use the help."

He waved off the thanks and abruptly stood and walked over to the balcony doors. His whole body was keeping time to that song now. Without taking his attention from the view past the balcony, he said, "Nothing like a good move to make me glad I write for a living."

He roamed the apartment, taking in my few pieces of furniture and small number of boxes. "This really wasn't that generous of me. I figured you traveled light and, as I see, I had you pegged pretty well. This move is gonna be a piece of cake. One trip. Two if we don't pack the truck well."

"You seem like an expert at this. Do you moonlight for Allied?"

He shrugged. "Guess I am an expert. Seems like I'm always being recruited. Actually I think it's the truck and not my renowned abilities as a packer." He crumpled his can of beer and tossed it in the trash. "Let me get rid of this beer and we can get started."

As soon as he closed the bathroom door, I opened the dish box and removed the envelope containing Anne's photos. On the one hand I thought he really was trying to be a friend to Anne and on the other he must have been real curious about the photos. I didn't doubt that he'd give them to Anne and I guess I couldn't blame him for being curious.

"Well, where do we start?" Jeff clapped his hands as he came back into the room. I handed him the envelope. He hesitated, then put it in his jacket pocket.

I decided not to call his bluff and was turning toward the boxes when Jeff said, "Who am I kidding, anyway?" and pulled the photos out. As a reporter, even on a local paper, it probably took a lot to surprise Jeff Barlowe. I wondered if Anne would have been pleased with his response. "Holy shit," he said, dropping onto the couch. "This I can't believe." He went through them again slowly. "How did you recognize her?"

"The nose."

"God, she's a knockout." He shook his head and returned the photos to his pocket. Then he looked at me. "Who was this guy? What did he have? I mean I can't believe what it would take to get Anne to brush her hair out of her face, let alone look like that." He took the photos out again and went through them, shaking his head.

"What I have to wonder about is what he did to keep her from looking like that all the time."

Jeff nodded slowly. "Good question."

"Do you know when they had their affair?"

"Yeah, it's been a while. About a year and a half ago I guess."

"Did you notice any change in her appearance or the way she acted while it was going on?"

"I didn't know when it was happening. She didn't confide in me until after it was over. Guess she figured she had to trust someone. But when she told me, I tried to think back that far. I asked myself the same question. And the only thing I can come up with was maybe she started paying less attention to herself when it was over. Became even more introverted." He shrugged.

"That'd make sense."

"Well," Jeff said, turning to me, "thanks. Like I said, I owe you." He put the photos away again.

I gestured toward the apartment. "This'll set us even."

The move took one trip and we finished just before noon. Louise was leaving to open the small shop she owned in town and insisted that if we needed anything we should call her there. Jeff said he wished that everyone he helped move used lawn chairs for living room furniture.

We were finishing off the last of the sixpack. I was inspecting the apartment, relieved that the move was over, and Jeff was in the canvas director's chair he'd taken a liking to. I had decided I'd made a good move. The place had some interesting angles and if I didn't spend much time at the south end of the living room, the slanted ceiling wouldn't be a problem. Louise had explained that the apartment had been carpeted in remnants and they all went together pretty well. It was kind of jarring when you went from the royal blue hallway to the chartreuse bedroom, but I could live with that. It sure as hell beat solid beige walls and solid gold carpeting.

When I stepped back into the living room, Jeff ambushed me with, "You sure there weren't any more photos?"

Peanuts was investigating the more interesting corners in the living room.

"That's what I said."

"If there were more, would you tell me?"

I sat on the couch. "Probably not." Then I tried to soften it with, "You're a reporter."

He shrugged and peered in the beer can's opening. "I'm a pretty decent guy. I'd keep quiet."

"I'll keep that in mind if I run across more pictures."

He looked at me. "There are more, you know."

"How do you know that?"

"Logic. If he could talk Anne into taking her clothes off, he could convince just about anyone."

"Yeah, but what difference would it make? The guy killed himself. The women in his life and how he posed them don't have much bearing now."

He chuckled and shifted in the chair. "But you don't think he killed himself. Do you?" I didn't answer and he continued. "Why? What made Markham immune to serious depression?"

"Would you kill yourself if the suicide clause in your term life insurance policy were still in effect?"

Jeff whistled softly and shook his head. "Not bright." Then he arched an eyebrow and said, "Who's his agent?"

"John Dieken."

Nodding as though it all made sense now, he pulled his reporter's notebook from the inside pocket of his jacket. "Call this guy," he spoke as he wrote. "Name's Bob Miller. He's over at City Mutual. He's a good guy and he might be able to tell you a few things about Dieken."

I took the paper. "Like what?"

He drained the beer and shook his head. "Don't know for sure. I've heard he misrepresents his companies. Don't know any details." Gesturing toward the paper he said, "Call him. Tell him I gave you his number."

I folded the paper and put it in my pocket. "He won't hang up on me?"

Tossing his beer can into an empty box, Jeff smiled and said, "He owes me.

"You talk to Janet Miraldi yet?" From the way he spoke, it sounded like an innocent question.

"Yeah, yesterday."

"What'd she think?"

"Like you said before, she's not real happy about things."

Jeff nodded, and this time there was something in his expression that indicated he didn't think I was totally leveling with him, but he didn't pursue it. "You meet Jack Alden?"

"State's Attorney, right?"

"Yeah. Watch out for him. As far as I'm concerned he's bad news."

"Why?" I asked. When Jeff hesitated, I said, "Off the record."

"I'm not so sure he gets his entire paycheck from the state. The Markham investigation was Miraldi's idea. She listened to the complaints, got someone to go in. Alden dragged his feet, and, from what I hear, was more than happy to drop it when Markham died. I guess I shouldn't say the guy's corrupt. It may be that he knows he's nowhere near as competent as Miraldi, and he wants to make sure no one else knows it." He was silent for a minute and it was almost as if he were changing the subject when he said, "What'd you think of Miraldi?"

"Impressive," was all I said.

Jeff nodded but didn't say anything.

I treated Jeff to lunch and he went off to cover a protest at the site of a new housing development just west of town. "Actually they've been digging there for a while, but there's a protest today. We've got a bunch of hopped up environmentalists upset because the guy's bulldozing a bunch of rodents or something like that out of a home." He patted his breast pocket where he kept his notepad and said, "Pulitzer material."

On my way home, I stopped at the Foxport Library. Janet had said Markham had published two photography books, but I found only one there. I almost panicked when I realized I didn't have a library card, but I managed to get out of there with the book and a temporary card.

On my way home, I stopped at a pay phone, called the courthouse number and asked for Janet Miraldi. When I told her who was calling, there was a slight hesitation before she said, "I'm sorry. I'm in a meeting right now, I'll get back to you." She hung up before I could tell her that was not possible.

Then I tried Bob Miller. He was out.

Back in my apartment, I decided to get to know Markham the photographer, since I was having some trouble getting a grip on him as a human being. The book was called *Portraits of a Conflict* and beneath the bold lettering was a line in smaller type which read, "by award-winning photographer, Scott Markham." Although the book had been published in 1976, the photos were apparently taken during Markham's stint as a combat photographer in Vietnam. As I turned the pages of the book, I became more impressed with Markham's skill as a photographer and more curious about the dark side of the man's personality. He had recorded every bleak aspect of that war in a way I'd never seen before. He drew the viewer's attention to details that seemed at first innocuous, but as you looked closer, they deepened the dread and the impact. In one photo a soldier crouched over the body of another. In his right hand he clutched a rifle like a staff, butt dug into the ground to steady himself. The thumb and forefinger of his left hand were pressed against the bridge of his nose, the way you do when you've got a bad headache. At first glance he seemed to be praying or grieving over the body of his friend, but then I saw that his eyes were open and they burned with some unspeakable rage. Photos of the bombed out villages with their dazed, uncomprehending occupants were harsh and vivid in black and white. These photos weren't portraits of a conflict, they were portraits of madness.

I tried to put myself inside Markham to figure out whether taking pictures like these was a catharsis or an obsession. Or both. I'd been in Vietnam and like most everyone else there, I'd seen some awful things. I sometimes think I'm insensitive because I've managed to tuck those memories into a corner of my subconscious I visit only when I drink a lot of tequila or get stoned—and it's been at least five years since I've done either one of those things.

There was a grim fascination about these photos that compelled me to keep turning pages. But when I got to page 52, I stopped. There was no reason to go further.

I stared at the page for at least a minute before I said, "Holy shit." Then I unpacked the photos from the envelopes and placed the one of the woman posed as a corpse opposite the page in the book. Incredible.

I compared them detail for detail. They were as identical as two photos could be given that they were of different women in different rooms, presumably on opposite sides of the world. The caption in the book was simple: "Murdered prostitute, Saigon, 1971." I picked up the other photo, wishing it had a caption and wishing it were a larger print so I could see the size of the pupils in those doll-like eyes.

▽

Chapter Ten

I SEEM to spend a lot of time between a rock and a hard place. I guess I do it to myself, though I've yet to figure out the pattern. My options were limited. I could get the picture enlarged and maybe ascertain whether the woman in the photo was a corpse or just faking it. I knew something of dark room work, but in order to get a close up of the woman's face, I'd have to make a negative first. I didn't have the equipment for that and didn't know a photoprocessor well enough to have it done for me. There were people I could show the photo to who might be able to identify the woman, but I had a real sinking feeling about that. I was probably in trouble already and I didn't want to have to trust anyone more than necessary. The third option was to sit on it for a while and hope that I could identify the woman on my own. I considered who might be privy to the women Markham kept company with and decided it was a good time to rattle Mason's cage. If he would see me.

"Quint McCauley, what a nice surprise." Mason not only agreed to see me, he didn't keep me waiting. I proceeded with caution.

"Sit down, sit down," he continued. "How's the P.I. business?"

As if he didn't know. "Not bad. I'm looking into Markham's suicide."

Mason looked genuinely confused for a moment, then recovered. "Well, I guess I don't have to ask who you're working for, do I?"

I just smiled. "You think he killed himself?"

"I think it's entirely possible," Mason answered without hesitation and plucked a cigar out of the humidor. "Scott had a knack for finding the easiest way out of a problem. And it's no secret that Miraldi had a good case." He lit the cigar and puffed on it, examined the tip and continued, "At the time, of course, I couldn't see how depressed he was. If I had, I might have done something." He shrugged. "Don't know what, but when something like this happens to a friend, you always have to ask yourself if there was anything you could've done to keep him from pulling the trigger." He studied me for a moment then looked away. "And you know what happens?" He looked back at me and answered his own question. "They find a way to do it anyway. Ninety percent of the time."

He didn't appear to be under any particular emotional stress, but I had to admit that if he had come across as distraught, I would have doubted his sincerity. I figured Mason managed his emotions the same way he managed his money— letting go of just enough to complete a transaction.

"Scott had a lot to lose. His prestige, his profession. He was trying to make some other kind of investments, but meeting with brick walls."

"What kind of investments?"

"Oh, for example, he wanted to buy some property. I think he wanted to turn it into a wildlife preserve of all things. Around here property's being grabbed up real fast. Scott made a real attractive offer to Bill Langley for some land just west of here. No dice. Some pretty bad blood developed between them. Scott figured, and maybe rightly, that one person shouldn't own all that land. Be able to call all the shots.

"And, of course there was his son Eric. That may have been what pushed him over."

"What about Eric?"

Mason leaned back and rested his right elbow on the arm of the chair, rolling the cigar between his fingertips. A smile crept over his face. He was in his glory. "You don't know, do you?"

I studied a glass paperweight on his desk for a moment before returning my gaze to him. "I guess I don't."

"It has to do with deception and desperation. Why don't you ask Lorna?" He checked himself. "Oh, I forgot. Of course, you don't know Lorna Markham."

"How well do you know Eric?"

If Mason was disappointed by my refusal to pursue his statement, he didn't let on. "Why, I'm the boy's godfather. And believe me, I'm quite taken with the role. My wife and I don't have any children of our own, you know." He sighed and went into his thoughtful mode. "Eric was the one thing Scott could be proud of. God knows his marriage wasn't much and he'd compromised his career. But he might have been able to recover from that. Let me tell you, what Scott was accused of—bribery—well, it's not like everyone else is a stranger to it."

Mason liked nothing better than the sound of his own voice and I intended to use that to my advantage. If I just let him talk for a while, maybe between all the boasts, threats and meanderings he'd provide me with a nugget of something I could use. He was saying, "I mean no one would say they approve of it, but it happens. And it's usually overlooked. Just so long as you didn't get too greedy. There's plenty to go around. And then that Ms. Miraldi, so eager to set herself up as the next State's Attorney, decides to break the thing wide open. People don't take very well to that sort of thing. Things were moving along fine before she got there. She just had to make an example out of somebody. And that somebody happened to be Scott Markham. Well, I guess she needed a place to cut her teeth. Once they've grown in I suspect she'll move on to more challenging assignments. Maybe she'll be ready to take on organized crime." He laughed at his own effort at a joke. He was the only one who did.

"Did she have a case on anyone else?"

"Not without Scott's testimony."

He continued, "Now I've got to ask why Lorna cares how her husband met his maker." He gave it about fifteen seconds of serious thought before he slapped his hand on his desk as if one of life's great ideas had just occurred to him. "Of course, of course." He burst into laughter and there was nothing forced about it. He was genuinely enjoying himself. After an effort to get himself under control, he said, "Oh, that's rich. It really is." He nodded, savoring whatever it was he was thinking about. "I'll bet the lovely Lorna is hollering murder at the top of her pretty lungs." He glanced at me out of the corner of his eye. "Of course, Lorna Markham is no concern of yours. I almost forgot."

Mason continued to explain it to himself. He wedged his cigar into a notch in the ash tray and folded his hands in front of him on the desk. I thought he was going to call for a moment of prayer. Instead, he smiled and said, "To Lorna, the difference between having a husband who committed suicide and one who was murdered comes to a million dollars I believe." He leaned back and continued, without so much gusto, but there was no doubt he was still amused. "The very least Lorna expected to get out of this marriage was a good settlement."

I took my time lighting a cigarette. When I'd slid my lighter back into my pocket, I said, "Why would Scott kill himself now if he could do it in a year and a half and get paid for it?"

Mason shrugged and waved his hand like he was swatting a fly. "People who commit suicide don't think about things like that. They're messed up already. That's why they do it.

"You're still working for her, aren't you?"

I really didn't see any reason not to tell him. Except my own innate obstinacy. Burke viewed me through narrowed eyes, and with his mottled, ruddy complexion, he reminded me of a lizard sunning itself on a rock. I half expected a slender tongue to flick out and snag a fly. Instead, a smile broke out on his face and he said, "Damn, McCauley, you don't budge, do you?"

"This woman Markham was seeing. How serious were they?"

Mason frowned. "She was probably as important as all the rest. But I'll bet her shelf life wasn't any longer."

"What do you mean?"

"Every time Scott met a new woman, he thought that was it. The real thing. Every time. An incurable romantic. He never saw the pattern and I never pointed it out to him. My guess is that in three months, this new one would have been traded in."

"Why you? Why would Markham hire you to defend him in a criminal suit?"

If the change of subject caught him off guard, he didn't show it. "Because he trusted me," he replied without hesitation and with a touch of exaggerated offense.

"Was he planning to divorce Lorna?"

"Scott was always planning to divorce Lorna."

"If Markham's case had gone to trial, would you have won it?"

He retrieved his cigar, puffed on it several times and examined the lit end, which was doing just fine. Finally he said, "I don't know. We had many options we hadn't considered yet."

"Was he going to cooperate with the state?"

"Let's just say that was one option."

"If you were an attorney, concerned about being named, wouldn't you like nothing better than to wake up one morning and find out that Markham had been run over by the six-oh-five to Chicago. Or that he'd committed suicide?"

Mason nodded slowly. "I suppose there were a few people in this county that might fall into that category."

"Doesn't it bother you, even just a little bit, that Markham was stamped and filed as a suicide almost before his body was cold?"

Mason sighed and looked out the shuttered window onto the semi-busy street. There wasn't much to see besides a station wagon parked across from the building and the hedges behind it. When he finally spoke, he might have been addressing one of those hedges. "Scott is dead. I can't change that. And life is for the living. I have to protect the interests of the living."

"Especially your own hide. Right?"

He shrugged and found his smug, satisfied smile again. "It's as good as anyone else's. If not better."

After two puffs and one examination of the current length of his cigar he looked at me and said, "You know this McCauley boycott doesn't have to continue. And I can't imagine you'd want it to. You can't work for Lorna Markham forever." He giggled. "She's running out of money."

I didn't respond. After a minute, he leaned over to look at his calendar and said, "Well, this has been amusing. But I'm afraid I've got an appointment in five minutes. I'm going to have to ask you to leave."

I stood, irritated with myself for even imagining that Mason might come through for me. Mason only came through for himself.

"Now, Quint, I wouldn't spend too much time on this murder theory of yours. I know it's colorful and makes for excitement, but it's not a good idea. This community may be growing but we're still pretty provincial. People like it that way. That's why they came here."

There was that smile again. "Besides, truth shall win out." He winked at me. "You know I'm right."

I thanked Mason Burke and left without my nugget, not realizing that the simple fact that Mason had agreed to see me should have told me something.

I went over our conversation and tried to latch onto something that might be significant. Langley. Where had I heard that name before? What was his connection to Markham? Was there a connection to Markham or was Burke, at this very moment, giggling to himself as he thought about me spinning my wheels? Suddenly aware that I was staring at a green light, listening to the guy behind me sit on his horn, I popped my Honda into gear, turned north on Second Avenue and headed into town. Chances were that if Langley was significant to this case, then Janet could tell me what I needed to know. The key word there was "could." She hadn't been too eager to part with any of that information yesterday. And if Jeff Barlowe was half the reporter I thought he was, my research was done for me already.

I learned that the answers to my questions would have to wait. The receptionist at the *Chronicle* told me Jeff was still out covering the protest at the new development. I left a message for him.

It was one of those early spring days when you can smell things starting to grow. Even on this boulevard with the carefully manicured strip down the middle, colors were intruding on the dull gray left by winter. I stood next to my car parked at the curb, hands sunk in my pockets, and breathed in the changes, vaguely recalling that this was a great time to be in the city too.

"Quint?" Even though the person attached to the voice was only a couple feet behind me, it was only because the wind was blowing in my direction that I heard her.

Having gotten my attention, Anne looked down at the sidewalk and then back up to me. I knew what she was going to say, felt I should help her, yet on another level felt that I shouldn't. Her eyes met mine and held on awhile before she said, "I, uh, wanted to thank you. Jeff gave me the pictures." She looked away and laughed a little, but it was forced. "I guess that was pretty stupid of me. Posing, I mean." She sighed and crossed her arms over her chest and studied the sidewalk again. "Pretty damned stupid."

"People have done a lot more stupid things and gotten away with it."

She shrugged.

"Remember Anne," I said, "you're talking to the guy who was so lonely he wound up with the police chief's wife in his motel room and almost got himself lynched for it. Nobody gets through life without doing his share of stupid things." She looked up briefly from the sidewalk. "And you know what?" I continued, "I don't think I'm going easy on myself when I say that it's not always fair. The people who get caught are usually the ones who don't need to be caught to learn the lesson in the first place."

She nodded, but I could tell she wasn't at all convinced. "I guess it could have been worse. Someone else could have found them. I'm just worried now that maybe there were others."

"Did he take more than that?"

"No. I don't think so. I'm just worried about copies."

"Were there negatives?"

She shook her head. "He destroyed them. It was part of our agreement. But I suppose he could have made copies."

"I think if there were copies, you'd know by now."

"I hope you're right."

It took her a while to work up the nerve to hear the answer to her next question. Finally she asked, "Did Jeff look at the pictures?"

"What do you think?"

She reddened slightly. "God, how am I going to face him again?"

I shrugged and wondered if she'd taken a good look at the photos. "I wouldn't be ashamed of those pictures." She didn't respond, so I prodded. "Let me ask you this. Did you throw them away yet?"

Her smile was slow in coming and was a little on the sheepish side. "No. Not yet."

I started walking down the street, past the store fronts. Anne walked with me, as I thought she would, and we followed the curve of the street as it branched out into Crowely Park. She needed to talk to someone but talking, especially about this, didn't come easily for her. There was something so helpless and pathetic about this woman and I couldn't see any reason for it. I was tempted to grab her by the shoulders and shake her out of it. But that would have committed more of me than I was prepared to offer at this point.

And I sure as hell didn't see what she and Markham had offered each other.

"How did you meet Markham?" I asked.

"He judged a county-wide photo contest I had some of my work entered in."

"Did you win?"

She nodded and said, "Yeah," like it wasn't any big deal.

"Mind if I ask who broke it off?"

"I did," she said without hesitating.

I didn't want to push for a reason, but I really wanted to know. This time she hesitated. "Married men," she said, "they aren't worth the effort."

"Did he promise to leave his wife?"

"Oh, no. That was never the issue. Look," she finally said, "I just realized I was wasting my time."

That sounded like a real sensible reason for breaking off an affair, but for some reason I couldn't picture Anne Phillips telling Scott Markham to take a hike because she had better things to do. It didn't fit.

"How many others were there?" she asked.

"Several."

She nodded as if that didn't surprise her. "I think he hurt a lot of people."

"Probably."

I really didn't want to ask the next question. "Anne, when you were posing for him, did he ever suggest any, uh, poses that you found, um, objectionable?"

"Like what?" She looked at me from beneath scrunched up eyebrows.

"Never mind." If she had to ask, she didn't know. I had my answer.

After a few moments, she said, "You stopped by to see Jeff?"

"Yeah, he's out on an assignment."

"That's right. He's covering that Langley development."

I stopped. "What did you say?"

"Jeff's covering that protest over at the new housing development."

"No, what did you say about Langley?"

"Well, he's the developer."

"Bill Langley?"

"Yeah," she dragged the word out as if she thought by the time she got to the end of it she'd have figured out where I was coming from.

"Can you show me where it is?"

"Sure."

"Let's go."

I drove and Anne directed. She asked why I was interested in Langley. I couldn't give her a good answer.

The area of development was south of town and west of the highway that had previously been the division between suburbia and country. Twenty years ago this was farther from civilization than anyone wanted to be. Now it was prime property. The entire area, as Anne pointed out, couldn't have been much more than ten acres and a group of about twenty people had congregated at the extreme south end. Some carried signs and others just marched along with the sign carriers. A few people led small children as they marched in front of the back hoe, which was slowly digging its way toward them. At the rate it was going, these people wouldn't have to budge for a couple days. I spotted Jeff, standing next to a photographer, and pulled onto a dirt road for construction vehicles. I parked as close to Jeff as I could and as we walked to where he stood, Anne explained, "This part of the housing development is going to destroy a large area of prairie bush clover, which is a habitat of the Indiana bat."

I stopped. "Bats?"

The wind had picked up and she had to hold her hair back to keep it out of her face. She smiled. "Yes, bats. These people are trying to protect the species."

Jeff watched us with interest as we approached. "Trying to scoop me. Should have figured."

"This is the story you've waited a lifetime for, right?"

"You said it." He squinted into the sun then looked at the group of protesters. "They'll be a while."

"Bat people," I said. "Hard to figure why there are so many people protecting the creatures."

"They're actually part of a bigger conservation group that's trying to save natural habitats for all kinds of critters. Very well organized too."

"Was Markham involved in this?"

"He might have been. I know this is part of the property he wanted to buy from Langley. He tried to get an injunction to keep him from digging."

"What happened?"

Jeff laughed. "Langley just bribed some officials higher up than the ones Markham bribed."

"Where is Langley?" I asked.

Jeff turned toward the back hoe and nodded. "This guy coming over now."

At first I thought that the man approaching us was the foreman of the construction crew. I guess I expected a developer to wear a business suit and a hard hat. Not Langley. He carried a heavy corduroy jacket and wore a flannel shirt and jeans. His shirt sleeves were rolled up to his elbows, revealing long-sleeved thermal underwear. This guy must have been out here since early morning when he would have needed the warmth. He wasn't a big man, but, with the exception of the inch or two of his belly that crept over his belt, he was solid and hard. That hardness was repeated in the cut of his jaw and the set of his eyes. He apologized to Jeff for the interruption and ran a hand through his steel gray hair. "You know," he said, "I don't feel good about making a bunch of damned bats homeless. I told those people to go right ahead if they want to relocate them. But I'm sure as hell not going to touch one of those things and they'd better hurry up and do it before my guy gets here, because we're not stopping for them." I wasn't sure if by "them," he meant the bats or the people. He explained to Jeff how he'd even gone to the trouble of checking to see if these creatures called anywhere else home. "They're Indiana bats, what in the hell are they doing here?" He continued to defend his actions to Jeff, frequently adding that he really didn't have to. I watched the back hoe working on a foundation and decided you needed a lot of patience to operate one of those things. The operator was slowly removing dirt and depositing it in a truck which, once filled, would haul it off to someone who needed a hill instead of a hole.

One person from the bat group approached the man on the big machine. She was young and fairly attractive and I wondered how protecting the habitat of the Indiana bat had made it to the top of her priority list for the afternoon. Since the machine's noise prevented verbal communication, she pointed to her sign, which said something about bats needing homes too, then toward the area her little group meant to protect, then at the hole he was creating. The guy on the machine just shook his head and kept digging.

Langley was watching her too and, shaking his head, turned back to Jeff. "I don't want to have to call the police in here. That's going to give those people a lot more publicity than they deserve. But they're not going to stop this. . . ."

We could hear the woman's scream above the sound of the back hoe and apparently so could the operator because he halted the huge shovel in mid air. The woman kept screaming and our small group and the bat people converged on the pit at the same time.

None of us screamed, but we all gaped. Dangling from the shovel blade, like it had bit off more than it could chew, was a chunk of a human being.

Langley spoke first. "Son of a bitch. This is all I need."

Chapter Eleven

∇

MORE THAN TEN years ago, a plane crashed after take off from O'Hare airport, killing all on board and taking out a few on the ground as well. One of the witnesses was a young man who described to reporters what he'd seen. When he finished, he shook his head like he was trying to clear it, looked up at the sky and said, "I always wanted to see an airplane crash."

On the surface, the statement sounded like something a person with his brains on vacation would say, but I think I knew what he meant. It's what causes gapers' blocks at expressway pile-ups and it's why the police have to put up barricades at murder scenes and fires. We fear death, cheat it, court it and in the end submit to it. But, along the way, like a moth to a flame, we are drawn to it.

At that construction site on the west side of Foxport, there was a grim expectancy among the observers, myself included, that was disquieting. And, as the experts arrived and began to comb the area, I had to constantly remind myself that this wasn't some ancient Mayan city being excavated with human remains dating back some two thousand years. No. This person had likely died before his time and had been buried with less ceremony than you'd give a pet gerbil. Most deserve better.

Both print and broadcast media considered the grisly event worthy of coverage—Jeff had lost his scoop, but was unarguably the first reporter on the scene. Carver arrived not long after the unearthing and after avoiding him for almost an hour, I decided it was time to leave. He was bound to spot me eventually. Besides, after the initial discovery, new evidence would be slow in coming and most of the fact-finding would occur at the lab. Anne said she'd stick around a while and catch a ride with someone from the paper. I extracted a promise from Barlowe to report any findings and left.

I had no opportunity to talk to Bill Langley, he was much too busy telling everyone within earshot he had no idea where the body came from. I think he was wasting his breath. To have amassed the property, fortune and reputation he apparently had, must have required a good deal of cunning and common sense. A whole lot more than it would take to dig up the body of one of your victims in front of the press and a bunch of bat fanciers. Actually, I'm not sure what I would have discussed with him. I guess I'd just wanted to get a look at the guy and I'd wound up with more than I'd asked for.

Before going home, I stopped at Robyn Fosse's apartment. I figured I had nothing to lose in a confrontation. And it might prove interesting. It was not to be, however; she wasn't home and I was lucky to escape Wanda Buchholz and her dashing doberman. As I returned to my car I saw them heading toward the apartment building, probably from one of the parks. I had to smile. Here was this frumpy middle-aged woman whose only nod to fashion and fitness was her lavender sweat suit, and she was walking next to this lean, mean animal with its head held high apparently secure in the knowledge that while most dogs looked ridiculous wearing a bandana, he could pull it off.

My apartment had a private entrance on the west side of the building facing the river. It was just a wooden flight of stairs painted gray, but it gave me a porch that had room enough for a chair and a small grill. I parked my car in the half of the driveway Louise said I could use and lifted the two bags of groceries out of the trunk. I noted that Louise's car wasn't there. I was beginning to suspect that Louise had a more active social life than I did. It wouldn't have surprised me. As I walked around the side of the house I was wondering how Peanuts would look in a bandana and anticipating my first cookout of the year, smelling the burgers charring over the coals, and I didn't realize someone was sitting on the bottom step until I almost tripped over her. It was Janet Miraldi and she recovered faster than I did.

"I've heard of guys changing their phone number, but isn't this a little extreme? Disconnect your phone and move?"

I allowed myself a few moments and then said, "I've changed my name too. Call me Diego."

Without pretending to be doing something else, we checked each other out. She wore a white turtleneck under a lightweight jacket and gray corduroy pants. The brand-name athletic shoes made me wonder how she had gotten here. It was a long walk. I hadn't noticed a white Toyota parked out on the street. The fact that she had come to see me might be a good sign, but the guarded way she presented herself made me think there was more to this meeting than renewing acquaintances.

She stood and stepped out of my way. "We need to talk." It was an instruction, not a request. She crossed her arms over her chest, and moved some pebbles around with the toe of her shoe. I hadn't known Janet very long, but nervous gestures didn't look natural on her.

"Okay," I said.

She shook her head. "Not about last night." She wasn't exuding much warmth and I wondered if she wanted to put last night in the 'Let's forget it ever happened' file.

"I kind of figured that." No problem, I thought, noting that I wasn't the one who brought it up. I added, "Well, whatever we're going to talk about, I don't want to do it standing here with my arms full." I gestured toward my apartment. "You want to come upstairs?"

She looked at me and my two bags, then up the stairs, and back at me. "Okay."

It took a minor juggling act for me to dig the keys out of my pocket while holding onto the groceries. Arms still folded across her chest, Janet watched me in a detached manner.

Just to make conversation I said, "You hear they're digging up bodies on the west side of town?"

"I'd heard rumors. Any idea who it is yet?"

"No." I unlocked the door, practically fell into the apartment and still managed to hold the screen door open for Janet. She accepted the effort without acknowledgment. "They didn't find anything buried with the body that would identify it."

"You were there?"

I shrugged. "Yeah."

Peanuts greeted us at the door. I set the groceries on the counter that separated the kitchen from the living room and said to Janet, "I've got to take him out for a few minutes. You're welcome to join us or, if you prefer, you can help yourself to my Oreos or search my apartment."

She looked over the room briefly, most of its contents were still in boxes, then said, "I think I'll join you two."

I introduced her to Peanuts and the three of us walked the span of the yard down to the river. I didn't say anything, just walked. While I was real glad to see Janet, at least I had been at first, I hadn't come home prepared for company. I needed a few minutes of peace and quiet and my daily river fix. Janet seemed to respect that. I noticed that the willows across the river were reflected in the water as if the surface were a mirror. There was just a whisper of daylight left and the dusk had a rosy hue. The willows' reflection was black and the lights dazzled in the water like a hundred brilliant stars.

Finally Janet broke the spell, "It's beautiful here."

I nodded. Peanuts raced by us in pursuit of some real or imagined fauna. We both watched him. "If you're lucky, maybe he'll herd some ducks for you."

"You're kidding." She laughed and I had a flashback from the night before, recalling her laughter, deep and throaty.

That was the extent of our conversation until we got back into the apartment. She sat on the couch and scratched Peanuts' head as I got beers for both of us and put the groceries away.

"Last night you introduced me to a good spot for Italian cuisine. Will you let me show you some of my native delicacies?"

"I'm not sure," she said, then considered again and added, "What do the Irish eat?"

"Potatoes," I said, my head in the refrigerator. "Potatoes and Guinness."

"Sounds great." She probably intended sarcasm there, but I decided to interpret it as "Yes, I'd just love to have dinner with you."

I opened a box of dog biscuits and gave one to Peanuts. He tore himself away from Janet. With no dog to focus her attention on, she looked out the window, although she couldn't have seen anything but the darkening sky. She sat with one leg folded under her, tapping her nails on the side of the beer can. The absence of color in her clothing made the richness of her hair—dark and thick with traces of gold—all the more obvious. I couldn't help but compare her to Elaine. Elaine was spontaneous, responding to her thoughts and emotions without censorship; Janet was cool, controlled, acting in response to logical reasoning. Most of the time anyway. Then it occurred to me that I was something like a beggar comparing the relative merits of two twenty-year-old brandies. At best, it was an intellectual exercise.

I tried to push such thoughts from my mind, but I guess a few fragments didn't vacate because I was still distracted when Janet bushwhacked me. "You have the photos of Robyn Fosse in the buff, don't you?"

I didn't want to insult her intelligence by asking her what photos so I didn't say anything at first. And since she only mentioned Robyn, she probably didn't know about the others. I opened the package of ground beef, ripped off a portion, and began to create hamburgers. "Yeah," I said. "I've got them."

She finally looked directly at me and locked onto me with dark, accusing eyes. "You were holding out on me. Why?"

I wiped my hands on a dish towel. They felt heavy with grease from the meat and wouldn't come clean. I leaned on the counter and looked at her. She was in control, but had a tight grip on the beer can. Finally I said, "I guess I didn't think those photos were significant. Especially at the time. I thought it was suicide at first, remember. Here I was looking at photos of a nude woman found in the office of a married judge who had just committed suicide. As far as I knew, she was just his mistress. Then when I thought 'Hey maybe this isn't suicide', it was a little late to do anything with them. I couldn't very well hand Carver the photos and say, 'Here. You must have dropped these.' He'd have had me for breakfast."

Unamused, she continued to stare. It wasn't a friendly stare, and I was starting to feel like I needed to explain further. I stubbornly resisted. Finally she shifted slightly and said, "You sure you weren't planning to do anything else with them?"

I felt like I'd been slapped. "Now just what in the hell is that supposed to mean? I'm not into blackmail, lady."

She sipped the beer and said, "I don't really know you. I don't know what you're into."

"Well, just so you don't feel obliged to launch an investigation, it's not blackmail. So don't worry about having soiled yourself with a felon." Mentally I pounded my head against the refrigerator. Damn, she drew that response out of me.

She looked away. "If the thought never crossed your mind, I apologize."

"Hey, either apologize or don't, but don't start slapping conditions on it."

She looked back at me. "I'm sorry. Okay?" She sighed and leaned back into the couch, looking up at the ceiling. "But what else was I supposed to think? I barely know you. All I've got to go on is one night we spent together that probably never would have happened if I'd been in my right mind."

"I think I liked you better when you were in your wrong mind."

"Yeah, I'll bet you did," she said, then after a few seconds added, "I was just trying to think of a reason why you'd take them. Blackmail was the only one that made sense."

"Yeah, well it doesn't make sense to me. Maybe I was protecting my client. Maybe I was trying to . . . , ah hell, I don't know. But I do know if I was planning to blackmail Robyn Fosse, I wouldn't tell you she was Markham's mistress."

Neither of us spoke for a few minutes. If it had been Carver accusing me of blackmail, I would have laughed it off. But not Janet. Our relationship, for better or for worse, had progressed past the "just business" point. And whatever we had become the morning after, we'd shared a lot the night before. I tried to remind myself that this was a possible murder investigation and there wasn't room for hurt feelings. Any shot was a fair shot.

Janet got up and walked into the kitchen, apparently in search of the garbage bin. She tried the cupboard under the sink before she spotted the brown grocery bag with the ground beef wrapper in it. She placed the can in the bag rather than dropping it and stood with her back to me for several seconds. Then she turned and said, "May I have another beer?" This gesture was more an apology than the previous one.

"Help yourself," I said, thinking that wasn't my style but she had just accused me of blackmail and I had to suffer righteous indignation for a minute or two.

She snapped the beer open, smiled briefly then turned away like she was looking for some reason to stay here.

"You like onions on your hamburger?" I asked.

"Sweet?"

I picked up an onion that was shaped sort of like a Frisbee. "Hard to tell. But I say we go for it."

"Sure, why not." She took the onion from me and started slicing it. I went out to check the coals.

They were almost but not quite ready so I took my beer and sat in the director's chair and watched Janet working at the counter. Last night I'd thought I knew everything there was to know about Janet. I didn't. Now I noticed how long and tapered her hands were; she probably could have been a surgeon or a potter. "How did you know about the photos of Robyn?" I asked.

She considered my question while separating the onion rings. Then she said, "I went to see her."

I sat up. "You what? I told you that in confidence. It's not going to help me any if she knows she's being followed. I was working her from another angle. You probably blew it for me."

Unperturbed, she smiled and said, "Don't you mean to say 'You beat me you bitch'?"

"Don't tell me what I was thinking."

She shrugged, "I guess I was just projecting."

"Well, don't. Okay?"

"Okay."

Again, there was that silence. Finally Janet said, "I didn't tell her how I knew. For all she knows, Markham told me."

I tossed the beer can and opened another. "Yeah, and I'm sure she bought that. I only met the woman once, but my impression of her was that she's no dummy."

"She isn't. But I think she was willing to give a little to get a little. She said she was concerned about some photographs he'd taken. She thought he kept hers in his office."

"And you told her you'd find those photos."

"I said I'd try."

"Were you going to give them back to her?"

"Yes."

"Pretty confident."

"I had to be. If I'd weakened an inch, I'd have lost her."

"Which side of the fence does Robyn fall on? Murder or suicide?"

"Oh, murder. Definitely." She took a drink of beer and wiped a residual drop from her mouth. "He told her he was going to leave Lorna."

"According to Mason Burke, he was constantly on the verge of divorcing Lorna." When Janet didn't respond, I said, "Do you believe her?"

She sighed and wiped her hands with a towel. Then she sat on the couch, draped her arm over the back and said, "I believe that's what he told her. And, like many mistresses, she lived in hope. I'm sure she believed him. There's no doubt in my mind. She adored the asshole."

"So you offered her the photos. Then tell me, Janet Miraldi, Assistant State's Attorney, over achiever and barterer for bits of information. What did she give you in exchange for that favor?"

"What do you mean?"

When she said that, I knew I wasn't going to get it out of her. But that didn't mean I couldn't try. "You know what I mean. She'd owe you a big favor."

"Look," she tried again, "I just didn't think the woman should be put through that agony if it wasn't necessary."

I looked at her for a minute. I was already becoming aware of how her body spoke for her and right now it was telling me that she wasn't going to budge an inch on this. I got up and took the hamburgers out to the grill. When I came back in, I said, "I could leave your burger on until you tell me, you know."

"You wouldn't do that to a hamburger." She smiled and I found I was no less attracted to her today than I'd been last night. Maybe even more. Briefly I thought of Elaine and wondered what she'd think of Janet.

We ate the hamburgers on the coffee table while listening to Miles Davis, and she fed Peanuts scraps of burger and potato chips. He seemed to think that the bowl of dog food by the refrigerator was put there for someone else. It was probably too late to make a dog out of him. Janet asked me how I got to be as old as I was without accumulating enough furniture to fill a dentist's waiting room.

"You don't like to be tied down," she said, tearing a paper towel from the roll I'd put on the table. She wiped hamburger grease off her fingers and waited for me to respond.

"Not to furniture, anyway," I said.

We were starting on the Oreos when I figured it was time to get back to business. "I realize you're not going to tell me what kind of deal you made with Robyn."

"*If* I made a deal with Robyn."

"Janet," I said, "you don't need to be a genius to figure that neither you nor Robyn is about to offer something for nothing. Information is expensive."

She acknowledged what I'd said with a nod, then she said, "I'm sorry, Quint. It's not that I don't trust you, it's just that I have to do some checking on my own first."

I didn't challenge her, but I knew that, in part, it was because she still didn't trust me. "Once you've got it all figured out, will I be the first to know?"

"Yeah." She smiled but there was a layer of concern there.

Then she cleared her throat and asked if she could see Robyn's photos. I decided I wasn't quite finished. "Wait. I tell you about Robyn. I feed you hamburgers and beer. And what do I get from you? I get 'Later, Quint.' " I kept the delivery light but was only half joking.

She frowned and fidgeted with a shoelace, then she looked up at me. "Markham was being blackmailed."

"How?"

She shook her head. "Robyn didn't know. He wouldn't tell her what it was about." She shrugged. "Not with those photos anyway. If he kept nude photos of his mistress in his office, God knows what else he was into."

"How much was he being taken for?"

"She didn't know. He wouldn't tell her."

"How long had it been going on?"

"Since before they met."

Peanuts curled up on the floor next to me, sated with burgers and Oreos. We both watched him for a minute, then Janet looked at me and said, "Did you find photos of women other than Robyn?"

I swallowed. "No."

From the look she gave me, I could see she didn't believe me. But all she said was, "Can I take those photos of Robyn?"

"Are you sure she didn't kill Markham?"

"No, I'll hold on to one. That way if they turn out to be evidence, I'm covered."

I smiled and nodded my approval. Then I pulled the photos out of the drawer where I'd stored them. Fortunately, Robyn's were the first ones I checked. Janet put them in her purse.

"Well," she said, rising, "Thanks for dinner. You Irish really know how to eat. I'd better get going. I've got a couple hours to spend in the office before I can go home."

I was disappointed, but I tried not to show it. And before I could think of a reason for her to stay, other than to help with the dishes, there was a knock at the door. She grabbed her purse and jacket and whispered urgently, "Find out who it is."

I drew back the lace curtain covering the small window on the door. Jeff Barlowe waved at me. I dropped the curtain and turned to Janet. "Jeff Barlowe, intrepid reporter."

Janet hesitated, turning that over in her mind. Finally she sat down on the couch again, tossing her jacket and purse to the other side. "Okay," she said, "you can let him in."

"Why thank you," I said and opened the door.

Jeff erupted into the room. "Quint, Anne is eternally grateful to you for those photos. She thinks you're a hell of a guy, she thinks you're . . ." he saw Janet, and his expression changed dramatically, "shit."

Janet glared at me, "So do I."

"It's not the way it looks," I said.

"No, it's not," Jeff added.

Once again she grabbed her jacket and purse. "Well, you do a pretty good indignant. Damn you, I should have realized." She hadn't raised her voice once, but her inflections must have been effective because Peanuts fled into the bedroom. She looked at me. "How many are there?"

"You don't need to know that." I crossed my arms over my chest and held her glare.

"Oh, and I suppose you do?"

"Don't worry. Yours wasn't one of them."

She slapped me. I didn't blame her.

I barely heard Jeff say, "Hey, did I interrupt something?"

Turning away from Janet, I apologized. "That was out of line. I'm sorry. But I don't think either of you has to see those pictures. Turn me in. I don't care. Nobody is sorrier than I am that I didn't leave those photos where I found them, and wouldn't it be nice if my life were on video tape so I could reverse to Sunday night and tape the whole damned thing over."

I finally looked at Janet. She seemed both amused and angry; a strange combination, but one that worked.

"Why don't we all sit down and relax for a minute." Although I had suggested that she turn me in, I felt compelled to convince her that it wasn't a good idea.

"Uh, guys." We turned to Jeff. "This is all real interesting, but I have some news you might like to hear."

I assumed he was talking about the body. "Did they find anything after I left?"

"They didn't find anything else, but they made a few theories based on what they had."

"Like . . ." I prodded.

"Well, the body, what was left of it, was relatively intact and a pathologist took one look at it and said it was probably the remains of a woman about 5 feet 6 inches in height." He shrugged, "Apparently they can tell that by the size of the pelvis. Also, the skull and teeth were intact so they may be able to identify her through x-rays."

Both Janet and I nodded, and waited. Jeff just smiled and you could practically see the feathers in the corner of his mouth.

Janet and I glanced at each other and mentally drew straws. She lost. She cleared her throat and said, "Okay, Jeff. Do they have any idea who it is?"

Jeff hesitated and watched Janet for a minute. "No one said anything, but I've got my theory."

Janet and I leaned toward him.

"Well," Jeff said, savoring the attention, "without tests it's impossible to be certain, but judging from the amount of decay to the body, the pathologist believes it's been there about a year."

He looked at Janet who was waiting for him to continue. "Go on."

Jeff rubbed his chin and smiled, "Can you think of anyone who was missing about a year ago?"

From the look on Janet's face, she was coming up blank.

"Think about it. Someone you'd have been talking to recently if she were still around."

Janet was staring at Jeff but her mind was somewhere else. Then her eyebrows went up and her mouth dropped open. "Susan Connors."

Jeff smiled, pleased with his student. "Yep. That's who came to my mind, but you know us journalists, we're just a bunch of speculators." He jumped up, walked over to the refrigerator and helped himself to a beer.

"Excuse me," I said, "but can you share this or is this woman someone you two got rid of?"

Jeff returned and, after taking a healthy swig of beer winked at me and said, "You're going to appreciate this."

"Jeff, all I want is a chance."

"Susan Connors disappeared about a year ago. She was Scott Markham's law clerk."

CHAPTER TWELVE

For SEVERAL MOMENTS we sat there, each in our own silence, considering the implications of Jeff's theory. Finally Jeff said, "It's gotta be her. I'd bet a month's salary on it." Then he reneged slightly. "Well, maybe a week or two, but I just know it's her." He leaned forward and lowered his voice, "No one actually saw her get on that plane and she never got to her friend's place in Stevens Point."

After the initial thrill of recognition, Janet was less enthusiastic. "I don't know, Jeff. The authorities were pretty well convinced that she didn't disappear here, but in Wisconsin. I mean, whether or not anyone saw her get on the plane, she used the ticket."

"*Someone* used the ticket," Jeff said.

Peanuts was eyeing the Oreos. I got another dog biscuit out for him and, after one long last look at the cookie bag, he took it. Then I sat down again and looked at Janet and Jeff. They each seemed lost in their own interpretation of this shady bit of Foxport history. I sensed that the uneasy feeling in the pit of my stomach would get worse before it got better. I cleared my throat. "Okay, is someone going to tell me about Susan Connors or am I going to have to wait until the movie comes out?"

Janet shook her head. "Jeff's the storyteller. I think he'd better fill you in. Even though I'm inclined to think he's full of it."

"Thank you counselor." Undaunted, Jeff bowed to Janet and then stood as if he'd been called on in class to describe the events leading to World War II. He started slowly and the closer he got to the end of his story, the more animated he became. "This was all about a year, thirteen months ago. Susan Connors was Markham's law clerk." He paced the width of the room as he spoke. "She was very good—I think she was just finishing her degree from uh, where was it—Loyola?" He hesitated, then dismissed it with a wave of his hand. "Doesn't matter. Anyway, one day she just disappeared. She was flying into Central Wisconsin Airport on a Friday morning to spend a long weekend with some friends in Stevens Point. She never made it. No one remembers seeing her on the plane and she never showed up at her friend's place. Sooo," he drew the word out for emphasis, "she must have disappeared here."

"Jeff," Janet said, "isn't this all academic? I think we're all over-reacting to your fired-up imagination. I mean, those remains might belong to Susan Connors, but then again, they might not. And just because a corpse was found here doesn't mean the victim was from here."

"Okay, maybe it isn't Susan Connors. Let's just say it is." Janet rolled her eyes and Jeff said, "Humor me. I mean, let's face it. If it's somebody else, we don't care about it. So let's assume that it is her. And if not . . . well, all we're wasting is our breath."

Janet didn't respond, she just turned away. She was either giving her tacit approval or she was disgusted. I was willing to pursue his theory, but there were a lot of holes. "You said the ticket was used?"

Jeff tossed that notion off like a used tissue. "Yeah, but it was made out to S. Connors. Not Susan Connors. Anyone could have gotten on that plane posing as S. Connors. And it was a commuter flight so there were no seat assignments."

"Was there any evidence that she packed for a trip?"

"Yeah, I guess some of her clothes and personal stuff were missing. And her mom thought maybe there was a small suitcase gone. I guess it looked like she packed."

"You're grasping, Jeff. You're grasping," Janet said.

The exchange ended in a sullen, uncooperative silence.

I wanted to keep them both talking because I believed something might come out of this debate, but I didn't want to appear to be siding with one or the other. I briefly wondered how Ted Koppel would have handled it.

"Did anyone on the flight remember seeing her?" I asked.

"One guy said he saw someone who looked like her but wasn't sure. None of the crew said they saw her."

Janet countered with: "Yes Jeff, but they also said they don't remember the faces of every person who gets on one of those commuter flights. Most people have their noses buried in their newspapers anyway."

"Where was the investigation centered?"

"Both here and in Wisconsin," Jeff said, then reluctantly added, "mostly Wisconsin I guess. Around the airport and Stevens Point."

"Were there any leads?"

"Oh, the usual missing person sightings, but nothing that came to anything."

"She have any boyfriends?"

"She'd dated this guy who was some kind of freelance consultant. I think his name was Dwight Adams," Janet said. "More recently she was dating Knox Ferris."

"Were they questioned?"

"Yes, they were." She thought for a moment. "As I recall, neither one had much of an alibi. I think Adams was holed up in his apartment doing some work for a client and Ferris was biking somewhere. But then there was no real reason to suspect foul play. Not on this end, anyway."

"Not until now," Jeff interjected.

I turned to Janet. "Isn't Knox Ferris the guy who was your case against Markham?"

"Yes," she was talking to me and excluding Jeff as much as possible. "In fact it was something that Susan said to Knox about Markham's spending habits that made us think we could make a case."

"Was she going to help in the investigation?"

"Knox thought she might be able to, but she disappeared before he ever talked to her about it."

I didn't want to state the obvious, so I waited for Jeff. "Sounds like a good motive for Markham." I knew he wouldn't disappoint me.

"So what you're telling me is that the body they dug up this afternoon was probably put there by Scott Markham." I hoped for a straight answer.

Jeff shifted on the couch, helped himself to an Oreo and tossed another to Peanuts. "Now, I didn't say that."

"Well, it's a cinch she didn't plant herself."

I turned to Janet. "Do you really think this is all that farfetched?"

She sighed and glanced at Jeff. "I don't know. If they prove that *is* Susan Connors buried out there . . . ." She paused, "Maybe it isn't. But it's all so neat. Tie it up and file it away." Turning to Jeff she said, "And I just don't like to see anyone— even Scott Markham—being accused of something like that based mainly on rumor and innuendos."

Jeff shrugged, somewhat subdued. "You gotta consider it," he said quietly.

"There's a big difference between bribery and murder. I guess I'm not so anxious to make the jump without a damned good reason."

I leaned back in the small chair and put my feet up on the coffee table. "At least one thing about this theory bothers me. Why would anyone bury a body, whether it's Susan Connors' or not, that close to town?"

Janet looked at him. "Good question."

Jeff shrugged. "I don't think it's that incredible. A year ago Langley was negotiating for the land. I don't think it was common knowledge at the time. The guy he bought it from had planned not to develop it, you know, donate it to the park district or something. Then he ran into some money troubles and figured it was better to sell the land than starve." Jeff leaned forward with renewed vigor. "And remember, that piece of land is part of the area that conservationist group was trying to get set aside for a wildlife preserve. Apparently, in addition to being a bat refuge, they were making a case for it being an important source of wetlands. Guess who was part of that conservationist movement?"

"Scott Markham," I said, quick study that I am.

Point made, he leaned back and added, "Maybe he had his own personal burial ground." Nodding to himself, he continued, "And that piece of land the conservationists were trying to set aside for the bats was the last to go the way of the back hoe. They lost the battle and Markham knew it was a matter of days before they dug up his law clerk."

"Interesting," Janet said.

"Interesting!" Jeff leaned forward. "If that is Susan Connors and if Markham did put her there, what better reason could he have for trying to block construction? A body is hard to explain."

Janet sighed. "Well, like I said, this is really just academic until they determine whose body it is."

None of us spoke for a minute. Peanuts was snuffling around for more Oreos and the thing that had started out as a knot in my stomach now had a grip on most of my intestines. I swallowed. "What did Susan Connors look like?" I was asking no one in particular.

Janet answered. "She was pretty. Beautiful hair. Very long and thick."

"She was kind of fat," Jeff added.

Janet started to get on Jeff's case about being superficial and neither seemed to think it odd that I had asked for the woman's description.

I listened as they tossed around ideas as to who might be buried out there if it wasn't Susan Connors, but neither had any decent theories and the discussion deteriorated. Jeff made the first move to leave and he did it in a hurried way that made me wonder if he wasn't trying to get out of our way and leave us alone. That wasn't any part of Janet's plan, however. She quickly gathered her things together and asked Jeff for a ride to her car, which she'd parked a couple blocks away. I wondered if she wasn't being overly clandestine.

All the same, I was relieved she hadn't stayed. Maybe I was getting old, but something was telling me to put the brakes on. Besides, I had to figure out what to do with those pictures. I studied them again. Damn, she was looking deader all the time. And from the description of Susan Connors, I figured we had a match. But, I reasoned, if it was her body, there would certainly be a picture of her in the paper. Then I'd know for sure. Who was I kidding? I knew for sure now. The thing was, this all seemed so convenient. I find the photos and a few days later a matching body appears. And it was especially interesting when I considered the fact that I shouldn't have been the one to find the photos. That notion posed so many other questions, that without more information than I had it was impossible to consider them all. So I made an effort not to.

I tried to occupy myself with something mundane. At first I thought about unpacking some boxes but then I decided that was a daylight activity. That was when I should have gone to bed. But it just sat there looking at me, unmade, its ugly blue mattress ticking echoing the bareness of the walls. Besides, I knew I'd just lie there thinking about that damned picture. I wanted to forget about it. For a while anyway. I glanced at my watch. Ten thirty.

Peanuts was sacked out on the couch and briefly lifted his head as I entered the room. Apparently he wasn't interested in going out. I was. One added benefit to my new residence was its location—within easy walking distance of the Tattersall Tavern.

Some people never appreciate the atmosphere of a good neighborhood tavern. I feel sorry for them. The smell of cigarettes, spilt beer and popcorn may not be universally appealing, but for me it's like coming home. I'd only been to the Tattersall once before, but it had the feel of a good place.

I'd been there about fifteen minutes and was finishing off a Guinness when Mike Richardson walked in. He saw me and we had a moment of recognition, but he greeted two guys sitting at another table before unhurriedly walking up to me. "See you took me up on my suggestion."

"Actually, I've taken you up twice. It's a good place."

"How's that Frisbee-catching dog of yours?" He had a quiet, almost gentle way of talking that didn't seem to match his size.

I told him Peanuts was settling in and asked him about his Irish setter. He smiled and shrugged as he sat down. "Beautiful but dumb."

"You better not be talking about me." The waitress was at Mike's shoulder.

"God no, Ginny. I was just talking about my dog."

Ginny nodded skeptically and then looked at me. "You got to watch this guy." When I first sat down, she had served me my beer with impersonal efficiency. My knowing Mike must have moved me up a notch. She favored me with a nice smile.

"You're Quint, right?" Mike said. I nodded and he continued, "And I can't remember your last name."

"McCauley."

"That's right," he said and told me his name.

I smiled. "I remember. And your dog's name is Dallas."

"Hey, he's all right," he said to Ginny. "My dog doesn't

even know what his name is." He introduced Ginny and me before she left to get Mike's beer. I ordered another.

I looked around the room and remarked that the place wasn't very crowded.

Mike said something about how it was seldom packed but never empty. "Sammy does a good, steady business," he said.

Ginny brought our drinks. She had a slight drawl that sounded like it might have come from southern Illinois or Missouri. She was small—not much more than five feet—with wispy blonde hair that was pleasantly disheveled. She wiped the table with one sweep, dropped napkins in a second and topped each with a drink on the third.

"So, how's the P.I. business?" Mike asked.

I shrugged. "Not bad today. At least no one asked me to leave town."

"That's good to hear." He was eating popcorn and, as he talked, he frequently glanced over my shoulder at the bar.

He talked some about his job, then we talked sports. He said this was the best place to be for the Cubs' opener. After about twenty minutes, he said, "There's a guy sitting at the bar. He's got short, light brown hair and he's wearing a brown leather jacket."

I looked. The man he referred to was very young—probably not into his twenties—and was drinking what appeared to be a Seven-up or club soda. He was watching the wide screen television, which was showing a rerun of a cop show.

"What about him?"

"Do you know him?"

I glanced again. "No. Don't think I've ever seen him."

"Well, he's real interested in you."

"What do you mean?"

"He's been watching you. He's being cool about it. Not staring or anything. But, for sure, he knows you're here." He leaned forward on the table. "This got anything to do with your job? Maybe he's here to run you out of town."

We both laughed at that one. The kid didn't look like the stuff of nightmares.

After we talked for a while longer and each drank another beer, I glanced at my watch and saw it was going on midnight. I put money for my drinks on the table and told Mike I'd see him around. As I left, he took his beer and joined his two friends at the other table.

The night was crisp and cool—a reminder that, although it was spring, it was barely spring. I walked to the end of the block where, in the shadow of a building, I watched the entrance. A figure emerged within a minute and, without hesitation, headed in the direction I'd taken. I crossed the street and walked one block toward the river, stopping again when I'd rounded a corner. The size was right for the guy at the bar but maybe my being a P.I. had simply fired Mike's imagination and this kid just happened to finish his drink a minute after I left. I could hear his footsteps now. Maybe he lived next door to me. It wouldn't hurt to find out.

He rounded the corner and pulled up abruptly. We stood, no more than three feet apart. He was, as I had thought, slight of build and at least four inches shorter than me. Now was a good time to apply pressure.

"You looking for me?" I said and before I could form another word, I was flat on my back trying to get my breath back. I felt like someone had used a battering ram against my chest. Maybe he'd overreacted to a perceived threat. I moved up slowly onto one elbow.

"What if I am?" He punctuated his question with another kick.

From my new perspective, he seemed a lot taller. Again, I tried to get up. As I did, I grasped for his ankle. I missed by a mile and he stunned me back to the concrete. With the tenacity and brains of an inflatable boxing clown, I pushed myself up again. I was almost to a sitting position when the next kick came. It caught me in the jaw and the pain flashed white and hot. I began to seriously worry about getting out of this.

Now he laughed. It was a high-pitched sound, bordering on hysterical. He leaped back, and danced around me, kicking in the air above me like I was the sacrifice on the altar and this was all part of the ritual. "Got any more questions?" He backed up now, prompting me with his outstretched hands to get up.

I did so, slowly, and only because he decided he'd let me. Then, like I'd learned way back when I first started defending myself and none of the kids knew karate, I raised my fists in the classic boxer pose. Under the circumstances, I felt a little silly.

I dodged and feinted and managed to block a couple kicks, which only served to inflict damage on my arm rather than my chest or my face. The next kick connected and as I started to reel against the side of a building, he delivered another. He must have been slightly off balance because I jerked out of his way and grabbed his ankle. He crashed to the ground but was up again so fast that the fall might have been defensive. Then he came at me in earnest. Using every part of his anatomy that could deliver a decisive blow, he worked on my head and torso like he was whittling away at a sculpture. Slammed up against the brick wall, I wondered, because it was all up to him now, when he was going to stop.

Then, as abruptly as the first blow had been delivered, it did stop. Just like that. One second I was being turned into ground beef and the next I pitched forward onto the pavement. I took a quick physical inventory. The parts of my face that weren't numb were hot and there was a metallic taste in my mouth. And it felt like there was an elephant sitting on my chest. Otherwise, I felt pretty good.

"Hey man, you okay?" Someone had his hand under my arm and was pulling me up. One eye was swollen shut but the other was working well enough for me to recognize Mike Richardson. "You okay?" he repeated.

I spit something out of my mouth. It was either a tooth or a piece of flesh. "I got my ass kicked."

Mike nodded. "Yeah, I'd say so."

"Where is he?" With Mike's assistance, I staggered to a standing position.

My assailant was held in place by the two guys I'd left Mike sitting with at the tavern. They were each about Mike's size and it took two to hold this guy. Each locked one of his arms behind him. The kid was showing no fear, just raw, unadorned fury.

One of Mike's friends said, "You wanna take a couple swings? Even up the score a little?" They shoved him toward me, inviting. "Go ahead man, you owe him."

I realized, too late, that Mike's friends had only disarmed part of him. Faster than anyone could react, the kid got me with two successive kicks to the chest and hurled me back into a solid object, which turned out to be Mike. After Mike righted me again, I saw that his friends were now standing on the kid's feet. One of the men said, "Sorry about that."

I turned to my attacker. "So, what were you hired to do? Follow me or beat the crap out of me?"

"I'm just trying to set things right." His voice was remarkably calm now and he wasn't at all out of breath.

I reached behind him and pulled his wallet from his back pocket. That got a bigger reaction than a left to the gut might have. He squirmed in the grip of the two men.

Out of my pocket, I pulled a disposable lighter and ignited it over his wallet, thumbing through its contents until I got to his student ID. A gust of wind extinguished the flame. Maybe I was missing something. I looked at him and said, "Is this supposed to make sense?"

Instead of responding to my question, he said, "I'll get another shot at you. When you don't have these goons around to run to your rescue."

I nodded, certain of his sincerity.

I couldn't tell where they came from, but the flashing lights were, at this point, not welcome. I wondered where they'd been five minutes before; it was easy to figure that what the police were seeing now didn't bode well for the good guys. Here was this short, thin kid, being held by two guys who could have been linebackers for the Bears. Mike and I were standing in front of him and we were both trying to look threatening. Mike was doing a better job of it than me, but I was way ahead of everyone in the self-incrimination department—I held Eric Markham's wallet in my hand. As the two cops approached us with their guns drawn, I briefly thought of that ugly blue mattress ticking. It was starting to look awfully good.

▽

Chapter Thirteen

MIKE SAT on a narrow cot and looked around the cell as though he was scoping out his first dorm room. Then he said, "I've never been in a jail before."

"Me neither. Not from this angle anyway." The pain in my ribs wasn't easing any and I shifted to a less uncomfortable position and tried to ignore it. The walls were concrete and the cold went right to the bone. I wondered where Eric Markham was and what line he was giving the cops. I hoped that my face would serve as an effective visual aid in supporting our side of the story.

I must have sounded as despondent as I felt, because Mike said, "Ah, relax. Once they figure out what happened, they'll be falling all over themselves to keep us happy."

"You think so?"

"Sure."

I studied him. As big and mean-looking as he was, there was still something naive and trusting about him. He had a vulnerable look, the kind that only comes from a sincere belief that, after all is said and done, life really *is* fair. It would never occur to him that possibly none of us would see daylight until well into the 21st century, at which time we would be wheeled directly into a high-security nursing home. Of course he'd never imagine that.

Maybe his was the kind of attitude to have. Not five minutes later, a cop unlocked the two adjoining cells the four of us shared. "You, you and you," he indicated Mike and his friends, "can go." Then he looked at me. "Someone wants to talk to you."

120

Mike started to protest and I quickly said, "It's okay. I think I know what's happening next. It's okay."

"You sure?"

"Yeah, and thanks. And, again I'm real sorry about all this."

They waved off my apology and one of Mike's friends said, "I'd sure like to get a crack at that little wimp. See how long he's kickin'." They left laughing at that image. Somehow the humor was lost on me.

I sat in the cell and waited, figuring they were saving me for Carver. I was right. After a few minutes, a cop led me into his office where he sat, unshaven, with a steaming cup of black coffee. When my escort left and closed the door behind him, Carver said, "I don't like being called away from my family at two o'clock in the morning. And I like it even less when I find out you're involved."

I figured the only reason he'd been called was because I was involved, but I bit my tongue and waited for him to continue. "What's going on? Huh? You wanna tell me? What are you hounding Eric Markham for?"

That was too much to take. "Hounding Eric Markham? Do I look like I was hounding Eric Markham?"

Carver smiled. "You look like you were getting on his nerves."

"He was following me. Mike Richardson and his friends can tell you that. All I did was confront him. In no way did I physically threaten him. And all of a sudden I'm flat on my back trying to pick out the Big Dipper." I paused. "Why don't you ask him?"

Carver eyed me coldly. The chill registered in his voice as well. "We already did. He says you were harassing him. You provoked him."

"I'm sure." I leaned back in the chair and the pain in my ribs jolted me forward again. Either Carver believed me or he didn't. He wasn't fence sitting on this one. Nothing I said would change his mind. "Am I under arrest?"

Carver continued to stare at me, trying to read behind my eyes. Finally he said, "He didn't press charges."

"That was downright decent of him," I said and added, "Then why am I still here?"

He took a drink of coffee and set the mug down. "You're

here because I want to give you some advice. And don't interpret it as friendly advice. I can't throw you out of town, but I can make life for you real unpleasant. And I'm here to tell you this: Leave the Markhams—both the living and dead—alone. Is that understood?''

I wasn't about to agree with him and I considered further protest, but it occurred to me that breathing was not as effortless as it used to be. When Carver paused to collect his thoughts, I said, ''I'd appreciate it if you'd wrap this up as soon as possible. I should be getting to the hospital.''

He leaned forward, as if getting closer to me might help him decide if I was serious. Then he said, ''You're pushing it McCauley. You're really pushing it.''

Apparently he needed some convincing, so I continued, ''I know it'd just make your day if I were to die, but I don't think you want me to do it here.''

Carver relented and grudgingly ordered one of his cops to take me to the hospital.

It was almost dawn when I got home. Markham had managed to crack one of my ribs and bruise several others. It felt like the elastic bandage the nurse had wrapped me in was all that kept me from coming apart. I didn't care if he was my client's son and was probably confused and disturbed. I wished I'd blackened an eye or relieved him of a couple of his teeth.

Peanuts was seriously starting to wonder about this guy who'd adopted him and he gave me a thorough sniffing before demanding to go out. Frisbee throwing was out of the question, but the two of us sat by the river and watched the sun come up. And when I finally lowered myself onto the mattress, my last conscious observation was of Peanuts stretching out across the foot of my bed and using one of my ankles as a pillow.

I was dreaming. In the dream, I was chasing something, but I couldn't get close enough to see what it was. I was running through a green, rolling meadow banked by tall trees, beside a highway. I was running toward those trees and, although the tall grass made my progress slow, I wasn't tiring. In fact I was surprised at how easy it was. I just kept running, like some antelope, bounding through the grass, toward that line of trees. I knew once I got to the trees, I'd be able to see what I was chasing but even though I could feel my speed as I ran, I never got any closer. Then I heard a sound that didn't belong in the dream and I slowed down and finally stopped running. I looked around—first at the trees that seemed close, yet no closer than before—then back toward the highway, which was so far away it was as if I were viewing it through a special lens. And I couldn't figure out where that sound was coming from. Then I woke up and groped for the telephone.

"Hey, your phone's working." I wasn't sure, but it sounded like Jeff Barlowe.

I sat up in bed, wincing at the pull on my ribs. "Yeah, just in time." I tried to get the juices in my mouth working. "What time is it, anyway?"

"Late night, huh? I read all about you on the police blotter."

It was definitely Barlowe. "You calling for a quote?" I fumbled for my watch on the nightstand. One P.M. My body wanted more sleep, but realistically I couldn't afford it.

"You got one for me?"

"Not right now. I'll get back to you, though. You wouldn't happen to know who picked up Eric Markham?"

"I sure would."

"Who?"

"None other than Mason Burke."

That figured. I thanked him and started to hang up, but I could hear Jeff hollering for me to wait a minute. I put the receiver back to my ear. "What?"

"You okay?"

"Yeah. Considering."

"One other thing."

"What's that?"

"I was right."

"What are you talking about?"

"That was Susan Connors they dug up yesterday. They made a positive ID based on dental records."

Silence.

"Quint? You still there?"

"Yeah, I'm here."

"What d'you think?"

"I think I need to wake up before I work on that one."

"Okay. Well, call me then. And don't go giving your story to the *National Enquirer.*"

"No, Jeff. All you gotta do is match their price. I'll call you tonight."

Half an hour later, as I was drinking a cup of coffee, I heard the rumble of thunder in the west. I poured myself another cup. The sky was heavy with clouds and the day uninviting and as I thought of the two things that I absolutely had to do, it got even worse. I had to pick up a copy of the *Chronicle* and I had to see Lorna Markham. I decided to see Lorna first. I was supposed to be investigating her husband's death and her son was doing his best to discourage that. And the thing was, I was actually starting to sympathize with Eric Markham. I'm not sure what I would have done to some guy who was getting paid to sneak around and take pictures of my father sneaking around. God knows what Mason had told him about me.

Before I left, I called Bob Miller, the insurance agent Barlowe had mentioned. I sensed that Miller's dislike for John Dieken extended beyond business, but he restricted his criticism of the man to Dieken the professional. And apparently he wasn't much of a professional. He'd been dropped as an agent by a number of insurance companies and Miller agreed that Metro wouldn't have been pleased about the million dollar policy Dieken sold Markham. He asked why I was interested and I told him I was working for Lorna Markham.

"She thinks he was killed?"

"We think it's a possibility."

"Wouldn't that be interesting?" I could hear the smile in his voice.

The Markhams lived about three miles west of town in one of the clusters of homes that were popping up in the middle of cornfields. These settlements were invariably connected to the highway by roads with names like Shagbark Lane and Charlton Place. The Markham home was on a rise at the end of Surrey Lane.

Just as I had imagined in the worst case scenario, Lorna answered the door. Distraught was the first word that came to my mind and at first I thought she was upset over her son's antics. Then I realized that she seemed genuinely surprised to see me and my battered face.

The day she'd hired me to follow her husband seemed like years instead of days ago, but death hadn't changed the house, not physically anyway. The same cathedral ceilings trapped the dim afternoon light as if the room were a world all its own. The same sleek, cold furniture invited you to sit but not to feel too much at home.

Lorna's hair was pulled back off her face with an elastic band but thick strands had escaped its hold and hung straight and limp against her neck. She observed me with some interest, then asked, "What happened to you?"

"I ran into the karate kid."

Her brows bunched together and she apparently didn't connect that description with her son. "Eric," I said. "Your son happened to me."

It took a second before her mouth dropped slightly and another second before she said, "Eric did that?"

I nodded.

She stood and walked to the foot of a spiral staircase. "Eric. Get down here." I was surprised by the sharpness in her tone. She'd gone from distraught to angry in a matter of seconds.

"I'm not here to get him in trouble," I said. "I just want to talk to him."

Giving no indication that she'd heard me, Lorna hollered up the stairs again. After a minute or so, a door slammed shut and I heard the floor creaking as someone walked down the hall.

Lorna turned to me and said, "We haven't exactly been communicating lately."

Eric Markham made his way down the stairs with an attitude that James Dean would have admired—slowly and with measured disdain. When he finally arrived on our floor, he crossed his arms over his chest, and cocked his head. "What?" he said to his mother.

Lorna gestured toward me. "Mr. McCauley tells me you two had a little run in."

He looked at me as though he'd just noticed that I was sitting in the living room. "Shoulda' known you'd come squealing."

"Eric!" His mother's reprimand only helped to make him more surly.

He sighed and shook his head.

"Mr. McCauley would like a word with you."

"Yeah, well I don't wanna talk to him."

It gave me little comfort, but I couldn't help noticing that Eric regarded his mother with only slightly less contempt than he reserved for me. There were a lot of similarities between them. Eric had his mother's slight build and the features were the same, only more masculine. He also apparently had her gift for spontaneity.

"Get out of our house," he said.

"That's right," Lorna said to her son, "it's *our* house. You aren't the only one who decides who gets to be here."

Eric shoved his hands into his pockets and, after studying his mother for a few moments said, "Well, I don't have to talk to him." He turned to go back up the stairs.

"I've got one question," I said, standing. Eric paused but did not turn around. "Last night you said you wanted to set things straight." Still no response. "I don't understand. What did I do to you?"

He laughed, his back still to me. "That's right. Play dumb. It figures."

"Humor me," I said.

He finally turned around. "My dad was set up. Everybody knew that. But his friends wouldn't help him out. Even she," he gestured toward Lorna, "turned against him. Hiring a two-bit detective to follow him around. People like you and her drove him to what he did."

"Suicide?"

"You ought to be charged with his murder."

"Someone ought to be, but it's not me."

"Oh yeah. The murder theory. It doesn't work. My dad blew his brains out because people like her and his so-called friends betrayed him. He had everything then all of a sudden it's all gone. His money, his friends, everything. And now he's dead and they want everyone to think he killed that woman out in the field." His face was red with emotion and he seemed to be fighting the tears when he said, "My dad wasn't a killer. No way."

"You said none of his friends helped him out. What about Mason Burke?"

Eric brought himself under control before he answered. "He was his only real friend. He had the guts to defend him. He didn't desert him, or hire some creep like you to follow him." He started to go back up the stairs.

Lorna stopped him. "Did it ever occur to you that maybe my life wasn't exactly a bed of roses either?"

Eric turned. "Yeah, well you drove him out. You were such a goddamned, frigid bitch."

She took one step forward and slapped her son. His eyes widened but he didn't turn away. She slapped him again—harder this time, leaving a smear of red across his cheek. Still no reaction.

"How dare you. How dare you presume to know about your father and me. How would you know? Your father saved the best parts of himself for you. All he ever offered me was leftovers."

A long moment of silence passed between them. Then Eric said, "Are you finished?"

Lorna only missed half a beat. "No, I'm not. Get out of here."

Eric's glare faltered and he started to say something but stopped.

"I said get out of here. I don't give a damn where you go. Just get out." Neither moved for several seconds; then, abruptly, Lorna turned and strode to the closet in the foyer. She pulled a jacket from one of the hangers and threw it at him.

He reached up to catch it. Then, gripping it in his fist, he wrote both Lorna and me off with a scowl and left.

For a moment, Lorna stared at the space where he'd been. Then she said, "I'm sorry you had to be here for that." She curled a loose strand of hair with her forefinger. Her voice was weak when she spoke again. "I suppose I'll be sorry I did that." Looking up at me, she continued. "But I don't need someone reminding me how lousy my life is right now." She paused and said, "I wonder how loyal he'd be to his father if he knew he'd been stealing money from him."

"You haven't told him?"

"No," she said, collapsing into a large chair. "The more I find out, the worse it gets. He sold some of our stocks, made withdrawals from our savings account. Cashed in some certificates. That son of a bitch forged my signature." She pounded a fist against her chest. "He robbed us. I can't believe I was living every day with a man who was stealing from me."

"Do you know what he did with the money?"

"I have no idea. What do you think, he left me a note? The bastard checked out without a suicide note. Oh, God." Her last words crescendoed into a wail and she leaned against the closet door, hands covering her face, and began to sob.

Taking her arm, I led her into the living room and lowered her into a chair. Then I looked for the liquor cabinet. There had to be one. On a low table to the right of the fireplace, I found a crystal decanter amid a group of brandy snifters. Its contents smelled like brandy. I poured a good-sized dose in a snifter.

She didn't drink from it at first. Tears streamed down her face and dripped from her chin. Her mouth was red and contorted and she spoke between the sobs she seemed to have no control over. "He couldn't have left me in a worse way if he'd tried. No money, no way to collect the insurance. And he leaves me with the one thing I never wanted in the first place. His son." She took several deep breaths and the sobs became less severe. "So what do I care if someone killed the bastard?" She took a gulp of brandy and looked at me. "I don't suppose you came here to tell me who killed him."

I shook my head. "Sorry. But I'm working on it."

She nodded without much confidence.

"What can you tell me about Susan Connors?"

"She was a nice girl. I liked her." Turning to me, she said, "I don't think they were having an affair or anything. Theirs was more a, uh, father-daughter kind of relationship." Pausing for a bitter laugh, she added, "What the hell do I know?"

When I stepped out into the afternoon the wind had picked up and the clouds seemed even closer to the ground. There was an occasional splinter of lightning in the west.

I saw the figure as I pulled off Surrey Lane and onto Route 38. He was about a half mile down the road heading into town. As I neared him, I noticed he'd put on his jacket. I slowed and pulled over to the side of the road. "You need a lift anywhere?"

Eric barely turned his head toward me. "No."

I continued to keep pace with him. "I can take you to Mason Burke's office."

He hesitated, then continued at a faster rate. What would it take to get this kid in the car? As if on cue, the skies opened up. The rain didn't start as a sprinkle. It poured from the clouds like it'd been doing it for an hour. I tried one last time. "It's dry in here."

Eric stopped, looked back toward the west where the clouds were darker still, then east toward town where, if he was going to Mason's office, he had at least a five mile walk. From the look on his face, it was apparent that he'd rather eat grubs than get in the car with me, but he did it. Getting him to talk would be another thing.

We drove in silence for about a mile. From his brief time in the rain, Eric was just about soaked, but he made no effort to wipe the moisture from his face or hair. He just sat there dripping. He reminded me of his mother, sitting on the couch, tears streaming down her face. I said to Eric, "This thing with your mom will probably blow over in a day or so. She's just distraught."

"She's a bitch."

At least we were communicating.

"You know, I wish I saw the world the way you do."

Silence for another half mile. Then, "What do you mean?"

"Pardon?"

He heaved an irritated sigh. "What you said. How do I 'see the world'?" He mimicked my inflections.

"Well, you figure a person is either good or bad. Right or wrong. Guilty or innocent. Once you put a person in the correct slot, it's so much easier to deal with him. Or her. And you never have to worry about being wrong about someone. You'd never admit to it anyway.

"Take your dad for instance." I could feel him watching me. "He probably wasn't as bad as they're saying."

"No kidding."

"But you're making him out to be some kind of martyr. He wasn't that either."

"What d'you know anyway?"

I shrugged. "Not much I guess. Not much at all. But at least I admit it."

This line of discussion obviously wasn't going to draw him out, so I tried a different one. "Back there at the house, you said your dad didn't kill Susan Connors, that woman they dug up yesterday. You sounded pretty convinced. What makes you so sure?"

"My dad wasn't a killer."

"How do you know?"

He turned to look out the window. "If he was, he woulda' killed my mother years ago."

That was the first time it occurred to me that Eric Markham might have a sense of humor, but when I glanced at him all I saw was the back of his head. Maybe not.

I dropped Eric off at Mason's office. He muttered something that was either a "thank you" or another phrase that ends with "you."

▽

CHAPTER FOURTEEN

I STOPPED to pick up the *Chronicle* and confirmed what I'd known already. The photo I'd found in Markham's office was Susan Connors' and I was going to have a tough time digging myself out of this one. What to do? The least likely scenario had me marching into Carver's office and dropping the photos on his desk. I'd calmly explain what had happened and he'd say something like "That's okay. These things happen." A more likely option would be to send the photos to Carver anonymously. Or write a brief note and sign it "A Concerned Citizen." In the end, I decided to approach the law from a slightly different angle. I knew the Assistant State's Attorney and sometimes she liked me. She might not want to hang me for my offense. On the other hand, I may have been overestimating my charm.

It took me quite a while to come up with that solution and, just so I'd feel free to chicken out, I left the photo at the apartment, taped to the inside of a record album. It was well after six before I got to the courthouse. Janet's car was parked in her assigned space. Even though there were hardly any other cars in the lot, I pulled into one of the visitors' spaces. I didn't want to risk doing hard time in Foxport for impersonating a clerk.

When I walked into her office she took one look at me and said, "Ouch."

I nodded and sat in one of the vinyl chairs. "No kidding. Parts you can't even see feel worse."

She smiled and raised her eyebrows. Then she said, "You going to tell me what happened?" She seemed happy to see me, which was nice, but not quite what I'd expected. Not after yesterday. I decided to explore her mood further before mentioning the photos.

"Don't tell me you haven't heard?"

She held either end of a pen with her thumb and forefinger and now she looked at it and gave a little shrug. "I guess I'd just like to hear your side."

I told her about the incident and tacked on the part about my meeting with Lorna and her son a few hours ago.

"The missing money. Do you think it might have been extortion money?"

"It's possible."

"You think that's something the cops should know about?"

"Sure," I said, crossing my arms. "There's probably lots of things the cops should know about." She looked puzzled and I added, "Things *we* don't even know about."

She gave her head a little shake. "What are you talking about?"

"Nothing. Just babbling." Then, in an effort to sound sane, I said, "Do you think that maybe after all he did kill himself?"

"If I were convinced that he killed Susan Connors, I'd say he had a good reason to. Being indicted for bribery is one thing, but murder too. That might have been too much for him." Pausing, she added, "But I'm nowhere near convinced that he had any reason to kill her."

"Jeff seems convinced."

"That made me wonder too."

Neither of us spoke for a few minutes. I knew I should mention the photos, but I waited. She drummed the pen against the desk blotter and seemed to be involved in a distant thought. At that moment, I didn't know how to reach her. Then she cleared her throat and said, "About yesterday. The way I accused you of blackmail. That was a lousy thing to do."

That was the last thing I expected to hear. "Yeah, it was. But it's okay. Really."

"No, it's not okay. Sooner or later you have to trust someone."

I watched her wrestling with some thought, trying to make it work for her. I wasn't sure where she wanted to go with this. On a hunch, I said, "That's what this is all about isn't it? Trust."

She looked at me, nodding slowly. "Everything depends on

it." We watched each other for a few moments. Then she said, "I have this absurd sense of justice. It's absurd because there's no such thing. Not really. If you have money and influence, there's no way you're going to do the same amount of time as someone with no money and no influence. And that's not fair." She paused and it was like she wasn't trying to convince me of her point, but rather herself. As she continued, she spoke faster and with increasing emotion.

"And then you get a Scott Markham. What he did was despicable. I mean if you elect someone to an office, you put your trust in him or her. But you don't necessarily do time for betraying someone's trust. I guess that's why this case was so important to me. Bribery is one thing I can do something about. I have no more respect for an official who solicits bribes than I do for someone who robs a bank. Less really. Usually a bankrobber does it because he needs the money." She looked away and said, "I know this sounds hopelessly idealistic, but I was brought up to believe that just because you wanted something real bad didn't mean you could screw the rest of the world on your way to getting it."

At that point, she seemed to want a response, so I said, "Sometimes you want that thing so bad you're not aware of what you're doing."

She gave me an odd look and didn't respond.

I figured I needed to explain myself so I said, "I guess I'm just trying to understand. When I saw Markham lying on his desk with a hole in his head, I remember thinking that I had never wanted anything that bad; had never felt the loss of something so deeply that I'd even consider cashing it in. And maybe in a way that makes me a lesser person, I don't know. I'm not saying I wish I felt rotten enough to end it all, but sometimes I wonder if I'm ever going to be committed to anything." She was watching me with intense interest and suddenly I felt quite naked. "Then I think that maybe I should leave the philosophizing to people who get paid for it. Or at least until I'm half in the bag. I make more sense then."

Her expression didn't change and she said, "What do you want?"

I sensed that this wasn't the time to tell her I wanted someone to take the damned pictures off my hands. Her question deserved a thoughtful reply, but I didn't think I could give her one. It wasn't like I never asked myself that. I guess I'd always managed to change the subject. Finally I said, "I don't know. I just hope I'll know when I see it."

"Don't cheat yourself out of it." Then she cocked her head and looked at me with that curious smile of hers. "Is there something you want to tell me, Quint?"

I took a deep breath and opened my mouth. Then there was a knock at Janet's door and it opened before I got a word out. A man stepped in, smiling like he knew he'd interrupted but hoped she'd let him stay anyway. She did. "Knox, come on in."

I couldn't tell whether I was relieved or disappointed. It was probably a combination. I decided I'd make sure we had time together later.

Janet introduced me to Knox Ferris and he took the only other seat in the room. I'd finally met the Foxport mole and bribery ring smasher. He'd set himself up as a defense attorney open to a judge's suggestions—willing to pay the going rate to get his client the most lenient sentence possible. I wondered what had driven him to expose the system. Bribery was a crime that was real easy to overlook. He was probably about Janet's age with boyish good looks and a slightly unorthodox way of dressing—a muted plaid shirt, and sports jacket. He was quite tall, I estimated six four or six five, but his clothes hung on him as though they had been custom tailored. As I observed him, I noticed his manner was casual, and slightly self effacing—traits which probably helped him bag Markham.

"I was in the neighborhood . . ." he started to say, then looked at me. Janet nodded, "He's okay." That made me feel good.

He continued, "What's this I hear about you giving up?"

I looked at her, not comprehending.

She gave me an apologetic smile and explained. "I had a talk with my boss, Jack Alden, this morning. Or, I should say, he had a talk with me. I've, uh, had finer moments. He lectured me. I'm not used to that, but I guess I'll live. Apparently I wasn't being as clandestine about my little investigation as I thought. He told me I was taking this too seriously. I needed to let go." She shrugged and her eyes averted mine. "I suppose he's right."

Then she looked at Knox, "How did you know?"

133

"Courthouse scuttlebutt travels fast." He paused then said, "I don't have to tell you that, do I?"

She smiled, "I guess not. Quint and I were just talking. What with Susan Connors being found and all, well, it is starting to look like maybe the guy really did kill himself." She brought both hands to her mouth as though she'd let some terrible secret slip. Then she said to Knox, "God, what an oaf I am. You two were dating. I'm sorry. Sometimes I don't think before I open my mouth."

He attempted a smile. "That's all right." Pausing, he looked away briefly. "I guess I never held out much hope for her being alive. I mean, she had no reason to disappear or anything like that. Still, you do hope. . . ." He stared at his folded hands and continued, "You know, they always say it's better to know. And I used to believe that was probably true. I'm not so sure anymore."

I gave him a few moments, then asked, "Do you think Markham might have known she was going to cooperate, you know, help set him up?"

He studied me briefly and shook his head. "I don't know. I'd hinted to her about it. Never came out and asked or anything. She might have known though. She was pretty sharp." He hesitated. "But if he was suspicious of her, that suspicion didn't extend to me. Obviously. I mean, how could I have pulled this off if he'd known I was trying to nail him?"

"Do you think it was suicide?" I asked.

Shrugging, Knox said, "I think that's likely."

I shook my head. "I still have a problem with where he buried her." Then I looked at Knox, "Didn't anyone know that area was going to be developed?"

Knox paused before he said, "Some people did. I did. I know Bill Langley. He was trying to keep the negotiations as quiet as possible. He anticipated trouble."

Janet rubbed her temples with the tips of her fingers. "It's just that it was all so convenient. Here we are, ready to burn the guy and he's just about to cough up some interesting names. And bang, he's dead." It was as though she hadn't heard our last exchange.

"Yeah," Knox said, then crossed an ankle over his knee and leaned forward. "But I guess I just can't believe that any of those guys—and I think I know who he was about to name—would kill a man for that reason."

Janet regarded him, slightly amazed. "We're talking careers here, Knox."

"I know, I know." Then he shrugged. "Maybe I'm wrong. It's just that it takes a certain kind of personality, pushed to an extreme, to kill someone in cold blood like that. Bribery's one thing, but murder. That person's playing by a whole new set of rules."

"What kind of personality are you talking about?" I didn't mean to sound like I was trying to put him on the spot, but I was curious.

Knox answered without hesitation, "Amoral. As opposed to immoral. Someone like Markham himself. I don't know how well you knew him, but there was a lot under the surface there."

"For instance?"

"You ever see some of those photos Markham got published?"

I told him I had.

"Well then you know what I was talking about. He was a combat photographer and a very good one. But some of his photos seemed to revel in death. Of course a combat photographer is going to shoot a lot of photos of people dead and dying, but it was the way he captured those images. It was like it was a religious thing with him. You know what I mean."

I knew what he meant, but I kept my mouth shut.

Janet rested her chin in her cupped hand and tapped her pen against the desk. Finally she said, "At any rate, I've got my sights set on a few more members of this legal community. Don't want them getting complacent."

Knox smiled. "Don't know that I can help you out any more."

She returned the smile. "You've done enough." Then she glanced at her watch and said to him, "We're going to grab a bite to eat. Why don't you join us?"

I liked this woman's presumption, but I wished she weren't so quick to be polite. I grinned and nodded but otherwise made little effort to let him know he was welcome.

He glanced at Janet, then at me, then looked down at his hands. My body language must have been working. Still, I felt a little guilty. If Janet had invited him, she must want him to come.

"Why don't you?" I tried to sound enthusiastic.

I think he appreciated the gesture, but he shook his head. "Thanks, but I've got plans." He walked with us to the parking lot, at which point he seemed to sense that he had become a third wheel. My placing a hand on Janet's shoulder might have had something to do with that. He told us to have a nice evening then walked across the lot to his car.

Janet stopped at her car, and looked up at me, smiling. "I'm glad I invited him. I'm glad he said no too, but I'm glad I asked." She looked across the lot and watched him get into his two-seater sports car. "I really feel sorry for him. He's alienated himself from a lot of the people in his profession and for no reason at all anymore. Some people admire what he did but most feel he broke one of the unspoken rules." She looked back at me. "He told me the other day that he's probably going to move. I don't blame him. But it's really too bad."

I felt I should say something. "He knew what he was doing. I'm sure he can live with it. He doesn't strike me as the kind of guy who lets life get the better of him."

She smiled and straightened my jacket collar. Then she said, "Why don't you come to my place for dinner?"

"Gee, I don't know. I thought you said you couldn't cook."

She shrugged. "I didn't say it would be a good dinner."

"That's fair."

I opened her car door for her and told her I had to go home first to feed Peanuts and let him out.

"That's right. Why don't you bring him along?"

"Thanks, I will. He'd like that." I paused and added, "I've got something you need to see."

She put her briefcase in the back seat of her car. The rain had stopped, but the night was still windy and as she turned to me, her hair blew in front of her face. "That sounds interesting," she said. I pushed her hair back and held it there, framing her face with my hands. Then we kissed. There was nothing passionate or promising about it. It just seemed the thing to do. I watched her slide into the car's seat. "I'll see you two in a little while then," she said. I closed the door and then began walking back to my car.

"Quint." I turned and continued walking backwards as she

finished the sentence, "what kind of wine goes with chicken pot pies?"

"Leave the wine to me," I yelled back to her.

She smiled and opened her mouth to say something else. Then she was gone. In a flash of metal and glass, the sky cracked wide open. I thought the world had ended and I'd been made a witness. Then it was like someone shut the sound off and, with an incredible sense of calm, I figured it was ending for me too.

CHAPTER FIFTEEN

THE NURSE was fat and smelled like talcum powder. Embracing her would be like burying yourself in cool cotton. She reached up and squeezed a clear plastic bag filled with some liquid that was dripping into my body. She didn't know she was being watched.

"What am I doing here?" I asked, my voice sounding cracked and foreign.

She started, but recovered quickly. Grasping my wrist with the fingers of her right hand and speaking to the second hand of her watch, she said, "It's nice to have you back with us Mr. McCauley."

"Where was I?" I asked, and that made her laugh.

She jotted something on a chart and gave me the briefest smile. "I'll get the doctor," she said and left before I realized that she hadn't answered my question. Either one.

"I'm not waiting up for him," I muttered. My mouth felt dry and gummy but the effort involved in getting a sip of water seemed insurmountable. Lying there, staring at the white ceiling, I decided this wasn't the time to sort things out. I drifted back into sleep.

The next thing I was aware of was pain. My bones felt like I'd spent the last twenty-four hours being stretched on a rack and my head hurt with the ferocity of an unchecked hangover. I tried to recall what had put me here but kept coming up empty. Janet was constantly in my thoughts so I knew it had something to do with her. But figuring it out was like sitting down to the Sunday crossword puzzle and finding the clue for 7 Across was a fifteen letter word for an obscure Turkish expression meaning "have a nice day." You might as well chuck the whole puzzle.

The light in the room was fading when I noticed Jeff Barlowe sitting in a blue plastic chair with his ankle crossed over his knee. At least I assumed it was Jeff. He was reading a copy of the *Chronicle,* which he held out in front of him so I could only see the hands gripping the paper. I couldn't read the headlines either.

"Did I make the news?"

He dropped the paper to his lap, looked at me and smiled. "Hey. You're back." He stood and approached me, carefully folding the paper so that it fit under his arm. "So. How you doing?"

"I have no idea," I said. Jeff shifted and jammed his fists into the pockets of his jeans. His gaze wandered to the IV, to the window then back to me. He reminded me of a kid who had wrecked the family car and didn't know how to break the news to his dad.

"I don't remember what happened," I said.

Jeff released a sigh of resignation and ran a hand through his hair. "Oh, boy."

I watched him for a few seconds. "Do I have to buy the paper?"

He shook his head, hesitated, then said, "It was a bomb blast. Practically leveled you."

That didn't trigger anything so I prodded. "What about Janet?"

"Yeah. She was there. It was her car. She didn't make it." He turned away and shook his head, like he was trying to clear it.

But for me there was still nothing. "How? How'd it happen?"

Jeff was rocking on the balls of his feet. He looked at the floor then back to me and cleared his throat before he said, "A couple sticks of dynamite were rigged to the engine of her car. They say it was a homemade thing. Went off when she started the car." He watched me for a reaction. I felt something but was unable to recognize it so I just nodded. Abruptly he turned away and kicked at the chair. "Damn. I can't believe this happened. Not to Janet. And not here. This is Foxport, for Christ's sake. We're not exactly in the grip of organized crime." He looked at me sharply. "What was she doing? Whose cage did she rattle?"

I shook my head. "I don't know." Then I added, "Or if I did know, I don't remember."

He looked at me out of the corner of his eye and spoke slowly. "Would you tell me if you did?"

"I don't know."

There was something in his expression that made me uncomfortable. "There's more here," he said. "I know there is. But I can't get at it."

"I know how you feel."

The look of skepticism was gone now and he smiled. "Yeah, I guess you do."

A tall, slender nurse wearing white pants and a tunic walked in. She raised her eyebrows when she saw Jeff standing next to me. Jeff said, "I'd better go. You need anything, let me know, okay."

"What about Peanuts? Is he still waiting for me to let him out?"

Jeff smiled and shook his head. "Don't worry about him. Louise has got him with her. He's doing fine."

I nodded my thanks and gestured toward the paper folded under his arm. "Can you leave that?"

He hesitated then said, "Yeah, sure," and put it next to me on the bed. "It's my story."

"Thanks."

"See you tomorrow," and he left.

As it turned out, there wasn't much wrong with me except for a concussion, a multitude of abrasions and what appeared to be a bad case of sunburn on my face. They thought at first that I'd also cracked a rib. I assured them that was a previous injury that had happened at least a lifetime ago.

The *Chronicle*'s account told the story—what there was to tell, anyway. In addition to Janet's car, part of a wall was blown out and someone was quoted as saying how fortunate it was that it happened after normal work hours and not when the parking lot or the building was full. There was an eyewitness who said I'd been thrown at least ten feet and might have gone farther had I not slammed into the side of a parked car. The police were following several leads, but would not specify.

My own memory couldn't add much to that account. I remembered she'd asked me what kind of wine went with chicken pot pies, but after that I went blank. The doctor said I might never remember. So, like a film director, I played different scenarios in my head until the images became a riot of sounds and colors.

I kept seeing Janet sitting in her car, its window rolled down and her arm on the door. She was one of those people whose car was an extension of their own anatomy—gear shifts were like mood changes and the brake was a last resort. I was sure that the little white Toyota was the last place she expected to die. It was certainly the last thing I expected. I doubt I'll ever understand how one moment can promise a thousand tomorrows and the next can blow them all away.

They let me leave the following afternoon. In the morning, Carver came to see me. I wondered what had taken him so long. He didn't sit down and the closest he came to settling in was when he unzipped his jacket. "You want to tell me what happened?" He was leaning against the wall when he asked that, arms crossed over his chest.

After I told him what I remembered, he looked at me for a long time, and not for a second did I think he believed I was telling him everything. Then he cleared his throat and slid his hands into his jacket pockets. "Tell me, McCauley, what were you doing with Janet Miraldi?"

"We were friends."

"Friends," he repeated, nodding as though amused.

"That's what I said."

"That's news to me."

"I didn't say we were old friends."

"Well, since you two were such good friends, I imagine you know what she was working on."

"Funny. I don't remember."

He wasn't taking notes or anything, which seemed odd. And he was beginning to act as though this interview were an imposition on his time. His silence made me uncomfortable. "Why don't you ask Jack Alden what she was working on? She worked for him."

He scowled and looked away from me. "Don't tell me how to do my job, McCauley."

"Then what did he say?" I was determined not to let this guy get to me.

"Well, as a matter of fact he said all she had been handling was the Markham bribery indictment. After that, nothing. Seems she was a little, what's that line those yuppies use—stressed out."

"I wouldn't know. I don't seem to be upwardly mobile."

"Yeah, but you think you are. Same thing."

I waited for Carver to continue. Finally he asked, "Did Miraldi share your half-assed theory about Markham being murdered?"

"She had some doubts about it being suicide." I smiled. "As any thinking person would."

"What about evidence?"

"No hard evidence." I hesitated then continued, "But, from what I've heard about Markham's indictment, a large part of this town's legal community didn't exactly mourn his passing."

"You got anything to back that up?"

"I don't."

"Did Miraldi?"

"I don't know."

"You've been a big help, as usual." He zipped his jacket. When he spoke, it was as if he were talking to himself. "To tell the truth, I'm inclined to think her death's got nothing to do with Markham. It was probably a vengeance killing. Pure and simple. She'd been pretty successful in getting convictions. Some of those guys don't take too kindly to being put away. Especially by a woman." He stepped toward the door.

I leaned forward. "I'll bet there are a lot of folks in town who would rather see you follow that lead than dig around the Markham case."

He had his hand on the door's handle. "Yeah. Well, right now that looks a little more promising to me."

He was halfway out the door when I said, "I can't figure you out, Carver. Are you really that stupid or does someone have your number?"

He stopped and turned toward me but didn't come back into the room. "Mister, you're lucky you're laid up in the hospital beat up so bad I can't find a new place to make you hurt." Then he smiled and added, "Oh, I never thought I'd hear myself say this: Don't leave town."

Jeff Barlowe gave me a lift home. Since Louise was at her shop all day, she'd brought Peanuts up to the apartment. He was all over me. There's nothing like a dog to make you feel wanted.

She'd also left some kind of casserole and a couple of sandwiches for me in the refrigerator. And there were three bottles of ale.

"Not bad for a landlady," Jeff said as he viewed the contents. "Mind if I have a sandwich?"

I told him to go ahead and help himself to the beer as well.

He set a place at the coffee table and I declined a sandwich but accepted an ale. Peering between the slices of bread he announced that Louise made a pretty decent meatloaf.

My body didn't look as bad as it had a couple days ago, but it ached like hell. I lowered myself onto the couch and glanced at the copy of the *Chronicle* Jeff had brought with him. Janet's murder wasn't on page one anymore; instead there was a large photo of some beauty contest winner. I dropped the paper onto the couch and watched Jeff eat his sandwich. Finally I said, "I think Carver's revenge theory is full of hot air." Jeff looked at me. "This is connected to Markham and I want whoever did it. And I'm not just talking about the guy who strapped the explosives to her engine." I paused, "I don't care how many were involved."

Jeff nodded. "I hear you."

"It had to be connected to Markham." I shook my head. "There's no way this is a revenge killing. How many dangerous felons could she have put away in this county?" I shook my head. "No way."

We didn't say anything for a few minutes. Jeff worked on the sandwich and I sipped the ale from its bottle. It was cold and refreshing. Then I noticed that Jeff was tapping his foot on the carpeted floor and bobbing his head to some unheard tune.

After another minute I said, "What is it, Jeff?"

"What d'you mean?" His eyes widened and he stopped fidgeting.

"Jeff, whenever you start attending concerts in your head, it's a sure sign that there's something going on in there besides music."

He dropped a sandwich crust on the plate and brushed the crumbs off his hands. His smile was sheepish. "Damn," he said.

I shrugged.

He looked at me and seemed to make an internal decision. "Okay," he said, "here goes." I leaned forward. "I know it's none of my business and if you want to tell me to go to hell, go right ahead . . ."

"Get to it, Jeff."

He took a deep breath. "Were you and Janet involved?"

I studied him and wondered if this question was off the record, but somehow felt he'd be offended if I asked. After several seconds I said, "We had been."

He slumped back into the chair, hands resting on his thighs. He nodded. "I kind of thought so."

I continued, "We didn't have much of a history. I mean," I hesitated because I had been trying to work this out for myself as well, "maybe something could have come of it in time." I paused and looked at Jeff because I wanted to make sure he understood. "But only part of this is personal, you know. We—this town, everyone—owes her this."

From Jeff's expression, I could see I needed to clarify.

I took a long swallow from the bottle and tried to link it all together. I thought about what Janet had said to me that day over the two bottles of Chianti and I said to Jeff, "You know, you see so much corruption—like Janet said, bribery makes the world go 'round—that you start to accept it. You figure if a politician's just a little corrupt, that's okay so long as he does good things. But where do you draw the line? When do you accept so much of it that you become part of it? And her dying. It's like saying those we can't break, we eliminate. So no. This isn't a personal thing. I'm not out to get whoever's ass needs to be gotten because they killed 'my woman.' They killed Janet Miraldi. And if we don't say 'No, we will not let you destroy the people who are trying to make us better' then we might as well be the ones doing the killing. And . . ." I stopped short. "Damn," I leaned back into the couch, and looked up at the ceiling. "I sound like I'm reading from a Frank Capra script, don't I?"

"Jimmy Stewart couldn't have done it better."

"It's just that she was so damned committed. Most people aren't. That's all." I looked at Jeff. "You know what I mean?"

Jeff nodded but didn't say anything for several seconds. He pulled a cigarette from my pack and lit it. I didn't comment on the fact that I'd never seen him smoke. He took a couple of drags and looked down at it absently as though trying to recall who put it there. Then he looked at me and said, "You make her sound like Joan of Arc."

"What's that supposed to mean?"

He tapped out the cigarette the way someone does when he

thinks he might get back to it. Then he removed his glasses and wiped the lenses with his knit tie.

"What're you saying?" I leaned toward him.

He put his glasses back on and shrugged. "Maybe nothing." He looked at me, hesitating, then continued. "But when you start spouting off about people making us better, I get concerned. And you should too. I've been a reporter long enough and I've seen enough of corruption and idealism to know that neither is absolute. And when you start talking about Janet in those terms, I get nervous. 'Cause I'm here to tell you, if they'd had decent media coverage back when Joan of Arc was making headlines, she never would have made sainthood. *Everybody's* got *something* to hide."

I stared at Jeff for several seconds and he began to look uncomfortable. "What aren't you telling me?"

He shook his head. "Nothing. Just rumors really."

"What rumors? What are you talking about?"

"Okay," he sighed and leaned forward. "Some people are saying her motive for going after Markham wasn't all for the good of the court system."

"Then what was it?" Was I being incredibly dense?

Jeff waited a beat then said, "I heard it was personal."

"What's that supposed to mean?"

"I don't know. The only conclusions I've heard drawn are just guesses. But," he hesitated then continued, "the popular theory is that she was acting as the woman scorned."

I stared at him for a minute, letting that sink in. Then I slammed the bottle down on the table. Peanuts jumped. "Oh c'mon Jeff. Janet and Markham? No way."

Jeff just looked at me. I stood and began pacing the room. After several laps I said, "No way. There's no way." I stopped next to Jeff. "Where'd you hear that crap?"

Shaking his head, he looked up at me and, locking onto my gaze, said, "I can't tell you that. Confidential source. And like I said the Markham-Miraldi connection is the speculation part. My source just said it was personal."

"Reliable source?"

He nodded. "Unimpeachable?" he said and made a wobbly-boat gesture with his hand. I walked to the window and looked out on the river. Jeff sighed. "I don't know if I believe it either. But I've gotta consider it now and you should forget your personal involvement here long enough to consider all the implications."

I tried to do that, but my head either wouldn't function or refused to. "What are you talking about?"

"Well, I may be playing the devil's advocate here, but if it is true—if Janet and Markham were an item, then she might have heard about some of the courtroom corruption from the horse's mouth, so to speak. And certain lawyers who were nervous about being named by Markham might think the problem was only half solved when Markham died. And, if you let your imagination wander, you could take it a step further. In order to prove what she'd heard from Markham, she could probably use the services of a private investigator."

I finally turned to him. "Yeah, well if that's true, then why am I alive?"

He leaned back and laced his fingers behind his head. "I don't think you're supposed to be."

I looked out on the river again and tried to figure out if any of this made sense. I wasn't sure. "You're talking about a lot of 'ifs'."

Jeff stood. "Maybe." Then he smiled. "Maybe I'm just looking for a story here."

"Oh, there's a story, all right. There's a story."

He glanced at his watch. "Well, I hate to tell you you're on someone's hit list and run, but I've gotta get back to the paper." He gestured toward Peanuts. "Guess you don't have to worry about life threats with him around." The dog yawned. "Yeah. He's not sweating it."

Jeff hadn't been gone more than five minutes when someone else was at the door. I opened it without looking. I've never slammed a door in a woman's face, but when I opened this one and saw Ellie Carver standing on my porch, I came real close. She must have sensed that too, because she quickly said, "Please. I need to talk to you. I'll only be a minute and it's very important. I won't cause any trouble. Really." The words tumbled out.

I looked down the steps and as far into the driveway as I could see. No one seemed to be lurking anywhere so I stepped back and let her enter.

I always thought there was something to the axiom that you

could gauge a person's true personality by the way a dog reacted to him. I was beginning to wonder if Peanuts was that discerning. He greeted Ellie like she was an old friend and not the woman who was at least partially responsible for the state of my relationship with Carver.

Ellie perched on the edge of the director's chair and kept a firm grip on the small leather clutch she carried. When I sat across from her on the couch, I lit a cigarette and offered her one. She hesitated, then took it. I lit it for her and she held it the way someone who only smokes on occasion does—fingers straight and spread. It didn't look natural in her hand. What was it about me that made non-smokers lapse? She smiled nervously and sighed.

"First," she inhaled and released a thin stream of smoke, "I guess I should apologize for the way you've been treated by my husband." She hesitated. "I've heard he's been kind of rough on you."

I shrugged. "In a way I can't blame him."

"I'm sorry. Really. I was pretty messed up then." She wet her lips and gave me another nervous smile then looked away. "Ed and I are trying to work things out. It's not easy, but we're trying. At least I am." She shrugged and turned back to me. "He's not the kind of man who accepts help from others. But I am. I have to. And we will work it out. It's just," she examined a nail, raised her shoulders in a slight shrug and looked at me straight on, "well, he's not always an easy man to love."

"You get no argument from me there." I smiled at her, wanting her to feel more at ease. I hadn't noticed this mousey quality in the bar that night. All I remembered was that she'd laughed easily and liked Margueritas. Not much to build a relationship on I guess.

She continued, "But he's a good man. He really is."

I nodded, not in agreement, really, more to keep her going.

"This is very," she took a deep breath and blinked her eyes rapidly. ". . . Oh damn." She burst into tears. "It's everything. First this god-awful mess with Ed and then Janet. Oh God." She was crying harder now and rummaging through her purse, presumably in search of a tissue. I brought her the box from the bathroom. Nodding her thanks she sobbed for a minute until she got herself under control. Then she blew her nose with one tissue and wiped her eyes with another. Even though she wore no makeup, she dabbed at her eyes the way women do when they don't want to smear anything. I offered her a glass of water and she accepted.

I set the glass in front of her and asked, "Ellie, why did you come here?"

She extinguished the cigarette and, with an effort, looked me straight in the eyes. Then she swallowed and said, "I know about the, uh, photos."

I knew by the look in her eyes and the strain on her face that she wasn't talking about just any photos. "Who told you?"

"Janet."

I tried to figure out where she was going with this, but couldn't. For lack of a better question, I asked, "What about them?"

There was a moment of confusion then anger flitted across her face, but she suppressed it. "Do you want me to beg? All right, I will." She swallowed hard and, from somewhere deep inside, pulled up some pride. "No, I won't. You're a cruel man, Quint McCauley. Well, this is one person you're not going to be able to blackmail. No sir. I'll tell him about them first." I tried to interrupt but she wouldn't allow it. "You know, when I met you that night at the East End, I thought you were a nice guy. And I felt bad about the way things worked out for you. Not anymore . . ."

I didn't need another concussion to figure out what was going on here. I held my hands up. "Wait a minute. Just one second." My head was starting to hurt. The doctor had said not to exert or excite myself. "There were no photos of you, Ellie."

She froze, on the verge of continuing her barrage. "What?"

I leaned toward her. "None of the photos were of you."

"You're sure?"

I nodded. Her look changed from disbelief to skepticism and I quickly said, "I swear, Ellie."

She leaned back in the chair and started to cry again. She had been staring at the wall behind me, but she brought her eyes to focus on me. "Then where are they?"

"Look. If they haven't turned up by now, what with Markham's death and all, I'd say they aren't going to turn up at all. They were probably destroyed."

She seemed relieved for a moment, then puzzled or, more likely, hurt. "Why would he destroy them?"

I shrugged. "I don't know. But wouldn't that be for the best?"

"Yes. Yes, I guess so." She was silent for several moments and

I was afraid she was going to burst into tears again. She plucked a couple tissues from the box and stuffed them in her purse. "I've got to go," she said. "I'm sorry I troubled you."

"Ellie?"

She stopped.

I knew I was courting another outburst, but I had to know. "What about the negatives? Do you know what he did with the negatives?"

Her smile was unarguably one of relief. "He destroyed them. In front of me. All of them." She seemed convinced anyway.

"What was he like? Markham?"

For a moment, I thought she was going to tell me it was none of my business. Then she seemed to think better of it, and with a shrug of resignation said, "He was exciting. Sensual. Moody. Violent."

"Did he ever hurt you?"

"No," she said quickly, then added, "He wasn't violent that way."

"What do you mean?"

She looked like she was trying to grasp a thought that was just out of reach for her. "I guess," she paused, "I guess it was what fascinated him, you know. He liked violent movies. I remember one night he had a tape of that movie *Bonnie and Clyde*. You know, the one with Warren Beatty and Faye Whatshername."

I nodded.

"Well, he kept playing that scene where they get killed. You know, ambushed. Gunned down. It fascinated him. He played it over and over again. Rewind and replay." She shuddered and shook her head. "Yuck."

"But he never hurt you? Threatened you?"

"Oh no." I looked at the wide-eyed woman and wondered if she was lying through her teeth.

"Why did you pose for those pictures?"

She smiled. "You never met Scott Markham, did you?"

"Very late in his life."

"He was a good photographer. And," she shook her head and broke eye contact with me, "I know you're going to think this is the dumbest thing you ever heard, but, well, when I was posing for him, I felt glamorous. Like I was the world's highest paid fashion model."

"Nothing dumb about that."

She shrugged and moved toward the door. "Really, I have to go."

I stepped between her and the door. She stopped abruptly and for a moment she looked frightened. "Just one more thing. Was Janet ever involved with Markham?"

She looked at me in undisguised shock. "Janet and Scott? Of course not. Where did you hear that?"

I shook my head. "Just some crazy talk." I held the door for her and before she could ask any more questions, I gently guided her out.

After Ellie left, I decided I needed some music. Setting up my modest stereo system seemed like an insurmountable task, but I had to have music. The boards and concrete slabs and the boxes with the components were in the living room, so it didn't take too long to set the unit up. The hard part was getting the wires in the right places so everything worked. There's nothing more disconcerting than watching those red and green lights that let you "see the music" bob up and down while there is nothing but silence emanating from the speakers. Your music's trapped somewhere inside the stereo. Every time I move, I vow to take notes on which plugs go into which sockets, and every time I tell myself, what the hell, I'll remember. I never do. So, it was only after considerable trial and error that I finally got the thing working. I popped in a Gordon Lightfoot cassette.

The whole time I was setting up the stereo, in the back of my mind I was thinking about those photos. Aside from the Susan Connors pictures, there were only two groups left. I needed someone to talk to who wasn't involved in this. I thought of O'Henry in Chicago. After ascertaining that the Connors photo was still taped to the album I dug the photos of the two women I hadn't yet identified out of the kitchen drawer. Nope. No Ellie. I dropped them on the coffee table and ordered Peanuts off the couch. He looked hurt, but I was beyond caring. Exhaustion took over. I tossed the *Chronicle* to the floor, lay down on the couch and stretched my sore joints. Resting his chin on one of the cushions, Peanuts indicated that perhaps I could atone for my manners with a riverside stroll. "Just give me twenty minutes," I said to him.

The next thing I knew, it was dark and some loud noise had roused me. The cassette had finished playing and the green lights were still. I listened and the noise repeated. Someone was pounding on the door. Peanuts was growling. I sat up and turned on a lamp. It seemed like the middle of the night but a glance at my watch told me I was off by about six hours. It was just before eight.

"Yeah, yeah, yeah, I'm coming," I muttered and opened the door to Carver and Henninger. Carver said, "We need to talk, McCauley," and without waiting for an invitation, he motioned the cop into my apartment. Peanuts sniffed at their boots as they pushed past me.

Chapter Sixteen

I MAY HAVE BEEN woozy with sleep and medication, but there was enough of the gray matter still working to warn me that I was one small discovery away from an exceedingly awkward situation. To say the least.

Carver and Henninger moved into the center of the room and did a quick surveillance, checking out the kitchen and the hallway. In what I hoped would appear to be a casual movement, interpreted only as a man straightening up for unexpected company, I picked up the copy of the *Chronicle* from the floor and tossed it onto the coffee table. Not wanting attention drawn to the action, I counted to five before checking my accuracy. When I ventured a glimpse I felt a guarded sense of relief. From where I was standing, it looked like the paper had, in addition to covering half of Jeff's sandwich plate, landed right on top of the photos.

Carver and I sat on the couch and there was a moment of suspense as Henninger lowered his huge build into the director's chair on the other side of the coffee table. It creaked and held. I glanced at the table and my mouth immediately went dry. From my new vantage point, the edge of one of the photos was just barely visible beneath the newspaper. A minor earth tremor could do me in. I leaned back into the couch and crossed my ankle over my knee. "What can I do for you gentlemen?"

"You can start with a few straight answers," Carver said and Henninger pulled out a small notepad and a pencil, the end of which was chewed.

I shrugged and said, "Shoot," instantly regretting my choice of verbs.

Carver smiled a little and cleared his throat. "You knew that Markham was being blackmailed."

It wasn't a question. I nodded.

"Who told you?"

"Janet Miraldi. She learned it from Markham's girlfriend, Robyn Fosse. Why?"

"What was he being blackmailed for?"

"That I don't know." Henninger was scribbling something on his pad and Peanuts was nosing around his food dish.

"You sure?"

"That's what I said."

"If you were so damned convinced that he was murdered, why didn't you tell me about this?"

I couldn't believe he was asking me that with a straight face. "Two reasons," I said. "One, I only found out myself the day before Janet was killed. I guess I didn't beat tracks over to your office because you don't seem to have either an open door or an open mind." I gave his question a little more thought and continued, "Two, when I saw you at the hospital, Scott Markham's problems weren't exactly foremost in my mind."

Carver stared at me for several seconds, glanced at Henninger and dropped his gaze to the table. I leaned forward, "Carver, why are you interested in the blackmail of a guy who committed suicide when you've got the murder of an Assistant State's Attorney to work on? Seems to me you need to get your priorities straightened out." The glint in his eye said he knew something I didn't. And he wanted me to ask. I said, "Okay, Carver, I'll bite."

"Well, you see we aren't so convinced Markham committed suicide. Never were actually. But for the sake of propriety we weren't mouthing off about our suspicions until we had some hard evidence. The way some folks did."

I smiled, pulling at a frayed lace on my jogging shoe. "Careful, Carver, your nose is going to grow."

Henninger shifted his bulk but a barely suppressed scowl was the only indication that Carver had heard me. He continued, "But you see we now have reason to believe that your good friend Miss Miraldi may have had a motive. And you're looking like a pretty good foil for the lady."

"Yeah, well why was she hollering murder before any of you geniuses started to listen?"

"Was she? We only have your word on that. What we do know is that she was acting awful strange after Markham died. Unbalanced some say. I got a hunch you might know what made her that way. Why she was all fired up to throw the book at him and why all of a sudden she's keeping company with the likes of you. Got any theories?"

I folded my arms across my chest and stared at my shoe for a few moments. Then I looked at Carver. "You're fishing," I said. "And the lake's empty."

Carver sighed and looked over at Henninger who appeared to have drifted off into a more pleasant world. When he realized he'd been caught, he leaned forward and tapped the pencil against his knee. Carver stared at the squirming policeman, but it wasn't the kind of stare that connected. Henninger might have been a blank wall. Finally Carver said, "Okay, tell me this. Why were you so intent on keeping the investigation open? Who else was interested?"

I hesitated. Not because I was trying to come up with a defensive block, but because I was watching Peanuts out of the corner of my eye with growing concern. He looked as though he'd convinced himself that there just might be something worth his time on that sandwich plate on the coffee table. But the newspaper was in his way.

"Who else?" Carver prodded.

I looked at him and my panic must have come across as incomprehension. Then he said something I didn't catch because Peanuts had decided the plate plan was a good one and was nosing at the crumbs. "Get away from there." I tried to keep my tone even and was only partially successful. Both Henninger and Carver were watching me.

I laughed. It was a nervous laugh, but I threw in a nonchalant shrug for emphasis. They continued to stare. "They say the really bright ones can be tough to train. You have to use psychology." No response. To Peanuts, I said, "SIT!" He did, but only because I'd caught him off guard. Then he watched me, waiting for me to say I was just kidding. "LIE DOWN!" I hoped, what with the momentum I had going, he would obey without hesitation. He didn't. "DOWN!" I repeated and now Carver was giving me an odd look. Peanuts glanced at the plate, which was no more than a foot from his nose, then back to me. I would have given him a thousand dollars to lie down.

"Peanuts," I spoke low and dragged the word out, hoping I could convince him I meant business.

"Peanuts." It was Henninger. "What the hell kind of name is that?"

Dogs have incredibly short attention spans and this interjection was all it took to get Peanuts' mind off the plate. He jerked his head up toward the voice and Henninger must have interpreted it as an act of aggression. At first I thought Henninger was scared. But he must have made a quick calculation of the amount of damage a forty pound dog can do to a 250 pound man because with one big slab of a hand, he shoved the dog away from him. The movement wasn't harsh enough to hurt the dog, but apparently it was enough to offend him because he snapped at Henninger. And for a second there I was afraid Peanuts would become the first dog in Foxport to die of multiple gunshot wounds.

"Lighten up, Henninger," Carver demanded. "For God's sake, it's just a dog."

Henninger leaned back into the chair and reddened slightly. "Yeah, a dog named after a comic strip." He shook his head and glanced at Peanuts. "Little wimp dog."

I cleared my throat. "Just for the record, he was named after a former Cubs outfielder."

"Looks like he belongs in a comic strip," Henninger paused and looked at the dog, then shook his head and said, "Mutt."

"He's a border collie," I corrected.

"What's he good for?"

I was about to elaborate on Peanuts' virtues when Carver said, "Lowrey? Peanuts Lowrey?"

"Yeah," I looked at Carver and he smiled. It was the closest he'd come to approving of something I had done.

Peanuts had moved around the table and was sitting next to me, leaning against my leg. I felt reasonably confident that the crisis had been defused. I turned my attention back to Carver's insinuation. "What's this hard evidence you have on Janet? And who is this 'we' you've been talking about?" While Carver was eyeing me, I glanced at Henninger and was surprised by the intensity in his expression. It was like he knew this question would be on the final.

"No," Carver said. "You're going to have to come up with something I can use before I start sharing names with you."

"You're accusing me of being part of some conspiracy someone's dreamed up. The least you can do is tell me who you're talking to."

Carver didn't respond for several seconds. He just sat there glaring at me. Finally he said, "Hope there's at least one lawyer in this town you haven't made your enemy. You're going to need him."

"I knew a good lawyer. She's dead now."

"Find another." He looked at Henninger and gestured toward the door. They both stood. They were leaving. I felt like one of those American POWs in the WWII movies. He's cut through the barbed wire and it's a matter of a mere fifty feet to the wood line, out of the sight of the guard tower. Freedom.

No sooner had that image flitted through my mind than Henninger said, "Hey, did you see this?" He bent over and picked up the newspaper, pointing to the beauty queen on the front page. "She's my sister-in-law. God, what a fox."

Carver didn't take note of Henninger's find. His eyes never left the place where the paper had lain. He got one look at the top photo, then he did a strange thing. He grabbed the newspaper out of Henninger's hand and threw it down on the pile. I don't think Henninger ever knew what he'd uncovered. "I don't give a damn about your relatives. Go out to the car. I'll be with you in a minute."

Henninger didn't move at first. He knew something was up, but when he made perfunctory attempts at communicating with Carver, he was ignored. Carver was too intent on drilling a hole through my head with his glare. I could already feel a spot between my eyes getting warm. Finally Henninger muttered something about starting the car and left.

Carver slowly drew his gaze from me and sank into the couch. When he lifted the newspaper from the table, it was like he was uncovering some kind of dead, rotting animal. I stood with my back toward the door. Without a word and with only one menacing glance, Carver picked up the pile of photos.

I placed one hand on the kitchen counter and shoved the other in my pocket. I waited, thinking that it could be worse. The picture of Susan Connors could have been in that pile. As I watched Carver study each photograph, his expression never changed. He might have been reading the obits. He went through the pile twice then threw them back on the table so they skidded along its surface. A couple dropped to the floor. He looked up at me, leaning back into the couch, and placing a booted foot on the edge of the table. When he spoke his tone was calm and even. "So. What were you planning to do with these?"

"I don't know," I crossed my arms over my chest. "Probably destroy them."

He nodded and tipped the table so the side nearest him was a few inches off the ground. The plate and the rest of the photos slid to the carpet. He eased the table back down. Then up again. Up and down, up and down. He never took his eyes from me and I didn't see him blink. Finally he said, "I suppose blackmail was the furthest thing from your mind."

"If you're talking about Markham, I don't think those photos would have done it for him. He's not in any of them."

"You've got more then."

"No. I don't," I lied.

"Where'd you get these?"

I went with the truth.

When I finished, Carver said, "Who the hell made you defender of these ladies' virtues?"

I shrugged. "It just seemed the thing to do at the time. I'm not saying it was the smart thing to do."

"I wouldn't say that either." The table was bobbing up and down at a faster rate now. "Were there photos of any other women?"

"Just one." The lies were getting easier. "Robyn Fosse. Janet returned them to her."

"No others?"

"Nope." I knew he wasn't talking about the one taped inside the album.

"You sure about that?"

"Yeah." I hesitated then added, "Ellie's picture wasn't there."

He stopped rocking the table, but didn't take his boot from it. The muscles in his jaw tightened, he braced himself against the back of the couch and jerked his leg straight. The table shot across the room, scoring a direct hit on my makeshift stereo cabinet. The receiver tumbled over the table, pulling wires loose and taking one of the speakers down with it. I turned to Carver, about to order him out of my home, and saw that he'd drawn a .38 revolver and was pointing it at me. Something snapped.

I pointed my finger at him. "I have had it with you, you son of a bitch." I started pacing. "I'm tired. Tired of cutting you a mile-wide berth. Tired of your threats, of being treated like some kind of felon, and really tired of you blaming me for your lousy marriage." I stopped pacing. "So either use that fucking thing or put it away and get the hell out of here." His grip on the gun seemed to tighten. I wasn't even sweating. "Go ahead, Carver. You take me out, you probably take yourself out too. Or do your connections go up that high? I doubt it." I never took my eyes off him. After a long, thundering silence, his hand relaxed. A few seconds later he returned the gun to its holster. He never spoke and when he glanced toward the door, I knew I'd won this round. But that wasn't enough anymore.

He regarded the stereo and the coffee table in a detached way, as if he wondered how they'd wound up in a pile like that, but wasn't curious enough to ask. Then he adjusted his jacket and ran a hand through his hair. He nodded at me and said, "Later." Before he could get past me, I grabbed his arm. Turning, he looked at my hand then up at me. He didn't understand. "One more thing," I said. "You're not writing off Janet Miraldi as a neurotic and you're sure as hell not going to hang any crimes on her for the sake of convenience."

Carver moved fast, grabbing me by the collar and pulling up so I could feel his breath on my face. "You listen to me . . ." In what I could only describe as a reflex, I brought my fists up between his arms, breaking the grip he had on me and smacking him in the jaw. Neither of us moved for several seconds. Then a smile slowly came to Carver's face as he rubbed his chin. "You just assaulted a police officer." He shook his head, not believing his good fortune.

That was when I decided if I was going to spend the next twenty years making license plates, I might as well take some sweet memories with me. With every ounce of strength I could muster, I drove my fist into his stomach. His legs went out from under him, and he hit the floor with an impact that rattled the windows. But he was on his feet before I could gain an advantage and proceeded to nail me so hard I saw flashes of white.

There was nothing polished or artistic about the way Carver

worked at me. He was a street fighter with no qualms about beating on a guy who'd just come out of the hospital. In less time than I'd care to admit, I was on the carpet, and he was standing over me telling me not to get up. I wouldn't hear of it, though. Fueled by righteous fury, I was not going to stop until one of us was dead. I pushed myself off the floor and barreled into him head first. He made a retching noise when I hit and clawed at my back until he gripped my shoulders and shoved me backwards. His next blow came so close that I could feel its breeze. I caught him under the jaw so his head snapped back. He staggered a few steps and I threw myself at him again. For a few seconds, I thought I was gaining on him. It seemed as though his blows were losing their intensity. Or maybe I was just going numb. Then Carver got me square in the stomach—real close to the cracked rib. The blow sucked the air out of me and as I folded over, he grabbed one arm, then the other and before I knew it, he'd cuffed my hands behind my back.

It was a couple minutes before I worked my way up to a sitting position, my back braced against the wall. Carver was slumped against the door and didn't look like he felt much better than I did. We were both too old for this. Sweat poured from my face but I couldn't wipe it away. I blinked rapidly to clear my eyes. Carver was breathing hard and dabbing at his split lip with a white handkerchief. When he finally looked at me, he didn't say anything at first. No smile of victory. Finally he shook his head. "Dumb son of a bitch. You just got out of the hospital."

I rubbed my face against my shoulder, as best I could. Breathing was painful and I tried to take the air in small gulps. I still wanted to hurt him but there wasn't any part of my body up to it. Or maybe there was. When I had collected enough air to get me through a sentence, I said, "Ellie was here this afternoon."

Carver stared for a moment, his eyebrows coming together in a dark vee. Then he pointed at the floor and said, "Here?"

"Yeah," I think maybe I wanted him to attack me again. Finish me off this time. He didn't though. After a minute I continued. "She thought I had the photos too. I don't. Never did."

He continued to stare, not speaking. "She's scared shitless

you'll find out about it." Then I looked at the ceiling and laughed. "Great lines of communication you two have." Carver must have been too tired to argue. "But you know who's got it, don't you? Whoever's jerking you around like a marionette. You never did think Markham killed himself, did you?"

"Shut up, McCauley," was all he said. Then he stood up, brushed his pants, and walked past me into the hall. After a few seconds I heard water running in the bathroom. When he came back into the living room, he was blotting his face with a faded blue hand towel, which he tossed on the counter when he was finished. He regarded me for several seconds then said, "Just because I'm not running the police department or my marriage the way you would, doesn't mean it's not working."

I realized he was leaving and said, "Aren't you forgetting something?"

He picked up the photos scattered on the floor and jammed them into his pocket. As he opened the door, he turned to me. "Yeah. I forgot to arrest you for assaulting a police officer." Then he left.

Chapter Seventeen

With considerable effort I stood and walked to the door. Through a crack in the curtain I could see retreating headlights. Relieved, I leaned against the door. I didn't want to think about the places I'd hurt in the morning, but things could have been a lot worse. I slid down the door and my legs folded under me so I wound up sitting Indian style. Not a good move. Being handcuffed was bad enough. With my legs tangled up under me, I wasn't sure I could stand again. I tilted my head back against the cold surface of the door and closed my eyes. There were worse places to sleep.

Seconds later a cold nose in my ear brought me around. "Now you show up," I said to my dog who began sniffing at the crack in the door, taking in the draft of cool air. "Lassie would not have allowed this to happen." He looked at me, then pressed his nose up against the door, whined and scratched at the floor. When I didn't move, he looked to see what the problem was. I shook my head. "Sorry. You're going to have to hold it."

Standing up wasn't as difficult as I'd anticipated, once I got my legs straightened out. The real challenge came when I tried to slip my arms under my feet so my cuffed hands would be in front of me. It looked so simple in the movies. Maybe my arms were short or maybe the cracked rib didn't help any, but it was anything but simple. It felt like my shoulders were going to slide right out of their sockets. I'd slouch my way through the rest of my life being mistaken for the missing link. The steel cut and dug at my wrists as I wormed my torso through my arms. My hands went warm as the circulation kicked in. When

"

I looked down at my wrists, I was surprised they were only red and welted instead of gashed and bleeding.

Now what? Jeff Barlow had probably had all he could take of me for one day. Mike Richardson? He might be at the Tattersall. Right. Here, Mike, give this a yank. The two heavy links that connected the cuffs could be cut with the right tool, but I sure couldn't do it myself. Then, even if I managed to break the chain, I'd have a tough time explaining the silver charm bracelets I wore everywhere.

I spent a few seconds wondering what Carver was doing. Snickering to himself? Or was he about to unload on Ellie. Maybe I shouldn't have indulged my spiteful side.

Peanuts was starting to whine again and obviously could not have been less interested in my mental state. First things first.

I stayed close to the steps as I walked back toward the river, trying to stay out of view of Louise's dining room window. I thought I was successful. Peanuts dashed down to the bank and, not wanting to let him get too far away, I began jogging after him. Then I realized you lose a lot of your balance with your hands cuffed. It's also harder to get up once you fall flat on your face.

After he'd taken care of his business, Peanuts wasn't interested in going back. He stood, facing the river, his head raised. Taking in lungs full of air, he reminded me of an athlete preparing for an event. I watched him for a few minutes, thinking if my hands were free it would be a nice evening to spend down here. I turned back to the house and was halfway there before I noticed the pawfalls behind me. He trotted past me and began to climb the steps. I was about five feet behind him when someone called my name.

"Oh, Quint. Quint." It was Louise, and I froze. Perhaps I could convince her it was a bungled magic trick. "I saw you leave with Peanuts a moment ago." She came around from the front of the house where her entrance was. She could really cover ground when she wanted to. "I just wanted to see how you were doing. I was at the shop this afternoon when you came home. I'm so sorry. What an awful thing. Are you getting on all right?"

She walked right up to me, but didn't seem to notice my hands. Maybe it was dark enough. "Yeah, I'm doing okay. Thanks a lot for the food and the beer."

"Oh, that's all right. How are you feeling?"

"Okay," I nodded in an exaggerated way so she'd be sure to see that I meant it. "I'm fine." Then I yawned. "Just tired."

"If you just got out of the hospital, do you think it's a good idea to be moving furniture?"

I missed a beat before answering. "Uh, well, I guess not. Sorry for the noise. I was, uh, just setting up my stereo."

"I see," she said, but her eyes narrowed at the same time and she turned to look up the steps as though debating whether to assert her power as landlady and check out the damage. Then she turned back to me. I yawned again. I think it was the fact that I'd just yawned twice without covering my mouth that made her suspicious.

She started looking for something out of place and stopped when she saw the cuffs. Her gaze shifted from my hands, up to my stupid smile, then down to my hands again. "Oh, my," was all she said at first. She started to say something else, then hesitated. She'd probably seen a lot in her life and was trying to decide where this fit in.

"Uh, Louise." I quickly decided the truth was the best way to go with this. "This is real awkward." She was a pretty game little woman, but I figured that cuffs and chains went just out of bounds for her. "I'm sort of on the outs with the police chief. He was angry enough with me to cuff me, but not angry enough to arrest me. So he left me this way. He's probably having a good chuckle about it now." I tried to laugh like I too could appreciate a practical joke. "Probably with his wife. Or maybe not."

She looked at me for a long time before she said, "So that *was* Eddie Carver I saw leave here."

Eddie? "Uh, yeah, that was him. Eddie."

She nodded slowly, then cocked her head. "I didn't know you knew Eddie Carver."

"Oh yeah, sure. We've run into each other a few times."

It took her about fifteen seconds to convince herself that, while I might be lying, at least I wasn't dangerous. "Why don't you two come in with me. Perhaps I can help."

Louise's "family" greeted Peanuts like he was a favorite cousin, but they were a little more reserved around me. Maybe it was the cuffs. When she saw me in the light, Louise did a quick appraisal of my face and said, "Looks as though that stereo put up a fight."

I nodded. "It always does."

She ushered me into her kitchen and, without asking, opened a couple bottles of ale. As she poured them into two steins, I looked around the room.

If I had ever imagined a Louise Orwell kitchen, this would have been it. It was cluttered and comfortable with teapots and notes hanging everywhere. And pictures. She may not have wanted a kid living upstairs but there wasn't much wall space that wasn't covered with, I assumed, several generations of her family. A large space above the telephone was reserved for a photo of the queen mother. And there were snatches of artwork done in varying degrees of talent taped to the walls and stuck to the refrigerator with little fruit magnets. Louise placed a stein in front of me and I watched Peanuts and the pug exchanging good-natured growls and scrapping over a rubber ball.

She drank from the glass and used a paper napkin to dab her mouth. I held my glass up to her before taking a drink. Neither of us spoke for several minutes, but the whole time Louise was watching me, apparently not convinced there wasn't a good reason for me to be cuffed. Finally she said, "So these are Eddie's cuffs you're wearing?"

"Yeah, they are." I tried to laugh it off, but Louise was looking dead serious. "Maybe this means we're going steady."

"It must mean something. They're very dear to him." Then she looked away from me.

I decided to shut up and drink my ale.

She was sitting across from me at a little table covered with a flowered plastic tablecloth and seemed to be wrestling with a major decision. Not knowing whether or even how she was going to help me made me wonder if I shouldn't be trying harder to get myself out of my predicament. But the room was pleasant, the scuffling dogs weren't disruptive and the ale was good.

I had worked my way through a third of the drink when she asked, "Are you in trouble with the law?"

"*I* don't think so." I realized it was important to be as honest with this woman as possible so I added, "What's going on between me and Carver, well, I guess it's personal."

She nodded and asked, "Do you know Ellie?"

"We've met."

For some reason, that answer seemed to satisfy her for she placed her hands on the table, palms down, as if it were time to get down to business. Then she pushed herself up and walked over to a small table next to the refrigerator where she opened a personal phone directory, flipped to a tab, and glided a finger down the page, stopping midway. She picked up the phone and dialed a number. While she waited, she looked at me and winked.

"Chief Carver, please," she said and added, "This is Louise Orwell."

After only a few seconds, she smiled and said, "How are you, Eddie?"

A pause, then, "Well, I'm getting along all right. Haven't seen you at the shop lately." She nodded. "Ah, I see. Well, yes, I suppose you have been busy. . . . yes, well the reason I'm calling. I've got a gentleman sitting here. A Quint McCauley . . ." Another pause, then, "Eddie? Are you still there? . . . yes, well, he's here at my kitchen table and I must say you've put him in quite a predicament." He must have tried to get a word in, but Louise wouldn't have it. "Eddie," she spoke firmly and placed a hand on her hip, "I must take exception to what you're doing here. You are . . . don't interrupt me, Eddie. You are an officer of the law. Don't you take that seriously? . . . I don't care if it is personal. . . . I'm sure it is none of my business. . . ."

He must have been going on because she stopped talking and glanced at me. I'd been grinning over the picture of Carver squirming under the wrath of this English lady. I nodded my approval. Then something in her look made me wipe the smile off my face.

When she finally got her chance, she said, "Eddie, I want you to come over here and uncuff this man. It's a disgrace. . . . We're all busy, Eddie. If you don't come over here right now, I'm going to call Charlie Olson and tell him where you left your handcuffs. . . . Don't 'Louise' me. I mean it." While Carver responded she looked at me. Then she said to Carver, "I'll have a Killian's waiting for you. . . . Bye now."

She hung up and turned to me abruptly, an accusing finger targeting me. "And you. Don't you look so smug, sir. I've known Eddie for years now, and I know he's a good man. I don't know what you've done to set him off, but I'm sure it's no minor thing.

"He's coming over now and I want you two to straighten this out. Whatever it is." She pulled another stein out of the cupboard. "It's none of my business so I won't ask what it is between the two of you. Though I have an idea."

I wanted to change the subject. "How do you know Carver?"

Smiling, she took a Killian's out and poured Eddie's drink. "I've known him for fifteen years. Ever since I opened the shop. That was before he was police chief and before he married Ellie. He used to buy her things there. Still does. Though not as often."

I started to ask her about Carver, but before I could form the question, she gave me a look of sudden anticipation and asked, "Do you play backgammon?"

Smiling, I said, "Yeah, and I'm tough to beat."

"Oh, good. I enjoy a challenge."

Standing on her toes, she drew an open board down from the top of the refrigerator. Aside from a little shifting, the stones were in place.

I rolled a three and Louise came up with a ten. "Oh, good." She rubbed the dice between the palms of her hands and tossed them onto the board. Two sixes.

I was on my way to losing a second game when Carver arrived. I was almost relieved. I stayed in the kitchen and tried not to look like the kid who'd squealed to the principal. I heard their voices in the other room but couldn't make out what was being said. Whatever it was didn't take long. In less than two minutes, Louise entered the kitchen with Carver in tow. While she set the ground rules, I was careful to keep my hands in my lap.

Carver probably measured in around six four. I'd be stretching it if I put Louise at five three. But it was the way she stood—feet planted, fists on her hips and her chin defiantly raised to Carver—that left no doubt as to who had the upper hand. "All I ask is that you take your handcuffs off Quint. And you both," she moved so she could address both of us, "sit here and drink your ales. It would be an excellent idea if you would try to communicate, but that may be too much to ask of men exhibiting less than mature qualities. However, neither of you leaves here until you finish your drink." Without time for either of us to voice a protest, Louise left the room. We both watched the doorway she'd exited through. After a long minute, Carver took a seat at the table and stared at the full stein of ale.

Being careful not to betray any kind of emotion, I offered him my cuffed hands across the table. He regarded me and the cuffs for what seemed like a minor eternity, then pulled out his keys and made me a free man. I rubbed my wrists and sat back in the chair. I didn't thank him.

He didn't make any effort to communicate so I turned my attention to the view from the window. I couldn't see much because I was looking through gauze curtains into a dark yard, but it beat staring at Carver. I wanted to clear the air with him, but I sure as hell didn't want to go through one of those male bonding things where we'd get incoherently drunk on beer with whiskey chasers and wind up arm in arm singing old Irish drinking songs. No thanks.

I ventured a glance at Carver. From the looks of it, he didn't see any bonding in our future either. He'd pushed his glass of ale so that it was within his reach but only with a fully extended arm. Then I thought of something that might cheer him up.

"Looks like I won't be around to bother you much longer."

A smile came to Carver slowly. "You dying?"

"Not that I know of. But Mason Burke's got the word out on me. There's not a lawyer in town who'll do business with me."

After a minute he said, "Mason's a powerful man. Hard to believe a little weasel like that could hold all the cards. But he does."

"Why is that?"

He didn't answer and I persisted. "I don't get it. The guy's no great shakes as a lawyer. What's he got?"

He eyed me as though he were trying to figure if I was bluffing. Then he said, "I wish I knew," and I couldn't tell whether he was being straight with me.

The refrigerator clicked off and the ensuing silence seemed to magnify the tension. Carver finally picked up his glass and took a drink. When he returned it to the table, he didn't let go. I almost sighed with relief.

"Tell me something," he said. "At first. Before Miraldi died, what got you into this? Why did you care if Markham committed suicide or was murdered? What is it to you?"

"Nothing. But Lorna Markham cares. Scott's insurance policy won't pay off if it was suicide. There's a two year 'self destruction clause.' After that you can feel free to blast away. Or whatever. Markham's policy was only six months old."

Carver looked away. He moved his stein in small circles so that the liquid sloshed up the sides. Without turning to me, he said, "So Lorna Markham would have no good reason to want me to close this case in a hurry."

"Not that I know of." I considered whether it was time to take the gloves off and decided that since I had Louise to protect me, I had nothing to lose. "Who's got Ellie's picture?"

He studied me, fingers tracing the corners of his mouth. Shifting in his chair he said, "I don't know. I got a copy of it. And a typed note. That's all."

"A duplicate?"

He shook his head. "No. It was like a Xerox or something. The note said as long as Markham was considered a suicide, nobody'd see it."

I nodded and waited.

Carver shrugged and picked up the glass. "Thing was, until I got that, I figured he was a suicide. No reason not to."

"When did you get it?"

"Morning after Markham died I found it on my car. Stuck under the wiper." He hesitated, the glass halfway to his mouth. "Like a goddamn parking ticket."

"You know," I said, "if Markham had a picture of Ellie, why wouldn't he have kept it with the others? Whoever has her photo took it from Markham's desk before I got there." When that didn't get a response, I asked, "By the way, who were the women in the photos you took from me?"

He stared at me without any expression and finally said, "Some rich guy's wife. Didn't know the other."

"What're you going to do with them?"

"Nothing unless I have to."

"What about that guy I saw going into Markham's office? You ever get anything on him?"

Carver shook his head. "You were the only one who saw him and you didn't give us enough of a description to go on."

He looked at me. "You saying that whoever sent me that copy killed Markham?"

"Not likely." My mind was scrambling ahead and all my instinct said to follow my hunch. "If he was murdered, it wouldn't make sense for his killer to even suggest that it might not be suicide."

"Who else you got in mind?" He said that like he was skeptical but he looked like he was interested.

"But it wouldn't hurt to have someone else urging the chief of police to close the case."

"Who?"

I glanced at Carver. "Someone who might be desperate enough to consider blackmailing a cop and self righteous enough to believe he could pull it off."

He studied a nonexistent spot on the tablecloth, his features tight and intense. I could almost see him flipping through his mental filing system. After a minute he focused on me and said, "Who cut that policy for Markham?"

I drank an inch off the beer, set it down and said, "John Dieken."

Carver raised his eyebrows slightly and leaned back into the chair. Resting his folded hands on his stomach he nodded to himself the way you do when a bunch of the puzzle pieces all of a sudden drift together. Under his breath he said, "Desperate and self righteous."

▽

CHAPTER EIGHTEEN

IT WAS NOT a day I greeted with open arms and a fervent desire to get on with the rest of my life. In fact if it hadn't been for Peanuts demanding I attend to his personal matters, I doubt that I would have gotten up. Ever. And then after being up for fifteen minutes, I couldn't believe how sore I still was. This must have been how the tin woodman felt right after Dorothy oiled him. I also felt incredibly ineffectual, and I was certain there wasn't an oil can big enough to get all my parts working right.

The night before, Carver and I hadn't parted as friends, but we were doing an excellent job of tolerating each other. And when he said he was going to see a man about an insurance policy, I assumed he would handle the situation in his own way.

I wanted to talk to both Robyn Fosse and Knox Ferris. Knox's place was on the way to Robyn's, so I stopped there first. He'd been there when Janet was killed. Maybe he could tell me something I didn't know. Besides, I'd heard from Jeff that he'd stopped by the hospital that first day when I'd been too out of it to notice.

Knox Ferris lived in an old house that had been divided into three apartments. His entrance in the back was the only one that opened onto the small square of yard. The house's paint was chipping some, but I'd seen worse.

When Knox opened the door he was wearing only a towel around his waist. I've never had the nerve to do that, so much depends on your not sneezing. With a smaller towel, he was drying his hair and cleaning the water out of his ears. They

170

were red with his efforts. He didn't seem surprised to see me and stepped back, waving me into the room.

"Make yourself comfortable." He turned down the volume on his stereo which was blasting an old song by The Band, "The Night They Drove Old Dixie Down." "I'm gonna put something on. Be with you in a second."

Knox's living room was not unlike Sears' electronics department. It was decked out with gadgets I didn't immediately recognize. And the fact that it was a small room made the accumulation of equipment overwhelming. One wall was devoted to just about any form of entertainment you would care to imagine. There was a stereo with countless components, a projection screen television and the requisite VCR. A metal bookcase was filled with video cassette tapes. On the opposite wall were posters that hinted at the titles of some of those tapes: film classics like *Mister Roberts, The Maltese Falcon* and *Citizen Kane*. Beneath those framed posters was a pile of large boxes, some filled with books and some empty.

A dining room was off the living room and I suspected he didn't do much eating in there. It was filled with sophisticated recording equipment and the only table was the utility variety, which was piled with books, papers and clothes. Judging from the furniture, which looked comfortable and old, and the clutter, which was almost but not quite overwhelming, Knox Ferris was making no pretense of being an upwardly mobile attorney.

Across from the dining room was what appeared to be a sunroom. I stepped in and realized that it was, in fact, a game room. Two light-weight touring bikes leaned against the south wall. There were three pinball machines and a computer with game diskettes stacked next to it. The pieces on a chess set were frozen in mid-game with the king one move away from being checked.

I stepped up to one of the pinball machines. It was called "Time Riders" and had all kinds of strange elements of the universe protruding from its board. I gripped the rod that propels the steel ball into the game, pulled it back and sprang it. A single ball shot straight up the right side, looped around a black hole, eluded the flipper I was frantically wagging, paused, then picked up momentum as it rolled off the board and out of play. The pinball wizard strikes again.

"I don't think anyone's ever scored a zero on that thing." Knox had come into the room and was standing with his hands on his hips, smiling. He had swapped the towel for pleated slacks and a vee-necked sweater.

I shrugged and turned away from the game. "I guess I spent too much time sitting at the bar instead of developing my motor skills."

Stepping back into the living room, I walked with Knox toward his kitchen.

I'm just enough over six feet to allow for shrinkage as I age. That isn't extraordinarily tall, but I'm seldom around people who make me feel short. Knox did.

"This is quite a place you've got."

He nodded, surveying the apartment like it was a garden he'd spent a season growing. "Yeah, it's home. You read briefs and mess with the dirty side of people's lives all day, you need something big time to unwind.

"Want some coffee?" He was pouring himself a cup so I accepted. As he handed me the mug, he cocked his head and regarded my battered face. "Saw you in the hospital the other day and I hate to say it, but you look worse now."

"Yeah." I sipped the coffee which was strong and hot. "I guess I should've stayed another day." I sat in a leather armchair that smelled as good as it looked. It was probably harder to move than a canvas director's chair, though. "I heard you stopped by. Guess I wasn't much of a host, but I appreciate the effort."

Knox shrugged. "No problem." Then he added, "You were lucky."

I set the mug down. "I understand you were the witness to the explosion."

He looked away briefly. "Yeah, it was me." Then he shook his head. "I'm still dreaming about it. Can't imagine what it must be like to have lived it."

"I don't remember much," I said. "I hoped you could jog some of those memories."

"Why? Why would you want to do that?"

"Because I want to know who killed her. And I think maybe there's something important I don't remember."

Knox didn't speak for several seconds. He seemed to be sizing me up. Finally he said, "I'd just pulled out of the lot and

172

looked back at the two of you." He leaned back and rested his elbows on the arms of the chair. Then he smiled and looked a bit sheepish. "Hell, I'll admit it. I thought maybe the two of you had something going. I guess I was just being an old lady. You see, I thought maybe you'd be stealing off in the car with her or something." He shook his head. "You must be thinking 'God is this guy hard up.' "

"No big deal," I said, amused by the idea that anyone would be remotely interested in my personal life.

"What were we doing?"

"Nothing," he said. "Well, I guess you were talking or something because you were walking backward—you know— so you were facing her car. Then you stopped for a second, and it looked like you were going to step back toward her car, but before you did, it blew up." He closed his eyes, leaned back into the chair and said, "I hope to God I never see anything like that again," as though he were reciting an oath. He opened his eyes and stared at the ceiling. "And then it took a couple seconds before I realized what had happened." Turning back to me, he shook his head. "You know, like my brain couldn't take the shock all at once. You were thrown back a good ten feet and slammed into Alden's Mercedes." He smiled. "I think you dented it some too."

"Alden was still there?"

"Yeah, I guess so. Though, come to think of it, I didn't see him until after the cops arrived and the, uh, coroner."

I nodded. "Anything else?"

"Not much." He took a noisy sip out of the steaming mug and set it on a marble coffee table. "Carver showed up and . . ." he hesitated.

"He kicked dirt in my face?"

Laughing, he rubbed his clean shaven chin. "No, nothing like that. He talked to people, did his usual bit.

"That's about it. I suppose that doesn't help you much."

"Well, I guess if you'd seen who planted the bomb, you'd have mentioned it to someone already."

"It probably would have come up."

Knox looked at me for a long time before he spoke again. "Have you heard what they're saying about her? About Janet?"

"Some. What've you heard?"

"Janet and Markham. She was out to get him because he wouldn't leave Lorna for her."

"You think that's true?"

"I didn't. But now, I don't know. When I think about it." He leaned forward and continued. "See, when Janet came to me about flushing out Markham . . ."

I interrupted. "I thought you came to Janet."

He laughed a little and looked puzzled. "She told you that?"

"Yeah."

Still chuckling to himself, he said, "No. Not me. I know how that kind of thing can alienate a person from his colleagues. I wouldn't *ask* for that. But when it was put to me, I was forced to think about it. And then there was no way I could not do it." He paused and I waited. "Truth be told, I wasn't convinced I'd do it until Susan disappeared. Then I had to."

This had the makings of an interesting story. I sat back to listen.

"You see, Susan and I had been dating on and off for a few weeks—nothing steady—when Janet approached me. And when I think about it, just her coming up to me and starting a conversation, well I should have known she was up to something. A bunch of us were up at The Docket. And that's another thing. Janet never went to places like that. You know, Janet just isn't the bar scene type." He paused. "But then I guess I don't have to tell you that. You knew her pretty well."

I didn't say anything, believing even deeper now that I'd only gotten a snapshot of Janet instead of the entire roll. I'd spent one night with her and thought I'd tapped into her essence. I was actually light years away.

Knox was continuing. "After a few visits we got to talking about our social lives. I remember she laughed and said hers was nonexistent. I talked a little about Susan. We hadn't been dating that long, but she was special. Well, eventually Janet led the conversation to Susan's boss, Scott Markham." The telephone began to ring and, instead of answering it, Knox nodded to himself, confirming his own theory and continued. "Yeah, and I think that was when I realized what she was after. Because, you see, Susan had said a few things that had started me wondering."

He saw me looking at the phone, which was hooked up to the most elaborate answering machine I'd ever seen. Smiling, he said, "Ignore it. I put it on record while I was in the shower. It'll take a message."

"From the looks of it, it does your talking for you too."

He laughed. "Just about."

Before he chose to elaborate, I put us back on the track. "What was it that Susan said?"

"Well, nothing damning or anything, just suggestions really." I started to prod him further, but he held up a hand. I curbed my impatience. "Well, once I mentioned something about a guy with a known drinking problem and a couple arrests for DUI still being out on the streets and she said something about 'thanks to my boss.' Well, I didn't think much of it at the time. We'd been at a wedding and Susan had had a few glasses of champagne. But later I started doing a little digging on my own."

"Did you run across the story about the man Markham shot?"

Knox stopped and stared at me for several seconds before he said, "I'm not sure I know what you mean."

I shrugged. "I don't know the particulars. Janet told me about a man who believed Markham was responsible for letting a DUI off who later killed his child in an accident. Happened seven or eight years ago."

Knox said, "Well, I didn't go back that far. Though I guess that's one I shouldn't have missed. And I've never heard of the incident myself." He smiled. "It may be part of Foxport's mythology."

"Maybe," I said. "Go on with your story."

"Well, when Janet asked me if I'd consider going undercover, I told her I'd have to think about it. Then I think I made a big mistake."

He looked down into his hands. I waited and after several seconds he continued. "I sort of prodded Susan about it. You know, casual questions. Nothing specific. Right after that, she disappeared." It was a full minute before he said, "I've never been able to convince myself that there wasn't a connection."

Something wasn't quite working for me. "If your suspicions are true, then why would Markham have taken the bait from you? Doesn't make sense. If he knew you were dating and he knew his clerk was suspicious, then why would he risk it?"

"I posed that question to Janet. She seemed to think it was

worth a try. And she was right. Once I got in, once I started working with him, I saw it wasn't going to be a problem. You've got to realize that among his other fine qualities, Markham was very arrogant. He thought no one could touch him. Especially someone as inconsequential as a minor league attorney.''

"He had a lot to lose."

"Did he? What did he really have? A lousy marriage. I'm not sure he was so in love with the law anymore either."

"Did you know his girlfriend?"

"Robyn? Hell yes. I introduced them."

It was my turn to look surprised.

Knox smiled. "Yeah. Actually she was a friend of Susan's."

"You talk to her lately?"

He shook his head. "I did try to call her after they found Susan, but I couldn't get hold of her. What with Markham dying too, she's probably in seclusion somewhere."

He got up to pour himself more coffee. I waved off his offer for a refill and glanced at the half-filled boxes. "When are you moving?"

"Probably next week. Actually I think I'm going to put everything in storage." He paused. "Haven't looked for a job yet. Probably won't for a while. I think I'll bike out to the West Coast. That's something I've always wanted to do. Now seems like a good time."

"You mean bicycle? The kind you have to pedal?"

Knox smiled. "Yeah. I do a lot of that. Cross-country biking. That's how I unwind. Never ridden out to the coast though. I know of one guy who rode around the world. Maybe I won't stop at California or Washington."

"Maybe you'll have to. I've never ridden out there either, but I hear once you get past California, it gets pretty rough."

We talked for a while longer and before I left, Knox said, "You know, Quint, I think you should at least consider the rumors about Janet. Rumors sometimes have their basis in truth. And, when you think about it, it makes sense."

"Not to me."

He shrugged. "It puts a whole new light on motives for killing Janet."

I regarded Knox for a few seconds, trying to figure out what he was getting at. When nothing came to me, I said, "What are you talking about?"

"Let's say it is true about Janet and Markham." He leaned forward and gestured with his hands as he spoke. "Her motive for getting him convicted isn't that he's a corrupt public official. It's because he's dumped her. So she talks a lot about ethics and codes of honor because she wants everyone to believe that's why she's so committed to convicting Markham. When she pulled me in, she knew there were more indictments out there. But I don't think that bothered her. Oh yeah, she made a few noises about losing the others, but all she really cared about was getting Markham. When Markham puts a bullet in his brain—and it does look like he had better reason than anyone else to pull the trigger—Janet's got nothing. She is deprived of exacting her revenge on the guy. She's mad as hell and figures since she can't make things worse for the guy, she might as well make his family suffer. So she digs up dirt on him that would humiliate the people he left behind—Lorna Markham, his son, maybe even his current girlfriend or his friend, Mason." He paused and seemed to be waiting for input from me. When he didn't get any, he continued in a quieter tone. "Maybe someone decided that having Janet around was too big a risk."

"What do you know about Mason?"

Knox paused, evaluating, then said, "He's smooth, slippery and very formidable."

"What makes him so formidable?"

"He's powerful. The power is inherited, but he knows how to use it. He's also rumored to be quite well connected. Supposedly he's good friends with businessmen who make large profits from other people's vices."

I nodded and considered the other names he'd mentioned before I said, "I don't know. No matter how hard I try, I just can't picture Lorna Markham wiring a bomb to Janet's car."

Knox dismissed my objection with a wave of his hand. "There are a lot of guys out there more than happy to do that for a few bucks. And they never ask questions. Her son might even have done it for her."

I shook my head. "No. Eric and Lorna Markham working together on something? No way."

"Even if it meant keeping what was left of Scott Markham's reputation intact?"

I didn't know Eric Markham well enough to answer that.

"Look, Quint, I'm not saying the rumors are true, all I'm saying is you have to give every conceivable option due consideration. I don't know whether to believe what's being said about Janet. She was a bright, talented, committed attorney." He paused then added, "And a friend, I guess. So, I don't want to believe it. It's just, well, since you're still looking into this, perhaps you should think about it."

"Tell me this. What did the other attorneys think of Janet?"

"Not much." He had answered quickly and took a few moments to consider my question before continuing. "Most of the time she stuck to herself. Didn't go out of her way to make friends. Strictly business. I think that was partly because she was real insecure, though she did a good job of hiding it. Did she ever tell you about her family?"

"Not very much," I admitted.

"Well, she had two brothers and one sister. The brothers got all the attention and encouragement as far as building a career goes. One of them owns a bakery and the other is some kind of media consultant. I don't think either of them is as bright or as hard a worker as Janet was. Her sister's the wife of an attorney. They live in a big house in one of the northern suburbs. And, well, Janet's parents felt that's what she should have been. The *wife* of an attorney. Not an attorney, for God's sake. And a prosecuting attorney, to top it off. Hardly a feminine calling. So she was always fighting that image her family had of her. Taking herself very seriously. And sometimes it made her seem aloof, even cold. I don't think that was the case though."

When he stopped talking, the silence in the room was heavy and I wished that the tape were still playing. I crossed my arms over my chest. "She told you all that. About her family."

He chuckled and said, "Yeah, last Christmas I took her out for a couple drinks. We just sat in a bar, drinking Scotch and swapping law school stories and such." Then he glanced at me and quickly added, "That's all it was. Just dumping our souls to a sympathetic ear."

When I left Knox's place, I had my first nagging doubt about Janet. I attributed it to jealousy and dismissed it. But like I said, it was a nagger and the harder I worked at convincing myself that she'd never been Markham's lover, the more I realized that I should not totally dismiss the possibility. I tried putting it all into perspective. Here I was fighting anything that messed with Janet's character but I needed absolutely no convincing that Mason was "heavily connected" right up to his little spotted head. I resolved to do whatever I had to do to keep my mind open and my head on straight.

Robyn wasn't home and I was starting to get concerned. However, I wasn't concerned enough to check with Wanda. Instead, I drove across Foxport and into the next town east to The Nordic Loft. Fortunately they featured a Sunday brunch so they were open. The hostess told me Robyn wasn't there and asked me if I'd like to wait for the manager. I did.

I was admiring the rustic, log cabin type interior to the restaurant when the hostess directed a small, attractive woman around fifty to me.

We shook hands. "I'm Gail Heulit. I understand you're looking for Robyn."

I told her I was and she said, "You're not the only one. We haven't seen her since last Sunday and, I'll tell you, I don't care to see her again. As far as I'm concerned we don't have a thing to discuss."

"She hasn't called or anything?"

"No, she hasn't. And unless someone is holding out on me, she hasn't talked to any of the waitresses either." She shook her head, her mouth in a grim line. "She's making it tough on the other girls too. They were trying to cover for her at first, but not anymore."

I asked to talk to a couple of the waitresses who knew Robyn. Their attitude ranged from concerned to disgusted.

Before I left I asked the manager if anyone else had been looking for Robyn.

She thought for a moment before saying, "Well, I believe there have been a few phone calls for her. A man who never identified himself. That's all that I know of."

I thanked her and left.

I picked up Peanuts before going to the Tattersall for lunch. Sammy MacTavish, the guy who owned the place, didn't mind having animals brought in occasionally as long as they behaved themselves. And, more than once Sammy had noted that usually the only trouble he had was with animals of the two-legged kind.

Before we left for the Tattersall, I spent a few minutes wrestling with my conscience. Finally I retrieved the photo of Susan Connors and stuck it in the book of Markham's photographs. Maybe it was time for another heart to heart with Carver. He knew I'd taken some photos from Markham's office. I could tell him that he forgot to take one with him.

I opened the door for Peanuts. "Let's go get a sandwich."

We never made it. On the way to the Tattersall, I passed the library. As I approached it, I made a mental note to find that news story about Markham that Janet had mentioned and Knox had known nothing about. As I drove past the building, I saw something that made me forget all about old newspaper articles. Bounding up the steps of the library two at a time was, I was certain, the same person I'd seen leaving Markham's office the afternoon he died. As before, I was too far away to recognize him, but there was something about the gait and the way he carried himself, head slightly bowed, that clicked immediately. It took me a fraction of a second to superimpose this image over the one I'd seen a week before, but then I knew I had a match. I was about to come face to face with the last person to leave Markham's office. I could not believe my luck.

I parked in the library lot and decided to wait outside rather than force a confrontation in the building. The library was in an old building with lots of rooms. It would be easy to miss the guy if I went in. I could wait him out. Leaving Peanuts in the car with the window cracked, I decided to loiter around the entrance so I wouldn't have to dash across the lawn. I'd noted what he was wearing—a short khaki jacket and gray slacks—so, unless he changed while inside, I had him.

Waiting is tough, no matter where you do it. Waiting on the library steps for what I hoped would be a major break in this case, I could hardly stand still. I smoked two cigarettes and was about to start my third when I saw him coming down the stairs from the library's second floor. It was fortunate that I had a whole flight of stairs to recover and get my act together. When I saw who it was, a voice in the back of my head said of course, dummy, you knew you'd seen that walk and that posture since Sunday.

▽

CHAPTER NINETEEN

WHEN JEFF BARLOWE got to the bottom of the stairs, he walked straight for the door. Noticing me standing in the foyer, he stopped, and smiled. "Hey, Quint. What're you doing here?" His surprise seemed genuine. But then, why shouldn't it at this point?

As he approached me, I looked him up and down, just to make sure it hadn't been a mistake. Then I said, "I'll tell you if you tell me what you were doing at Markham's office last Sunday afternoon."

His mouth formed a number of words before he came up with one. "What?"

"C'mon Jeff. Don't do this to me. You know I was sitting outside his office. You know I saw someone go in there."

We were in the way of people entering and leaving the library so we moved out and onto the large concrete stoop. I leaned against the brick wall and Jeff stood a few steps back facing me.

He cocked his head, then looked back into the library. "What gave me away?"

"That bouncing step of yours. I saw you going into the library. At the time I didn't know who you were, but I knew you were the guy I'd seen before."

Jeff nodded and ran a hand through his hair. "He was dead."

"When you left or when you got there?" Part of me felt like a jerk and part of me wanted to know why he hadn't told me any of this.

"Knock it off." He shook his head, laughing. Then he looked at me again and his expression changed. "You think I killed the guy?"

181

I didn't answer.

He pushed back his jacket and put his hands on his hips. His reporter's notebook protruded from a breast pocket. "I don't believe this." Then he shook his head in disgust, turned and walked down the steps. So much for kicking ass.

I followed him to his pickup truck. He started to get in and I grabbed his arm. "Then what were you doing there?"

He turned abruptly and yanked his arm from my grasp. "You mean, if I wasn't there to kill him, what business could I possibly have had with the guy?"

"Something like that."

"I don't believe this," he repeated.

He turned his back to me, put both his hands on the roof of the cab, and looked like he was waiting to be patted down. Apparently he was weighing his choices. Finally he turned, leaned against the truck and crossed his arms over his chest. "I was following up a lead on a story. They were going to start digging in that field west of town, where they found Susan Connors. Markham had tried to get an injunction. You knew that. Anyway, I got there and he was dead."

There was a real sour note in that chord. "What stopped you from calling the cops? Either way, you would have had your scoop."

He started to say something but stopped and eyed me for a minute. Then he said, "I'm not sure I should tell you." Pausing, he nodded to himself. "Yeah. Here you are, ready to nail me for killing the guy and then you want me to level with you. Why should I?"

"Because I need to know."

His expression didn't change.

"Look," I said, "I don't think you killed the guy. Okay? But you gotta admit that your being there raises a whole bunch of questions. You discovered his body for God's sake. Why didn't you call the cops?"

Jeff shifted his weight and looked away. "Anne," he said and when he turned back to me the look in his eyes made me believe him. "We had talked the night before. She told me he had taken those pictures of her and that he still had them. It made her real uncomfortable. I told her to go get them back. That idea seemed to scare the hell out of her so I offered to go myself. She seemed relieved, but then the next morning—Sunday—she called and told me it was something she had to do herself."

"Did that seem strange to you?"

"No," he said as though he'd already debated that possibility with himself. "No, not really. Anne is real shy. Mousey really, but she's a damned good photographer and in order to be a good photographer, you have to be intrusive. She's not afraid to do that for a picture. Well, maybe I shouldn't say she's not afraid, sometimes I think it's torture for her. But she does it. You know, sticking the camera in the face of a person whose house has just burned to the ground. She hates to do that but she believes what she does is important. Anyway, I could see how she could psych herself into going to see Markham."

"Did she go?"

"Yeah. But he told her he didn't have the pictures in the office. Said he'd send them to her."

"But he did have them there."

"That's not what he said."

"What did Anne think?"

"She said she thought he was giving her the bum's rush. He had the pictures but just didn't want to give them to her."

"If Anne thought the photos were there why didn't you look for them? I mean, especially if you thought she might have killed him. They weren't that hard to find. Why didn't you spend five minutes looking for them?"

"I freaked."

I was surprised by his abrupt reply and the show of anger. "You what?"

"I freaked, okay? I've got a real problem with dead people. I don't like being around them." The anger dissipated and when he spoke again it was in a quiet, almost apologetic tone. "Besides, I'd had a pizza for lunch and I was about five seconds away from losing it all over his desk."

He seemed to be waiting for me to give him some grief, but I didn't say anything. I've never taken the measure of a man by the way he reacts to a corpse.

Jeff thrust his hands in his pockets and looked away as he spoke. "I'd appreciate it if you wouldn't spread that around. It wouldn't exactly help my career as a crime reporter." Then he laughed a little and dismissed it with half a shrug.

I studied Jeff for a minute. He didn't look like he was lying, but I wasn't supposed to trust anyone.

"Why didn't you tell me any of this?" I was more hurt than angry.

"Why the hell should I have?" Jeff, recovering quickly from his humbling confession, was more angry than hurt. "I don't know you from Adam. You had the photos and you didn't turn them over to the cops. You gave me the ones of Anne, but how do I know you weren't just trying to get a reporter in your pocket?"

"What?"

"It happens. And you were sitting outside Markham's all afternoon. That sure puts you within striking distance."

"Why would I kill Markham?"

"How the hell would I know. Why would I kill him?"

We could have stood there for a long time, shooting accusations at each other. And it wasn't like either one of us was going to confess. There was an awkward silence before Jeff said, "Maybe we should go see Anne."

I nodded. "Good idea."

Jeff turned to open the truck's door. "Might as well take mine."

"No," I said. "Let me drive. I've got Peanuts with me."

As we walked across the lot to my car, Jeff muttered, "Maybe the dog did it."

"You really think Anne could have killed him?"

"Ah, hell, I don't know. When I saw him lying there, that was the first thing I thought of and well, Anne acted real bent out of shape. Said it was because of the pictures." He shook his head. "What am I saying? I know Anne. She couldn't kill anyone."

I pulled the car out onto the street and Jeff gave me directions to Anne's place.

"You know Anne pretty well, huh?"

"Sure. We've worked together for years."

"You know her interest in you is more than professional."

Silence. Then he laughed and said, "Yeah, sure."

I glanced at him. He was smiling and shaking his head. Neither of us spoke for about a mile. Then Jeff said, "You really think so?"

I sighed. Now I knew what my sister meant when she'd say "Men are so dense."

After a minute, Jeff said, "You know, we've got to be really careful with Anne. She's the kind of person who would have done well a century ago. You don't need much in the way of street smarts to survive in Foxport, but sometimes I think she's barely making it. Seriously."

As I turned onto Anne's street I wondered if Jeff was giving her enough credit, but I kept my mouth shut. However, Jeff apparently needed some feedback. "You know what I mean, don't you?"

I glanced at him, then back at the street. "Yeah. We leave the bamboo shoots in the car."

Anne lived with her mother and sister in an older section of Foxport. There were lots of trees and the streets were held together with veins of asphalt. Right off, she seemed nervous, but then there also seemed to be a calm under the surface that I hadn't noticed before. She wore jeans and a red blouse, which set off her dark hair and the color in her face. Mumbling something about her sister and mother going shopping, she led us into the living room. It was small but bright with lots of windows. The sparse furnishings were dwarfed by a grand piano in one corner of the room. Jeff and I sank into the couch as she perched on the edge of the piano's bench. I left Peanuts on the screened-in porch because, as Jeff had said, this was a cat house.

Then, as though she suddenly remembered she'd left the iron on, Anne leaped up. "Can I get either of you something to drink? Or eat?"

I declined her offer but Jeff asked for a Coke. I reconsidered and said that sounded good to me. Anne fled the room. Jeff and I exchanged looks but we didn't speak. Not at first anyway, but after about five minutes of flipping through magazines and watching a black cat clean itself, I said, "Was it a pepperoni pizza?"

"Yeah." One corner of his mouth moved up slightly and he added, "With extra cheese."

Before I could respond, Anne came back into the room. She carried a tray which held more than drinks. There was one plate lined with soda crackers next to a tub of spreadable cream cheese. Another plate was piled with sliced sausages. I turned to Jeff and smiled. He just swallowed.

Anne took her time setting the tray on the coffee table and placing our glasses in front of us. She gave us each a napkin and a small china plate with a busy pink design and chipped edges. Taking one of the sodas, she returned to the piano bench and reclaimed the same position, as if the center foot on the bench was its only habitable space. She didn't ask why we had come.

I don't have much use for a soda cracker unless it's crumbled into a bowl of cream of tomato soup, but I spread one with cream cheese and popped it into my mouth. All I could taste was the dryness and I washed it down with a couple swallows of the Coke.

I cleared my throat and smiled. "I've never been in this part of town. It's real nice."

Smiling in agreement, Anne said, "Yes. We like it very much."

The silence began to accumulate again and although I wasn't the reporter, it looked like I'd have to be the one to ask the questions. She had to know why we came. I cleared my throat and leaned forward. Both Anne and Jeff were watching me with more intensity than my actions merited. "Anne," I said and they seemed to move forward slightly. "How did you learn that Markham was dead?"

She glanced at Jeff, puzzled, before she said, "Jeff called me."

"When?"

Jeff started to say something, but stopped. Anne looked at him and he nodded to her. Turning back to me, she said, "Sunday night. Real late."

"What was your reaction?"

"To Scott's death?" She still didn't know where I was going with this. That made two of us.

I nodded and she shifted on the bench. "Well, I guess I was shocked. And scared."

"Because of the photos?"

Again, she seemed to receive some sort of sign from Jeff. "Yes, I was worried someone would find them."

"What else did you feel?"

"Shock. At first. I mean I didn't think he was the kind of

man to take his own life. But then when I started to think about it, I guess I never really knew him that well."

"Tell me about him."

"I guess he had two sides to him. One could be sensitive and charming. Funny almost. He could be very loving and supportive."

"What a prince," Jeff muttered. This time Anne shot him a look.

"What about the other side?"

"Moody. Very moody. Depressed really. I didn't like being around him then. And, I might as well not have been around then. He'd ignore me, everyone, when he got like that."

"What was he like the day you went to get the photos back?"

She gave Jeff a look that probably made him feel like a slug. He shifted uncomfortably and made a helpless gesture with his hands. "He saw me at Markham's office that Sunday. After you'd been there."

Her look of shock seemed genuine. "You were at Scott's office? Why?"

Raking his hand through tangled hair, Jeff wasn't just uncomfortable now, he was squirming. "It doesn't matter, Anne. It was about a story."

Now Anne looked confused. "I don't get it. What does your being there have to do with me?"

Jeff wasn't ready to lay that one on her, so to speed things along, I said, "Markham was dead when he got there."

"I see," said Anne, although from the expression on her face, it was obvious that she didn't. Not at first, anyway. But during a long count of ten, her look underwent a three step transformation, from confusion to understanding to disbelief. When she hit the third stage, she turned to Jeff. "You think I killed Scott?"

"I didn't say that."

"You didn't have to." She stood and approached Jeff, her arms crossed. "You didn't tell me you'd been to see Scott because when you got there, he was dead." Shaking her head, she finished with, "And you figured old Anne was so rattled she killed the guy."

Rising from the couch, Jeff confronted her. "Well, first you wanted me to go see him. Then, out of the blue, you call me and say no, 'I want to do this myself.' I thought it was a little weird, but I didn't think much of it until I got to Markham's office and found him with a hole drilled in his head." He shoved his hands in his pockets. This hunched his shoulders up and he reminded me of a kid taking a bawling out.

Anne's hands were at her sides now, fists clenched. "I'd think you'd give me the benefit of the doubt rather than assuming I was a murderer."

Eyes fixed on the floor, Jeff said, "I'm sorry."

"Anne," I said, and they both looked at me. "There've been a lot of accusations flying around today. Maybe we just need to pool what information we have and go from there."

They looked at each other, then separated; two boxers returning to their corners.

"Why did you go to Markham's office, instead of Jeff?"

She paused for a moment, then took a deep breath and looked at me when she said, "I was a long time getting over Scott Markham. Even though I was the one to end it. I suppose he knew he could get me back if he tried. He didn't. I thought if I went to get those photos, he'd see that he didn't have any power over me anymore. Not that he cared or anything."

"What happened?"

With a little shrug she said, "He told me he didn't think they were at his office. He said he'd send them to me."

"What did you say?"

"I guess I was worried about them coming to the house with my mom and all, so I kind of pushed it. I said, 'Are you sure you don't have them?' "

"What did he say?"

She looked at me and for a second I thought I saw some of the anger she must have felt. But she suppressed it. "He kind of snapped. He said something like, 'I'll get them for you, goddammit. Do you think I care about them anymore?' " She tried to smile but didn't quite make it.

No one spoke for a minute, then I said, "When you left his office, did you think the photos were there?"

After a few seconds of studying the grain in the wood floor, she said, "I guess I wasn't sure. He seemed distracted."

"The way he was acting. Was it sort of like 'maybe they are here, maybe they aren't. But I don't have time to look now'?"

"Yeah." She nodded slowly. "It was kind of like that."

"Have you ever seen this book?" I handed her Markham's
collection of photos. She took it and regarded the cover without opening it. "Yes. I have a copy. Scott gave it to me." Jeff
moved from the couch and looked at the book over Anne's
shoulder, careful not to venture into her space.

"The photo on page 52," I said.

Obediently, she turned to it and nodded in recognition.
"What about it?"

I gave her the photo of Susan Connors.

"Oh my God," Anne gasped.

Jeff took the photo from her. "Where did you get this?" He
paled a little and handed it back to Anne.

"Markham's office."

"You were holding out on me."

"Sue me," I said.

Anne placed the photo next to the one in the book and I
imagined she was comparing them, detail for detail. Without
looking up, she said, "Who took this one?"

"Like I said, I found it in Markham's office. I assume he
took it."

Her eyes widened as she looked to see if I was being straight
with her. "But are you sure this is his?"

"It was with the others. You know . . ." I started to explain,
but she wasn't listening anymore.

Shaking her head, she looked up at me, holding out the
photo of Susan Connors. "I don't think Scott took this one."
Then, as though I'd asked her to, she re-examined them. But
when she spoke again, it was with even more conviction. "I'm
sure of it. It's not his work."

189

CHAPTER TWENTY

Anne was on her knees at the coffee table where she had laid out the book with the photo next to it. She tapped her finger on the photo. "This one was taken by an amateur. Or at least not by Scott Markham. Notice the way not everything's in focus." Running her finger along the fuzzy lines of the bedside table and the pattern in the worn-looking rug, she added, "I don't think that's intentional either. Just sloppy. And the lighting. In the book it's very dramatic, but I know he didn't have any time to set it up. He just used what was there." She hesitated then said, "He was good at that. Working with very little, I mean. I saw a photo he shot of a man in a darkened auditorium. The only available light was the exit sign the guy was standing under." She shook her head the way people do when acknowledging something so impressive that words are inadequate. I was beginning to understand how Markham could have seemed the answer to this shy photographer's dreams.

I needed a cigarette, but there wasn't an ash tray in sight. "Is it all right if I smoke in here?"

Anne shook her head as though to clear it and murmured, "Sure, just a second." She pulled an ash tray out of a small, dark wood table next to the couch. I could hear Peanuts whining on the porch.

I lit a cigarette and said, "What if Markham were under a lot of pressure. Nervous. You know, like someone might be if he'd just murdered a woman or was thinking about it. Isn't it possible that his focus would be a little off? That he might not be so worried about shadows and lighting when taking a picture of a woman he had just killed."

Anne didn't answer right away. And when she did, she admitted the possibility only to dismiss it with a wave of her hand. "It's possible, but I can't see it happening." She drew her knees up to her chest and wrapped her arms around them.

"What part are you having trouble with? Scott forgetting to focus or Scott strangling a woman?"

"Both," she said without hesitation, then seemed to remember that the subject wasn't entirely about photography anymore. She looked at the floor and finished her thought without half the conviction she'd started with. "Well, I don't know. I mean, I never saw him violent, but, well, I guess he had a fascination with it. Still, that doesn't always mean anything."

I remembered what Ellie Carver had said about Markham's fixation with slow motion violence.

"He was fascinated with violence," Anne continued. "I mean, you can see that in his book. And he did like violent movies and all. You know, it's weird, but I really think he saw a beauty in it. Scott believed there was something both horrible and beautiful about an act of violence and he considered it a real challenge to capture that essence on film."

Jeff snorted in disgust and abruptly stood. He moved to the door, looking out onto the porch, hands thrust into his pockets. Anne was watching him with a scared look as though she'd said something unforgivable. But when he spoke, his disgust wasn't directed at her. "What a challenge. Capture the essence of death in all its glory. Make violence a thing to be admired, maybe replicated. Refine it, massage it enough and you've got a work of art." He turned back to Anne and me. "What bullshit. Dangerous bullshit. Someone who believes something like that's got the makings of a Charles Manson in him. If someone did kill him, maybe he—or she—did us all a big favor."

Anne seemed to have forgotten that Jeff once thought, and perhaps still thought, that she was a murderer. Her concern had shifted to making Jeff understand that she hadn't wasted her affections on a sick man. Either out of politeness or obligation, she tried to include me. "No. You don't understand. Really. It wasn't like he worshipped it. Not at all. It was like he understood it. I don't know, it's really hard to describe."

Jeff said, "No shit." I said, "Try."

"He believed that we can't change things. Ever. That we're

sort of doomed to play out our roles. Everyone is. And the most you can ever do is to understand.''

Jeff couldn't contain himself anymore and his bundles of nervous energy were forcing him to pace along a short, tight line. "Why are you defending this jerk? I'm really not impressed with people who use their own personal philosophy of life to defend every goddamned thing they do. I think you should only be allowed to take Philosophy 101 if you pass a psychological test first. And I suppose his taking bribes was something he just went ahead and did so he could understand it.''

Anne wasn't trying to convince me anymore. I wasn't even there. She was putting all her energies into convincing Jeff that Markham was a decent human being. And I sure couldn't figure that one out. "You didn't know him. He was so committed.''

"Committed to what? His profession? Hardly. His marriage? That's a laugh. His community? Apparently the only reason he was pushing for a park west of town was so nobody'd disturb Susan Connors' grave. Seems like the only thing he was committed to was himself.''

Anne was becoming flushed and frazzled. Jeff was clenched and determined. Anne took a couple deep breaths and said, "He was betrayed by his profession and his marriage. And as far as that woman they dug up, I don't believe, not for a second, that Scott did it.''

Jeff shifted his weight to his left hip and crossed his arms. "Okay, I'll bite. How was he betrayed by his profession and his wife?''

"I don't believe that Scott ever wanted to take those bribes. I think he was coerced into it.'' Shaking her head, she added, "Don't ask me why. It's just a feeling. And as far as Lorna goes,'' she delivered the line looking at me, "she didn't deserve him.''

Jeff was the first to respond. "And every other woman in Foxport did? What made her different?''

Anne looked away, confused. "I don't know. I'm not sure he knew. He hated the way she treated Eric. He felt like she was in competition with Eric for Scott's affection.''

"Maybe that was true,'' I said.

Anne looked away and Jeff stepped toward her. For a second

I thought she was going to back up to maintain the distance between them, but she held her ground. Jeff said, "Why are you defending this guy? I still don't get it."

"Because it wasn't all bad. Yeah, I fell for his line but maybe I'm not as stupid as you think. He made me feel really special. And maybe I deserve to." Her voice dropped and she finished on the defensive. "Just because it ended up bad doesn't mean something good can't come from it."

Jeff looked at her for a long time.

Before any of us could get the discussion going again, two car doors slammed, one right after the other. Peanuts barked. Anne's family was home.

"Will you come down to the police station with me and tell Carver what you just told me about this picture?"

Nervously she looked from me to Jeff then back again. In a small voice, she said, "Yeah. I guess so." Then her eyes went wide as she heard her mother and sister on the porch. "Tomorrow."

What Carver didn't know wouldn't hurt him for a few more hours.

"Morning?" I said and she nodded.

When I drove Jeff back to his truck, he spent the first mile or so staring out at the passing scenery and tapping a rhythm on his leg. Abruptly he stopped and looked at me. "You're still not convinced she didn't do it, are you?"

"Are you?"

Instead of answering, he said, "Are you convinced I didn't kill him?"

"Yeah," I said and added, "no offense or anything, but I don't think you've got the stomach for it."

I owed Peanuts a long walk and he wasn't going to let me squirm out of it. When we got home, we went straight down to the river. We made our way south along the bank.

It was late afternoon, but there were still people picking off the end of a cool, clear, spring day. And geese. God were there geese. In late March, Foxport must be to the geese population what Ft. Lauderdale is to the college crowd. And Peanuts had taken it upon himself to make some order out of the chaos. He hunkered down in the grass about twenty feet from a flock of the noisy creatures and studied them.

As beautiful and graceful as Canada geese are, they can be downright unpleasant when they feel like it. Not so different from people, I guess. And a few of them were watching Peanuts with growing suspicion. Word spread through the flock and soon they were all aware of this black and white dog giving them the eye. One of the ganders spread his wings and came at Peanuts, hissing, but he backed off when the dog didn't budge. Then Peanuts began to move, low to the ground, around the flock until he had them all heading upriver as one unit.

Confident that he had them under control, Peanuts glanced at me as if asking, "Where do you want 'em, Quint?"

I figured this was a good time to end the game. I called to him and he hesitated, then turned and with only one backward glance, trotted over to me. I wasn't sure, but he seemed to be relieved.

I was so busy admiring my dog that I didn't see her approaching us.

"That's quite a dog you have there."

I looked up and saw Lorna Markham standing about ten feet from us at the end of the yard that connected Louise's house to the river.

"Yeah, he is," I agreed and walked up to her. Peanuts followed.

"Does he do that with any group of ten or more?"

We began walking toward the house. "It's instinct," I explained. "I was reading that they'll even try to herd cars and children."

"Children," she echoed, then smiled. "We need more dogs like that."

"How's Eric?"

"I wouldn't know. I imagine he's still with his uncle Mason, but that's just an educated guess. I haven't heard one word from the kid since I sent him packing."

As we climbed the stairs to my apartment, she said, "When are you going to get an office like a regular detective? I feel like I'm party to a tryst every time I have a meeting with you." What could I say? She added, "Maybe once you prove that Scott was murdered, you'll have enough mad money to set yourself up in a nice little place in town."

That offended me, but only a little. It was true. The last time I'd thought about the fifty grand I'd figured I owed myself a shingle.

Lorna took in my new apartment. "I like this. It's more you than that other place."

I asked her if she wanted a drink and it occurred to me that that would be one of the nice things about having a real office. I wouldn't be obliged to make people feel at home. She sat on the couch and rubbed Peanuts' head. He really liked her. I wasn't sure if I did. But she was a client, it wasn't necessary for us to click. She refused the drink, but I remembered the last time she'd been at my place. She'd refused it then too, only to take me up on it when things started to get tense.

"What can you tell me about Scott's death?"

I told her everything without naming unnecessary names. She was familiar with Markham's book and when I handed her the photo, I asked her if she thought it was Scott's work. She studied it dispassionately and dropped it to the coffee table, apparently unmoved. "It could be his work. I don't know photography that well."

"Do you believe your husband was capable of that?"

"Maybe, I don't know," she said. Then she stood and moved over to the window. Lorna Markham was normally a tightly wound person. But standing there, arms folded in front of her, holding on to herself as if she were afraid of letting go, she seemed even more tense than usual. I kept talking. I told her about the connection I believed there was to Janet's death and went on about the likelihood that Janet's and Markham's killers were the same person.

It had been so long since she'd spoken that I was a little startled when she turned and said, "Don't you understand. I don't care about that woman. And you shouldn't either. I'm not paying you to find out who killed Janet Miraldi. You're working for me and I'm paying you to find out who killed Scott Markham."

Right then I decided that I didn't care much for Lorna or for anyone who would consider Scott Markham's death more important than Janet's. But when I said, "You're wrong. I'm not working for you anymore," I realized immediately that I might have been a bit hasty. Just to dig myself in deeper, I added, "You figure out who killed Scott Markham. You keep the fifty grand."

"Are you crazy?" She stopped short and apparently did a more thorough reading of my mind than I had thought her capable of. She continued with an annoying little smile, "You and that lovely State's Attorney. You're doing this out of devotion to that woman, aren't you? Well, there are a lot of men out there thinking with their crotches instead of their heads because of that woman.''

Since I'd already tossed my fee back in her face, I figured I had nothing to lose. ''You know, everyone is real fond of telling me that Janet was involved with Markham, but nobody will give me the name of their source. I'd sure like to hear it.''

''There are probably a lot of people singing that tune, but I heard it from Mason Burke.''

''And you believed him?''

''Why shouldn't I? If Scott didn't have a thing going with the good State's Attorney, she was the only attractive, available woman he missed. I don't know how that would have happened.''

I wanted to hit her. Not with an open hand either. I grabbed my clenched fist with my other hand and took a couple deep breaths, trying to figure the fastest way to get her out of my apartment.

Then she was sitting on the couch across from me, leaning forward, elbows on her knees. ''I'm sorry,'' she said. In less time than it takes to turn off a radio, Lorna had gone from malicious to contrite. If it was an act, it was a good one. She buried her face in her hands and heaved a deep sigh. I relaxed and waited. When she'd collected herself, she said, ''That was uncalled for. Just because my life's turning to shit doesn't mean I can become a shrew.''

I offered her some scotch and she accepted. I poured myself one too.

She didn't speak again until she'd taken a couple sips. ''I've put the house on the market.'' She turned away and said, more to herself than to me, ''I just hope I don't have to sell so fast I don't get what it's worth.''

''How much money did Scott take?''

''About four hundred and fifty thousand.'' Pausing, she shook her head. ''What could he have done with it?''

''Was it possible that he was being blackmailed?''

She seemed genuinely surprised by my question. ''I can't imagine. I mean he had been indicted for bribery. What more could there be?''

''What if he had killed Susan Connors and someone knew about it?''

She drank some more scotch and scratched Peanuts' head. ''I don't think he did.'' She stopped attending to Peanuts and he nuz-

196

zled her hand. Ignoring him, she continued, "Oh, hell, what do I know? Sometimes I think if I learned that field was studded with corpses, I wouldn't be shocked."

"Is Eric Scott's son?"

My question didn't generate anywhere near the reaction I'd thought it would. Without missing more than half a beat, she said, "Where'd you hear that?"

"I don't actually know it for a fact, but something Mason Burke said . . . I don't recall exactly what . . . something about deception and desperation . . . made me wonder."

"That bastard," she said under her breath.

She seemed to wrestle for a time with an internal decision, then she heaved a resigned sigh and began. "Scott wanted a child more than anything else in the world. And I say that unequivocally. We tried. Nothing. After three years of trying, we went through the usual tests and it was then that we found out it was Scott's problem. Very low sperm count. We were told I could get pregnant but it was highly unlikely. That was when I started to lose him. I could see it happening. I think he stopped caring. About everything. I had to do something," she focused her eyes on mine and held my gaze, "so I got pregnant." She looked away. "Brilliant. I chose a young man who resembled Scott, who was intelligent, and who had generally admirable qualities. At least I thought so at the time."

I interrupted. "Did he understand his purpose?"

"No. He thought he was just getting lucky. Of course, I let Scott think the child was his and of course he wanted to believe it so badly, that was easy."

"What happened?"

A smile came to her face slowly and it was a bitter one. She leaned back with her drink and crossed one leg over the other. "Of all the horny law students in the world, I had to pick one destined to become Mason Burke's brother-in-law."

She nodded as it all clicked for me. "Mary Lord Burke's brother. Apparently he wasn't as bright as I'd hoped." Smiling at her own expense, she added, "I guess that shows in the offspring."

"So Mason knew?"

"Oh, yes. Well, after he and his brother-in-law shared secrets, he suspected." She stopped then and was silent for a minute before she said, "He didn't tell Scott until just recently. Mason had this thing hanging over my head. He knew that I knew that he knew." She smiled. "You know what I mean. But he never told Scott until just a couple months ago. I don't know whether Scott believed him at first, but we had blood tests run and the rest, as they say, is history."

I lit a cigarette and smoked part of it before I said, "Why didn't you tell me this before?"

"It wasn't exactly one of my finer moments."

"It would have helped to know."

"Why?"

"Maybe that's what pushed him over the edge."

She looked at me and didn't respond.

"Did Eric know?"

"I didn't tell him. I don't think he knew." Then she looked at me, long and hard. She needed me, but it was important to her that she not be required to descend a rung in order to keep me. "I still don't think he killed himself." She sounded tired and not at all certain of that, but she added, "Are you still working for me?"

I still wasn't sure whether I liked Lorna Markham, but maybe I was beginning to understand her. And I was also beginning to allow that perhaps she was motivated by something more than a million bucks. "Yeah, sure," I said.

She nodded and drank from her glass, the ice cubes giving up the last of their liquid.

∇

CHAPTER TWENTY-ONE

Just when I think my body's about to fail me, it comes through. The aches and pains were still there when I got up the next day, but they seemed to be receding. What made me sick that Monday morning was thinking about what Carver would do to me once he found out about the photo of Susan Connors.

On the way over to the police station, Anne suggested telling Carver that she had found the photo in Markham's desk that last day. "Or maybe I could tell him that he gave me my pictures back then and this one happened to be among them."

I was touched by her offer and ashamed of how seriously I considered it.

Now Carver sat, stone faced, staring at the photo of Susan Connors as Anne explained the discrepancies between this and Markham's work. Once again, she came across as though she really knew what she was talking about, and once again as soon as the subject turned from photography she rolled up mentally into her little ball.

"So, what are you saying?" Carver held up the photo and Anne stared at him wide-eyed.

I tried to help, "She's saying that . . ."

"I didn't ask you," Carver shut me down. When I'd explained how I'd found the photo with the others, he hadn't reacted. When you can't read a man like Carver, you might as well assume that you're in serious trouble. No sense underestimating the situation.

Anne cleared her throat and pulled at the cuffs of her blouse. "I don't believe he took that photograph."

"You can say unequivocally that Scott Markham had nothing to do with this," Carver pressed her.

In a small but clear voice, Anne said, "He didn't take that picture. I don't know whether he had anything to do with it."

He turned back to the photo and muttered, "Wish I could be that certain about something." Then he leaned back in his chair and studied Anne for a minute. Finally he said, "How do you know so much about Markham's skill as a photographer?"

She lifted her chin a notch and said, "I learned a lot about photography from Scott Markham. We were lovers."

Carver looked at me and I confirmed what she'd said with a nod. He shook his head and dropped the photo onto his desk as though dismissing it. "We don't even know if she's dead here."

"Maybe we could enlarge it enough so we can tell if the pupils are dilated?" I suggested.

Both Carver and I looked at Anne. I was sorry to see that she was shaking her head. "I don't think you can get a clear enough photo. You'd have to take a picture of this one," she nodded at the three-by-five on Carver's desk, "then using that negative, enlarge it. I think it would be too grainy by the time you got it large enough to see the pupils of her eyes." She slumped in the chair. "I'm not saying you shouldn't try it. I just don't think . . ." her voice trailed off and she avoided Carver's stare. I wanted to tell him to lighten up with her, but I didn't.

Carver sighed and rubbed his face with his hands. He looked tired and I wondered if he'd seen John Dieken the night before. "We've got a lot of ifs here. If Markham didn't take the photo, then someone else did. If she's dead in that photo then whoever took it probably killed her."

"That's the way I see it." Carver's look implied that he could continue without my prompting.

"Whoever killed her planted the photo in Markham's office after he killed Markham."

"He or she," I corrected. Sometimes my mouth runs away on me.

Carver looked at me, his smile oozing with sarcasm. He gave me a moment to appreciate it before he said, "Who do you have in mind?"

I shrugged. "No one. You want me to do all your work for you?"

The smile faded and with some effort he put on a more neutral expression and turned to Anne. "I appreciate your coming forward, Miss Phillips. I don't suppose it was easy for you. The fact is, I'm not sure how we can use this photo. Testimony regarding where this was found is, at best," he glanced at me, "questionable. This was probably taken right after she was killed, but we can't prove that. I mean, maybe she was into some weird stuff." He looked thoughtfully at Markham's book of photography, then shook his head. He turned back to Anne. "And I hate to put it this way, but your saying this isn't his work just might not hold up in court."

His manner was starting to irritate me. "So why did I bother bringing this to you?"

"Why did you bother stealing it in the first place?"

Touché.

He lifted the photo off his desk. "What if he did kill her? They were about to dig up the spot where he buried her body. There's your motive for suicide."

"I don't know," I said. "Coincidences really bother me. A couple days before they unearth Connors, Markham kills himself, leaving behind a photo of the woman they're about to find. And the police were supposed to find it. Not me. Sounds awfully neat."

Carver shook his head and said to Anne, "Why don't you wait outside for a minute. McCauley and I need to talk."

She nodded and, with a concerned glance at me, got up. Before she was out the door, Carver said, "And thanks."

There was silence in the office for a few seconds after she closed the door. I took the time to decide that if he wanted to arrest me for godknowswhat, he'd have to change the subject to do it. "Was it John Dieken? Did he have Ellie's photo?"

From the look on Carver's face, I figured this wasn't the way he had planned for the conversation to go. But he went with my lead. "Yeah. The man cracked after a couple well placed . . ." he paused and finished with "questions."

"He say where he got the photo?"

"Oh, yes. It was given to him."

"Yeah? Who?"

"God."

That made sense. It really did. I gestured toward the ceiling. "I suppose *He* told Dieken to use it to blackmail you."

"Something like that."

"When did God make the delivery?"

"Sunday night. Dieken found it when he got home. It was stuffed in his mailbox."

"A note?"

Carver shook his head. "God doesn't write notes."

I nodded. "I suppose not."

"The thing is," Carver said after a moment.

"What?"

"He really believes it."

A thought, or more likely a hope occurred to me. "Think maybe Dieken killed him?"

Carver shook his head. "I doubt it."

"He had the photo."

"You have some too, you know."

I leaned forward. "If nothing else, doesn't this prove to you that Markham didn't kill himself? Whoever killed him sent that photo of Ellie to John Dieken. Unless I'm missing something. I can't think of any reason Dieken would want Markham dead. But if he were to die, he'd sure want the death certificate to read suicide. Maybe whoever did kill him was using Dieken as his own insurance. Dieken knows Lorna's going to make a stink about it. Why not have the cop who's heading the investigation on his side?" Carver didn't respond so I continued with a final push. "He gets the photo Sunday night. That same night, Markham's death is on the radio. On the radio they say it appears to be suicide but the police haven't ruled out foul play. He spends all night praying that Markham offed himself and by morning God has convinced him that he'd better nip this thing in the bud. If they don't wrap a suicide up fast, more questions start to come up."

Sighing, Carver said, "You're not telling me anything I haven't thought of already."

"Well?"

"Well, what? Just what in the hell am I supposed to do with evidence I get more than a week after we're supposed to have it? What am I supposed to do with a picture of my wife that's been used to blackmail me? A picture I had to work some holier-than-thou asshole over to get? What in the hell do you want me to do?"

I smiled and folded my arms across my chest. "Would you consider backing my investigation?"

Now it was Carver's turn to gaze up at the ceiling.

The intercom clicked on. "Who's there?"

Desperate men take desperate measures. Wanda Buchholz was my last link to Robyn. "It's Roger Kafka. I came by last week looking at apartments."

She was quick to respond. "Don't give me that Roger Kafka line. I know who you are, mister."

"Oh? Then who am I?" How could she know?

Pause. "Well, I don't know your name, but you're some private detective type. I know your kind. Snooping around in other people's business. Why don't you get a real job? A respectable one."

"I need to talk to you, Wanda. It's really important."

"You'd better leave or I'll call the cops. I mean it."

"Have you seen Robyn Fosse?"

"You stay away from that poor girl."

I love conversing with someone over an intercom. "I just need a few minutes of your time, Wanda."

Silence.

"Wanda?"

More silence.

I consulted my wallet. "I'll give you thirty dollars for three minutes."

Click. "What?"

"Thirty dollars. I need three minutes."

No response. I went back into the wallet. "Fifty dollars. That's all I've got."

Buzz. I had gained entry.

When I got to Wanda's apartment, the door was cracked just enough to poke her arm through. I started to hand her the money. "Three minutes," she said. "That's all you get."

I jerked my hand back. "Fifty dollars. I get five minutes."

I could see one heavily shadowed eye through the door. It was wrinkled and untrusting. "All right." I gave her the money and she opened the door just enough to poke her head out. About two and a half feet below her face, a pointed black nose thrust its way through a space between Wanda's leg and the doorway.

"Hello Fiscus."

"You wanna talk to me or the dog?"

I smiled at Wanda. "It's very important that I talk to Robyn. Can you tell me where she is?"

She eyed me up and down. "How would I know where Robyn is?"

"Well, I just figured since you live across the hall from her and she seemed to like you, you know, trusted you maybe, I figured . . ." I let the sentence drift off.

"Yeah, well you figured wrong. The clock's running, mister." Before I could come up with another insightful question, she asked, "Why do you need to see her?"

"It's my fifty bucks. I get to ask the questions." I paused, half expecting her to slam the door in my face. The fact that she didn't encouraged me. I tried a simple bluff. "She might as well talk to me. The police are going to be here soon and they'll be even more insistent on finding her and talking to her."

Her hesitation made me believe the bluff had worked, at least partially. She pulled her head out of the door, started to look back into the apartment, thought better of it and said to me, "Well, I don't know if I can help. But I just might run into her, you know, I think she's moved, but I'm holding onto a few things for her."

"Then you know where she is."

Wanda studied me for a minute then said, "I don't know where she is. Maybe she's just out of town."

"When's the last time you saw her?"

"Uh, I think it was Wednesday."

"Where'd she go?"

"She said something about going away for a long weekend."

"Where?"

"I think it might have been Galena or some place like that."

"Without her car?"

Wanda faltered briefly then recovered. She drew herself up and raised her chin. She must have been at least five feet three inches. "Well, Mr. Smartypants, it ain't as suspicious as it looks. She went with a friend."

"Did she say who?"

"No, she didn't say who," Wanda snapped. "Now I don't know who you're trying to make a liar out of—Robyn or me—but I don't have to stand here and listen to this."

In an effort to keep Fiscus in her apartment, Wanda had wedged his neck against the door's molding with her leg. I glanced at him and he looked extremely uncomfortable. "Can he breathe?" I asked.

She looked down at the struggling animal, then realizing that he was in a bad way, made an alarmed noise and jumped back, releasing her hold on him and pushing the door open. In the microsecond before Fiscus came barreling at me, I saw a flicker of someone in Wanda's apartment. Then Fiscus pinned me to the wall. He was a big dog and I could feel and smell his hot breath on my face. Before he could figure out what to do next—he'd probably never actually pinned his quarry—Wanda gripped his red bandanna and hauled him off me.

"Shame on you, Fiscus." She was simultaneously scolding the dog and petting him. No wonder he was maladjusted.

She turned to me and said, "You must forgive Fiscus, he's very protective. If you were to come into my apartment, he would accept you as a guest and wouldn't bother you."

"Oh, then can I take that as an invitation?"

Her mouth dropped open. "That wasn't any invitation."

She hesitated and I added, "It would be a shame to find Fiscus' name on the dangerous animal list down at the police station. I can do that, you know."

"You wouldn't." She was sputtering.

"I can and I would." I was reduced to bullying Wanda and Fiscus Buchholz and I wasn't proud of it.

Wanda gaped at me, praying, no doubt, for a well-placed bolt of lightning.

"That's all right, Wanda." Robyn Fosse stepped from behind the door. "I'll give him the rest of the five minutes."

Wanda looked from Robyn to me, then back to Robyn. "It's time for Fiscus' walk."

We watched her cross to the kitchen and collect a red leather leash, and attach it to a chain collar concealed beneath the dog's bandanna. Before walking out the door she said to Robyn, "I'd leave the door open if I were you."

Robyn's smile was genuinely fond as she watched the woman and her dog go down the stairs, but when she turned to me, not a trace of softness remained. She stood, with her arms crossed and when she spoke her voice was even. "I don't have to talk to you and I don't have to talk to the police. And don't you dare threaten Wanda."

"Why are you hiding?"

She stepped into the living room but left the door open. In a short-sleeved pink sweater and a cotton flowered skirt and sandals, she didn't look like she was ready to leave town. From the way she nervously paced the room, I guessed she'd been cooped up here for several days. She kept giving me these quick, angry glances, and it seemed she didn't really want to talk to me. But she must have really wanted to talk to someone for finally she stopped her pacing and, standing right in front of me said, "I'm hiding because I don't trust anyone in this miserable town. And why should I?" She turned and took a glass from a kitchen cupboard and put it on a two-seater table in the kitchen. I moved over for a better look. It was half filled with water and in the bottom was what appeared to be a small listening device. Better known as a bug. "God knows how many more of those are in my apartment."

I looked at her. "Where'd you find this?"

Her eyes narrowed. "As if you didn't know. I suppose you're going to tell me you didn't put it underneath my table when you were apartment hunting last week."

"Would you believe me?"

Her glare faltered and she sank into a chair at the table. "I don't know. There haven't been many people in my apartment since I've moved in."

"Maybe someone broke in."

She turned away and I continued. "Do you have any idea how long it's been there?"

"I have no idea. I found it as I was packing to move."

I sat across from her. "Look, I can understand your thinking it might be me. I assume you know what I was doing there." From the look she shot me, I knew I was right on that one. "But realistically, why would I? And when could I have done it? You were in the room with me the whole time."

She heaved a deep sigh and shook her head. She wasn't ready to concede the point but she'd run out of arguments. I leaned on the table and tried to draw her out of her anger enough to communicate with me. "I don't think he committed suicide either."

She turned to me slowly. "What makes you think I think it wasn't suicide?"

"Isn't that what you told Janet Miraldi?"

She swallowed and looked at the glass of water. "Janet Miraldi had something I wanted. I told her what she wanted to hear."

I decided to wait to process that bit of data. "Why would Scott Markham leave your apartment and go to his office and blow his brains out?"

She suppressed a shudder and, still staring at the glass said, "It was something I told him. What it was is none of your business."

I nodded and leaned further onto the table. "He killed himself because you upset him?"

The glare came back. "It wasn't just that. There was a lot going on in his life. That was just the last straw."

"What about the blackmail? Was that true?"

She looked toward the door and allowed herself a few moments. Her tone was calmer when she spoke again and it was as though she were explaining something to a slow learner. "I only know that he was being blackmailed. That's all. I don't know how much or for how long."

"Why'd he bother to tell you?"

She got up and poured herself a small glass of soda. She didn't offer me any. When she returned to the table she said, "We shared a lot. He felt I should know but he didn't want me involved. To tell me the details would involve me." She hesitated. "That's what he told me."

I leaned back and looked at the glass of water with the bug and thought about Janet. How far would she go to get a conviction on Markham? Then because I didn't want to believe she'd resort to this, I managed to think of someone else who had a vested interest. "You know Knox Ferris, don't you?"

"That bastard," she said and meant it. "I've got him to thank for ruining Scott."

"From what I hear, you've also got him to thank for introducing the two of you."

Her laugh was bitter. "Yes, that's true. Ironic isn't it?"

"What can you tell me about him?"

She shrugged, "He dated Susan. That's all."

"Was he ever in your apartment?"

She gave me an odd look. "Yes, once. Right after Susan disappeared. He was asking me questions about where I thought she might be. He was real upset."

"Was he ever alone with your dining room table?"

"How would I remember that? It was a year ago."

"Just think for a minute."

She looked away, disgusted with me but giving my request some thought in spite of herself. Then, slowly, she nodded and said, "Yes. I think he was." Turning to me, she paused in mid thought then said, "I think he asked if I had a picture of Susan. I keep photos and things like that in my bedroom. So, yes, I suppose he was alone for a minute or two."

Neither of us spoke for a minute. Finally Robyn asked, "Why would the case be so important to him that he would plant a bug?"

"That's a good question." Knox had not seemed overly ambitious and I couldn't imagine any other reason for the stakes to be so high for him. "You sure there's nothing you can tell me about him?"

Lifting her shoulders in a shrug, Robyn said, "I hardly knew him." After a moment she added, "Susan sure liked him."

"Enough to help him get the goods on Markham?"

"No way." Her response was immediate and assured. "She worshipped Scott. Considered him her mentor."

"Do you think she might have been jealous of your relationship with Markham?"

"I don't think so." From the tenuous way she spoke, I assumed she had already considered this and hadn't fully convinced herself. But she continued, "You see, at the time Susan disappeared, Scott and I had just started seeing each other. I don't think she even knew."

"What if she did? Just suppose. Would that have been reason enough for her to help the State's Attorney's office?"

She didn't answer for a minute. Then, as if she'd come to the decision she was going to stick with, she shook her head. "No. I honestly don't think she would have. I don't think she ever looked at Scott as anything but a mentor. And she'd been with him a long time. She worked for him through law school, college too I think."

"Was she working for Markham when he shot that guy in self-defense.

She gave me an odd look. "No, she wasn't. But why are you asking about that?"

"I'm not the first?"

"Janet Miraldi asked me if I knew anything about the incident."

"Janet? Do you?"

"I'll tell you the same thing I told her. I asked Scott about it once. He just said it was an awful tragedy and he didn't want to talk about it. Then he was real moody the rest of the afternoon. I never mentioned it again."

Just then a black creature bounded into the room, shot me a nervous glance and licked Robyn's extended hand. From the doorway came a raspy voice: "Is that awful man still here?"

Wanda and Fiscus were back.

Chapter Twenty-Two

I HAD BEEN at the doors of the Foxport Library when they opened at nine o'clock. It was two and a half hours later now and I was driving north of town to an area of Foxport I'd never seen. I proceeded with the caution of a man who thought he was onto something big but was afraid to dwell on it because it could just as easily be nothing.

The newspaper accounts of the shooting incident between Scott Markham and Michael Tyler were on microfilm, and since the library carried both the *Chicago Tribune* and the *Foxport Chronicle,* I had two sources to compare. It had all taken place within a two-week period during a particularly hot June almost ten years ago. A local businessman, Howard Fisher, had been charged with driving under the influence. Apparently it wasn't his first arrest. He had plowed into a mailbox while weaving his way home one Friday morning at one o'clock. He was defended by my buddy, Mason Burke. Scott Markham had been the judge on the case. Fisher received a fine for his action and had to pay the Postal Service to replace its mailbox. No suspension of his license. No time to be served in jail or in some kind of community program. But that was ten years ago. Back then people still thought drunks were funny.

Fisher went out the next day and bought himself a new Cadillac to replace the one he'd wasted. Two days later after a multi-martini business lunch, Fisher got his directions confused, turned down the wrong road and before he found his way out, swerved to miss a pothole and struck and killed Melissa Tyler, age three, who had been playing near, but not in, the street. That was Fisher's final offense. After hitting the child, according to witnesses, his car went out of control, shot across the road and into a gully. Fisher was thrown from the car and, without the ton and a half of metal to protect him, died of injuries sustained when he wrapped himself around a tree. No one mourned the loss of Fisher, but the child's death was a tragedy made all the worse by the fact that she'd been killed by a jerk who had no right to be driving a car. And apparently the child's father, Michael, took it upon himself to even the score.

I imagine he would have started with Fisher if he'd been alive. But he wasn't, so Tyler went after the judge who had let Fisher off with a slap on his wrist. Tyler drew a gun on Markham in his chambers and Markham shot him with the .25 he kept in his desk. I wondered if ten years later Markham had died by the same weapon. Although there had been no eye witnesses, it was clearly a case of self defense and charges were never filed against Markham. It just went down as a senseless tragedy.

The *Chronicle* had painted an interesting profile of the Tyler family—tight knit and well liked. As I looked at the family's photo I wondered what had become of Karen Tyler and whether she could add anything to the newspapers' account. When I found that she wasn't listed in the phone book, I reasoned that she might have gone back to her maiden name.

My next stop had been the clerk's office where I'd learned that Karen and Michael hadn't been married in this area—so there was no marriage license, but Melissa had been born here and there was a birth certificate, which included her mother's maiden name. But it wasn't her mother's name that piqued my interest; it was Melissa's middle name: Knox. Knox is an unusual name: as a girl's name it's practically unheard of. And since I had run out of leads, I couldn't afford to call this coincidence. I figured my best source was still Karen Tyler, wherever she was. But she wasn't listed in the phone book under her maiden name either. So that was why I was turning down this lousy little road. Maybe one of her former neighbors could tell me where she'd gone.

As I drove the road where Melissa K. Tyler had died, I realized that not everyone in Foxport enjoyed the good life. The houses here were small and the lawns scraggly. Occasionally I'd pass a house painted an outrageous shade of blue or green. One out of every three driveways contained a rusted-out car perched on cinder blocks. There were no sidewalks and the yards ended in gravel as they met the street.

I tried the houses on either side of the Tylers' former residence, figuring a neighbor might know where Karen had gone. No such luck. At one place no one was home, and at the other the woman was convinced I was selling something, and I didn't have the chance to state my case before being ordered off her property. Then I tried the place where the Tylers had lived and had better luck.

The woman who answered the door was young, early twenties maybe. Two toddlers were hanging on her and I heard the cries of an infant coming from another room. While the noise was piercing to me, she didn't seem to notice it. If given the chance, she might have been pretty. She was small-boned with nice features, but her hair was dry and a harsh shade of blonde and her eyes looked tired and defeated. She had a nice smile, and when she couldn't answer my question, she shook her head regretfully. "I'm sorry. I think there were a couple families living here since she left." She gestured outside. "Most of the people living around here rent. I really don't know who could help you." She caught her breath as an idea came to her. "Oh wait." She stepped outside, dragging one of the children with her. Directing me west, she said, "About four houses down there's an old man named Luther. He's been here forever and seems to know everything that's going on. You might try him."

I thanked her, grateful for her advice and for the sweet silence when she closed the door behind her.

Luther was sitting on his porch and as I approached him, I realized he'd probably been watching me since I stopped on this road. And I knew that if this man couldn't help me, no one here could. He smiled and nodded as though he'd been expecting me. And I guess he had.

With some effort, he leaned forward in his big rocker and switched off a small black and white TV. Then he motioned for me to sit in one of two other chairs on the porch. I did, realizing that while I might pick up some valuable information from this man, I would not pick it up quickly. Luther looked to be in his seventies. His face was weathered and deep lines fanned out from the corners of his eyes. His gray hair was a bristle against his scalp, and even though it was turning into an unseasonably warm day, he wore a blue flannel shirt open over his Cubs t-shirt.

"So, what can I do for you?" he said as if all roads led to Luther's porch.

I told him I was trying to find Karen Tyler.

He studied me, nodding to himself. "You a cop?"

"No. I'm a private investigator," I said, then added, "licensed."

He nodded again and looked away as he began talking. "Nice couple, the Tylers. And that poor little Missy." He turned back to me. "I saw it, you know."

After a few seconds, I said, "Can you tell me about it?"

"Awful thing. That little Missy Tyler didn't have a chance. Don't think she knew what hit her either." He paused and chewed on that for a second. "Suppose that's a blessing. Anyway that drunk's car goes flying across the road and down into that ravine." I followed his gesture as he pointed toward a spot off the road about a block away, right in front of the house that had been the Tylers. I noticed there was a guard rail. "They put that rail up right after the accident. I'm glad it wasn't there when that son of a bitch came through here. Might a' saved his life." I glanced at Luther and saw that he'd meant that. "Man like that's got no right being alive. Especially not after he killed Missy.

"And I'll tell you. You won't find anyone on this street who was here when it happened that was sorry to hear that judge blew his brains out."

A gray tabby jumped up on the old man's lap and rubbed its head against his chest. He stroked the animal with a big, gnarled hand. I waited. Then he turned to me and his smile seemed self conscious. "What were you asking me first?"

"I'm looking for Karen Tyler. You know where I can find her?"

"Ah, let's see. Where did Karen go after that?" The cat jumped down and Luther rubbed his jaw. After a minute he said, "Seems to me she went to live with her sister in Wheaton for a while. And let's see, what was her sister's married name? Something like Porter, no that's not it, let's see, maybe it was Potter. Potter. I think so. Yeah, that's it, Potter."

Thirty minutes later I was back in my apartment dialing the three Potters listed in Wheaton. This was one of my least favorite things about being a detective. Calling strangers and being a nuisance. Fortunately Karen's brother-in-law's name was Allen.

"Why do you want to talk to Karen?" her sister asked.

"It's regarding the Scott Markham suicide. He was . . ."

"Yes, I know who he was," she cut me off. "I'm not sure Karen would want to talk to you about that."

She didn't rush me off the line so I said, "I understand. Tell you what. Can you reach her now?"

She hesitated. "I think so."

"Okay. What if I give you my number? You call Karen and ask her to call me."

No response. I added, "If I don't hear from her, I'll assume she wasn't interested in talking to me. I won't bother you again." I had my fingers crossed.

After a few seconds she said, "All right. I guess Karen can make up her own mind."

I unpacked the rest of my belongings and got a load of clothes together to take to the laundromat. When I'd first rented the place, Louise had mentioned something about letting me use her washer and dryer, but she hadn't brought it up since then. I'd already tested her good nature quite a bit, so I wasn't going to be the one to mention it again. Maybe I'd wait until she was out working in her garden so she'd see me haul the load of laundry out to my car. Next I checked the state of my finances, which was depressing but didn't take any time at all. My down payment from Lorna was just about gone. I briefly wondered if I'd still be eligible for the fifty grand if I confessed to murdering Scott Markham.

I managed to kill an hour and a half with weird notions like that and finally conceded that Karen had decided to ignore me. I made myself a sandwich and was chewing my first bite when the phone rang. I washed it down with some milk, crossed my fingers and answered the phone.

"Hello. This is Karen, uh, I used to be Karen Tyler." Before I could say anything she continued. "Who am I talking to?"

I told her my name and said I was a licensed P.I. "I appreciate your calling and I only have a few questions." Judging from the sound of our connection, this was not a local call. She waited and I said, "Do you know Knox Ferris?"

There was a long pause before she said, "Yes, I do. He was a friend of Michael's."

"A good friend?"

Instead of answering she said, "If you're a private investigator, then who are you working for?"

"I'm investigating the murder of a friend." It wasn't a total lie. She didn't say anything so I prompted her. "How close were Michael and Knox?"

She answered my question with one of her own. "That friend of yours. Who was that?"

"Janet Miraldi. She was Assistant State's Attorney in Foxport."

If it hadn't been for the noise on the line, I would have thought she'd hung up. Although I wondered why Janet's name had drawn the silence, I tried to steer her back on track. "How close were Michael and Knox?"

It felt like a full minute before she said, "Very. They were very close. They grew up together. Went to school together. Grade school. High school. College. Mike dropped out after his freshman year. We got married and moved to Foxport." She paused and I waited again.

This was going to be difficult. Maybe there was another way. "Would it be possible for you and me to meet? I could come to wherever you are. Or we could meet halfway. Wherever you . . ."

"No," she said, adding, "I really can't talk now." I was moments away from losing her.

"Please don't hang up. I just want to understand what happened." No click. I kept going. "Do you know that Knox was going to be the state's witness in convicting Scott Markham on bribery charges?"

She sighed deeply and I hoped it was one of those sounds that signifies resignation. "Yes. I knew that. I know what's been going on there."

"Knox going after Markham. Was that a revenge kind of thing?"

Another pause. "Of course it was."

"Well then can you explain their relationship to me. Knox and Michael's. I need to understand how deep it went. Please," I said. Other words failed me.

After a few moments she said, "Knox sort of looked on

Mike as a kid brother. They were the same age and all but, you know, sometimes one is more mature than the other. Mike worshipped Knox. And Knox, well Knox was always there for Mike." She paused then added, "and me. He was there for me too. Mike and I didn't have an easy time of it at first, you know."

"Yeah," I said. "I think so." I tried hard to picture Karen and wondered if she looked at all like the young woman living in her house now, only ten years older and that much more tired.

She continued, "Well, after Mike and I got married, it was okay for a while between them. Then gradually it changed. Mike saw how different things were for him now, what with the baby and all. He got resentful of Knox. The worship turned into jealousy. Mike had always wanted a law degree. Knox was getting his. Mike envied Knox his freedom." She sighed and added, "But really, Knox never did anything to make Mike resentful. He just made the right choices. That's all. And I guess in a way Mike felt he'd let Knox down."

"How did Knox feel about all this?" I had been standing, facing the window to the river. Now I lowered myself onto the couch.

"He was hurt. He came to see us a few months before Missy was killed. He was real glad to see Mike, but I think Mike was ashamed of how we lived, you know, how far we were from making it. Mike had a factory job. Knox was in law school at the U of I. I think it bothered Knox too. He hated seeing Mike not living up to his potential. Knox only stayed a day and a half. I didn't blame him. That was the last time they talked . . . " She hesitated then said, "Until Missy was killed. Knox called, then came right out. Mike needed him then. So did I, but Mike needed him more." There was a long pause and I could almost see her chewing on her lip or twisting a strand of hair. "He should never have come."

"Why?" My voice was barely a whisper. When I got no response, I said, "Tell me Karen, did Knox in any way feel responsible for Mike's death?"

"He might have." She seemed relieved that someone had said it for her. When she continued, it didn't seem so painful for her. "Yes, in a way he did feel responsible and, though I've never said this to him, I think in a way he was."

216

"How's that?"

"Well, he told Mike that bribery had gotten that Fisher man off. He said if Markham hadn't been bought, Fisher wouldn't have been driving. I'm sure Mike had considered the possibility, but when Knox said it, well, it was like he suddenly had to do something about it. You know, it's one thing to have this notion that something fishy went on, but when someone tells you 'This is what happened, what are you going to do about it?' well you have to do something."

"Are you still in touch with Knox?"

"Yeah, some. Not so much at first. I'd hear from Knox every now and then, you know, like you hear from an old friend you don't have much in common with anymore. You keep in touch, that's all. Knox told me at Mike's funeral that people like Markham shouldn't have the public's trust and that he was going to see him disbarred someday. He said he was going to prove that the system works."

She stopped talking then and I asked, "When's the last time you heard from him?"

Instead of answering me, she said, "You know, it all started out as this really noble thing that Knox was doing. And maybe I'm the one who's wrong, but I just wanted to forget the whole thing and get on with my life. Mike and Missy are dead. That man never should have been driving. Markham never should have let him off. That Burke lawyer never should have bribed him or whatever he did. But I can't change any of that. I just wanted to get on with my life. Put it behind me once and for all."

She waited and I said, "There's nothing wrong with that. That's the only thing you can do if you want to get through it." Everybody needs to be told it's okay. But there was something more than guilt going on here and I had the feeling she was about to tell me. I leaned back into the couch and propped my feet on the coffee table.

Finally she continued. "About a year and a half ago Knox moved to Foxport. He said he was moving in for the kill. Or something like that. But it was like he was joking. At least I thought he was, but Knox has a way of making you think everything is just fine when actually it is anything but. It got so he'd call about once a month and I thought things were okay.

He told me about the investigation and everything. I'm sure he wasn't supposed to, but he did. And I was interested.''

The next pause lasted a long time, but I was afraid if I asked her a specific question she would lose her train of thought. I clamped my mouth shut and waited and finally was rewarded.

''Then things changed. If I had to tell you when the calls started getting strange, it would be hard. Maybe last April or May. You see, at first the changes were subtle and it was a while before I noticed that things were different. You know what I mean?''

She seemed to want an answer here. ''Yeah, sort of like not being able to see the forest for the trees?''

''Yeah. I guess it was something like that. Anyway his calls started getting more frequent and it was 'we' this and 'we' that. You know, 'We're going to put him away,' things like that.

''After several months of this, I just came out and told him to forget the whole thing. I told him I didn't want this thing to destroy him and couldn't he see what it was doing to him. He went nuts. Said things like 'Doing to me?' He repeated that several times, then he said 'Don't you mean doing to us? . . . I'm doing this for us, Karen.' I told him I wanted no part of it and he told me I already was part of it. I had been from the beginning.''

''What did he mean by that?'' I wasn't sitting back in the couch anymore.

''I'm not sure. But like I said, he wasn't making a lot of sense.'' She paused.

I was about to ask her something about Knox when she said, ''That friend of yours, Janet Miraldi.'' She hesitated and, again, I was afraid to prompt her. ''She called me several months ago.''

Now I was standing again, staring out the window. But I wasn't seeing anything this time. ''She knew about the connection between Knox and Markham?''

''She suspected. I could tell she was kind of concerned about Knox. I told her some of what I've told you. I didn't see anything wrong with telling her. He was acting strange, but that doesn't have to mean anything, does it?''

''No, it doesn't have to. What else did Janet say?''

''Not very much. But she seemed to be satisfied that Knox wasn't acting real unusual given the circumstances.''

"You didn't tell her your concerns about Knox?"

"No."

"Why are you telling me?"

She sighed. "That woman was murdered. If something Knox did . . . made it happen, well, I don't know." She sighed again, deeper this time.

"Did you tell Knox about her call?"

"Oh no." She sounded as though the prospect horrified her.

I paused, not sure I should pose the next question. Then I figured what the hell. "As angry and vengeful as Knox was, do you think he would have liked to kill Markham?"

"Liked to? Yes. Done it? No. Not unless he had run out of legal options." She'd answered quick enough for me to figure she'd already asked it of herself.

After a few more minutes, I realized there wasn't much more she had to say, or was willing to say, so I thanked her. Before she hung up, she asked, "What has he done?"

"I don't know. Maybe nothing."

"Maybe nothing, but probably something."

"Yeah," I admitted.

"He's really a good person. Please remember that."

Chapter Twenty-Three

I STARED at a water ring on the coffee table for a long time after I hung up. Janet had known about Knox's connection to Markham, and she had gone ahead and used him as her undercover man. Yet if the defense had known about that incident, it probably would have destroyed her case. In a way it didn't surprise me. She was looking for someone as driven as she was to put this guy away. Knox was it.

I took Peanuts for a run and cleared my head by tossing the Frisbee for him for thirty minutes. By the time we climbed the stairs back to the apartment, I had reasoned everything out to the point where I figured I might have no motive for Markham's murder—if it was murder—but I did have one that might work for Susan Connors's. And if I worked at the one long enough, maybe I'd be able to reason out the other. And maybe it would all eventually lead to Janet's killer. I needed to try my theory out on someone, so I went out in search of a reporter. I found the one I was looking for at the *Chronicle*. He was tapping out a story on a green-screened computer and glanced up at me as I stopped next to his desk. "Be with you in one second," Jeff said and went back to his work. I was surprised that his desk was as neat as it was. It wasn't empty by any means, just neat and organized. The in and out baskets were full, but there were no papers on the desk's blotter, although it looked like he used it as a notepad when the situation called for it. A baseball signed by several Cubs players rested on a paperweight, and there was a coffee mug with a cartoon of a dizzy-looking reporter sitting in front of an old manual type-writer above the caption: "Not tonight dear. I have a deadline."

Jeff shook his head in humble acceptance of his own abilities and muttered, "Damn, I'm good." Then, with a small flourish, he punched one last key and turned to me. "And what can I do for you?"

"What do they have on the Susan Connors murder?"

He got comfortable and collected his thoughts. "Well, there is a very strong movement at city hall and everywhere else to attribute her murder to Scott Markham. Especially after you were kind enough to supply the photographic evidence. Incidentally, I'm going to have to get a statement from you on that. People will wonder why you sat on it for so long. Carver is spending his time explaining why he hasn't put you in jail yet." He regarded me for a moment and shook his head. "You amaze me."

"You think Markham killed her?"

He sighed, then said, "I don't know. I mean I know Anne said the photo wasn't his work, but well . . . "

"Well?"

"I don't know. I'm not so sure Anne's very objective when it comes to Markham." He paused, frowning, then with a small shrug continued, "So he forgot to focus. I mean the woman was dead. He killed her. Maybe his hand was shaking. Hell, I don't know."

"How do you explain the sequence of events surrounding her murder?"

"How'd he do it, you mean?"

I nodded and Jeff leaned forward. Taking a pencil from behind his right ear, he began to make notes on the blotter. "First he kills her. Then for some sick reason he poses her like the picture of that murdered prostitute. Who knows. Maybe they were doing some reenactment of the whole scene and it got out of hand. Anyway, he takes a photo of her, hauls her body west of town, and buries her. Then, since she was leaving town the next morning anyway, he takes her suitcase, drives to the airport, parks her car, checks her bag, checks in at the flight, maybe even gets on board the plane for a minute, then leaves the car there and goes home."

I was sitting in a wooden chair in front of Jeff's desk, looking at the back of his computer as he spoke. I turned to him and after a few seconds said, "Problem: even when there are no seat assignments, they still keep track of how many boarding passes are turned in and how many people are on the plane."

Jeff chewed on his lower lip for a minute. Then he said, "Okay. He took the flight and came right back. That's not much more than a thirty minute flight."

"How'd he get back? They sometimes use the same crew for the return flight. He couldn't risk that."

Waving off my question, Jeff said, "I don't know. He rented a car. How come I'm answering all the questions?"

"Because you have a devious mind," I said and went on, "You need a credit card to rent a car. How can you do all that without a paper trail?"

"Train? Bus maybe?" He took the souvenir baseball in his hands and began kneading it. "Yeah, a bus. How much more anonymous can you get?"

"Maybe, but then you'd be at the mercy of lots of schedules."

"He deals with the schedules." Then, seeing my skeptical look, he added, "Okay, Einstein, you tell me. How did he get home? Walk?"

I leaned forward and rested my arms on Jeff's desk. "Or rode a bike."

Jeff's eyes widened. "Are you nuts?"

I didn't say anything.

"We're talking, what . . . a couple hundred miles? Probably farther. Markham was in okay shape for a guy pushing fifty, but he wasn't exactly into cross-country pedaling."

"Markham wasn't. But Knox Ferris was."

"Knox Ferris? Why Knox Ferris?"

"First play this theory out with me."

Jeff appeared doubtful, but nodded. He set the baseball back on its paperweight, looked at me for a minute, then shook his head. "I don't know. You've got some convincing to do. Central Wisconsin. That's at least 200 miles. A long way."

"Yeah, for you and me it is. But an experienced cross-country bicyclist can cover 60 to 100 miles in a day. I checked with the bike shop in town. And Knox Ferris was an experienced cross-country biker. It's how he unwinds." I couldn't get a read on Jeff from his expression. "And remember Janet said Knox was biking that weekend."

"Yeah, I remember." Jeff removed his glasses and absently polished them with the end of his tie. "Why not take the bus?"

"He'd rather ride his bike. Remember he just killed someone. What better reason is there to unwind?"

"What was the weather like?"

"Mild and clear all weekend. High fifties to low sixties. Perfect weather. He stays at little out-of-the-way, flea trap motels, paying cash as he goes. He makes up his own route so he'd be tough to trace."

Jeff leaned back and stared at the blank computer screen. Finally he said, "I suppose he could have carried his biking gear with him on the plane." He paused for a moment. "But he couldn't bring his bike along. So you must be thinking he bought a bike up near the Central Wisconsin Airport."

"Would it interest you to know that Knox has two bikes— they both look like touring bikes—in his apartment?"

"I don't know. If he's the fanatic you say he is, he might have a back up."

"Maybe." Unphased by his logic, I continued to explain my theory. "I'll bet somewhere near the airport there's a bike shop that sold a bike to a guy who paid cash and walked in wearing biking clothes, carrying a backpack. Maybe he gave the guy a story about how his bike was stolen or something."

"It's a year later, genius. How's he supposed to remember?"

"Maybe he doesn't have to. Each bike has a traceable serial number."

Jeff looked away, rubbing the bridge of his nose, his glasses pushed up on his forehead. Then, abruptly, he grabbed his coffee mug and walked to the back of the room where there was a coffee and a vending machine. I watched him pour himself a cup and stare at the wall for a couple minutes. Then he came back to his chair and set the mug on the desk. "Okay. Maybe that's all true. But wny Knox?"

I told him about Knox's friend Michael and what had happened to Melissa Knox Tyler. Jeff said he'd heard of the incident, but it was before his time. "So why would he kill Connors?"

I prefaced my theory with "This is just an educated guess. But maybe Knox started dating Susan Connors to get to Markham. And maybe she figured that out. Knox didn't want her,

he wanted her boss and mentor's ass. Maybe Knox overesti-
mated her devotion to him. Asked her to choose between a
lover and a mentor, and she went with the mentor. Knox knew
she was going to spill her guts to Markham." I paused and
went over the possibilities I'd considered before I said, "The
way I see it, it could have gone two ways here. One: he meant
to kill her. If Markham knew that Knox was out to get him, not
only would it ruin Knox's chances of avenging his friend's
death, it would ruin his career in Foxport. So he kills Connors,
figuring he's eventually going to frame Markham for it, copies
the photo in Markham's book, buries her, drives her car to the
airport, takes her flight, buys a bike and rides home."

Nodding, Jeff said, "I might buy that. Tell me your other
theory."

"Well, maybe it wasn't premeditated. Maybe they got to
talking about Markham, she realized what Knox was up to, she
went nuts, they fought, she died."

"Why the elaborate charade? How could he have considered
all the details?"

"That's where I have a little trouble," I conceded. "Although when you think about it, the fact that she was leaving
town might have been a stroke of luck. The rest—the photo
and all—he could have come up with that pretty fast. It's
amazing how creative you can be when your ass is on the
line." Pausing, I went over the scenario again. Then I said, "I
guess that's what I like about the bike theory. It's not only
something Knox is capable of, it's the first thing he'd think
of."

Jeff took half a minute to digest that before he asked, "What
makes you think he was going to frame Markham?"

"Three reasons. One, he photographed her; two, he planted
the photo in Markham's desk; and three, he buried her on
property he knew they were going to develop."

"How'd he know that?"

"Janet, Knox and I were talking about Connors's murder,
saying most people didn't realize that piece of land was going
to be used. But Knox said he knew Langley pretty well and he
knew it was just a matter of time before they started digging
there." I stopped to light a cigarette. "If it was Knox it had to
be a frame."

"Why did he wait a year to frame the guy?"

"Suppose that after the initial inspiration, it didn't seem like such a hot idea. Maybe Markham had an alibi for that night. Or maybe Knox wanted to be sure he couldn't argue in his own defense."

"Maybe that's why he killed him," Jeff suggested.

"Maybe. But I've got a feeling there's more to it."

Jeff nodded slowly, apparently in agreement. "Yeah, there's gotta be more. Like why would he kill Markham at that time? Especially when he had him dead to rights on that bribery charge."

"That's the question. If he wanted him dead, why did he wait so long to kill him? Something changed."

"Like what?"

"I don't know," I said to Jeff while thinking about the tapes. If that was Knox's bug, there might be some interesting conversations on those tapes.

Jeff pushed his glasses up the bridge of his nose, and looked at me. "What about Janet's murder?"

I shook my head. "I don't know. I try, but I don't see a connection."

"She knew what was motivating him."

"Markham was dead. What difference did it make anymore?"

"Maybe she thought he killed him. And he knew it."

I had thought about that myself, but couldn't get it to work. "I saw them together right before she died. She genuinely liked the guy." I looked for an ash tray and Jeff handed me a styrofoam cup with an inch of cold coffee in it. "All I've got now is a theory about Connors's death. That's what I've got to go with." I dropped my cigarette in the cup and it hissed out.

Jeff smiled and shook his head. "I don't know. I guess it makes sense, but I don't know."

"What would it take to make a believer out of you?"

He shrugged. "That serial number business. That'd clinch it for me."

"Okay." I stood. "I'll get it."

"How?" Jeff looked at me and must have read the answer on my face. "Don't tell me. I don't want to know."

If there was a legal way to get what I needed out of Knox Ferris's apartment, I couldn't think of it. That was why I was standing outside his apartment on a late Monday afternoon trying to figure out the least conspicuous way to break in. It made sense to wait until dark, but I needed the daylight. And I figured he'd be at work at least another hour. That was my theory anyway.

I had the feeling that Jeff knew where I was going when I left him at the paper, but he chose not to ask. I didn't blame him. I'd never been on this end of breaking and entering and it wasn't exactly tops on my list of ways to kill an afternoon.

The door to Knox's apartment faced the backyard, which was good. The huge bushes that defined the yard's perimeter were just starting to get their cover back, but the branches themselves did a pretty good job of concealing my actions from the neighbors. So all I really had to worry about was a passing car.

The first floor windows of the house, being not much more than a yard from the ground, seemed the best way to go. I chose as my point of entry a window that he'd been considerate enough to leave open. The screen was held in place by small, retractable pegs that popped into holes in the window frame. I was delighted to see that the peg in the lower left corner was missing. Piece of cake. If I could free the bottom part of the screen, I would have enough room to squeeze in. I pried back the corner and inserted my arm far enough to release the middle peg then slid down to release the right corner. Once I released the last peg, the entire screen fell out. They just don't make those little pegs like they used to. No problem, I assured myself. I glanced toward the street to make sure there wasn't a line of cars stopped to watch the show. The street was clear, but there was one wide-eyed kid, age about seven, standing halfway between me and the street. He had loud, knee length pants and a t-shirt that came down almost as far. His hair was short and bristly and he wore dark sunglasses.

I nodded to him, "Hi. How's it going?" I don't know kids well, but I've heard if you treat them like regular people, they appreciate it.

He didn't say anything, continuing to stare.

I propped the screen against the side of the building. "Locked myself out."

He glanced over his shoulder ensuring that nothing stood between him and the safety of the street. Turning back to me, he folded his arms over his chest and cocked his head. This kid wasn't about to be fed a line.

I proceeded as if nothing were unusual. They say you should

do that with foaming dogs and children. Just pretend you barely notice them and they won't attack you or run home and tell their parents that there's a weird guy breaking and entering down the street. The window slid up without protest and I hoisted myself into the apartment.

I could have used his help but I didn't want to encourage him to assist people committing felonies. By the time I got the screen in place and the window adjusted, the kid was gone. I hoped he'd just gotten bored and moved on to some other form of entertainment.

Knox Ferris was a lot closer to that great bike ride across the country than he'd been a few days ago. Just about everything he owned was in a box, including all the elaborate recording equipment. Not that I had the time to sit and listen to the two boxes full of reel to reel tapes. I wouldn't know where to begin. Besides, I was hoping the serial number would be all I'd need. The number was right where the guy at the bike shop said it would be and it only took a couple minutes to get it off both bikes.

Then, because I figured I had some time, I decided to look around. In case my bike theory was all wet.

Systematically, I looked in every box in his apartment, glossing over the ones with kitchen supplies and dishes. I wasn't sure what I was looking for, I just hoped I'd know when I found it.

Then I came to a box labeled "Projects," which would have been more accurately labeled "Scott Markham." Everything you would want to know about Scott Markham and then some was in it. And there was his book *Portraits of a Conflict*. If I was looking for the page with the murdered prostitute to be dog-eared with Susan Connors' name scribbled across the top in Knox's handwriting, I was disappointed. But at least he had the book. There were clippings from numerous publications on the Tyler incident. And photos. He had dozens of pictures of Markham. Lorna Markham should have hired Knox to tail her husband: he probably had enough incriminating photos on file to set her up for life. And speaking of tailing, who was this good-looking guy with the Honda and the dog in the back seat? So much for being inconspicuous.

I went through every room in the apartment. Apparently Knox's bathroom doubled as a dark room. It was there that I found boxes packed with aluminum tanks, bottles of solutions and an enlarger.

When I'd finished going through rooms and boxes, I figured if the bike theory didn't work there was nothing here to help me. I was just about out of light and my luck wasn't doing much better. Nothing I'd found had been damning or surprising. Then I noticed his sophisticated answering machine. The message light wasn't flashing, but I rewound the tape just to see if he had gotten any interesting messages. When I played the tape back, I realized this was no ordinary answering machine. Knox Ferris was either so paranoid or so infatuated with the art of recording that he taped his phone calls. And when I heard who the last call was from, I could not have cared less what motivated him.

"Hello, Knox. Mason Burke here." This must have been one of his "important" calls.

"What can I do for you?" His voice was calm but there was an edge to it.

"You and I need to talk, don't you agree?"

"What about?"

Mason took his time answering, savoring the moment. "Oh, it's something to do with exterminators getting rid of bothersome insects. One in particular."

Mason gave Knox about five seconds, then said, "I really don't think you've got too many options. You know what I mean?"

"When?"

"Eight o'clock tonight. At my home." He gave Knox his address and added, "Now don't keep me waiting."

"Of course not," Knox said with unmistakable sarcasm.

The call disconnected then. I glanced at my watch. It was five o'clock and time to get out of there before Knox got home from work. I left Knox Ferris' apartment by more conventional means than I'd entered.

CHAPTER TWENTY-FOUR

Two hours later I was driving down the west side of the river toward Mason's home. I hadn't quite figured out my game plan. For a guy who found it so distasteful, I seemed to be doing a lot of breaking and entering. I was wearing black jeans and a black turtleneck and there was a black ski mask on the passenger seat. I couldn't decide whether I felt like a cat burglar or an extra from a James Bond movie. In the glove compartment was the .38 Smith and Wesson I'd reclaimed from the bottom of the box where I'd packed it several months before.

Mason's home was on the west bank of the Fox and it was one of the older homes that had laid claim to the river before Foxport had been invaded by yuppie families. I parked my car about three blocks north of Mason's house in a small asphalt lot next to a riverside park. I clipped the revolver's holster to the right side of my belt, pulled the ski mask over my face, and made my way through the darkened backyards of Foxport's wealthy. It was still fairly warm, but fortunately no one was taking advantage of the combination of the weather and the inviting river bank.

I had counted the number of houses between Mason's and the closest east-west street and was pretty sure I was in his backyard, but wished I had a way to be certain. It's got to be hell breaking into the wrong house. But here I was and I had to go with my best guess. Now I just had to get in. I was pretty sure the windows of Mason Burke's home weren't the kind with little broken pegs. They looked like they were all shut too. So much for windows. The doors looked more promising. French doors opened onto a second floor balcony, and a set of sliding glass doors led out to a big deck on the first floor. There was a light on in the room behind these doors. As I moved up through the yard and around to the north side of the deck, I saw that the room off the deck was the kitchen and I also saw someone in it. That was the bad news. The good news was that the glass doors were open. I had almost reached the deck when someone approached the door. I moved back into the shadows. It was a stocky, gray-haired woman wearing an apron over a plain looking dress. She opened the screen and waved a dish towel in the air as if she were surrendering, then stepped back in and shut the screen, but didn't lock it. As I was trying to hatch a plan, the phone rang. I climbed up onto the deck and edged up to the door with my back against the house. The ringing stopped.

"Burke residence." A pause while she listened. "Mrs. Burke's not home now. She's not expected back until late this evening. Mr. Burke should be home shortly, though." Another pause. "What? Oh, yes, Mrs. Blalock. Well, I don't know where she keeps it. Wait, let me check one place." She set the phone down and moved across the tile floor until I could no longer hear her footsteps. It was now or never. A quick reconnaissance convinced me that the maid wasn't crouched next to the screen doors with a baseball bat. I slid the screen back and stepped into Mason Burke's home.

Moments after I entered I heard someone approaching from the hallway. Aside from the patio doors, there were only two ways out of the kitchen and she was coming back through one of them. I moved straight ahead into what turned out to be the laundry room. There I crouched next to a clothes dryer. From this position someone would have to step into the room and turn around to spot me.

The maid got back on the phone and told Mrs. Blalock that she couldn't find whatever she was looking for. Apparently Mrs. Blalock put up a bit of a stink because the maid kept apologizing and assuring her that she would leave a message for Mrs. Burke. After she finally hung up she muttered, "Bitch." Then I heard her sigh and move around the room. I removed the ski mask and tucked it into my waistband. After about ten minutes, during which time I thought she sat down and had a cigarette, she finally turned the light above the stove on, the overhead light off, and left the room. After about thirty seconds, I moved out of the laundry room and into the kitchen.

Moments later I heard the sound of a heavy door shutting. Silence followed.

I glanced at my watch. It was seven forty. Where the hell was Mason? I moved down the hall. There were two rooms to my right, and a foyer and staircase to my left. I checked out the room at the end of the hall first. It was a bedroom suite illuminated by a small table lamp on a bedside table. There was a fireplace cut out of the wall on the north end, which had apparently been cleaned out for the warmer months. The carpet was thick and the big four-poster bed seemed to have sprung from it. I lifted the corner of the spread and on my hands and knees quickly ascertained that the space beneath the bed was a good place to stash a private investigator. I moved on to the next room.

This had to be Mason's study. It smelled exactly like his office. And only Mason Burke would have a study that looked like a lounge in a Swiss chateau—talk about pretentious. If he were going to have a showdown with Knox Ferris, it would be here. The room had a vaulted ceiling and was richly carpeted in a muted red plaid. A massive dark wood desk with a leather swivel chair befitting Mason's opinion of himself dominated the room. It probably seemed even bigger when little Mason was sitting there. A row of windows overlooked the backyard and the south wall of the room shared the fireplace with the bedroom. It was a cinch that Mason and his wife didn't have to deal with children.

The room was surrounded by a second-floor loft. I figured there were rooms to the north and south and a hallway on the east side. I couldn't see much up there except for some plants against the heavy wood railing. The stairs to the second floor were off the foyer and I was about to climb them when I saw lights and heard a car in the driveway. I took my place under the bed. Just as I was crawling under it, I thought I heard the floor above me creak, as though someone had shifted his weight or gotten up. Maybe I shouldn't have assumed the house was empty. I paused, but heard nothing else until Mason entered his home.

I tried to imagine the rituals Mason Burke performed when he walked through the door to his castle. Maybe he lined up his calf skin briefcase with the legs of the hall table, and took a moment to work on his "freeze them in their tracks" look in the wall mirror. What sounded like a closet door opened and closed. He probably didn't need that coat today. Would he bother to check the mail? After a couple minutes, he approached the bedroom and I could hear him whistling something that sounded like Beethoven's Ninth. He entered the bedroom, presumably to exchange his suit jacket for his smoking jacket and left without looking under the bed for goblins. It was seven fifty. Cutting it a little close, Mason? Or did Mason have this meeting so well rehearsed that he wasn't sweating it? Then I heard him in his study, opening desk drawers, still whistling. With the fireplace connecting these rooms, I couldn't have asked for a better surveillance point.

I waited. Mason waited. Eight o'clock came and went. Mason stopped whistling at eight ten. I lay beneath the king-sized bed, my chin resting on my folded hands and my gun cutting into my waist, thinking about how I was getting hungry and wishing I'd raided Mason's refrigerator while I'd had the chance. And as the minutes crept by, I worked on the problem of getting out of the house. Unless an opportunity provided itself, I might spend the night under Mason's bed. What a concept.

Strange. It had never occurred to me that Knox might not show up. Apparently it had never occurred to Mason either. I could hear him pacing in the next room, occasionally muttering something incoherent. He made a couple of phone calls, slamming the receiver down when he got no answer. Mason Burke did not like to be kept waiting. I'd have to remember that.

By nine o'clock, I was expending most of my mental energy convincing myself that the bed was not getting lower. It would not suffocate me, crush me, or both. In order to get my mind off grim thoughts, I tried to plant a telepathic suggestion in Mason's head. "Go upstairs. There's someone upstairs." When the doorbell rang, I almost cheered.

Mason muttered something about it being goddamned time but he didn't hurry out of the study. He moved deliberately as though he'd measured this all out ahead of time and couldn't rush the cues. As he opened the front door, I heard him say, "Need a new watch? . . . " Then there were about five seconds of silence followed by the sound of someone crashing to the tiled floor, heavy footsteps and then the voice of Knox Ferris.

"My watch is working just fine, Mason."

I pictured Mason scrambling to get his footing like a lizard on ice and I heard an uncharacteristic tinge of panic in his voice as he said, "There's no need for weapons, Knox. Let's just talk about this. I don't know what you're . . . "

Mason must have hit the floor again because the next thing I heard was Knox saying, "I'm going to talk. You're going to listen."

"That's fine. Why don't we go into my study?" From the strain in Mason's voice, I imagined Knox was lifting him by his collar.

At first I was surprised that Knox agreed so quickly, then I began to wonder if that wasn't just where he wanted Mason. Gentlemen always commit suicide at their desks.

Once I heard them go into the study, I belly crawled from under the bed to the fireplace's hearth. I pulled myself up enough to see through the fireplace, but the desk was not in my line of sight. And apparently that was where Knox had deposited Mason, who was still protesting. "Why Knox, I thought you and I could talk like reasonable men." The panic was gone and Mason the charmer was back. "Now tell me. What is this all about?"

"It's about paying for the crimes you commit."

Mason didn't respond and as the silence between them extended, I moved toward the bedroom door.

"Now, what's all this about, Knox?" If Knox had upped the threat, it wasn't registering in Mason's tone. He even summoned up enough arrogance to say, "Don't you think two suicides in as many weeks is going to be a little difficult for anyone to buy? Even that inept bunch of jokers that calls itself a police force might see through it."

"This isn't about suicide. It's about murder," was all he said in a voice as calm as a doctor's when he gives you the bad news.

After several moments of harsh silence, a less than charming Mason said, "What are you talking about?"

"You heard me. You killed her and I know it. And you're going to have to die for it."

I eased my gun from its holster and began to move out of the bedroom into the hallway. Even as I did it, the notion of my lifting a finger to save Mason Burke's life didn't connect with reality. But he was about to be summarily executed for the death of a three-year-old girl. And even card-carrying assholes like Mason were supposed to get their day in court.

"For God's sake, Knox, grow up. This is the real world, not Sunnybrook Farm." The irritated tone in Mason's voice froze me. How could someone with a gun drawn on him maintain a state of constant arrogance? But it was what he said next that really made my insides go cold. "If Ms. Miraldi had been a team player, she'd be down at The Docket with the rest of the young lawyers nibbling on Brie, sipping white Zinfandel and bitching about her case load." Maybe I should just keep walking. All the way home. Maybe farther. Never hear the gunshot, never look back.

I took a couple deep breaths and checked myself. Mason must have interpreted Knox's lack of a response as a sign that he was getting through to him because he kept going. "You don't mess with the system." It was as though he were lecturing a group of sixth graders. "This one works better than most. But even as it stands, the prisons are overflowing with murderers, rapists and thieves. There's not enough room for the drunks and there sure isn't enough room for a judge who's just doing his job the best he can." Mason stopped.

At first I heard nothing, then what sounded like sobbing. And suddenly I realized Knox was working his way up into hysterical laughter. As I moved down the hallway, I heard Mason's tentative laugh: at best it was never very credible. He tried to find Knox's enthusiasm, but couldn't. Finally he stopped trying and said, "You see, I knew you'd understand once I explained it. Now that we both know where you're coming from, our talk can proceed at a more civilized level."

Knox stopped laughing. I moved closer to the study door. Knox said, "This is going to be a lot easier for me knowing that you killed Janet too. I thank you for that." He giggled.

Mason took a few seconds before he asked, "Then who in the hell are you talking about?"

"I'm talking about Melissa Tyler." Knox wasn't giggling anymore.

"Who in the hell is Melissa Tyler?" I could have told Mason that was the wrong thing to say.

"She was a little girl. She was three years old. And you killed her." Knox sounded like he was talking through clenched teeth. I stepped into the doorway, finding Knox and taking aim at him before either he or Mason could react. When they did, it was hard to tell who was more surprised to see me, Mason or Knox.

Knox stood next to Mason who sat in his swivel chair. The barrel of a nine millimeter automatic was pressed to Mason's temple. Mason's jaw dropped when he saw me and he moved it up and down a couple times as if he were trying to jump start it. His eyes were wide.

Knox and I stared at each other. My gun was drawn on him, but his was drawn on Mason. A stand off. Knox spoke first. "Put it down, Quint."

Shifting slightly I wondered if I could get a shot off before Knox pulled the trigger. Then I conceded that even if I could, it was an action I was not capable of.

"This son of a bitch killed Janet." Knox spat the words out.

My gaze dropped down to Mason for a fraction of a second. He looked away.

"Here it is, Quint." Knox's voice was calm, but there was something in his eyes that scared me. "The only way you're going to get me to put this down, is to shoot me."

I moved further into the room.

"This man's a lunatic. You can see that."

"Is he, Mason?"

"Listen to me, Quint." Knox's voice rose. "If your gun isn't on this desk by the time I count to three, Mason is one dead son of a bitch." He held the gun to Mason's head with one hand and rested the other on his shoulder, apparently exerting pressure. "I've got no quarrel with you."

I was near the desk now. "That's far enough," Knox said and continued with "One . . . "

"If you're not going to shoot him, for God's sake put the damned thing down." Mason had lost some of the color in his face, and his freckles had taken on a gray cast.

"Shut up, Mason," I said.

Knox said, "Two." His breathing was heavy and his jaw clenched. Did he mean it? Should I let him anyway? In the split second I took to analyze the veracity of his threat, I convinced myself that he was serious. Slowly I lowered my gun to Mason's desk. They both looked relieved.

Then Mason seemed to remember that he was the one being

inconvenienced here and, as if he were changing the subject said, "Who in the hell is Melissa Tyler?"

"She was killed by a drunk driver named Howard Fisher," I said to him. "Name familiar? He'd gotten off on a DUI charge just days before. You'll never guess who his lawyer was and what judge heard the case."

"Oh, so that's what this is all about." It was as though he'd just heard the answer to a mildly annoying riddle and I wondered if he wasn't trying too hard for nonchalance.

"You've done your homework, Quint." Knox increased his gun's pressure on Mason's temple. Mason bent with the pressure of the gun and Knox leaned down to wrap his left arm around Mason's scrawny neck to hold him still. Then he looked up at me. "The little bastard killed Janet too. He just said so. He deserves to die."

Did he need my approval? My mouth had dried up and I didn't have enough spit to wet my lips. "Probably. But why don't we let the courts decide that?" The second that was out of my mouth, I knew it was the wrong thing to say.

In less time than it takes to pull a trigger, Knox went from calm to crazy. The veins in his temples stood out and his eyes were wide. "What the hell do you mean?" He raged. "Let the courts decide? Let the courts decide? You're talking about the system. It's *his* fucking system. You heard him."

"It'll work. This time." I didn't sound very convincing.

"Bullshit." He was in genuine agony, stooped over Mason with the gun still at his head. "Nobody's ever going to make him pay for all he's done."

"What else has he done, Knox?"

"Are you going to listen to this idiot?" Mason found his voice again and both Knox and I ignored him.

"What else has he done?" I repeated.

"Well," Knox kept his gun in place but looked up at the ceiling, then back to me. He kept moving his weight from his left foot to his right as if he couldn't stand still. He reminded me of a little kid forced into a confession. He was in such agony, he couldn't contain himself anymore. "Susan Connors."

Mason jerked his head, unsuccessfully trying to break Knox's grip. "What in the hell are you talking about?"

"You killed her." Knox squeezed Mason's throat tighter.

I moved closer to the desk and my gun. "No. You killed

Susan Connors, Knox. I know that." Mason was the one with the gun at his head, so I didn't care how agitated Knox got.

Sweat was streaming from Knox's face and he shook his head as he tried to find words, but failed.

"Tell me about it, okay?" I had to work at keeping my voice even.

"That wasn't my fault. She was supposed to help me get Markham. She used to tell me all kinds of stuff about the guy. That's how I knew about those photos he liked to take. I mean, she knew he was into some weird stuff. But then when I brought it up, when I asked her to help me get the guy, she freaked. Even after I explained it to her. All of it. She didn't care. All she cared about was Scott Markham." Mason was clawing at Knox's arm, trying to get him to relieve the pressure on his throat. His face was red and his eyes were bulging. But this was life and death for Knox and he had to make me understand. And as far as he was concerned, Mason was just an animal to subdue. Knox's sentences were choppy, the words coming in torrents or not at all. "I sat there half the night. Just looking at the poor girl. I just hit her. That's all. . . . It was the way she landed. Twisted like that photo Markham took. You know the one. . . . And that was right. Because Markham really did kill her. It wasn't me. People would have to know that. It wasn't my fault."

Mason must have squirmed an inch because Knox looked down at him and forced his head back with his left arm. Mason squeezed his eyes shut to keep them from popping out of his head.

"So Markham had to die too?" I said.

Knox turned to me, puzzled. "He wasn't going to do time for what he'd done. Don't you know that?"

"No, I don't. Explain."

"Oh, for God's sake," Mason's abruptness surprised both Knox and me. And he managed to get enough air to keep going. "Scott had nothing to do with Susan's death or, for that matter, that little girl and her stupid father."

Knox released his grip around Mason's neck, swung him around in the chair, grabbed his collar and yanked him up in the chair, arching his back. Mason groped at the edge of his desk, trying to support himself.

"You know what that bastard Markham, your buddy, did?

You know?" He tightened his grip on Mason who croaked something unintelligible. "He begged me. And then he started to cry. And that's when I did it. I thought it would be more authentic if the guy was crying before he blew himself away. You know, instead of a note, tears."

I was moving closer to my gun when Mason croaked, "Sounds like everybody in this world but you is guilty of something." Knox wrenched Mason's neck in a way that should have made it impossible for him to breathe let alone speak, but he kept going and was almost smiling when he added, "Share the guilt, Knox. There's plenty of room."

Knox swung his gun up to smack Mason across the face with its butt. He wasn't ready to kill him yet. I made a move for my gun, but Knox saw me. He released Mason, took a step back, shifted his gun, and froze me inches from my goal. During the seconds it took to convince myself that Knox would kill me if he had to, Mason brought his arm up from beneath the desk. He held something hard and shiny, and before my brain activated my body, he'd leveled the object at Knox and pulled its trigger.

Before the sound of the gun's blast dissipated, Knox staggered back a step, as though he wanted us to see the look of shock and a terrible understanding that registered on what was left of his face. Then, like a giant redwood, he toppled, crashing the back of his head against the hearth.

I thought I heard someone moan. Maybe not. Or maybe it was me.

Then Mason was turning in his chair, still holding the .357 Magnum. Before he completed the turn, I scrambled across the desk, grabbing his wrist with both hands. He locked onto me with his beady eyes, then smiled. His fist sprang open and the gun fell heavily to the desk. Retrieving it with one hand, I slowly released my grip on Mason with the other and eased myself back across the desk. Mason regarded me with frank amusement and, removing a white linen handkerchief from his back pocket, began to dab at his face making certain Knox hadn't gotten any blood on him.

"Disgusting," Mason grimaced as he glanced at Knox.

I wanted to tell Mason it was going to get a lot more disgusting for him. But all I said was, "Don't think you're going to get away with this. You're not."

He raised his eyebrows. "Why Quint, it was self defense. Even you aren't that blind. Hell, I might have saved your life too. What are you bitching about?"

"Janet Miraldi. I suppose you're going to tell me that was self defense too."

"No. That was self preservation. The difference is subtle, but I know you can appreciate it." He leaned back in the big chair and rested his elbows on its arms. "And that conversation you overheard. It never happened." Smiling and confident, he continued, "It's your word against mine. And you know what? I'm not too worried about whose story they buy." He laughed and gestured behind him. "After all, the late Mr. Ferris was right. It *is* my fucking system."

CHAPTER TWENTY-FIVE

I CALLED the police and Mason poured himself a drink. After I'd hung up, he said, "Where are my manners? You look like a Scotch drinker." I just shook my head and after holstering my gun, swung open the chamber on Mason's Magnum and dumped its bullets. Then I dropped the gun on his desk and pocketed the bullets. Mason laughed and said, "Can't be too careful, can we?" I sat on the edge of a black leather chair on the opposite side of the desk from Knox's body, lit a cigarette and waited.

Mason walked over to the fireplace and sipped on his drink as he regarded the body in his study. It looked as though he was making a judgment on decor and ambiance. Finally he shook his head and turned to me. "Well, if you'll excuse me, I can think of places I'd rather be." As he was leaving the room, he smiled and added, "Remember. Don't touch anything."

In less than five minutes the first squad car rolled in. Mason was standing in the foyer when I stepped out of the study. He looked angry or maybe just distracted, but brightened up when he saw me. "Nothing like a prompt police force, don't you think?" He set his drink on the hall table as he opened the door.

Carver arrived minutes later, took one look at me, and shook his head. I couldn't tell what his disposition toward me was at the moment. One of the uniforms was directing him into the study when Mason stopped him, "I'd like a word with you, Ed."

Carver hesitated, then said, "I'll get your statement in a few minutes," and walked into the study.

Mason wasn't pleased, but said as he followed, "This was

clearly a case of self defense. The man had gone off the deep end, I'm afraid. Even Mr. McCauley will back me on that.''

A half hour later when Carver finally got to me, I'd had plenty of time to think about the situation. And I'd reasoned that if Mason stopped to figure out how I got in the house, I could be arrested for breaking and entering.

I was sitting on the steps leading to the second floor, watching the activity when Carver motioned me into the kitchen. Two patrolmen were in there shooting the breeze. Carver's glare was enough to send them scurrying to the study. We sat at a small table with four chairs. Carver was looking pretty tired and he seemed to get even more tired as he gave me the once over.

"What were you doing here?" It was apparent from his tone of voice that he was going to cut me no slack. We were even in the favors department and he didn't owe me a damned thing. But he didn't seem to be particularly taken with Mason Burke, so maybe there was hope.

I rested my hands palms down in front of me on the table. "This is really very interesting."

"Let me decide that."

"All right. That's fair." I cleared my throat. I didn't want to have to say this twice. "This afternoon I heard a telephone conversation between Mason and Knox Ferris during which Mason asked Knox to come to his house."

Carver stared at me and nodded. When he realized I was finished, he said, "You want to tell me where you heard this conversation?"

"Sure. On Knox's telephone answering machine. It's actually a tape recorder."

"So you saw Knox this afternoon?"

I crossed my arms over my chest. There was no way out of this gracefully. "Actually I didn't. No. You see, I came across some information that made me believe that Knox might have killed Susan Connors and Scott Markham. And in order to get the proof I needed, I uh, I had to be there when he wasn't."

Carver nodded, jotting something in a small notepad. "You broke in."

"Not exactly. The window was open."

I leaned forward. "But let me tell you what I learned." And I proceeded to tell him about the bug in Robyn's apartment, presumably put there by Knox. I told him about the Tylers and my theory as to how Knox made the round trip. And I finished with, "And, as Mason probably told you, Knox did admit to killing Connors."

Carver nodded. "And Janet Miraldi."

Knowing Mason, I don't know why that stunned me. Once I got over the initial shock, I realized that must have been part of Mason's plan from the beginning. "No," I said to Carver, "Knox didn't admit to killing Janet. Mason did."

Now it was Carver's turn to look stunned. I continued. "Knox told Mason he knew he'd killed her. He was actually talking about the little Tyler girl, but Mason thought he meant Janet. So Mason told him why he'd had to kill Janet. She was messing up his system."

"You're saying Mason Burke planted a bomb in Miraldi's car?"

"I doubt it. He probably hired someone to do the job."

Carver looked at me with a surprisingly thoughtful expression. Then he shook his head.

I persisted. "It makes sense, doesn't it? Here's this State's Attorney who's trying to clean up his system. That's what he called it. *His* system."

I couldn't tell whether Carver was buying any of this. So for good measure, I added, "You want to hear what he said about the police department?" Carver glanced in the direction of the study then back to me. "An 'inept bunch of jokers' was, I believe, his choice of words."

I could see the muscles in Carver's jaw working. Finally he said, "Too bad nobody else heard that confession."

"Maybe someone did."

Carver raised his eyebrows. I continued. "I think I heard someone upstairs. Whoever it was might have heard the whole thing."

"Who?"

I shrugged and Carver motioned into the hall. One of the loitering uniforms was there before three seconds had passed. Carver told him to check out the rest of the house. "See if there's anyone else here." The patrolman nodded and left.

Carver jotted something down in his notebook, and then pressed his thumb and forefinger against the bridge of his nose. "Tell me about the rest of it. What happened here tonight?"

I told him and he took notes. Nothing I said seemed to surprise him. But then Mason would have no reason to lie about most of what had happened tonight. When I finished, he said, "So it looked like self defense to you?"

"Not really. But it would be tough to prove otherwise. Knox did have a gun on him. But I don't think it was a coincidence that Mason shot Knox just as Knox was about to say why he killed Markham."

Carver's eyebrows gathered in a dark vee. "Good timing?"

"I think so." Carver nodded as though he'd expected me to say that. In a gesture of good faith, I gave him my last lead. "But I think Markham's girlfriend, Robyn Fosse, might be able to clear that up."

"Excuse me, gentlemen." Carver and I looked up and saw Mason standing in the doorway. I had no idea how long he'd been there.

"Ed, I want you to arrest this man for breaking and entering."

Before Carver could respond, I said, "Why don't you check out the tapes in Knox's apartment. It's all there." I ventured a glance at Mason and could tell from the look on his face that he wasn't a bit concerned. "Forget it. It's too late." I turned to Carver. "Now we know why Mason invited Knox over."

Carver looked from Mason to me. "What about the tape on the answering machine?"

Mason's expression changed and I smiled at him. "Knox taped all his phone calls." To add to his consternation, I said, "That's why I'm here."

Abruptly, I stood. "Well, if you gentlemen will excuse me, I've gotta find the can."

As I walked out of the kitchen I heard Mason. "I want you to arrest that son of a bitch for breaking and entering. He was probably in on this with that idiot Ferris."

"Oh, and you think this inept bunch of jokers is up to it?"

Regardless of what Carver thought of Mason, I was inches away from getting thrown in jail. I edged out of the house. One of the cops who'd been caught gabbing in the kitchen was on the porch. He was one of those really young, intense-looking types who can make you feel as if you're getting ticketed by the coach of the high school debate team. A few reporters, among them Jeff Barlowe, were congregated on the walkway. I stepped up to the cop. "Carver wants to see you."

He glanced around nervously, from the reporters, to the door, then back to the reporters. I leaned toward him and spoke so only he could hear me. "He sounded like he really meant it. He's sending someone else out. I'll wait here until he comes."

Reluctantly he went in the house. I really am ashamed of myself sometimes.

I jumped down the steps and up to Barlowe. "I've gotta get the hell out of here. Can you give me a lift?"

Barlowe quickly sized up the situation and decided that the story was with me. Minutes later we were speeding toward Robyn Fosse's apartment in Jeff's pick up. If the cops or Mason's people got to her first, it might be too late. She'd either clam up or be removed from the picture permanently.

Jeff agreed to wait in the parking lot if I promised him an exclusive.

I tried Robyn's apartment first. When I got no answer, I cursed and rang Wanda's apartment.

"Who is it?" came the scratchy voice. Here we go again. Maybe Robyn didn't need to be warned. Maybe Wanda was all the protection she needed.

"It's Quint McCauley. I have to talk to Robyn."

"What's it worth this time?"

"It's probably worth Robyn's life." Buzz. I gave Jeff the okay sign and entered.

Even though it was almost midnight, both women were up, Wanda in a pink terry-cloth robe and Robyn in jeans and a t-shirt. Fiscus was still wearing his bandanna. He probably slept in it. Both women were leery. Robyn was doing the talking, though. She stood with her arms crossed and a set and determined expression on her face. "I thought we'd done all the talking we had to do yesterday."

Wanda settled into a green vinyl recliner to watch the action.

"You forgot to tell me you were going to call Mason."

"I didn't call Mason." I didn't know Robyn Fosse well enough to tell when she was lying, but I figured if she had an idea of what had gone down, she'd lie through her teeth to save herself.

"Okay. Let me tell you what's happened since we talked.

Then maybe you'll want to help me fill in the blanks." Robyn remained standing as I began the story. I paced back and forth as I spoke. When I got to the part where Mason all but confessed to Janet's murder, she put her hand to her mouth and quickly found one of the dinette chairs. She went about three shades paler when I told her that Knox admitted killing Markham. I was glad she was sitting when I told her about Knox's violent death. I didn't spare the gory details. She had to know how much trouble she was in. When I finished she didn't say anything, just sat at that little table, her forehead braced in her hand. Finally she breathed, "Oh, God." Fiscus came over to her and rubbed up against her leg. She dropped one hand to his shiny black head and began stroking him.

I sat down on the table's other chair and leaned toward Robyn. "I don't mean to scare you, Robyn, but you've got to see the whole picture here. You should be scared. You told Mason that Knox planted the bug. Right now he's saying he doesn't know anything about tapes and he has seen to it that they've been disposed of. You know too much. I've seen the way he disposes of people, Robyn. He doesn't lose sleep over it." She didn't respond. "In fact, you're a bigger liability to him right now than I am. Nobody believes me."

She shook her head, still not understanding. "But what do I know that could ruin Mason?"

"Knox Ferris might have let Scott Markham pay for his crime by going through the system. At one point he believed in the system. But he also believed in high tech surveillance and something he heard, probably the same Sunday afternoon he killed him, something he heard made him believe that Scott had to die. What did he hear?"

"I don't know."

"I think you do."

"Honest. I don't."

If I'd thought it possible to shake it out of her, I'd have done it. "You know he was listening to whatever was being said that afternoon. What was it? What did you say that made Knox think Markham was going to get off?"

At first she didn't know. That became apparent when it did finally dawn on her. Her eyes widened and she looked away from me. "What was it Robyn?"

She was staring at nothing. Then she turned to me. "I think I know."

"What was it?" I tried to keep my voice even.

Finally she said, "When Scott was here that Sunday, he had a new plan. We were both going to disappear."

"How does a Scott Markham disappear?"

She swallowed. "He dies in a boating accident. Mason could get all kinds of witnesses lined up."

"Of course." I was miles ahead of her. "Let me guess what he was going to use for money after he died."

Robyn looked down at Fiscus, and I thought I'd guessed right. "The money he'd been taking out of his and Lorna's accounts."

When she wouldn't look at me, I knew I was right. "Markham was never being blackmailed. You just told Janet that to explain the money disappearing from his family's accounts. Even after Markham died, you figured it was yours."

"It was ours. He meant for me to have it. Even now." The words had come in an outburst but no sooner were they out than she was subdued again.

"Where is the money?"

She shook her head. "I don't know. Mason put it in some accounts that Scott could get to."

"I'll bet."

She looked up at me, ready to defend her lover. "Scott was going to provide for his family. He'd taken that big insurance policy out."

"Salt of the earth."

"Oh, God." She buried her face in her hands and her long hair fell forward, brushing the table. "He just wanted to get away from everything. He didn't want to be a judge anymore. He didn't like what he'd become. We were going to start over. You know, do something totally different."

"Sit on the beach somewhere and string puka shells?"

She sat up and pushed her hair back, wiping some moisture from her cheeks. Then, with a wry smile she said, "Yeah. Something like that."

"Tell me, Robyn. You must have realized, you and Susan being friends and all, and her working for Markham, you must have known that Markham wasn't exactly a one-woman kind of guy."

She stared at me, daring me to finish my thought.

"What made you think that Scott wanted to throw it all away with you?"

"Scott loved me."

"I'm not saying he didn't, but . . . ."

Before I could finish, she interrupted, "He loved me. But more than he loved me or any woman for that matter, he loved this child of his that I'm carrying." She put her hand to her belly. She must not have been very far along because she sure didn't look pregnant.

I recalled that Markham had been so desperate for a child that his wife knew their marriage depended on it. Maybe that was all he ever really wanted. But the situation Robyn described did present an obvious question.

"He believed you? No offense, but he's been taken before."

She nodded. "He said that deep inside him, somewhere he'd never been before, he knew that the child was his."

"Aside from that gut feeling, I suppose he also wanted to verify everything with blood tests."

She shrugged as though it hadn't bothered her in the least. "After the child was born."

"What would he have done if the two of you were building a grass hut on the beach in Pago Pago and he found out the kid wasn't his?"

Her gaze never faltered. "I never considered that. It is his child."

"So Sunday when he asked you to go with him, that was the first time he'd mentioned it to you?"

"Yes."

"And you said yes."

"I didn't hesitate."

"You know that Mason was involved?"

"That's what Scott said."

"Can you prove it?"

"I suppose he's got Scott's money somewhere."

"Will you tell this to the police?"

She paused, then nodded, opening her mouth to verbally affirm. Before she could get the words out, Wanda said, "That's not a good idea, honey."

Wanda stood robed and slippered in her bedroom doorway, holding a shotgun and looking grimmer than usual. Fiscus moved from Robyn's side and went to stand next to his mistress.

"You know, mister," Wanda said, "you're nothing but trouble. Everything would've been fine if you hadn't butted in. You take that gun off your belt and bring it here."

I did as I was told. There was nothing I didn't think Wanda capable of.

She sidled her way into the kitchen and kept the gun trained on us while she picked up the telephone receiver, punched a number and put it to her ear. After two or three rings she hung up. One minute later the phone rang. "Hello. . . . Yes. This is Wanda Buchholz. I'm supposed to call you if there's a problem. Well, there is. I think you'd better get over here." She listened for a few seconds. "That's right. Okay. Bye now."

She looked at Robyn. "I'm sorry, honey. I hate to do this, but an old woman's got to make a living."

"Wanda," Robyn still didn't look like she believed all this was happening. "You and I talked after he left." She gestured toward me. "And then you called Mason. Didn't you?"

Wanda didn't answer.

"You told him that Knox planted the bug, didn't you?"

"Oh, don't give me that shocked and innocent look, honey. You're no saint yourself. Easy for a pretty young thing like you to make her way in life. I'm not doing anything awful here."

"That number you called," I said, "you think he's just going to come over and escort us out of town?"

She wagged the gun at me. "You shut up."

I said to Robyn, "This is probably the same guy who planted the bomb in Janet's car."

"Shut up, I said. I don't want to hear a word out of either of you. You hear me?"

I nodded. We waited. And waited. Between the ticking of the kitchen clock and the sounds of canine personal hygiene, I was ready to give away troop positions.

When the doorbell rang, Wanda scurried over to the intercom and buzzed the visitor in.

I tried to imagine what this grim reaper would look like, and I wasn't prepared for the face on the other side of the door.

Wanda was behind the door as she opened it, so Jeff Barlowe didn't see her when he stepped in. He saw me and Robyn and said, "Sorry to bother you, but there's a squad coming down the road and I got a feeling he's headed here."

Wanda's mouth dropped and the gun sagged in her arms. That was when Jeff first noticed her and he sized up the situation with amazing clarity. Slamming all his weight against the door, he pinned Wanda to the wall. Fiscus was on him, chomping down on his right arm. Before I could get to my gun, Wanda lost her grip on the rifle. It met the floor butt first and went off with a deafening blast. If I thought the blast was loud, it was nothing compared to the yelping coming from Fiscus who lay in a heap on the floor.

"Oh, my baby." Adrenaline pumping, Wanda pushed Jeff and the door aside and rushed to the dog.

When the bell rang, I hit the buzzer and opened the door for the police.

I was sitting outside Carver's office with Jeff Barlowe, waiting for him to finish questioning Robyn Fosse. Jeff had a makeshift bandage on his forearm. He'd have to get it looked at later, but he wasn't about to miss the scene that was unfolding.

He saw me looking at his arm and said, "You think this is bad, you oughta see the other guy." We laughed a little. Although Fiscus's injury was not as severe as it could have been, he'd taken a pretty bad hit to the shoulder. Wanda was being held for questioning.

Robyn's statement would help make Mason's life miserable for a while, but there was still nothing to link him with Janet's death. It occurred to me that the only way to do that was to come up with someone to corroborate my version of the evening. I had an idea who might have been upstairs, but believing it was light years away from proving it.

Carver and Robyn finally came out of his office and he handed her over to a female officer saying something about wanting her to stick around for a while. Then he looked at Jeff who understood immediately what was expected of him.

He stood. "Yeah, yeah, I know. I've gotta get my ass out of here." Turning to me he said, "Remember. An exclusive. I'll be waiting in the lobby." He bowed to Carver and left.

Carver watched until Barlowe had left the area, then sat on the bench next to me. "I've got an officer bringing Mason down here and he's got plenty of things to answer for, but I'm afraid Janet Miraldi's death isn't one of them."

"What about the tape on the answering machine?"

Carver's smile was bitter. "It was blank." He shifted on the bench and added, "That was the only tape they found. Not even an unused one."

"Mason should think about giving his help a raise." And I added, "It's too bad he didn't show up at Robyn's the same time the cops did."

Carver nodded.

"I suppose Knox was the one who sent those photos to Dieken."

He eyed me briefly then turned away. "That's what I'm counting on."

I was almost afraid to ask the next question, but I did. "You find anyone else at Mason's house?"

Carver shook his head. "Nobody." Then he shifted on the bench and added, "Mason said that Eric Markham had been staying there. But he also said that Eric was with his mother tonight."

"Anything out of the ordinary upstairs?"

Carver hesitated before he said, "The upstairs balcony door was unlocked. But the maid said she might have left it open."

"I doubt it."

"I don't know. The maid didn't hear Eric come in the house."

"Yeah, well what does that mean? The maid never heard *me* come in the house." I hurried on before Carver had time for questions. "If Eric had his own key and if she was in the back of the house doing dishes or laundry, she wouldn't hear him." I leaned forward, rubbing my face with the palms of my hands and tried to think. Finally I turned to Carver. "The maid didn't leave that balcony door open. Eric did. On his way out."

"You sure that's not just wishful thinking?"

"Yeah, I'm sure." After a few seconds I added, "I think."

My hunch had been right, but there was no way to prove it. I had delivered Eric to Mason and he'd chosen to stay with him rather than deal with his mother. I was certain he was the witness I needed to put Mason away, but my word didn't seem to count for much around here. "The maid didn't leave that door open," I said and turned to Carver. "Did you talk to Eric?"

Carver snorted in disgust. "Of course I talked to him." Then he mellowed some and added, "He says he wasn't there. He was back at his mother's house."

"What does Lorna say?"

He shrugged and looked doubtful. "She backed him up."

"Damn. I know he was there. I could feel it."

"Hey, maybe you're right, but I can't torture it out of him."

"Yeah, well, I can't let it rest. I don't know about you, but that sonofabitch killed Janet and I'm not going to let him get away with it."

Carver stood and looked down at me. "McCauley, you think you're the only one around here who gives a damn? You think I like being the only guy around here who plays by the rules?"

Carver was on his way to a personal best soliloquy, but he stopped when Mason Burke was escorted into the squad room.

Mason was saying very loudly that this was all an inconvenience for him and how everyone would pay for that. He was sweating, but not as much as he should have been and I didn't want to stick around. As I walked past him, he started hollering at Carver. "Why isn't this one locked up? The bastard broke into my home, probably intended to kill me." He was still singing my praises as I left the room.

"You know where there's a bar open?" I asked Jeff as we walked out of the station.

He consulted his watch. "Three A.M. in Foxport. Not likely."

Jeff climbed into his truck and flipped the lock open on the passenger door. As I opened it, a flash of red pulled into the empty space to the left. I turned and looked at the red Jaguar. Lorna Markham rolled down the window. "Wait." It was an order.

Jeff and I exchanged looks. As I waited for her to get out, my mind was running through a preliminary list of the thousand things I'd rather do than talk to Lorna Markham. But I forgot about the list when I saw Eric Markham climb out of the passenger side. He straightened up and looked at me over the roof of the car. I couldn't read his expression.

Lorna glanced at Eric, then me. "He has something to tell Carver."

I closed the truck's door and followed them in. Jeff was right behind us.

Mason was still threatening the police force with a law suit when I followed Lorna and her son into the squad room. When he saw Eric the threats stopped. He gaped for a moment, then found his voice. "Why, Eric. What brings you here?"

Carver opened the door to his office. "Nice to see you, Eric." He motioned him inside.

When Eric hesitated, Lorna laid her hand on his shoulder. After a moment he moved ahead. As he passed Mason, Mason said, "So, the little bastard really is a mama's boy." Lorna marched right up to Mason and slapped him, and when he turned back from the blow with that indelible smile of his, she slapped him again. Then she started to follow Eric into Carver's office, but Eric stopped her. "I can do this myself." Although it wasn't a question, he waited until Lorna nodded her approval before walking into the police chief's office.

Lorna glared at Mason, then turned to me. I smiled and said, "Where's a glass of cheap scotch when you need one?"

I offered to buy Lorna a cup of lousy coffee. She went with me to the vending machine. As I searched my pockets for change, she said, "It looks as if I'll get the insurance money now, so you'll get your fifty thousand." She paused. "You earned every penny."

Except for four pennies and a piece of lint, my pockets were empty. "You got a quarter?"

She smiled and dug two out of her purse. "I'm not going to drink that crap alone. I take mine black."

I handed her the steaming cup and sipped my own. I looked at the cool, composed, but strained woman next to me and figured there was more to her than I'd given her credit for. I gestured toward the squad room. "How'd that happen?"

"I'd finally broken down and called Eric. I guess I thought we might be able to talk things out. I had to do something. He agreed to have dinner with me. I was my usual cool, composed self for all of about five minutes. We had words and he stormed out of the restaurant. What could I do? It was useless to follow him." She took a sip of coffee then looked up at me. "Sometimes he's so much like Scott it scares me." After a few moments, she continued, "I ate dinner and went to a movie. When I got home, Eric was there. He wouldn't talk to me, but I knew he was upset. I couldn't figure it out. I couldn't imagine that our fight would have done that to him. Then the police showed up. Started asking him questions. He denied being at Mason's. I backed him up." She shook her head. "I knew he was lying, but I also knew if I challenged him, I'd lose him for good. So I lied. After the police left, Eric went up to his room. A little while later he came down and confronted me. He demanded to know if Scott was guilty of the bribery charges. He wanted the truth," she gave a half shrug and let her hair fall forward, "so I gave him the truth. *All* of it."

"Including the part about Scott not being his father?"

She nodded. "I think hearing those things about Scott coupled with seeing the real Mason Burke in action did it."

"Well, he must trust you. He'd probably be carrying it around for the rest of his life if he didn't."

Then she laughed and looked away for a moment, blinking her eyes rapidly. "Yeah, sure. I just wish I could tell you that all of a sudden my mothering instincts kicked in. But then . . . " smiling, she shrugged, "maybe we're both starting to come around. We're both realizing we're all each other's got. Not much for a mother and son to build a relationship on, is it?"

"There's lots worse reasons." And then, because she seemed to need more than that, I added, "Who knows. This mothering thing. Maybe you're just a late bloomer."

I don't know if that made her feel any better, but she laughed again and we walked back into the squad room to wait for her son.

Chapter Twenty-Six

Not so long ago I thought someone who'd spend fifty thousand dollars on a car seriously needed to re-examine his priorities. Now that I had fifty thousand dollars, I was starting to think maybe I deserved an expensive car. Hell, I could even get a telephone put in it and use it as an office. Yeah, I needed an office. Quint McCauley, Private Investigator on Wheels. Expensive wheels.

It was another unseasonably warm day and Louise, Jeff, Anne and I had decided to give ourselves the afternoon off and picnic in Louise's backyard by the river. Louise was in the house concocting her secret salad and Jeff was tossing the Frisbee for Peanuts. Anne was taking photos of Peanuts who was so into it I figured in a previous life he was either a model or a child actor. I was stretched out on a lawn chair cooking hamburgers and wondering how much of a car I could buy. We were all a lot better off than Mason Burke who had been charged with conspiracy to commit murder. Eric Markham had not only corroborated my story, but had seen and overheard enough around Mason's house to help the police locate Mason's trigger man, who was still providing the authorities with lists of jobs he'd done for Mason.

Mason wouldn't hang for his crimes, but he'd do a stiff sentence and lose most everything he had. He had promised me that he and I weren't finished conducting business. I told him by the time he got out of prison he wouldn't be able to afford my rates. His wife had already filed for divorce. He deserved a lot worse, but I'd settle for whatever the courts decided. It was tempting to think of extracting my own personal revenge, but I'd seen enough of that in the past couple weeks to last a lifetime. The most I could do was trust in karma and hope that on the day he gets out on parole, some drunk in a big car will come along and mow him down. I'm not proud of these thoughts, but it's probably unhealthy to repress them.

Although Mason still insisted that Markham and Janet had been an item for a while, no one but Mason claimed ever to have seen them together. I chose not to believe him, confining my thoughts of Janet to those that fit with what I'd known. I went back to La Primavera, the restaurant she'd introduced me to, and was served by the same waiter. He remembered me and, since it wasn't busy, he sat and talked with me for a few minutes about Janet. She'd usually come in alone and he re-called how she often brought a book along. She'd liked mys-teries and an occasional fantasy. It's those kind of memories I'll collect about Janet Miraldi.

I'd finally called Elaine after finding the birthday card I'd forgotten to mail her. She'd sounded different and seemed glad to hear from me. When I asked her what she'd done on her birthday, she said something about eating a hot fudge sundae and going to bed early. And she suggested that maybe I'd like to come out and visit. Maybe next week when I gave serious thought to moving from this lawn chair.

"Quint, can you give me a hand here?" It was Louise, bal-ancing dishes and bowls as she made her way down to the river. I jumped out of the chair and relieved her of most of her burden. She was wearing red checked knickers and a long red t-shirt with a drawing of the Eiffel Tower on it. I don't think many people could pull off that look, but Louise did.

We set the salad, chips and paper plates out on the table. Peanuts saw there was food and left Jeff to retrieve the Frisbee himself.

Somewhere between the burgers and the s'mores, Louise said, "So, Quint, what are you going to do with your windfall?"

"I don't know. I'm thinking about a car."

"What about the rest of it?"

I didn't have the guts to tell her after I bought the car I wanted, there'd be no more. Jeff didn't mind telling her, though. "You don't understand Louise, he's thinking about one of *those* cars. You know, the ones you see on the street and wonder how someone can afford a car payment that's bigger than your rent payment."

Louise made an "O" with her mouth and didn't say anything for a minute. She looked like she was trying to figure out if she really knew me after all.

I shrugged. "It's just a thought. You know, I could use it as a kind of office. With a phone and all."

Anne laughed and we all looked at her. "I'm sorry. The picture of you in this expensive little car with all your files, maybe a typewriter and a coffee maker, I don't know, it's kind of funny."

Jeff was getting into the spirit. "Yeah, maybe an electric pencil sharpener that plugs into the lighter and a tiny fax machine."

Louise was laughing now too, and, in spite of myself, so was I. Maybe it wasn't such a hot idea.

"Have you thought about making an investment?" It was Louise.

"I don't know. What kind of investment?"

"Well, I know of a shop owner with quite a successful business who's looking for a partner. And now that I think of it, the building has a room in the back which might work nicely as a one-man office."

Jeff's eyes widened. "Better than a Porsche with a telephone?"

Anne was looking at Louise oddly, as though she wanted to say something but thought maybe she shouldn't. Now I was starting to get suspicious. "What may I ask does this shop specialize in?"

Louise broke a potato chip in half and ate the larger piece. "Imports."

"Wouldn't happen to be jewelry, jade and oriental art, would it?"

"It might be."

"And I don't suppose it's called The Jaded Fox."

When she didn't answer immediately, Anne said, "Aunt Louise, you're not selling the shop, are you?"

"Oh, heavens no. Not all of it at any rate." She turned to me. "I'm looking for a partner. I still enjoy the shop, but I don't want all the responsibility anymore." She drank some of her ale and wiped her mouth with a paper napkin. "You know,

I'd like to do some traveling. And it's not that I don't trust the people who work for me, because I do. But I want a decision maker to be there when I'm not.''

This was nuts. "Louise, what in the hell do I know about the retail business?''

"Well, honestly, what did you know about being a detective a few months ago? But you're doing nicely. There would really be very little for you to do. You know, you'd be one of those silent partners.'' When she didn't get a response, she quickly added, "I don't need an answer right now, just think about it. Before you spend all that money on a splashy car.''

"Think about it, Quint,'' Jeff said. "You know what it costs to insure one of those things?'' He shook his head. "You spend that much on a car, you start getting paranoid. You find yourself parallel parking in angle spaces at the food store. You haven't got a garage. You gonna let it rain on a fifty thousand dollar car? You gonna take a car like that out in a blizzard?'' I was scowling at him and he shrugged. "Gotta think about things like that.''

Louise nodded. "It would be different if you made that kind of money every day. But, honestly, how much do you plan on charging clients?''

"Well, at least he's got clients again.'' Leave it to Anne to see someone squirming and change the subject. And business had picked up since Mason had been locked up. But Louise was right. It might take me more than a year to make that much money again. Well, a guy can dream.

It was getting dark and we cleaned up the table and brought the food and dishes back into Louise's kitchen. Anne started to wash the dishes and Jeff and I, not wanting to appear anything other than liberated, picked up towels and dried.

By the time we'd said our goodnights, it was almost seven. Before I got out of the house, Louise took my arm and said, "Think about it, Quint. I'm serious. Wouldn't hurt you to settle down a bit.'' I promised her I'd give the investment serious thought.

As I began to climb the steps to my apartment, I noticed that Peanuts was back on the grass with an "Aren't you forgetting something?'' look about him. "Ten minutes,'' I said and followed him as he raced down to the river in search of unsuspecting waterfowl. I wondered as I walked what it was about me that elicited Louise's trust. Still it was worth thinking about. Hard to figure how a guy gets to be my age with nothing to show for it but a few sticks of furniture and a sound system he doesn't understand.

It was quiet and the reflections in the river were calming, almost hypnotic. Tonight I could get away with a lightweight jacket, but they were predicting an end to this warm spell before morning. Tomorrow it wouldn't be enough.